Rosalind Miles is the prize-winning author of 18 works of fiction and non-fiction, including *The Women's History of the World*. Born in Warwickshire, she wrote her first story at the age of ten. In 1990 she won the Network Award for outstanding achievement in the field of writing. Her most recent work of fiction was the highly acclaimed *I, Elizabeth*. She now divides her time between Los Angeles and Faversham, Kent.

Also by Rosalind Miles

Fiction
Return to Eden
Bitter Legacy
Prodigal Sins
Act of Passion
I, Elizabeth
Guenevere: The Queen of the Summer Country
Guenevere: The Child of the Holy Grail

Non-fiction
The Fiction of Sex
The Problem of Measure for Measure
Danger! Men At Work
Modest Proposals
Women and Power
Ben Jonson: His Life and Work
Ben Jonson: His Craft and Art
The Female Form
The Women's History of the World
The Rites of Man
The Children We Deserve

GUENEVERE

THE KNIGHT

of the

SACRED LAKE

a novel

ROSALIND MILES

POCKET
BOOKS

LONDON · SYDNEY · NEW YORK · TOKYO · SINGAPORE · TORONTO

First published in Great Britain by Simon & Schuster UK Ltd, 2000
This edition first published by Pocket Books, 2000
An imprint of Simon & Schuster UK Ltd
A Viacom company

1 3 5 7 9 10 8 6 4 2

Simon & Schuster UK Ltd
Africa House
64–78 Kingsway
London WC2B 6AH

Simon & Schuster Australia
Sydney

A CIP catalogue record for this book is available
from the British Library

ISBN 0-671-01813-2

Typeset in Palatino by SX Composing DTP, Rayleigh, Essex
Printed and bound in Great Britain by Omnia Books Limited, Glasgow

For the One Who Roams the Astral Plane

FAMILY TREE

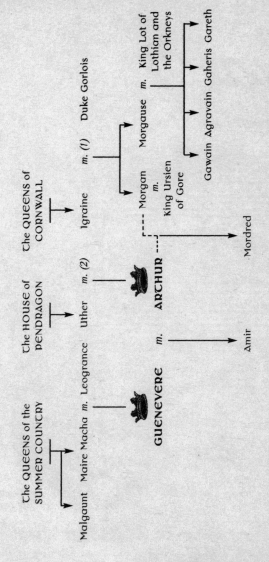

The QUEENS of the SUMMER COUNTRY

Malgaunt   Maire Macha m. Leogrance

GUENEVERE m. ⟶ Amir

The HOUSE of PENDRAGON

Uther   m. (2)

ARTHUR

The QUEENS of CORNWALL

Igraine   m. (1)   Duke Gorlois

Morgan m. King Ursien of Gore

Morgause m. King Lot of Lothiam and the Orkneys

Gawain Agravain Gaheris Gareth

Mordred

IT BEFELL IN THE DAYS of Uther Pendragon, King of all England, that he loved the Queen of Cornwall, a fair lady by the name of Igraine. So he came there with a great host, and Merlin raised a mist in which Igraine's husband Duke Gorlois was slain. Then Merlin brought Uther to Igraine in her castle at Tintagel in the likeness of Gorlois, and Uther lay with her and begat on her the child called Arthur.

Then Uther took Queen Igraine as his wife, and willed King Lot of the Orkneys to wed the Queen's daughter Morgause. Her other daughter Morgan Le Fay he put to a nunnery, because he would have it so. Then the Queen waxed great with child, and when she was delivered, the child was given to Merlin out at a postern gate to nourish as his own. Merlin placed the boy at fosterage with Sir Ector, a knight of King Ursien of Gore.

Within two years King Uther fell sick of a great malady, and died. And after many years, Merlin called all the people to London, to show who should be rightwise king of the realm, and Arthur drew the sword out of the stone.

And when Arthur was King, it befell that he would take him a wife. He said to Merlin, 'I love Guenevere of Camelot, that hath in her house the Round Table, and she is the most valiant fair lady alive.' And Merlin said, 'Sir, if you loved her not so well, I should find you a damsel that should please you more than this Queen.' And Merlin warned the King privily that Sir Lancelot should love Guenevere, and she him again, but the King's heart was set.

So they were wedded, and ruled together with good cheer. And a son was born to them that Arthur took to war, and the boy perished because he was too young.

Then the King cast great love to his sister on the mother's side, Morgan Le Fay, and lay with her and begot on her a son called Mordred. When she was found with child, Arthur gave her to King Ursien of Gore to wife, and ordered all the young infants of that age to be put in a ship and cast out to sea. And the ship was wrecked and the children drowned and their bodies cast up, save that the boy Mordred was never found.

And Sir Lancelot of the Lake, son of King Ban of Benoic in Little Britain, came to court, and in all tournaments and feats of arms, he passed all other men. Wherefore the Queen held him in high favour, and Sir Lancelot loved the Queen above all other ladies of his life.

Yet for the love they had of Arthur they might not partake of their pleasure, nor dishonour the noble fellowship of knights. So the Queen said to Lancelot, 'Fair sweet friend, break my heart, but I must desire you to leave . . .'

MORTE D'ARTHUR

CHAPTER 1

Igh on its crag, Camelot slumbered in the shining gloom. The owls drowsed in the bell-tower, and the round turrets with their pointed roofs, bright pennants and golden spires hung in the glimmering air. The guard in the look-out shifted himself on his haunches, and prepared for an easy watch. On these blessed summer evenings, a silver twilight lingered all night long, even in the dead hours, when the Fair Ones walked.

He chuckled softly. The Fair Ones, yes. Well, a June watch-man was never short of company. But a wise one learned to look the other way when he felt the Fair Ones near. And they'd surely be abroad tonight, what with the Queen's feast and all.

Thin snatches of sound came fleetingly to his ears, the chant of plainsong rising from far below. His eyes travelled down to the courtyard, where a long building huddled in the shelter of the outer wall. Through the high mullioned windows, a single light burned brightly in the dark. It was the flame above the altar, the symbol of unfailing hope and prayer.

Hope, was it? They'd need it, all those poor devils down below. The watchman shuddered as he pondered it. Ye Gods, to be down there now, and all night too!

Yet to the men inside the chapel, their night's work was not an ordeal, but a great honour, he knew. He scratched his head, and let his mind roam free. What must it be like, to be made a knight by the Queen?

The Queen . . . his senses misted with a fleeting memory of white and gold, a drifting shape, a shining smile. A haze of precious thoughts descended on him like a cloud of winged things. To kneel to her, and call yourself her knight, to touch her hand and swear to die for her – yes, any man would thrill to that destiny, that kiss of fate. And all the young men in the chapel had fought for this, chased after it for years. They had valued it above the love of women, above life itself. No matter then what they were going through. Some would endure, some wouldn't, that was all.

And afterwards, they'd have a feast to end all feasts. Gods above, he grinned to himself, what the Queen had commanded from far and wide! Wagons full of beer and wine, carts groaning with fresh meat, every home farm raided for miles around. The cooks had been cursing and tearing their hair for weeks as the Queen's orders flew like arrows from her high tower. 'Nothing but the best! There are queens and kings expected, and all our people from here and far away. Above all, we must honour our new-made knights.'

The new knights.

Well, their honour would be dearly bought.

With a sigh, he turned his eyes down again to pray for the sufferers below.

Inside the chapel the air was misty and cool. The young knight swayed on his knees, and lifted unseeing eyes. High on the wall, the Round Table hung suspended above the stout trestles that supported it when it was in use. The great circle gleamed with its own light like the face of the moon. The knight fixed his gaze on it and tried to drag his mind back from wandering in some lost realm of pain. Dear Lady, Queen of Heaven, bless my vigil, he prayed humbly. Let me not faint, let me not disgrace my new-found honour and Your sacred name.

At the back of the church the Master of the Novices viewed him sardonically, and echoed his prayer. Folding his arms, he leaned his back against the damp chill of the chapel wall, and surveyed the kneeling rows facing the altar, all silent now, and grey-faced like old men. They were all the same, these young knights-in-the-making, on fire to be the best in the land. But after the first hour on their knees on the cold stone, even the strongest was praying to survive.

They could lie down, of course. Every one of the twenty

young men kneeling now in prayer would spend some part of the hours between dusk and dawn prostrate before the altar, arms outstretched to form the sign of the Cross. After the first hour or two, when the stones they knelt on felt like knives of fire, the weaker vessels would fall on their faces and remain there all night long. Others would struggle repeatedly to remain upright, till the bell rang for first light.

The novice master smiled coldly to himself. Already he could tell which of them would fall, and even when. And he could tell too, from this simple fact, those who would make good knights, and who would not.

And most would not. His eye passed carefully over the serried ranks. He was too old a hand to sigh over young men's frailties and lost hopes. But every year at this time he remembered how ardently the new knights all embarked, and how few were destined to survive the course. Some would perish cleanly on the point of a lance or sword, often on their first outing from the court, as they sought the deeds of daring that would make their name. Others faced a messier, crueller end, the long slow death of hope and faith, as they measured themselves year by year against the dreams they once had had, and found themselves further back than when they had begun.

These would be the ones who had fallen on their faces at the first trial of strength. He could smell it on them now, the stink of fear and failure, the terror of a little pain. The novice master sucked his teeth, and rocked back on his heels. So many were called to knighthood, and so few would prove to be knights of any worth.

Take the Orkney princes now –

With a frisson of unease, he surveyed the three mighty forms shoulder to shoulder at the front of the church, still rock-solid on their knees. Not one of them would faint, he would take money on that, they had no fear of pain. And as nephews of King Arthur, they would surely be loyal enough. Loyal, tough, and brave. So what was it about the three sons of King Lot that made him wish they were not among his charges, not destined to become knights of the Round Table when the night was done?

Tenderly he explored the thought like a fresh wound. Sir Gawain had been the King's most faithful knight from the first, rough-hewn and pugnacious, yes, but as true as they come. Why then should his three younger brothers fail? Each of them was as big as Gawain, and as useful in a fight. But none would shape up like Gawain, there was no hope of that. Especially the dark one, Agravain.

Agravain –

The novice master felt a shadow he could not name. Yet every year there was one who gave him hope. His eyes returned to the frail youth he had seen before. Mador, it was, yes, Mador of the Meads. Young Mador would not fail.

With grudging approval the older man eyed the slight figure on its knees before the altar, rigid with terror, transcendent with desire. He was a good lad, Mador was, and no mistake. His brother showed promise too, holding on at Mador's side so grimly that he would swoon with agony sooner than give in. They were good lads both, Mador and Patrise. But Mador had felt the flame, he had the edge.

And he would make a perfect knight in time.

The novice master sighed. If –

If the lad survived the night with honour, according to his own high desire –

If he did not lose his head for love, and forget about tournaments and feats of arms –

If he could find a worthy knight to follow, one like Sir Lancelot, not a rough warrior like Sir Gawain, or a cynic like Sir Kay –

Lancelot –

The novice master sighed now in earnest, and deeper than he knew. Did anyone in the world know where Lancelot was, and when he would return?

Patrise! Don't fail, don't fall, hold on!

The young knight Mador leaned sideways to take the weight of his brother's swaying body, and tried urgently to drop the thought into his mind, Hold on, Patrise, hold on. Patrise stirred and braced himself, and shot back a glance of grateful love, I will, brother, I will. The comforting recognition passed between them, not long now.

Mador closed his eyes, and looked out through the thin flesh of his lids. He had discovered a while ago that he could see better that way. Truly it was the best way to see, in fact it was the only way to see her at all.

And there she was, dazzling his eyes as always, filling his soul with steel. She was all that any knight could hope to worship and adore. And now she was appearing to him in the dim chapel, shining for him, floating below the great Round Table of the Goddess where tomorrow her chosen knights would sit.

The knights of the Queen.

He swayed on his knees, drunk with ecstasy. Guenevere, his soul chanted, Guenevere the Queen. Every man here would give his life for her, if he could die in the light of her smile. But how could he dream of the Queen's favour, when he had done nothing to deserve her regard? How to be worthy? Mador groaned to himself. How to live up to her knight that was gone?

For a moment Mador's faith faltered, and his proud heart quailed. No man could surpass Lancelot, any more than another woman could hope to outdo Guenevere herself. They both seemed to have lived a thousand lives before this, when at last they came into their own. Mador's soul shrank further into itself. Lancelot was the best knight in the world, and would always be.

But any man could become better than nature had made him at the start, Mador reasoned humbly in the breaks between his fervent, wandering prayers. Another man could not be Lancelot. But he could try to emulate the knight the Queen loved. Loved so much, it was said, that he had had to go away. And it was certain he had gone, none knew where, nor when he could return.

But here or afar, Sir Lancelot was the star by which every young man set his course. Lancelot would not fail, and neither must he. Yielding again to the passion of his pain, Mador floated out of himself, above the fragile body kneeling on the stones. His spirit soared with the chanting of his soul, Guenevere my lady, Guenevere the Queen.

CHAPTER 2

The landlord knew what they were the moment they came in. They were modestly dressed for the road like any other travellers, but their air of dignity and quiet assurance was not to be missed. His eye quickened. The alehouse was packed, and the customers were drinking well, but that type had to be worth a week's takings or more.

'Look sharp!' the landlord hissed to his harassed serving girl, delivering a swift kick to her leg. 'Clear the table in the corner by the fire, and bring in three of the best goblets right away.'

'Yes, sir.' The sweat-stained girl pushed a strand of damp hair away from her forehead, and scurried to obey.

The newcomers stood on the threshold assessing the dim interior full of idle clamour, the low, smoke-blackened beams, the sour reek of bodies, the thick fug of beer. Only nightfall and a shortage of other accommodation would have brought them to his wretched door, the landlord knew. Best not let them get away.

'Welcome, sirs!' he cried, wiping his hands on his dirty apron, and bustling forward with an oily grin. 'It's not often I can welcome knights like your noble selves to my poor house! Step inside, come in! The girl will have a table for you in a trice.'

Behind him he could hear loud, drunken protests as the servant girl dislodged the drinkers at the corner table, and moved them to join the group standing round the fire. Covertly the landlord assessed the three men. Younger than they looked at first, and finer too, no knights of the road, living by their wits, but young men of the court, most likely companions of the King. Two of them were brothers, he decided, no mistaking that, though the shorter was neat, brown-haired and reserved, while the other was fairer, and more open-faced. But what to make of the tallest of the three?

It was plain that the brothers deferred to him, and that his abstracted nod decided what they should do. The short, dark-haired knight was watching earnestly for his word, while the fair one waited patiently in the rear. But the tall knight seemed not to care where he was. His burning brown eyes looked out on another world than this, and his lithe, slender frame stood half turning in the doorway as if reluctant to enter the place and leave the comfort of the dark outside.

Even the landlord, a complacent monument of common clay, could tell that the stranger was no ordinary man. He wore a soft green leather tunic patterned with silver studs, and a fine woollen cloak in the same woodland hue. His chestnut hair gleamed with a light of its own, and when he moved, every line of his form had grace. He stood on the threshold with an ardent, grieving air, as if searching for something he had lost and never hoped to find.

The landlord saw all this, and it twisted his heart. He remembered a knight like this, years ago, who went to the woods one day and never returned. That one had been a good-looker like this knight too, and all the town said that the Queen of the Fair Ones had taken him for her love.

Darkness and devils! the landlord cursed under his breath. Why was he letting this stranger knight put such tomfool thoughts into his head? And where was that idiot girl? He reached out, caught the maid by the back of her neck, and viciously wrung the scrawny flesh. 'Run to the cellar, dimwit,' he commanded roughly, 'and fetch the wine from the back shelf. You know the one.'

He raised his hand to speed her on her way. To his surprise he found the tall knight standing between him and his own servant, the silly slut he had only taken in out of the kindness of his heart.

'No need to make the maid run for us, landlord. We can wait our turn,' were the words he spoke. And do not dare to strike her again, was written in every line of the lithe body poised to enforce his pronouncement if the landlord disobeyed.

To the end of her life, the maidservant never forgot the look in the knight's bright eyes as he raked the landlord with contempt, then turned his thoughtful gaze on her. Great lord as he was, she knew in her small bones that something of her own sadness, the daily misery of a loveless life, hung about him too.

As she ran for the cellar, she could hear the landlord's grovelling tones. 'Just as you say, sir. Whatever you say.' He was angry now, she could tell, and a bleak acceptance settled into her soul. It was gracious and good of the tall knight to speak up for her like that. But where would he be when she paid for it later, as she'd have to, for sure?

Trust that mooncalf of a girl to show him up like this, the landlord thought venomously. Well, she'd pay for it, as soon as he got his hands on her after they'd gone. And even if he was handsome and well-made, what made the tall knight think he was better than other folk? The landlord's anger rose. What gives you the right to say a man can't be master of his own wench, Sir Precious? his ugly inner voice was clamouring, even as his mouth was saying fulsomely, 'I have a fat chicken in the pot, and some cold brawn on the side. What'll you take, my lords?'

The tall knight shook his head dismissively, and turned aside. 'Nothing for me, Bors,' he said to the elder of the two brothers. 'But you and Lionel order what you want. I'll see to the horses, and join you in a while.'

Sir Bors stood aside, and watched the tall knight retreating before turning back into the alehouse with the fair knight behind. 'Well, landlord,' he said, 'my brother and I will dine with you tonight. Let's have the best you've got.' The lightness of his tone did not disguise the concern he felt for the knight who had just left. And again the question fretted the landlord's rising spleen: who is this man? Why the great care for him?

But two birds in the hand –

Swiftly the landlord drew his new guests inside, and ensconced them at the rough corner board. A shout brought the maidservant hastening with the wine, and another good kick as she poured ensured that she spilled only a little of it, and none on the knights. He waited till they had both taken a first sip before easing slyly into what he wanted to know.

'It's good wine, this,' he began, 'best in the house. From France.' He paused. 'Like your good selves, unless my ears deceive me.' He smiled with what he thought was a jocund air. 'A trace of a French accent there, good sirs?'

Ill fortune be our speed, Bors thought wearily, a fawning publican, a tedious braggart and a fool, must be our host tonight. Well, so be it. We do not journey for our pleasure or delight. This country clown and his bad wine are our affliction now. Tomorrow we may wish ourselves back here.

He took another draught of the sour red wine, and shook his head. 'Not France. France is our overlord.'

The younger knight laughed. 'We are from Little Britain below France, sons of Benoic. But we have been here since our boyhood. We are knights of this island now.'

The landlord nodded. 'Then you'll be travelling to Camelot for the Queen's feast.' He jerked his head round the room 'Like most of these here. They've been thronging the roads this past week and more.' He guffawed. 'Not that this rabble'll be dining in the palace with all the knights and lords. But the Queen will make sure that there's plenty for all who come. And they'll see her and King Arthur and all his knights at the tournament, and come back as happy as birds on mating day.' He rubbed his hands, and showed a mouthful of rotten teeth in a reminiscent grin. 'Ten years they've been on the throne and ten years married. That's something to celebrate, eh, good sirs? Ten years! And peace and plenty for us all.'

'Sir?' Appearing silently at his elbow, the servant girl surreptitiously slipped a brimming flagon into the landlord's grasp. If she could keep him happy, or better still, get him drunk, she might escape the worst of what usually befell her in the cellar when the alehouse had closed, and his wife was asleep. The landlord's hands closed around the crock of ale, and he took a long pull before warming to his theme.

'You'll not remember how it was before, young sirs, you growing up in France so far away. Oh, the Summer Country was always safe enough under the rule of queens, and for my money, Queen Guenevere's the best of them all. But the Middle Kingdom was a wilderness after King Uther died, what with rogue knights and warring kings, and all. So when King Arthur came and claimed it back, we all rejoiced to see Pendragon on the throne again. And when Queen Guenevere took him as her king and married him, and then joined her lands to his – oh, yes, lords, we have plenty to be thankful for.'

The two knights exchanged a glance. 'We do not go to Camelot,' said Bors at last. 'We wish the King and Queen well on their great day, but our business calls us elsewhere. We sail for Little Britain by the first boat.'

The landlord stared. 'But they're making new knights this Pentecost, new brothers of yours in the Round Table, in a mighty ceremony. You wouldn't want to miss that, surely, young sirs?'

Unless – said his prying mind.

A dull light lit his eye. Unless they had left the court under a cloud. Banished and sent abroad, never to return. What would it be, their offence? Drunkenness, lewdness, dishonouring a lady or what? He reached eagerly for a chair to plump himself down with them. 'So you've left Camelot, lords? Tell me, then.'

What a fool he is, the little servant thought, with a sick recognition of her employer's ways. He can't help himself. He treats the finest knights that ever graced his house like his alehouse cronies, poking his nose into matters beyond his ken. He'll drive them away with his prying, then punish me.

A sudden uproar broke out by the fire. One of the drinkers, a large local lout, was threatening a traveller, a merchant by his dress. 'Who are you calling clot-polls?' he was shouting. 'There's as much brains in this village as where you come from!'

'One moment, sirs.' The landlord hurried off to deal with the affray. Bors looked at Lionel, raising his eyebrows in interrogation, and his brother gave a faint nod.

Both were on their feet as the tall knight re-entered the room. 'We go?' he asked, without surprise.

Bors nodded. 'Time to move on, I think,' he said quietly. 'There's no peace for us here.'

Lionel seconded him with a rueful smile. 'Better a night in the open, under the stars. It'll be warm enough tonight, and far sweeter there.'

'As you will.' The tall knight returned his smile. 'We've slept out often enough not to fear it now.'

The little servant flew forward in dread. 'Oh sirs, must you go? I beg you, tell him it's not my fault! And will you leave some money for the wine?' Tears stood in her eyes. 'Or else he'll –'

The tall knight fixed her with his gentle gaze. 'My cousin will give you silver for a whole barrel of wine, won't you, Bors?'

Sir Bors smiled and nodded, and reached for the money-pouch at his waist as the tall knight went on. 'And he will give you gold for yourself, too. You must leave this man who treats you like a dog. We are riding for the coast to take ship over the Narrow Sea, or else we would escort you away ourselves. But hear my words. Go to Camelot, and seek service with the Queen. She is the finest lady in the world. I swear on my soul that she will treat you well.'

He lifted his head and looked through the walls of the ale-hovel into some magic garden of his mind. 'There is a place for you there at court with her, a world of love and grace, and Guenevere is its heart. Say to the Queen that we send our humble wishes for her health and joy. Tell her that she is with us wherever we go.'

The maid nodded, huge-eyed, her chapped lips working as she struggled to fix the words in her memory. 'Thank you, sir,' she forced herself to say.

He tried to smile. 'May the Great Ones go with you. And may She who is the Mother of them all smile on your journey, and bless your new life.'

He turned, and was gone. Sir Lionel was already following him through the door. The maid found herself clutching a piece of silver and a large coin of gold as Sir Bors took his leave.

'Sir!' she gasped. 'What shall I say to the Queen?'

Bors's smile held all the sadness in the world. 'Just tell her that you come from Lancelot.'

CHAPTER 3

Low on the horizon, the love star bloomed in the evening sky. Guenevere moved to the window, and carefully lit the tall candle standing there. She stood for a moment willing the tiny flame to speed its message through the night. From her tower chamber, the light would be seen for miles. She raised her eyes to the full, smiling moon. *Goddess, Mother*, she prayed, *shine on my love –*

As the candle flamed, its honeyed scent of beeswax warmed the air. Behind her she heard the door opening, and the soft familiar footstep of her maid. 'So, Ina,' she said tremulously, 'what news?'

She heard the maid's gown rustling as she curtsied to the floor. 'King Arthur sends his compliments, my lady, and begs you to join him in the audience chamber. King Ursien of Gore has arrived.'

Uneasily conscious of smelling of weeks on the road, King Ursien stood in the low panelled chamber, and shifted from foot to foot. 'Why does the Queen want to see us the minute we arrive?' he growled to his knight.

You know why, sire, the young man's troubled glance replied.

Ursien waved him aside. 'I'm too old for this!' he groaned. 'The Gods know that I don't need to be welcomed with feather beds, and hot coddled wine. But I need my rest after a hard journey, and I can't play games with the Queen.' Removing his helmet, he ran a hand through his iron-grey hair. 'I can't give her what she wants, Accolon!'

The young knight bit his lip and turned away. Gods above, Ursien cursed, what's wrong with Accolon now? Mysterious moods, anger and storms had dogged every step of their long journey south. What was it all about? In his day knights did not act like lovesick maids. But face it, Ursien, he instructed himself bleakly, any old soldier who survives the wars of his youth, not to mention the jousts and tournaments of his prime, is condemned to live on into lesser, weaker days.

But then again, any young knight would feel it if the Queen of Gore vanished into thin air, when he, Accolon, was the only knight on guard. Of course Accolon blamed himself, it was only natural. And not only Accolon, but all his knights had been shaken to the core. It could hardly have inspired them with confidence in their master too, that king or no, he could not hold on to his wife. Look to yourself, Ursien, he thought, before you start blaming other men.

Well, he had failed. Ursien braced his tired shoulders and took a breath. Failing a High King usually meant death. Praise the Gods that Arthur was too magnanimous for that. He of all men knew what the woman was like. But she had had to be disposed of, and Arthur had chosen Gore. And for Ursien, the honour of an alliance with the King's sister was not to be refused.

The King's sister.

Morgan Le Fay.

Gods above, what a woman she was! Ursien's memory shrank to a hard kernel of desire, the lust that had been his undoing from the start. He had to admit that he had grown hot at the thought of bedding her when the time came. That thin body, chalk-white face and black hair, those terrifying eyes and huge mouth, she was a woman to thrill the loins of any man. As a hard-bitten old soldier, Ursien had found a special relish in the idea of risking his manhood in a witch's place of devils, in the most secret part of the she-devil herself.

Well, he had never had the pleasure, or enjoyed that risky sport. Indeed he had to smile at another grim irony, that he who had so desired her had never possessed his wife.

And he'd thought, hadn't he, that he was ahead of the game? He'd known there had to be a reason for Arthur's desperate message summoning him south. Of course he'd heard the palace gossip as soon as he arrived. Arthur was the last man on earth he'd have suspected of any such thing. But when he'd seen the sister, half-sister, whatever she was, he'd understood at once.

Of course he'd suspected that there might be more to hide than a forbidden love, however shameful that was. And with sons of his own, Ursien had no desire to rear another man's bastard, even a king's. So when he married Morgan and brought her back to Gore, he had kept her closely confined, surrounded by her women night and day, in case she proved to be with Arthur's child.

Before long the women had confirmed his suspicions, and the way ahead was clear. When Morgan had delivered Arthur's child, he reasoned, there would time enough for his long-awaited matrimonial rights.

Well, he was wrong. Instead, she had disappeared, and the boy she bore too, fled from the castle even though he had kept her under lock and key. He grinned mirthlessly. Now he was married and not married, a husband without a wife. He had no desire for whores, nor would he ever take a concubine. He wanted his wife, and his wife did not want him. What Morgan wanted was to play games with them all.

'Games,' he repeated, moving to the window restlessly. Across the courtyard, the low shape of the chapel loomed up through the violet dusk. At the rear of the building, black-gowned monks were passing to and fro, their hands in their sleeves, their bowed heads lost inside their capacious hoods. Snatches of plainsong floated through the air. Through the high window at the end, Ursien could see the altar light glowing red like a dragon's eye. A leap of memory took him inside, and he let out another groan. 'Ye Gods, isn't there enough misery in the world?'

'Sire?' The young knight Accolon moved to his side, following his gaze.

Ursien pointed. 'There.'

He could almost smell the reek of incense inside the chapel, the sweating flagstones, the mildew on the walls, all overlaid by the stink of suffering. 'In my day, knights were made up without this ordeal of pain. But since the Christians got their hands on the knight-making ritual, I've had to watch young men tortured in the name of faith. And I never saw that it made them better knights!'

He turned to Accolon with a reassuring smile. 'Not you, of course. You were Arthur's knight before you came to me.'

Accolon bowed. 'I was, sire.' A spasm of tension mottled his face and was gone. 'If only I had stayed with the King –'

'Nonsense, Accolon!' Ursien briskly cut him off. 'You had no choice, remember, the King sent you to Gore. He appointed you to guard Queen Morgan, and become her knight. He knows you never faltered in your trust. And none of what has happened is your fault, none at all.'

Accolon's face had taken on a glassy sheen. He licked his lips. 'Sire –'

'Enough of this! Don't look so wretched, man. You aren't the one who has to answer to the King and Queen.' Ursien turned back to the window with a harsh laugh. 'And it could be worse. You could be on your knees down there, proving your loyalty.'

He peered out through the pitted, greenish glass. In front of the chapel, a huge knight in full armour stood leaning on his sword. With his back to the closed doors, he stared out over the courtyard, keeping guard.

'It's Gawain!' Ursien said with interest, drawing up to the window, and beckoning Accolon to share his view. 'He must be keeping vigil for his three brothers inside. I knew they'd won their spurs at Le Val Sans Retour. I'd forgotten they would be made up this Pentecost.'

Accolon gave another sickly nod. 'They should make good knights.'

Ursien tugged his fingers through his grizzled beard, and gave the matter some thought. 'The younger two, maybe,' he said at last. 'But Agravain –'

'My lord!' Accolon cocked an ear. 'It's the Queen.'

There was a flurry outside, and the guard on the door sounded the royal fanfare. The heavy oak doors swung back, and both men fell to their knees. Ursien raised his eyes to see King Arthur handing Guenevere into the room.

She wore a long, full gown of cream-white silk, with sleeves of ermine falling to the floor. Her waist was encircled with a girdle of gold, and a golden cloak swung from her shoulders as she moved. Gold chains and bracelets flashed at her neck and wrists, and moonstones and crystals lit up her long pale hands. Around her head, containing its rainfall of bright hair, she bore the antique circle of the queens of the Summer Country, with its large pendant moonstone between the brows.

Behind her came Arthur in a tunic of fine red wool, and a cloak of royal blue silk edged with gold. A sword of state swung from his heavy gold belt, and a silver dagger in the shape of two dragons locked in combat snarled at his waist. His thick fair hair was held back by a coronet of gold, and deep bracelets of gold banded both his wrists.

Ursien stared in unaccustomed reverence. All his life he had seen women come and go, queens and camp followers, young and old, fair and dark, fat and thin. But the Queen was different, and above them all. How old was she now, he wondered. Thirty? Thirty-five? Her tall, shapely figure bore no trace of child-bearing, let alone of grief. Yet the Gods alone knew what she had suffered in her life. Any other woman who had lost her only son like that would have run mad. Still, her sweet face and luminous smile were just as he remembered them from her wedding day.

Whereas Arthur –

How long was it, Ursien wondered, since Merlin had come to Gore, and asked him to take in the unknown boy? The child who had later proved to be the only son of Uther Pendragon, the King of the Middle Kingdom and High King of all the Britons in his time?

Ursien groaned inwardly, and felt his age. It must have been thirty-five years and more since he had taken the child in, and placed him with his trusted knight Sir Ector as his foster-son. Thirty-five years! And he had to admit that Arthur was showing every one of them now. True, the thick head of dusty fair hair was only lightly sprinkled with grey. But the great bear-like frame was bowed with the weight of care, and deep lines marked Arthur's face from nose to chin. Yes, Ursien mourned, he was suffering for Morgan still, no doubt about that. As he would for a long time to come.

'Sire –' he said hopelessly.

Guenevere hastened forward to take both Ursien's hands.

'Welcome, my lord!' she said warmly, as she raised him to his feet. She looked at her husband with urgency in her gaze. *Arthur, Arthur, give a welcome to our old friend Ursien. After all that has happened, he needs our love too. And it was not his fault, he is not to blame.*

Arthur's face did not change. But his tone of voice as he said 'Come, Guenevere!' told Ursien all there was to know.

Arthur took up a position in front of the empty hearth, and drew Guenevere to his side. She shivered. *How cold he is,* she thought, looking at her husband's withdrawn face. The air in the chamber was chill, and a small wind rattled at the casement with a dismal whine. Guenevere drew her cloak around her arms. *This room is cold, we should have had a fire.*

Arthur waved Ursien and Accolon to draw near. 'So, Ursien, what news?'

Ursien planted his feet like a soldier, and fixed his eyes on the ceiling overhead. 'None at all, sire.'

Arthur stiffened. 'She can't have disappeared!'

Guenevere clasped her hands, and forced herself to be calm. *Arthur, you know she can.*

Arthur's colour changed. 'And the boy?'

Watching his face, Guenevere suppressed a groan. *Arthur, why ask, why torment yourself? Wherever she is, he's with her, we can be sure of that.*

'We've scoured the country from our borders to the sea,' Ursien returned. 'We searched into the Welshlands, and up as far as the shore looking over to the Druids' Isle.' He gave a harsh laugh. 'Without success. Anywhere in these islands could be home to Morgan Le Fay.'

Arthur flinched at the sound of the name. 'Don't remind me, Ursien! Do you think I'll ever forget what she can do – what she's already done to all of us?' He turned to Guenevere, his face working, and took her hand. 'Oh, my love –'

He paused, struggling to master his welling grief. 'I – I –' He shook his head. 'Forgive me, Ursien.' Abruptly he left the chamber, covering his face.

'My lady!' Ursien was aghast. 'Did I offend the King?'

Guenevere crossed to Ursien, and took his hand. 'Don't reproach yourself,' she said sadly. 'The King has never forgiven himself for drawing you into this . . .' she paused '. . . when he knew – when we all knew – what Morgan was like.'

Ursien nodded, recovering himself. 'Comfort yourself, madam, I did too. I thought I had the measure of the witch.' He laughed savagely. 'Never was I more wrong!'

Guenevere shook her head. 'The King does not blame you. He knows you did your best to keep her decently.'

'But there's no keeping a witch and a whore!' Ursien broke in violently. 'A thing of evil, who sucks out men's souls! The King must want to see her stripped and whipped in the marketplace, then broken on the wheel, joint by joint. Not only for all the men she has enslaved but for Amir.'

A faint sound escaped Guenevere unaware. She stood quite still.

Amir.

She hardly ever heard his name these days. The sound of it went rolling round her mind. Then her sight faded, and he came to her as he always did, his arms outstretched, his fair hair glinting like Arthur's in the sun, his face turning up to be kissed, his sturdy little body warm in her embrace.

Amir.

Lost and gone, years ago now.

Guenevere gave a violent shudder and came to herself again.

'Never fear, King Ursien, she said gently, laying her hand upon his arm. 'My son is worlds beyond any such revenge. And do not fear that King Arthur would ever take the life of a woman, still less of the Queen your wife. She is still his sister, and his own kin too. We are both hoping that she has finished with us now. The King prays every day that she has gone, never to return.' She paused, and nerved herself to say the name. 'But if Morgan Le Fay is found, I swear to you that the King will be governed by reason, not by lust for blood.'

Could any other woman be so generous to a rival who had seduced her husband, and plotted to take her place? King Ursien chewed at the mouth hairs of his beard. Yes, Guenevere could. Too many had died already against her will. From now on, she would end the march of death.

He looked at Guenevere with a new respect. 'And till then,' she was saying, 'let us make as merry as we can.' She tried bravely for a smile. 'Tomorrow we celebrate ten years of our marriage, and ten years of our reign. You must raise a glass with us at the feast, my lord, and drink to the honour of our new-made knights.'

Her eyes were glistening with unshed tears. Unexpectedly Ursien felt his old eyes moistening too. So beautiful, so sad, and all alone. What was it he had heard about Lancelot? Well, time enough for that.

With a sweep of the hand, Guenevere gestured towards the window and the world beyond. Outside a deep purple dusk had settled on the Summer Country's rounded hills and green pastures, its rich forests and wide woodland ways. Above the horizon, Venus the love star shed her blazing beams. Guenevere smiled.

'The night is clear, and tomorrow will be fine. My Druids tell me that the Old Ones plan to honour our celebrations with a run of perfect days.' She drew Accolon towards her and took King Ursien by the arm. 'And when the feast is over and the other guests have gone, will you take the King out hunting in the forest, good sirs, somewhere sweet and wholesome, far away?'

Ursien nodded towards his knight. 'Sir Accolon has already suggested as much.'

Guenevere pressed his arm. 'Will you ride out with Arthur then, old friend, and help him drive this wretched grief away?'

Ursien's sigh sounded like a groan. 'If we can, my lady,' he said heavily. 'If we can.'

CHAPTER 4

Was he dreaming, or was the sky paling towards dawn? Gawain blinked his bleary eyes, and felt a sharp stab in his back as he straightened up from leaning on his sword. Gingerly he flexed his heavy limbs. He was aching in every joint.

Gods above, he cursed softly to himself, but the night has been long! The courtyard in front of the chapel had been as damp and cold as the grave. The weight of his armour was grinding into his flesh, his mouth felt full of sand, and strange sights and sounds had vexed him all night long. What had possessed him to swear such a mighty oath to keep the vigil along with his brothers, hour by hour?

He groaned. What but the drink, and being a sentimental fool? He'd had no fears for the three of them, not even Gareth, the youngest of them all. Youngest? He laughed quietly to himself. Youngest and biggest of all the sons of King Lot, Gareth was, and that was saying a good deal. They were all great brawny lads, big and hard like their father, King Lot had seen to that. But Lot's death had left Gawain head of the family, and responsible for them all.

The family –

The big knight shifted his weight, dimly conscious that the simple everyday word came nowhere near to describing the tangle of his kin. Of course Uther Pendragon had been a hero, much beloved of the Old Ones, and no ordinary man. But to set his heart on a queen with a husband, children, and a kingdom of her own, and take all that from her in order to make her his – Well, that was not the highest act of chivalry, it had to be said.

Still, Gawain reasoned uneasily, who was he to say? Kings

were not governed by the rules of common men. And Uther's misdeeds had come to some good in the end. If he hadn't married Queen Igraine, Arthur would never have been born. If she had had to lose her husband in the battle as the two men fought for her love, well, those were the fortunes of war. And if her daughter Morgause had not been given to King Lot, neither Gawain nor his brothers would ever have been born.

So, then! Gawain's furrowed brow cleared, and his mighty frame relaxed. There was a purpose behind all this pain and suffering. All that had happened was written in the stars, and even cruel acts could have a good outcome if the Old Ones willed it so. Oh, it was true that King Uther had parted Igraine from her daughters so that he could have the Queen all to himself. But the girl sent off to the far Orkneys had delivered four sons who were now the most loyal knights of Pendragon, and devoted to Uther's son.

Uther's son, yes. Gawain sighed. It was his proudest boast that he had been the first knight to declare for Arthur when he drew the sword from the stone. He'd taken an oath that as he had been Arthur's first companion, he would be the last. And now his three brothers were joining the knighthood too. To add to their joy, their mother had travelled down from the Orkneys to witness the great event. So good had come out of evil after all.

Gawain shifted his aching body, and gave a soft groan. It was true that his mother had not been the happiest of women, married to King Lot. But the death of her husband had left Morgause ruler of the Orkneys in her own right, every bit as much a queen as she would have been if she had stayed at home, and succeeded to her mother's land. Now Morgause was free of King Uther, free of King Lot, and could call herself her own woman again. And he, lucky man, as King Lot's eldest son, had inherited the role of taking charge of them all.

Taking charge?

No, not quite.

Gawain grunted derisively to himself. No one, not even King Lot, had been in charge of their mother, Queen Morgause. Oh, she was quiet enough when her great black-bearded husband was around. They all were, for King Lot inspired fear, not love. And never had he heard his mother raise her voice, despite the harsh treatment the King gave her, or throw a single glance of resentment her husband's way.

But Morgause was a daughter of Tintagel, and the land of Cornwall still kept the rule of queens. She had been born and bred in a land where the Mother-right held sway, where the worship of the Goddess taught the faith of love, not fear. She had walked warily round her husband, for Lot worshipped at altars far older still, the Gods of blood and bone, and he loved to kill. But never had she crouched to him to live. Only where Christians ruled were women forced to bow to men. No one told a woman of the old world what to do.

And not even an elder brother could rule the three Orkney princes now, any more than he could the Queen. Gawain rubbed the back of his stiff neck and grinned to recall the pitched battles of their childhood, when none of the four boys would give in without a bloody nose, split lip or battered head. Even Gareth, the youngest, was a baby giant with a will of his own. Gaheris, the third-born, had a spine of iron too, for all his quiet demeanour, pale-blue eyes and milk-white skin. And as for Agravain –

Agravain.

Gawain sighed heavily. Well, he would think about Agravain another time.

Stretching, he raised his eyes to the east. Red streaks like infected veins were racing up the sky, and a dull glow lit the distance as if the whole horizon was on fire. Clouds and rain on the way after all the fine weather the Queen's star-watchers had promised for the feast? But bad or good, there it was, he rejoiced, true dawn at last.

And with it, the release of those inside. He turned back towards the locked doors of the chapel deep inside the low porch, and tired though he was, became instantly alert.

'Who's there?' he growled. He levelled his sword, and pointed it at the door. There was a slight movement in the darkness and a light Welsh voice. 'Gawain?'

'Bedivere!'

Emerging from the shadows came a lean, brown-haired man with mild hazel eyes. Behind him came a shorter, neat-made figure, showing signs of fatigue but still dapper after a night out of doors.

Gawain burst out laughing. 'And Kay, by all that's wonderful!'

'Who did you think it was?' Kay queried tartly as he limped forward into the light. 'You didn't think we'd leave you out here to keep this fool vigil by yourself?'

Gawain let out a guffaw of delight. 'So the two of you have been in the porch all night?'

Bedivere gave a tired smile. 'You kept watch for your brothers, and we watched for you.'

'And we've all wasted our time, and worn ourselves out for nothing!' Kay fretted. 'Your mighty brothers will have come through the ordeal with banners flying, I'm quite sure. It remains to be seen if we'll survive the night!'

Gawain surveyed his short companion lovingly. Kay had never been the same since he had lost the good use of his leg, stabbed through the thigh long ago by a treacherous dwarf. His drawn face showed that he was in pain now, and would be till the wine went round tonight. But Gawain knew better than to say a word. Kay had the small man's touchy dignity, and would not be consoled.

'So!' Gawain said lightly. 'I had you two wretches with me all along, did I? Well, we saw out the night. Let's hope they did inside.'

As he spoke, they heard the iron groan of hinges as the doors behind them opened on the day. Inside the chapel, moving like the risen dead, a ghostly group of swaying bodies met their gaze. First out through the arched doorway and into the rising sun was young Mador, with his brother Patrise. Mador's white face had a worn and waxy sheen, but the look in his eye was pure exaltation.

Half shouldering, half carrying his brother's stumbling form, Mador was gently coaxing Patrise forward step by step. 'Mind your footing, brother, easy now,' he breathed. Joyfully he hugged his brother to his side, and murmured in his ear, 'Take heart, it's over, we've done it, dear Patrise!'

The three knights watched them cross the courtyard, and pass through the cloisters to disappear from sight. Behind them came the rest of the novices in ones and twos. At the far back were three towering figures sized like Gawain. He pushed forward eagerly to greet them in the porch. 'Brothers, how goes it? How was the night?'

'How do you think?'

The speaker shouldered past him with a face like lightning hidden in a cloud. As tall as Gawain but much leaner, he was as dark as the rest of his brothers were fair. Of all the four sons of Lot, the world observed, only Agravain had inherited his father's colouring – a pity he had King Lot's black temperament too. Even clad in the white robe of a novice knight and blanched by the rising sun, Agravain carried with him a darkness of his own. Now, with a sullen glare and an angry shake of the head, he stalked off across the courtyard towards his waiting page.

Gawain turned to his brothers. 'What's troubling Agravain?' he asked in a low voice.

Gaheris threw a glance at Kay and Bedivere. Family matters, his embarrassed silence said. 'Oh – ' he shrugged. His voice trailed off.

Gawain nodded grimly, needing no further words. To be born the second son was a heavy curse of fate. Since childhood Agravain had raged against this spite of the Gods. It was as bad as being born male in a land like the Summer Country, where women were ordained to rule. Only the sudden good fortune of finding himself the head of the family would appease the hunger of Agravain's haunted soul. And Gawain had no intention of dying in order to set his sibling free from the torment of his rage.

And yet –

'Is that all?' he demanded, turning abruptly on Gareth, whose young face was an open book of his every thought.

Gareth flushed, and spread his hands. 'Brother – ' he said helplessly.

Kay took in the situation at a glance. 'Come, Bedivere,' he said briskly, 'let's get some rest.' Clapping Gawain on the back, he led Bedivere away. 'We'll see you at noon for the ceremony,' he called.

The three brothers stood in silence and watched them go.

'So?' Gawain demanded ominously.

Gareth looked in anguish at Gaheris, then back to Gawain again. But Gaheris only said quietly, 'Tell him.'

Gareth drew a breath. 'Our brother is unhappy to see our

mother here.' He paused uneasily. 'With only one special escort, when she could have been surrounded by her chosen knights.'

'Hah!' Gawain's face showed that he was not surprised. He took a heavy breath. 'She is a queen,' he said doggedly, 'and a great one too. She is sole ruler of our whole kingdom, from Lothian to the farthest Orcades. And a mother has a right to be at her sons' knight-making, yes?' He paused, then spoke with a fierce emphasis. 'With whatever company she chooses to keep.'

'Sole ruler, brother?' Gaheris frowned. 'If we were sure of that – But Agravain thinks her knight has too much influence. Sir Lamorak never leaves her side.'

'Gods above!' Gawain exploded. 'This is Agravain's poison speaking, not your own thoughts! I'll hear no more of it!'

Gaheris flushed. 'It's true that Agravain's concerned. He thinks our mother is under –'

'He can tell me himself what he thinks,' Gawain glowered. 'But for you, and you too, Gareth,' he repeated, fixing his younger brother with a fierce glare, 'let this be an end of it, d'you hear? She's the sister of King Arthur, she's the daughter of a queen, she's a great queen herself, and she's our sovereign lady and our mother too.' He paused. 'A queen must have her knights.'

'Knights maybe, brother.' Gareth looked distressed. 'But one alone?'

'Every queen has her Champion and Chosen One.' Gawain stuck out his chin. His face was dark. 'Enough, Gareth, or we'll come to blows. And tell Agravain the same goes for him if I hear another word!'

CHAPTER 5

Pendragon.

Arthur, then before him was Uther, then Gawther, then old Mauther, High King for a hundred years. Before him there had been Pendragons as far back as anyone could remember, and no one knew if they had been men or Gods.

Merlin sighed, and cracked his bony knuckles one by one. Men, or Gods, or both?

Not that it mattered to the eye of time. One blink, and they were gone. Merlin's eyes grew dim. How many bold, laughing, red-gold men had he seen go down to the world between the worlds?

And only old Merlin left to maintain the line. Well, so be it. The enchanter settled his scrawny frame in the saddle, and drew a deep breath of the sweet summer air. Above his head the trees met in a perfect arch, casting a greenish light on the path below. The narrow bridleway ran deep between high banks, and all around him the world was fresh with the green shoots of June. His patient mule trod at an easy pace, its every step in tune with Merlin's thoughts.

Pendragon.

The search was on for the next in the line.

The quest would be long, he knew. But to a lord of light as he was, time rolled in channels not known to other men.

Slowly he mused on.

Gore.

That was the place to start.

Merlin laughed. Strange to think how much had begun in Gore, the kingdom where he had himself hidden Arthur so long ago. The King of Gore had been a most faithful friend. No man had served Pendragon as Ursien did, and his knight Sir Ector loved Arthur as his own.

Yes, all that was well done. But now?

Merlin bared his yellow teeth. When Arthur was born, he and these others had laboured to save his life. But for Arthur's issue in turn – Gods above, who had taken account of that? And what to do now, when the line seemed likely to fail? The familiar pain began gnawing again in his breast. The old man reached out and tore a handful of heart's-ease from the steep wayside to chew as he passed, and lapsed into deep thought.

How to keep the line alive, when Arthur had no heir?

'Yet Arthur has had seed.'

Merlin raised his eyes. On the top of the bank, perched under a hawthorn tree, sat an aged woman, regarding him steadily with a kindly eye. Though she was clad from head to foot in black, her soft garments seemed to weave themselves into the shadows of the hillside, and he had not noticed her before. Her twinkling gaze was both merry and wise, and she waited with the composure of a woodland creature for him to speak.

Merlin smiled. He knew better than to say, 'Greetings, old mother, where do you live?' for she would only reply, 'Oh, here and everywhere, good son.' Yet the wrinkled face beneath the tall black hat was anything but vague, and her words were sharply echoing his own thoughts. He grinned at her. Truly the Great Ones sent their help at need.

'Arthur has had sons,' he agreed. His thin frame tensed as he prepared himself for his rage. 'Two fine ones – and the great fool lost them both!'

The old woman tutted softly. 'Any king would want to take his first-born son to war. Arthur was not to know.'

'Amir was only a child. He was too young!'

'Yes, Guenevere was right, and Arthur was wrong. But neither of them could have known that their son would pay for the sin that had brought Arthur into the world.'

'Sin?' Merlin's eyes flashed fire.

'Sin,' repeated the old woman equably. 'When Uther took Igraine, he broke the Mother-right. And to dispose of her daughters in the way he did –' She sighed heavily, and shook her head. 'That was a wickedness the Great One could not forgive.'

Merlin ground his teeth. 'We had to ensure that Arthur was Igraine's only concern.'

'So her daughters had to lose their mother and father, their sister-bond, and the life they knew? Was that not an offence against them both? From her marriage, Morgause at least was granted four sons to love. But Morgan had to live in a convent, beaten and starved for the sins of Eve. No wonder that she learned how to hate. Arthur has paid dearly for his father's deeds.'

Merlin could not deny it. He nodded helplessly and spread his hands. The old woman's indictment rolled on with the force of an incoming tide. 'All Morgan's sufferings sprang from Uther's desire for an heir. What better revenge than to rob Arthur of his son?'

'And to torture his wife,' Merlin said sombrely. 'Amir was her son too.'

'Morgan was too much for both of them. She told the Saxons where Amir lay concealed. Her malice guided the spear that pierced his heart.'

'Yet another boy could have taken Amir's place!' Merlin cried. 'Morgan destroyed Amir in order to give Arthur her own son instead. But then the great fool wanted all the newborn boys put down. He hated Morgan so much that he was ready to cast away his own flesh and blood!' He clutched at his head. 'Lost one son, lost another, he'll surely be the end of the Pendragon line!'

The old woman's eyes raked him from head to foot. 'But you don't believe,' she said softly, 'that Morgan's son was lost.'

'No!' The old man's face split with a sudden fierce joy. 'He lives, I can feel it, I know the boy lives!' He cackled with glee, and rubbed his leathery hands. Every inch of his skin was crackling with delight. 'Morgan would not let her son be killed.'

He cocked an eye wildly at the old dame. 'She called him Mordred, did you know that? She named him for a purpose, and her purpose is revenge. She means her son to bring *more dread* to the House of Pendragon than we shall ever know.'

A prophetic shudder passed through his withered frame. 'So I must find him, and bring him to Arthur again. That's the only way to turn aside Morgan's schemes. I know that she has saved the boy somehow. And now she has spirited him away, the Gods know where. But I will find him, if it takes ten years.'

'Where will you look?'

Merlin laughed harshly. 'Everywhere. Morgan could hide her son under a leaf.'

There was a gentle laugh. 'She may have hidden him under your very nose.'

The old man swayed in the saddle and passed a weary hand over his eyes. 'She can do anything.' He groaned. 'Anything!'

'The power of darkness is at her command,' the old woman agreed. Her ageless eyes rested on the old man. 'As you well know.'

Merlin's parchment skin took on a brownish hue. He clenched his teeth. 'I remember.'

His flesh crawled. How could he forget that Morgan had played on him till she awoke his lust, had sucked the soul out of his body, sported with him, and driven him mad with shame? And then while he was slowly mending his wounded wits, confined to the calm of Avalon's crystal cave, the black-eyed witch had had free rein with Arthur, and seduced him too. Yes, Morgan Le Fay was a thing of darkness indeed.

Merlin's voice rose in a high, fractured wail. 'I was not there when Arthur needed me!' He shook himself like a dog, in a vain attempt to cast her out of his thoughts. 'I opened the gate to let the evil in to him. But I shall make amends when I bring him his son.'

The old woman shook her head. 'Think, Lord Merlin, think! If you do that, Mordred is Arthur's heir. Do you want a child of incest to lead the House of Pendragon in times to come?'

'Arthur and Morgan were only connected on the mother's side,' Merlin said stubbornly. 'There's no reason why he can't be High King.'

The old woman's voice took on a stronger note. 'I beg you, think again. Remember, the blood of Queen Igraine flows in Morgan's veins. Igraine hated Uther with all her heart. And all that hatred Morgan will pour into her son.'

Merlin nodded unhappily. Once again the old woman had sensed his deepest thoughts. 'Yet he is still a Pendragon,' he insisted, 'and the only one left to rule when Arthur dies.'

The old woman fixed her clear green eyes on him. 'That is not written in the stars, Lord Merlin.'

Merlin sat up as if he had been stung. 'Will Guenevere have a child?'

The old woman shook her head. 'Grief has closed up her womb since Amir died.'

'How, then?'

She raised a wrinkled finger to her lips. 'Do not ask.'

'I must!' Merlin cried. 'Pendragon must rise in this land again! Or else – ' He tossed his head in pain, and his long grey locks moved round his neck like snakes.

The sadness of the ages breathed in the old woman's words. 'Or else it is all for nothing?'

Merlin clutched at his head. 'All my life – all my lives – I have worked for this end! To ensure that Pendragon will be High King by right, instead of having to make war in every reign. To restore our house –'

'*Our* house?'

The cool question stabbed Merlin like a knife. 'Our house!' he shouted. 'My mother was a princess of Pendragon, a virgin priestess, touched by a Holy One! I was the last of the line, until the time came when I could bring Arthur forward to claim his own.' His voice broke. 'I must make sure that it continues now.'

'But not with Mordred, not through that line.' The old woman's voice darkened and grew heavy as she spoke. She stood up, growing taller before Merlin's gaze. The black spire of her headdress seemed to weave its way up through the branches of the tree until it touched the sky. 'Hear me, Lord Merlin. Do not seek to find the boy.'

Merlin's face was transformed. 'So he is alive!' he hissed, clasping his wizened hands in ecstasy. 'I have had glimpses, caught words flaming in the sky, but my sight failed me, I could not see so far.' He dropped his reins. A trickle of tears ran down his wrinkled cheeks. 'Praised be the Great Ones,' he wept. 'Thanks to the blessed Gods! He lives! Pendragon lives!'

The figure before him was still growing and fading away. But her words reached into the deep places of his mind, like the echoing voice of thunder on the hills. 'Lord Merlin, it is not for you to know. Dead or alive, let the boy sleep in peace. Pendragon he is, but Morgan's creature too. She gave him half her name, and more than half of her own dark nature, the evil that you know. Do you still think to track down this changeling child? Think, Merlin – think of Arthur! Think of Guenevere, even though you have no love for her!'

The wind sighed, and she was gone. Merlin sat gazing at the shimmering air, his mind, his whole being washed clean of conscious thought. Praise the Gods, throbbed numbly through his frame, the blessed, blessed Gods –

Slowly, slowly he came to himself again. High overhead a golden eagle wheeled and danced in the sky. Behind it, and tracking its every move, flew the dogged shadow of a lesser hawk. Merlin cackled. More than one word was coming to him today. The old hawk's work for the royal eagle his master was not yet done, it seemed.

He breathed out heavily and took up the reins, urging the white mule on. His thoughts began again with its first steps. Pendragon must succeed. Arthur now, and after him – who?

CHAPTER 6

The Great Hall of Camelot struck cool in the midday heat. The sun poured through the windows, and fell in streams of molten gold to the grey-flagged floor. The brilliant light gilded the high white walls, and lost itself in the soaring vault of the roof above.

In the centre of the hall the Round Table stood in all its glory, surrounded by the sieges of its one hundred knights. Twenty of the names picked out in gold on the wooden canopies overhead were fresher than the rest. Each of the knights who had kept the vigil in the chapel was now to receive his sword from the King, and take the seat at the Table that he had striven so hard to win.

Many of the knights had already taken their seats. From his life-long place, old Sir Niamh surveyed the new gilt-work, and was swept with a sense of loss. There, where the scrolled letters read 'Sir Mador of the Meads', was the siege where Rotho used to sit, his dear old friend-in-arms, and over there, the hot-tempered Tirzel, never liked, but oddly missed once he was gone. Rotho had died in the infamous Saxon attack, when the young prince Amir had been killed. Tirzel had perished ignominiously when an evil lord had thrown him down a well. Now strangers would take their seats, and young ones too. Unfledged boys, Niamh mourned, filling the place of men.

Yet one seat at the Table was not filled. Niamh did not need to lift the red velvet cover over the canopy to read the words that every knight knew by heart. **'Here is the Siege Perilous,'** the gold letters read, **'for the Knight Who Is To Come. He Will Be the Most Peerless Knight In All the World, and When He**

Comes, the Prophecy of Merlin Will Be Fulfilled.'

Niamh sighed. He could remember when Merlin had made this prophecy, from the depths of his crystal cave. A boy would come, the old enchanter had said, who would be the son of the finest knight in all the world. He was destined for the highest adventure of all. They must call his seat the Siege Perilous, for he would face many dangers, and defeat each one. He would become the best knight in his turn. And when he came, the Table would be complete.

Of course they all thought it would be young Amir, who else? The Queen's son, and so like his father that every movement, even the way he held his sun-blessed head, was Arthur to the life – no one in the world could have a stronger claim. And who could make a better knight at the Table of the Great Mother herself than the Queen's own son? It had all been perfect, a cause of heartfelt joy.

Too perfect, Niamh reflected grimly. Fate had seen to that. He fingered the thick gold torque around his neck, the only badge of knighthood before the Christians had brought in this foolery of suffering, vigils and fasts. Was he the only one who remembered the glory days, the days of gold before Arthur came?

No, over there was Sir Lucan, a valiant knight of Queen Guenevere, and one-time Champion of the Queen's mother before. And Sir Lovell, Lovell the Bold the women used to call him, still as handsome as ever, damn him, not a scar to be seen. Niamh chuckled. The new knights would do well if they managed half of Lovell's triumphs with twice his wounds.

His eye roved on. Lovell was a hero, one of the old school, not to mention Gawain, Kay and Bedivere sitting next to Dinant, Tor and Sagramore, doughty warriors all. Sir Niamh sighed. Yet the Round Table needed new blood, there was no doubt of that. So it was right that the King and Queen were to make up a band of new knights today, with a fine feast to boot.

The King –

Sir Niamh frowned down the length of the Great Hall. Outlined against the whiteness of the far wall, Arthur sat enthroned with Guenevere in a blaze of gold and red. Above the dais was a canopy of scarlet silk, and on the wall above, their royal banners picked out in silver and gold, the crossed flags drooping limply from their poles. In the quiet space the Queen flamed in a crimson gown, with a cloak of white silk and a ruby-studded crown. To honour his new knights, Arthur wore the plain white tunic of knighthood over simple dark breeches and fine leather boots. Only his rich silk cloak of royal red, and the heavy gold crown of Pendragon proclaimed him a king. The sun poured down like a blessing on his fair head as he gripped the arms of his throne, the lines of resolution visible on his face.

Sir Niamh felt a stirring around his heart. What a man Arthur was, what a king! That ever he should have had to suffer so, both him and the Queen! Niamh closed his eyes, and a heartfelt prayer rose unbidden to his mind: Goddess, Mother, spare them more misery, help the King.

At the head of the hall Guenevere sat immobile on her throne, and did her best to stifle unwelcome thoughts.

If Amir had lived, we would be knighting him now.

No, not yet, he would not be old enough.

But still —

She gripped the carved arm-rests of her throne in an unconscious echo of Arthur's regal pose, and straightened up. She must not allow herself to envy Queen Morgause of the Orkneys, seated below her in the body of the hall. Tall and well formed, inclining to an ample fullness, Morgause shone like a midnight star in a gown of indigo velvet, with purple sleeves and a train of sweet viridian. A white veil floated down from her headdress to wind around her stately neck and shoulders, and the crown of the Orkneys glittered on her head.

Behind Queen Morgause's throne stood her knight, Sir Lamorak. She half turned, he leaned down towards her, and she whispered in his ear. He nodded, and a languorous smile passed over her face. In the same instant it came to Guenevere: *these two are lovers, she has had him in her bed.*

Morgause glanced up at Lamorak again, then her eyes sought her eldest son Gawain. Seated at the Round Table, finely dressed in green and gold, relaxed in careless manhood, Gawain's big body was almost beautiful, and Morgause's gaze caressed him with a fierce maternal pride. Watching her, Guenevere was seized by such a pang of envy that she almost cried aloud.

She held her breath, and tried not to feel or think. Morgause had suffered much in her marriage, Guenevere knew. King Lot was crueller than the Saxon pirates, who crucified monks on their own church roofs and played football with unborn babies ripped from their mothers' wombs. Yes, Morgause had suffered. But she had never lost a son. Least of all to the Saxons, men so cruel they would dig up a child from his grave to make his father grieve. So Amir had to be buried on the sea-shore, where his small grave would never leave a sign. Where not a soul, not even his mother, could find it again.

A horde of wounding thoughts came down on Guenevere like a swarm of angry bees. *And now I sit here childless, when I might have been like Morgause, revelling in a mother's joy. Even at seven Amir was so bright, so forward, so tall and bold that he would have been made a knight ahead of his time, perhaps even now, with the young knights here today.*

And every one of them will remind me of him. Arthur will feel it too. Every sword-stroke on every new knight's shoulder will be a knife in both our hearts. For there will never be a knighthood for our boy. The Siege Perilous will remain unfulfilled.

The first would be worst, they both knew that. The first young man who mounted the dais in his pure white tunic, scarlet cloak and shining mail would be the sharpest reminder that if Amir had lived, he would have been this and more. Shivering beneath her cloak even in the warmth of the sun, Guenevere pressed her cold hands together and echoed Sir Niamh's prayer: *Goddess, Mother, be with Arthur and strengthen him now, help my dearest man –*

A great fly buzzed against the window above her head. Guenevere shifted restlessly in her seat. Where were the novice knights? They had all been released from last night's ordeal long ago, revived with strong cordials, given bread and hot meat. How long did the attendants need to give each one the ritual bath, and robe him in the white tunic of purity, and the red cape for the blood that he must shed?

'Your Majesties? The novice knights are here.'

Guenevere started. For all her impatience, the approach of the Chamberlain had taken her unawares. She caught Arthur's eye, and he nodded impersonally. She bowed to the Chamberlain at her side. 'Yes, we are ready,' she said. 'Let the ceremony begin.'

The Chamberlain bowed, then turned and raised his staff. At the far end of the hall, the great double doors swung back. Waiting outside was the novice master, finely arrayed in chequered black and white. Beside him stood the first of the novices, his pale face burning like a candle flame.

Behind the novice master came the rest of the novices, walking in pairs. At the rear three mighty figures towered above the rest. Agravain, Gaheris and Gareth were set apart from their fellows, as princes of the Orkneys, and close kin to the King.

The small procession drew up before the dais. Arthur reached for the sword at his side, and rose to his feet. Guenevere stood too, and put her soul into her eyes. *Courage Arthur*, she willed him, *I am with you, take heart, my dear.*

Arthur felt her glance, and turned. *And I with you*, his grieving look replied.

'Approach the throne, Mador of the Meads!' called the Chamberlain. White and quivering, the frail youth mounted the steps, and knelt at Arthur's feet.

The silver sound of trumpets pealed overhead. As pale as Mador and beginning to tremble too, Arthur drew Excalibur from its sheath. The great sword murmured sweetly in his hand. Arthur inclined his head. 'Do your office, Chamberlain,' he commanded in a steady voice. 'Require the oath.'

'Mador, do you swear to serve your liege lady Guenevere with your life?' cried the Chamberlain. 'To honour your lord King Arthur with your last breath? To keep the Fellowship of the Round Table till your dying hour? To defend the weak, and give battle to the strong, and protect all women all your livelong days?'

Mador swallowed. His voice was a dry husk. 'I swear.' He reached for Arthur's hand, and brought it to his lips. Excalibur flashed through the air to touch Mador's left shoulder, then the right, then left again. Arthur's voice was clear and strong. 'Arise, Sir Mador, and glory be your name!'

The novice master stepped forward to pass a fine sword-belt to Guenevere, with a slim gold and silver sword dangling from its side. 'Draw near, Sir Mador,' she said.

For the rest of his life Mador never forgot the touch of the Queen's hands, fluttering like butterflies as she buckled on his sword. He was trembling so violently that he could hardly stand, and his head was filled with her as with a bewitching scent. Dazzled, he saw the sunlight slanting on her still burning-bright hair, casting fragments of light into her slate-blue eyes. He heard her speak, but did not know the words. Yet his soul sang to the music of her voice like the harmony of the stars, Guenevere my lady, Guenevere the Queen –

Mador –

Guenevere stood on the dais and watched him go. *Mador, yes, I know who you are. The son of a poor lady from Marches, who has spent all her widow's mite on sending her sons to be knights, to honour their own wishes and the will of her dead lord. You have a brother Patrise – is that his name? Yes, there he is, a younger, paler shadow of you, Mador, and the Gods know that you are pale enough.*

Yet you are brave, you wear it in your eyes. You will do well. All my knights will do well.

The ceremony wore on. One by one the knights were dubbed.

'Arise, Sir –'

'Arise, Sir –'

At last only three large forms remained in the body of the hall. Guenevere saw Morgause sit up eagerly, murmuring to her knight, the rich blue velvet rippling over her heavy mother's breasts as she watched her youngest, Gareth, moving down the hall. When he stepped up on the dais to receive his sword, Guenevere had to struggle to get the leather harness over his head, even though Gareth was shamefacedly trying to make himself as small as he could. She smiled to herself, and sadly acknowledged Morgause's glowing pride in her four fine sons. The Orkney princes, Arthur's nearest kin, were the only men at court who could stand shoulder to shoulder with him, and like him, block out the light.

Gaheris, too, had to stoop to receive his sword. Now only Agravain remained, standing alone. Guenevere glanced down, and hardly knew what she saw. The eyes raised to hers were pools of black despair.

No, not despair, her racing heart rushed on, but a sucking, seething hollowness, empty of all but hate. Then Agravain's face changed, and it was gone. With a downcast face and reverent air, he knelt before Arthur and bent his head. Arthur stretched out his arm, and Excalibur murmured faintly in his hand.

Suddenly Guenevere caught a sharp tapping sound behind. Above her head, perched outside the high window, was a raven, peering in. Its hooked beak ended in a cruel tip, and its round eye glistened with a blue-black sheen. As Arthur's sword fell for the third time on Agravain's shoulder, the hideous creature opened its mouth to crow.

Guenevere's mind spun. *A dark messenger from the Otherworld! Arthur must not see –*

'Bow your head, Sir Agravain,' she instructed hastily. Somehow she fastened the sword round his long frame.

'May your Gods go with you, sir,' she wished him through cold lips, 'and bring all your purposes to fulfilment, whatever they are.'

He raised his head, and his mouth formed a cynical smile. 'They will, madam, they will.'

'You are one of the Fellowship of the Round Table now. See that you serve it well.'

As she spoke, a loud crack came from the centre of the hall, followed by a groan, like life itself escaping from some mighty thing. To Sir Niamh it was as if the Round Table had let out a cry of woe. Gawain leaped to his feet, and supported the great wooden disc with both hands as he peered down to inspect the trestles below. 'It's only shifted on its base, there's no danger here,' he cried out reassuringly. 'You may carry on, sire, let the ceremony finish as planned.'

But another sharp rap from above distracted Arthur from his task. He turned to look up at the window where the raven on the ledge had launched itself into a dance. Puffing up its chest and flapping its wings, it strutted to and fro, clacking with glee. At last it lifted the blunt wedge of its tail and triumphantly voided the contents of its body before launching itself into the air. One, twice, three times it circled, darkening the sky, before winging straight into the sun, where it was lost from sight.

Arthur turned to Guenevere with an odd, strained laugh. 'So, Guenevere, she has returned, it seems?'

CHAPTER 7

The sweet mist off the water reached them on the highest crag. From there the narrow track wound down the sheer face of the mountain to the lake. Bors loosened the reins to give his horse its head, and noticed his two companions doing the same. Trusting to the sure footing of a creature born in these parts was their best hope now. He looked at the dizzy drop at the side of the path, and composed himself for the descent. May the Great One in all Her kindness see us safely down!

'And may this torturous journey soon have an end,' he added under his breath. He gritted his teeth. He had not expected the going to be so hard. As if the crossing of the Narrow Sea had not been bad enough! Brave as he was, Bors was no sailor in his soul.

It had not helped him to remember the time when they first left Little Britain and they first saw the sea. They had been only boys then, on fire with the thrill of accompanying their fathers to war. Sailing over to the island of the Britons to fight for the fledgling king had been the greatest adventure of their young lives. Well, Arthur's war had been won for a good decade and more, and never once had they sailed back to their native land.

Until now. Now Lancelot's stars had led him back to Little Britain, and wherever their cousin went, Bors and Lionel would go too. And in truth, rough as the terrain was, the beloved country was opening its arms to welcome them home.

Bors glanced at the rider ahead of him as the native ponies plodded stolidly downhill, nose to tail, and his heart eased. Here, if anywhere, Lancelot would find peace. Here, all would be well.

He looked around him with a stranger's eyes, and marvelled

at what he saw. He had forgotten how wild, how wonderful this
land could be. Massed eglantine ran riot down the mountain, its
tender pink laced with pale honeysuckle, their mingled scents
filling the hot dry air. Underfoot lay clusters of white thrift and
scrubby blue-green thyme. The sharp fragrance released by the
horses' hoofs reminded Bors of boyhood days out hunting, when
they knew no greater joy than to roast what they had caught with
a fistful of wild herbs, sage or rosemary. He sighed with deep
content. Here in the south-west of the ragged, sea-girt
promontory lay a secret world, a place made by the Old Ones,
then forgotten by time. And this was the end of their journey,
where Lancelot might find what he sought.

The going was harder now, and the rough ponies were
placing each stubby hoof with care. The mountain path had
narrowed till there was hardly a foot of land between the riders
and the craggy void. Bors schooled himself to sit deep in the
saddle, centring his weight in the hollow of his short-legged
mount's strong back. He fixed his eyes on Lancelot, and raised a
fervent prayer. Lady, spirit of this place, wherever you may be,
give peace to our cousin, heal his wound, console him for his
loss.

'Bors! Lionel! See there!'

Bors followed Lancelot's pointing hand. Far below lay a
hidden valley, a verdant green amid the rugged mountain crags.
As they descended they could see a waterfall cascading from the
peak, and above it a fragment of rainbow playing in and out of the
silvery mist in the midday sun. The plume of water danced its
way down the cliff until it plunged into a dark, still lake below,
spreading from the base of the rock to form a perfect mirror of the
world above.

Lancelot stretched his long legs in the saddle, taking care not
to disturb his horse's foothold on the vertiginous path, and gave
weary thanks. 'Descend from the crag by the narrowest way,' was
the memory he had carried with him for ten years. 'Though the
road shrinks to nothing beneath your feet, press on. Do not let
your gaze drop into the void. Raise your eyes to the heavens, and
you will see the sign you seek.'

The rainbow. That was the sign.

'If you return,' she had said when he left. And he had smiled with all the assurance of his sixteen years, and told her, 'Say not if, Lady, only when.'

He could hardly believe now in the confidence he had had then. How long had he known that the Old Ones had marked him out? All his life, it seemed. Other boys, like Bors and Lionel, had been the sons of kings, and others, too, had had been reared with the same care, brought up with boys of lesser birth, as the three of them had been, to give them respect for true worth, wherever it was found. But only he had been taken by the Lady of the Sacred Lake to foster as her own. '𝔜our son will be Sir 𝔏ancelot 𝔡u 𝔏ac, the most peerless knight in all the world,' ran the Lady's runic script when the summons came. 'Send him to me, that he may fulfil his fate.' Tears as big as diamonds had stood in his mother's eyes when she read the words. But she knew in her heart that she had to let him go.

So he had grown up a prince in this hidden valley, and the lake palace of the Lady had been his home. She had tutored him in knighthood and deeds of arms, and also schooled him in the book of love. Never did he forget his parents, King Ban and Queen Elaine, nor the two cousins who were like brothers to him now. But his place was here, and she, more than they, had made him what he was.

Whatever he was.

A bitter smile creased the handsome young brown face. Of course he was not the finest knight in the world: that honour belonged to Arthur, everyone knew that. But from six to sixteen he had studied with the Lady to become the best he could. And he was still failing, he reflected savagely, to approach his ideal.

His heart stirred, and he felt again the stabbing shafts of pain that came to him every moment, every day. A hundred separate sorrows made one endless ache, the grief that answered to the name of Guenevere.

Yet he could not blame her for what he suffered now. He knew she had been right to send him away. Not even that, he thought with a special pain. She had not dismissed him. They both had known that the time had come to part.

If only it did not have to be so. Each thought now came with a separate groan of pain. If only they were free to enjoy their love.

If only she were not the Queen – not married – and above all, not to Arthur, his own dear lord and king –

Enough! he castigated himself. They had both agreed that the fragile love growing between them must be no more. Together they had pledged themselves to murder the new growth, root it out and trample it underfoot. He must find another lady, she told him through dry lips. She must love and honour her lord, he told her, pale with the effort and fighting for control. And so it was agreed. They would be better strangers than lovers now, nothing to each other after one last kiss.

Yet love so butchered cannot die cleanly, but lingers on, a weeping, wounded, mutilated thing. What then had brought him here after ten years? What could the Lady do, what could she say? Yet still an inner voice told him that it had been time to return. Here, if anywhere, he would find his way.

The air had been getting warmer all the way down. Now at the foot of the track, the midsummer heat reached up to fold them in its shimmering embrace. Deep in the valley, not a breath stirred. Ahead of them lay the Lake, a perfect circle, no longer dark but silvery in the sun. Breaking the surface as they approached were the heads and shoulders of half a dozen laughing girls. Their bodies were clothed in filmy draperies, and their long hair floated out around them like water-weeds.

'Welcome, Sir Lancelot!' called the leader, striking out boldly towards them in a shower of glistening spray. 'We have been expecting you!'

'And Sir Bors!'

'And Sir Lionel!' chorused her sisters merrily.

The maidens trod water and held out their slender white arms. 'Come!'

The three knights dismounted, slipped their reins and allowed their horses to graze. Together they approached the water's edge. Golden king-cups and forget-me-nots as blue as the sky overhung the placid surface, smiling at their own faces below. The sun lay like molten bronze over all the scene.

The chief maiden leaned up and placed an arm on the grassy verge. 'Sir Lancelot!' she called, in a voice like water over stones. 'My sisters will take care of Sir Bors and Sir Lionel. You are to come with me.' She reached up, and took his hand in a powerful grip. One pull, and Lancelot found himself falling forward through the melting air. The waters parted and he entered the silent world beneath the Lake.

The cool water soothed his tired skin like balm. He felt the dust and grime of the roads leave his travel-worn limbs, and the weight on his soul lighten with his new-found buoyancy. Ahead of him he could see his guide carving her way through the water, a fine trail of sparkling bubbles in her wake. He swam after her like an eel, and could have laughed aloud in delight. With every fluid move, his body was remembering the natural element of his boyhood days. And more than that, the secret way back home.

Down they went, and down. Shafts of yellow sunlight poured through the greenish deep, and Lancelot laughed to himself again as he chased the slight form ahead as it went fluttering through the depths. Now the lake was growing darker as they drew closer to the crag looming above. The waters began to boil as they took the full force of the waterfall tumbling from the peak. Lancelot plunged into the maelstrom without fear. Once through the bubbling cauldron below the fall, he knew what he would find.

He swam until he felt the weight of the falling water, then floated free, allowing it to drive him down and down. Now his head and chest began to pain him, and his lungs felt squeezed by a giant hand. He fought the mad urge to inhale, and cursed himself for his earlier recklessness. He had been too careless with his breath in the excitement of coming back. Another misjudgement, and he would spend eternity at the bottom of the whirlpool, never to rise again.

His lungs were bursting, and his senses were beginning to fail. And still he was going down, pounded remorselessly by the waterfall.

Hold on –

Still further down –

Hold on!

Gods, let me breathe!

With the last breath in his body he flipped sideways out of the furious turmoil into the clear green water on the other side of the fall. And there it was, a great arch of underwater rock. He swam for it with the speed of desperation, then struck upwards with all his force, his lungs on fire.

He broke the surface scrabbling like a dog, tossing his head to get the hair out of his eyes. One stroke brought him to the rocky edge of the pool, and he heaved himself out. The blood thundered in his veins as he gulped down great draughts of air. Above it sounded the roar of the waterfall. Then a laugh like an otter's bark reached his ears. 'So, Lancelot, you have forgotten how to swim? Time, indeed, for my pupil to return.'

Lancelot raised his head as his eyes accustomed themselves to the light. 'Lady –' He stumbled over the word, confused by the strange yet familiar sight.

Before him yawned a great cavern, reaching into the heart of the rock. Wide but low, it held all the warmth of the sun-baked land above. Only where the rock pool lay behind the shining curtain of the waterfall, was the air cool and moist with dancing droplets of the breaking cascade. The cave rolled out before him, inviting him in.

In the distance, a female figure reclined on a long couch. Her silken gown of brown and gold clung to her lithe flanks like an animal's skin. A strange cap of crystals hugged her head, flashing with every broken ray of sunlight that made its way in through the dancing waterfall. Beneath the cap her shining hair fell like rain. She was young and yet ageless, knowing, and yet quite unmarked by time. She extended an arm to beckon him to her side, her body rippling with slumbering power. 'Come, Lancelot of the Lake. Welcome to Broceliande.'

The chief of her maidens stood at the head of her couch. A dozen or so other gossamer-clad girls stood or sat around their mistress's throne. Their eyes were bright with mischief, and their laughter tinkled like fountains in the wind as Lancelot approached.

'Hush, girls,' said the Lady indulgently, raising a hand. 'Be off with you now.'

Giggling, they all scattered back to play in the rock pool. The Lady waved Lancelot to a stool at her side. 'So?'

Lancelot fixed his gaze on her shining form with all the hunger of ten years away. The brown eyes that looked back held all the wisdom of a beaver, and the blithe sweetness of a water-vole. Her small muscular mouth moved with a mirthful twitch, and her teeth when she smiled were white and sharp. To

Lancelot, she had not aged at all since he left. And boy though he was then, it came to him with the shock of new awareness that she had not changed in the decade before that, when he had lived with her and seen her every day. He had known her then as a great teacher, and a woman gifted with the Sight. Now he knew that he had not known her at all.

He was dumbfounded, and suddenly at a loss. The Lady smiled. He knew she could hear his thoughts. 'You came here once to learn to be a knight,' she prompted. 'Do you come now to have your poor heart healed, so you may be your own man once again?'

He nodded, still tongue-tied. The thought of Guenevere pierced him so acutely that he could not speak. Gods above, he cursed, where to begin?

The Lady returned his nod. 'Then let me try to tell you your own tale. I am not as old in the ways of seeing as my sister on Avalon. But all this time I have watched you in the mirror of falling water, and seen many things. When you became a knight, you wanted to serve the best lady in the world. You did not know that you would come to love her too.'

Lancelot bent his head. The tears rushed to his eyes.

The strange rough-toned voice went on. 'And she did not know that you would offer her a love closer than her skin. A love a world away from the love she had for her lord.'

'Arthur is more than her lord!' Lancelot burst out. 'He is the High King, the leader of us all.' His heart contracted. 'And he is my lord too. As his knight, I swore to honour him to the death.'

'And instead –?'

'A knight kills his lord every time he lies with his wife.'

'But she sent you away, to spare you all from that shame. And you agreed to go.'

'And now I can hardly live.' Lancelot closed his eyes in a wretchedness too sharp to bear. Goddess, Mother, he prayed, take away this grief –

'If that is what you wish, it can be done.'

Once again the Lady was reading his raw thoughts. He looked up at her in dread.

'Oh, yes.' She smiled her timeless smile. 'Here at the Sacred Lake we have many ways to release you from your pain. I can charm you with the magic sleep of the Druids, so that your mind lies suspended in your body, and you hear only my voice. Whatever I tell you in this waking dream, you will obey. I shall tell you that you do not love Guenevere. And when I bring you back to yourself, that memory will remain.' She paused. 'Or my maidens can make you the cup of forgetfulness. Drink that, and it will wash your brain clean of all you suffer now. You will sleep many days, and when you wake, it will be as if you had never met Queen Guenevere. You may make your way merrily throughout the whole wide world, and never be grieved with the thought of her again.'

Lancelot had turned pale. 'No thought of Guenevere?'

'None.' The brilliants in her headdress flashed like shafts of fire. 'She will never trouble you again.'

The dull roar of water filled the echoing space. Lancelot surged to his feet and paced like a thing in pain.

Forget Guenevere ?

Forget her limpid eyes, her loving smile, the soft strands of hair curling at her temples, the sweet groove of her lip?

Live without the memory of her small hand placed confidingly on his arm, her hopeful smile, her face turned up to his to ask, 'Now, sir, what do you think?' Her child-like frown when she was crossed, her queenly rages when provoked?

Fool!

Why had he dragged himself all the way here to be free of Guenevere, when it was the last thing he could endure?

Double, triple fool!

He could not speak. At last he mastered himself, and turned to the Lady again. 'Forgive me, Lady. The love I have for the Queen is the most precious thing in my life. Without it, I am nothing.' He turned away in a spasm of self-reproach. 'I have wasted your time in coming here. I swear to you, I'll repent in time of my own.'

'A wasted journey, Lancelot?' The Lady shook her head. 'I do not think so. You are no fool.' She rose from the couch. 'Attend.'

In a daze he followed her sinuous figure as she moved down the cave. They came to a halt before the tumbling waterfall. The silver curtain of water splashed and shimmered before their eyes. The Lady composed herself, fixing her gaze on the ground and pressing her hands together palm to palm. Then she turned up her eyes and grew tall, uttering the words of power. 'See, Lancelot,' she intoned, pointing a hand. 'The waterfall!'

As she spoke, the dancing curtain of water shuddered and grew still. Strange figures took their place on its flashing surface, human shapes moving silently, yet speaking without words. Lancelot saw Arthur and King Ursien of Gore, riding with a knight he did not know. The three men were entering a valley in a dark wood.

The scene changed, and he saw a whitewashed, cloistered dwelling built around a central court. Above the courtyard rose a low bell-tower crowned with a Christian cross. The bell was chiming the service of the dead. And suddenly the white courtyard was full of black-clad nuns, flapping like crows around a body on a bier.

The dead man was shrouded from head to foot in white, ready for burial. Draw back the grave-cloth, cried Lancelot's inner voice, let me see who lies there! He knew he would know the man when the shroud went back. He only feared that the face would be his own.

'Lady!' he cried.

'Watch!' warned the Lady, with her angry otter's bark. 'Watch, and see!'

Now the moving picture had composed itself again. Two riders were making their way through the gathering dark. As they passed, the forest on both sides of the track shrank away from them in fear. The branches of the trees shivered aside, and the night-walking creatures scurried to their holes.

Then of the two riders, there was only one. He staggered from his horse, blood running from a gash in his head. The helmet that dropped to the ground bore a gold crown. And the blood-covered face raised in anguish to the stars was as dear to Lancelot as Guenevere's, or his own.

'It is the King!' he cried in agony.

Through the mist came the sound of the convent's passing bell. Then the falling water dissolved all the images and bore them away. Beside him the Lady convulsed as if a bolt of lightning had passed through her frame, and came to herself again. Lancelot stood in an ecstasy of distress. 'The King is in danger!' he cried. 'He has been attacked!'

'My pictures speak in riddles,' the Lady said huskily. 'But some bad omen threatens your lord, that much is clear.' Her face was full of sorrow. 'Will you return?'

Lancelot twisted away. 'The Queen ordered me to go.'

'But the King stands in peril of his life.'

'I swore an oath to Guenevere! For the love that lies between us, she has forbidden me the court.'

The Lady's keen animal's eyes never left his face. 'King or Queen, which loyalty is the greater? You must choose.' She gave her otter's cough. 'On your knighthood, Sir Lancelot, what will you do?'

CHAPTER 8

The raven of death appearing at the knight-making, just as Agravain was proclaimed – was it Morgan, as Arthur believed?

Or another dark messenger from the world beneath the worlds?

Or simply a passing bird, nothing at all?

Guenevere roamed her chamber in an agony of doubt and fear. She came to a halt at the window, and drew deep breaths of the warm summer air. The pounding in her head was more than she could bear. Would Morgan's malice pursue them all their lives? Surely the son of Uther had paid for his father's misdeeds? Would the daughter of Igraine always seek revenge?

She paused in her pacing, and forced herself to be calm. The knight-making was over, there was nothing more to fear. Arthur was out of harm's way in the forest, hunting with King Ursien and Sir Accolon.

She sighed.

Safe.

Arthur was safe.

And soon she would join them on the woodland ride. All that remained now was one last farewell. Queen Morgause was coming to take her leave, before embarking on her long journey back to the Orkneys, eight hundred miles away and more. Guenevere's heart revived. At least one of Igraine's daughters did not blame Arthur for all that had passed, but wanted to remain on good terms with him. Already Morgause had made her formal goodbyes, and received a royal send-off at Arthur's hands.

Behind her Guenevere could hear her maid Ina padding

softly around the chamber, preparing to receive the Queen. Every surface was gleaming with beeswax, Camelot's reddest roses were glowing in the hearth, and a flagon of honeyed wine was sweetening the air. Ina herself was on alert by the door. When the clatter at the foot of the tower announced the arrival of the Queen and her entourage, her sharp ears were the first to pick up the sound.

'Oh madam, they're here!' Ina's small, cat-like face lit up.

'Hush . . .'

Two pairs of feet were mounting the winding stairs. The ancient walls echoed to the low murmuring of two souls in close communion. Ina flew to the door. It opened to reveal Morgause, attended by Sir Lamorak, her knight.

Her full body was simply clad for the journey ahead, but there was no mistaking that she was a queen. The soft greys and greens of her wrap threw up the fiery tints in her long, curling hair, and she carried her head as if it still bore a crown. She moved into the room with an air of command, and her long, strong hands were heavy with antique rings. Only the sleepy-eyed look she threw over her shoulder at the knight coming up behind betrayed the woman beneath the queenly show.

If her knight caught the meaning in her glance, he kept it to himself. He bowed to Guenevere with a dignified restraint, and his handsome, expressive face showed his sense of where he was. Tall and raw-boned, his body was that of a young knight in his prime, shaped and hardened by horsemanship and deeds of arms. His straw-gold hair and clear skin were like that of Morgause's two younger sons, Gaheris and Gareth. It must surely comfort Morgause, Guenevere pondered, to have Lamorak with her when her sons were so far away.

'Your Majesty.'

Carefully Sir Lamorak handed his lady through the low arched doorway and into the tower chamber, then dropped on one knee to greet Guenevere. He knelt again to Morgause to kiss her hand, and bowed himself out.

'I shall attend you, madam,' was all he said. But his eyes, his body spoke for him without words. I shall wait for you, his glance said, till the sun and moon burn out. Though the oceans swallow the dry land, I shall be there. Call, and I will come.

There was a silence in the chamber when he left. Guenevere motioned Morgause to a seat in the window, where the wide bay looked out on the countryside below. Through the open casements, the fresh green scent of meadow and woodland came in with the morning breeze.

The sun danced over Morgause's strong hands as she folded them in her lap. She turned towards Guenevere. Her heavy gaze wandered to the doorway, where Ina had closed the door on Lamorak.

'Ah, Guenevere,' she said suddenly, 'you and I, my dear, we were never friends. Too much bad blood had flowed before we met. The wife of Arthur could never trust the daughters of Igraine.' She paused, looking back in time. 'It would have been better for all of us if my brother had not trusted Morgan too. But Morgan's spirit would always have its way.'

Guenevere did not move. *Why is she telling me this?*

Morgause met her gaze, and laughed. 'Never fear, Guenevere, I am not Morgan's messenger.' A flash of savage sadness lit her face. 'These days I don't know where my sister is, or if she's still alive. We were close once, in our childhood, we were happy then. But good King Uther took care of that.'

Guenevere leaned towards her. 'Arthur has tried to undo what his father did.'

Morgause shook her head. 'The clock of life runs forward, never back. And my life spun off into other paths. I thought I suffered when Uther gave me to King Lot. But the Mother rewarded me with four fine sons for my pains.' She gave a smile of pride. 'Knights now, my sons,' she marvelled, 'all four of them! I can hardly wait to have them back in the Orkneys with me.'

She gave an ironic laugh. 'And I thought I'd had the worst of it by far! I envied Morgan in her nunnery, free to call her soul her own, and her body too, all for the price of singing a few psalms. While all the time . . .'

She folded her hands, and tightened them in a knot.

'I know.' Guenevere rose to her feet, overwhelmed with distress. 'The convent Uther chose was a prison for unwanted girls, no more.'

'With a mother abbess who beat them all like slaves.' Morgause smiled bitterly. 'And Morgan was such a marvellous child when she was young. Strange and secretive yes, but she had the power. Our mother was going to send her to Avalon to study with the Lady of the Lake. We thought Morgan would become the Lady when the time came.' Morgause exploded into an angry laugh. 'And this child to be locked up, starved and whipped for twenty years? I tell you, Guenevere, whatever Morgan has done, I fear you have not heard the end of it.'

Whatever Morgan has done –

The room faded, and a host of dark visions invaded Guenevere's head. Morgan in the black, nun-like gown she always wore, the shy, tormented virgin, casting down her eyes. Morgan covering her mulberry mouth with her thin white hand to hide a smile, Morgan turning to Arthur for every little thing.

Guenevere moaned, and tried to open her eyes. Then in a torrent the nightmare scenes returned. Morgan caught unawares in Arthur's bed, a welter of naked, writhing flanks and long white legs, and a gaping, mocking sex, livid enough to make all who saw it turn to stone.

And Morgan conjoined with the powers of the night to betray Arthur, when he took Amir to war. All Arthur's careful plans to protect the seven-year-old, all, all in vain, when that implacable raven-black gaze saw it all, and calmly led them to the enemy.

'Ohh –'

Guenevere came to herself shuddering and drenched in sweat. Waves of nausea washed over her from head to toe. Was she wrong in thinking that Morgause was a friend? Or had she come here to renew the old torment too?

She rounded on Morgause in anguish. *'Why are you here?'*

Morgause shrugged. 'Not as Morgan's friend or confidante. Our bond of sisterhood was broken long ago. And since my sons are knights of Arthur now, believe me, she trusts me no more than she trusts you. But Arthur is still my brother, blood kin to me on our mother's side. I wanted to warn him to beware of Morgan, because I know she won't give up her revenge. But Arthur wouldn't listen to a word I said. He brushed it all aside, so I came to you.'

And Arthur never told me any of this. 'Did he tell you that Morgan stole his scabbard?' Guenevere burst out. 'The sheath I gave him for Excalibur?'

Morgause stared. 'Your mother's scabbard, which had the power to protect the wearer from the loss of blood? The one you gave him on your wedding day?'

'The very same.' Guenevere closed her eyes. 'It was the most precious treasure of the Summer Country, handed down our line of queens from the time before time.' She could hear her mother's voice as she told the tale. 'There was a queen of the Summer Country, and the King of the Fair Ones fell in love with her. Though she was a mortal, she made the sacred marriage with this king of the Otherworld so that all her children and all the queens of the Summer Country after her would be like him, tall and fair and well shaped, with shining brows.

'And he loved her so much that he made this magic thing. He wove a charm into the gold and silver of the casing, and whispered his will into the pearls and crystals that adorn the sheath. Being mortal, she could always lose her life. But wearing this she would shed no blood. It came to me when my mother died. I gave it to Arthur because I loved him so.' She could not hold back her tears. 'And he let Morgan have it. When she disappeared, the scabbard did too.'

Morgause did not speak. Her large eyes were fixed on Guenevere.

Guenevere clutched her head. 'I used to buckle it on him when he went to war. Without it, he will never be safe again.'

Morgause's lovely face had set like stone. 'I knew that Morgan blamed Arthur, and wanted to punish him. I did not know she wanted to see him dead.'

She paused for a while, deep in thought. 'But I am not so wasteful of my kin,' she said at last, turning her gaze full on Guenevere. 'Arthur must live. So if I hear where Morgan may be found, rely on me. I will let you know.'

'Thank you.' Guenevere took a breath. *Morgause means well, you must trust her,* came into her mind. If only she could like Morgause more, or fear her less.

'And if ever I can help you in return . . .' she said, without conviction, but trying to sound warm.

Morgause moved her well-covered shoulders uneasily. 'That may well be.'

A sudden knowledge flowered inside Guenevere's head. 'You're concerned about your sons?' She did not say, 'about Agravain?'

Morgause nodded. 'And my knight Lamorak,' she said simply. 'My sons are turning against him, after all. You know he's been with me since my husband was killed. Indeed, Arthur gave him to me with the aim of healing that very wound. Lamorak was like an older brother to the boys then, and they loved him, one and all.' She gave a wry smile. 'It wasn't surprising. After all, he was much nearer to their age than mine.'

'Morgause, you were a mother at fifteen,' Guenevere broke in. 'As a queen gets older, her knights must be younger men. And Lamorak is old enough to make his own choice. What's it to them how old your knight is now? Are they jealous?'

Morgause looked away. 'Not all of them,' she responded quietly. 'Gawain is as loyal as the day. Gareth is my baby, so in his eyes his mother can do no wrong. But Agravain has his own view of everything. And he works on Gaheris, which troubles them all.'

'What does he say?'

'That now they are knights, their honour is more important than it was before. And the honour of their mother is their main concern.'

Guenevere grew cold. She could almost hear Agravain's high, crowing voice.

'And their father's honour too,' Morgause went on monotonously. 'Agravain says that Lamorak's father killed their father, and Lot's death went unavenged.'

Another debt of honour in the eyes of a son of the Orkneys, where blood feuds never die.

'King Pellinore was a loyal vassal of Arthur, and of Uther before,' Guenevere managed at last. 'He had no choice but to fight at the battle where King Lot was killed. And it was all ten years ago and more. But if Agravain believes that vengeance is still due –' She broke off, defeated by the horror of it all. 'Honour is a word of death for men.'

'For women too. In men's eyes at least.'

Guenevere started. 'What do you mean?'

Morgause paused. 'Agravain's new-found honour embraces

his mother now. He has made that another reason to hate Lamorak.'

Hate the man who would die for his mother, do anything for her love? The knight who would champion her to his dying breath? Guenevere gave a snort of disbelief. 'Hate Lamorak? What is there to hate?'

Morgause took time to reply. 'I saw you watching the two of us in the Great Hall,' she said slowly. She looked Guenevere in the eye. 'And I could tell you knew.'

Guenevere looked away. 'Every queen is entitled to her knights.'

Morgause waved a hand. 'You knew.'

I knew you were lovers, yes, Morgause. Because of Lancelot, I knew.

Morgause was watching her keenly. 'Did you tell Arthur?'

'No.'

'Did he notice? Has he said anything to you?'

'Arthur has not said a word to me.' *There are many things he does not tell me now. And I too have secrets I keep from him.* 'But he has scouts the length and breadth of the isles. He may already know.'

Morgause shook her head. 'No one knows,' she said confidently.

Guenevere started. 'No one?' *When Lamorak looks at you like that? When you smile at him with bedtime in your eyes?* 'How can you be sure?'

'Oh, at home in the islands, yes, among those I can trust, there are a few who know. But we have been secret, for my sons' sake.'

'Why?' Guenevere was seized by an irritation she could not explain. 'You're a ruling queen, and free to choose for yourself. You have no husband to lay claim to your body, as the Christians do. You're older than Lamorak, it's true –'

'Many years.'

'But for love and war, an older woman should take a younger man. He's worthy of your love. He's the son of a king, he'll be king in his turn, and a match for any queen.' Anger pushed her further than she meant to go. 'Why don't you marry him, and make an end to all of this?'

Morgause sighed. 'He has begged me to, time and time again.'

'But you fear your sons?'

Morgause's face darkened with the shadow of a fleeting fear. 'Our islands are much closer to the Norselands than they are to Camelot. There, cruel feuds last a lifetime and more. Our menfolk follow the Norse blood-hunger, not your chivalry. No, Lamorak and I are best off as we are, living quietly and giving no offence. As long as my sons are here, we are safe up there with the secret of our love. In such a faraway land, who cares what we do?'

'And there, you are the Queen.'

And a queen must have her knights.' Morgause smiled, a long, full, radiant smile.

Guenevere turned her head away, scorched by Morgause's naked joy. She felt again the same wild envy as before. *Morgause has four fine sons and a lover for her bed, and I have nothing, nothing at all!*

'You understand me, Guenevere.' Morgause looked at her keenly. 'You are doing the same as I am, you are taking care,' she said abruptly. 'I heard as soon as I arrived at court that Lancelot was not here, and I knew that you sent your knight away before a breath of scandal could touch you both. With the Christians all around Arthur as they are, it's only wise. How long will it be before he can return?'

Guenevere surged to her feet and moved to the window, where the evening candle stood waiting to be lit. She could hardly speak for pain. 'He has gone back to France. He will not return.'

CHAPTER 9

Merlin went singing through the trees, weaving a thin web of notes into a chant of triumph as he rode along. 'Pendragon lives,' went his high, bat-like call. He was alive, the boy Mordred was alive. And every day brought him closer to where the child must be.

The old man cackled with glee, and flapped his bony heels against the sides of his mule. He had learned a lot in Gore. Oh, not the fear-laden gossip about how Queen Morgan had disappeared, fled from King Ursien like a shadow in the night. There was no clue to the child's whereabouts in that.

And little had come from the silent witnesses he was hoping would tell him all. Morgan's chamber dogs had fled from him, and her little cat would only scratch and spit as he approached. Even the mice, who must have heard her every word, did not dare to leave the wainscot to speak to him. Morgan had cast a spell against outsiders, and left them all in terror of their lives.

Merlin shifted restlessly on his mule. Well, she had the power.

Yet the human witnesses had told him all they knew about the boy. From the women of the Queen's bedchamber, he learned that the baby had been a prodigy when he was born.

'As big as a two-year-old child,' the leader proudly declared. 'And marked out for great things!'

Merlin's heart thrilled. 'How so?'

'He was born with teeth. Not just one or two, a full set. It's a sign.'

The sign of the dragon, rejoiced Merlin, and it won't be the only one. He did not need to glance down at his own wrists to see the fighting dragons tattooed there. Somewhere, he knew, Morgan would have put this mark on her son, the badge of Pendragon from the time before time.

'And our lady the Queen couldn't get enough of him,' the woman went on. 'How she loved that bairn! She hugged him and kissed him and whispered in his ear, and he understood every word she said to him too. Young as he was, he was born old in his mind.'

Her face darkened. 'But then they came and took him away from her.' Merlin could see the tears gathering in her eyes. 'You know the rest.'

In truth he had not known in detail then. But it had not taken long to track down the captain of the palace guard, a hard and wary man who had served King Ursien all his life. Yes, it had been a bad business, one of the worst, but the order had come straight from the High King himself. Not a single newborn boy to be left alive.

The man took a long, reflective pull on the ale Merlin had bought him to lubricate his tale.

'We wondered why all the newborns,' he said at last. 'Why not just the King's bastard, if that's what the poor kid was? But I suppose the King feared they might have done a switch. Got the Queen's real son away to safety and put another in his place.'

'No doubt,' said Merlin shortly. He had no intention of revisiting Arthur's fear of Morgan in the aftermath of the affair, the madness of his grief. 'Well, on with your tale.'

'We were ordered to put them all in a boat, and cast it adrift. Lots of them, there were, but one of them stood out. He had shiny black hair, a full head, and old sort of eyes. Big too, and quiet, didn't cry like the rest. Like he knew something they didn't know.'

Perhaps he did, thought Merlin, with a spurt of wild hope. Ye Gods, let it be so!

The captain took another drink and went on. 'A few weeks later, we had word that the boat had wrecked itself down the coast. We rode over there, and it was our boat all right. And all their bones washed up on the sand.'

'All?'

'Well, we didn't count 'em one by one,' the captain said

defensively. 'But there were plenty of legs, and arms, and skulls –'

'Skulls?' said Merlin, his eyes glowing fire. 'These skulls –'

'Yes, we gathered them all up and buried them. We made a cairn of stones to mark the place. The mothers all wanted to know where their babes were, see? It was terrible for them –'

'Yes, yes,' Merlin burst out in a fury, 'but hear me! Among these skulls, *was there one with teeth*?'

And the captain's answer had brought him down here now, Merlin reflected. For there was no such skull among the dead. When King Ursien learned that, he had sent his men-at-arms out time and again to hunt for the boy. Each time they had drawn a blank. So Morgan had contrived to save her baby's life, from the soldiers as well as from the sea. Where would she stow the child she had plucked from the deep?

Merlin lapsed into deep thought. The afternoon sun was warm on his back as the mule plodded west. Ahead he could hear the ocean's comforting roar. Underfoot he felt the pulse of the earth itself in every green shoot thrusting through the loam, and his heart picked up new strength. He caught the trill of a skylark on the wing, and wove it into an airy melody of his own. All the while his mind hummed like a hive of bees. Where would Morgan have placed her baby son? Who would she trust?

'No one,' said the blackbird in the hawthorn bush.

'No one,' agreed the snake slipping sideways through the grass.

'I thank you, sirs.' Merlin nodded to his helpers as they passed. Yes, they were right. Morgan had had no ally in her life. An abandoned child, a woman without a home, who could she call a friend?

So a stranger, then, must have been entrusted with the child. Someone ignorant of his parentage without doubt, but still able to give him what Morgan sought. And with a sentence of death on her infant's head. Morgan's concern would be for sanctuary above all.

He raised his head and savoured the salt air. From the pile of stones that marked the infants' remains, he had checked every village, every hamlet and isolated farm down the length of the coast. Time had stretched on, but he was not deterred. The child had been on the ship, that much was clear. And when it sank, he would have landed here. Merlin nodded, and renewed his song. He was somewhere near, and Merlin would track him down.

Yet when it came, he almost missed the place. Built into the hillside and roofed with the living turf, it seemed part of its surroundings like the dwellings of the Fair Ones in the hollow hills. On plain inspection, it proved to be a low, one-room hovel of the humblest kind. But neat and clean, Merlin noted, with a well of its own by the door, and what was that? A child's toy lying abandoned in the grass?

It was a carved wooden knight on the back of a horse. A grin of triumph split Merlin's wizened face. Hurrying down from his mule, he pounced on it, and approached the open door. The elderly woman inside was building up the fire, a year-round necessity for hill-dwellers, he surmised.

'Good day to you,' he cried. He waved the toy knight with false joviality. 'And where is your boy?'

In the darkness at the back of the room, an old man rose to his feet. 'Come in, sir,' he said doubtfully.

Merlin stepped inside. On the table he could see a child's wooden beaker, and a child-sized chair squatted beside the hearth. Every fibre of his being told him the boy was here. Mordred, his mind was humming, Pendragon, Arthur's son –

Rashly he threw caution to the winds. 'I've come for the boy,' he said, his voice cracking with emotion as he spoke. He nodded at the little chair. 'That's his, isn't it?'

The old couple shared a fearful glance, then the woman spoke. 'It's his, sir, yes.'

'Don't be afraid,' cried Merlin, 'I mean you no harm. The boy is my kin, and I've come here for his good.' He thrust out his skinny wrists. 'See these dragons?' He laughed confidently. 'The child bears this mark on him, am I right?'

The old woman smiled, and tears stood in her eyes. 'It's hidden – but he does, sir, it's true.'

'Then you see that he's no ordinary child. I promise you, he is destined for higher things.'

'We don't fear to lose him,' said the old man, shaking his head. He twisted his knotted hands as he spoke. 'He's been a joy to us, sir, but it's been a power of effort as well. And we've always been afraid of the soldiers coming back.'

'The King's soldiers?' prompted Merlin.

The old woman took up the tale with smiles and tears. 'We found him in the hedge by our door, not crying, just looking up at us with those eyes of his. His swaddling clothes were all wet and torn from the sea, and we didn't know how he got there because as big as he was, he was a baby, he still couldn't walk. So we thought he was a changeling, and we gladly took him in.'

The old man nodded. 'A child of the Fair Ones blesses any house. And it's many a year since we had babies of our own.'

The old woman chuckled in fond reminiscence. 'And he grew and throve with us from the very first. Such a child he was! Such a lovely boy.'

The old man frowned. 'But then we saw the soldiers on the shore. They were searching every cave, turning every stone. We knew they were looking for him. And we didn't want them to take away our boy.'

A sulphurous light gleamed in Merlin's eye 'Your boy?' he breathed dangerously.

'He's been happy here, sir, and doing well,' the old woman said simply. 'He can walk and talk, and understand all we say.' The light of mother-love shone in her face. 'That's how we saved him when they came for him.'

'How?' Merlin could hardly speak.

The old man grinned. 'We put him down the well. We knew the soldiers'd tear the place apart, and they did too, but they never looked down there. He sat in the bucket as cool as he sat here till we pulled him up again.' He gave a delighted laugh. 'He's got an old head on young shoulders and no mistake. It's time he was back with you, sir, where he belongs.'

Merlin was in raptures.

'You won't lose him, I promise, when I take him away,' he cried. 'We shall never forget that he is your son too.' He rose eagerly to his feet. 'Let me have him, then, and we'll be on our way.'

'But sir, you have him already,' the old woman cried.

The old man was aghast. 'You have, haven't you?'

Merlin felt a lightning bolt pass through his heart. 'Have him?' he mouthed numbly. 'What d'you mean?'

'Why, your kinswoman came and took him only hours ago!'

the old woman cried in fear. 'She said the same things as you about going to his kin. Don't you know where he's gone?'

'My kinswoman?' screeched Merlin. 'I have no female kin!'

'But she knew the secret of the dragons, just as you did. She –'

Merlin was frantic with fury and distress. 'Who was she?'

'Tall and queenly, sir, and royally dressed. She said she'd take him to her palace far away. He'd be safe there, she said, from those who sought him here.'

A storm of fury coursed through Merlin's head.

Morgause.

Morgan's sister, and queen of a faraway realm. Morgan would trust her. And it would be a fine trick to hide Mordred in the Orkneys, nine hundred miles and more away.

Well, so be it.

Merlin stood in perfect calm till he could silence the anger roaring through his head. Then he made time to reassure the old couple before he took his leave. At last he was able to heave himself up on his mule, and set its head due north, cursing all the way.

Morgause, of course. He had reckoned without the deadly sisterhood. He laughed bitterly. A precious ironic reversal, the house of Uther at the mercy of the daughters of Igraine.

But he would not be deterred. Merlin's eyes glowed as golden as a hawk. He would overcome.

To the Orkneys, then. The boy's destiny was not to be set aside.

For he was Pendragon, descended from the first Red Ravager of the Islands, and the next High King. And though the youngster did not know it, his destiny was approaching even now on an old white mule treading the Great North Way.

Gods above, it was cold! King Ursien grumbled roughly to himself. A raven croaked from a branch high overhead, and he eyed it askance. Call this June? What had happened to the warmth of the summer afternoon?

A good gallop would warm him up, but not on this pitiful nag he was riding now. For the hundredth time, King Ursien hauled up his horse's head as it stumbled through the grass, and cursed it from his heart. What was wrong with the brute? And come to that, was he ailing too? Why was he so uneasy here in this wood?

He looked around. It was only mid-afternoon, but evening came early in the shade of the trees. All the living things of the woodland seemed to have taken to their dens, the forest was so still. It was getting colder too, and a creeping dampness was rising from the earth. He shuddered involuntarily, and was disgusted at the weakness of his flesh. Face it, Ursien, he told himself grimly, you're losing your nerve. Yet what was there to be concerned about?

A day in the open air had seemed just the thing when they left Camelot a few hours ago. Queen Guenevere had held him and Accolon to their promise to take Arthur hunting, and they had been glad to do anything that might help to chase the King's sadness away. But the afternoon ride had been ill-fated from the start. First Arthur's horse had panicked at the sight of the wood, as if reluctant to take its master into the trees, and only a horseman of Arthur's exceptional skill could have made it obey. Then Accolon's horse had inexplicably gone lame, and he had had to lead it a good deal of the way, so ensuring that they only reached the part of the forest they were making for when the best of the day had gone.

Yet even when they had arrived too late to begin the chase, all had been well. An old crone on the road had told them that there was a convent nearby, the House of the Little Sisters of Mercy, where travellers could find hospitality overnight.

So Ursien had remained behind with Accolon's lame horse while the younger knight and King Arthur rode off in search of a bed. There would still be time for a gallop, Arthur had promised, when they got back. But now the sun was going down, and still there was sign of them at all.

Ursien shivered, and found himself wishing he was not alone. A chill was rising from the earth in thin white wisps, and a curious clammy smell invaded the air. Ursien's stomach turned. He knew that smell. The last time he had smelt it was in a charnel-house, where the rotting dead were groaning for burial.

His horse caught the scent and threw up its head, whinnying with distress.

'Easy, boy,' Ursien said, with an assurance he did not feel.

Now the rising mist was rolling through the still forest, making a ghostly landscape all around. And through the white silence it came to Ursien, I am in the land of the dead.

He sighed.

Undead as yet. But not for long.

He bowed his head, and made a brief peace with his Gods. Then he heard his own voice in the stillness of the night. 'I am ready. Come for me, then, if you must.'

He paused for an answer, and bade a tender, silent farewell to his sons. Then his thoughts turned to the beloved wife of his youth, long dead, and still mourned. His sent his spirit crying through the void, Make way for me, dearest, I am coming now. Then he squared his shoulders and lifted his old grey head.

And there it was straight ahead, looming through the trees, darkening what light remained. All his life he had prayed the old soldier's prayer, Gods, let me see my death. And now it had come true.

'Ha!' He grinned at his savage luck, not only to see his death, but to know it too.

'You!' he said, with a total lack of surprise, as the darkness deepened and covered the earth, then took shape and leaped snarling for his throat.

CHAPTER 10

'The High King here? King Arthur and his knight? Well, don't just stand there staring like a natural, girl, show him in!'

Jesu Maria, what fools these young nuns were! The Abbess Placida sucked on her few sour teeth, folded her hands on the lower slopes of her belly, and cursed them in her heart. She had long ago stopped trying to live by her chosen name, when all these new young nuns tried her patience so.

Half the time now, she did not know who they were. Time was when she knew every nose on every face in this House of the Little Sisters of Mercy, formerly known as the Convent of the Holy Mother herself. And not only their faces, she smirked to herself. It was her proudest boast that she ruled her convent with the rod, and no novice so high-born but was forced to bare her body for the good of her soul.

The rod, *yesssssssss* –

The old woman's fingers itched, and her rheumy eyes took on a yellow gleam. She had belaboured the daughters of queens and kings. She had beaten the fat wrinkled buttocks of the old cast-off wives of good Christian lords, and their young ones too, discarded if they did not prove fertile inside a year. Her house was known as a Christian sanctuary for all unwanted females, or those for whom the Good Lord God had not ordained a place in the outside world.

And God had smiled on her endeavours, rewarding the convent for her pains. She gave a righteous smile. Of course, the kings who saved fortunes on royal dowries by giving their girls to Christ would want to make some donation to the house. And of course, they had something back in return. They knew that when they died, they would be laid to rest in the peace of a cloistered courtyard, beneath a bell-tower crowned with its Christian cross. They loved the idea that the pale hands of virgins would toll their passing bell, and ranks of black-clad nuns would chant the service of the dead.

So why did it have to change? The Abbess moved her wimpled head fretfully from side to side. Hers had been the first house of holy women in all the isles. Oh, it was true they were surrounded by the wicked on all sides, and they still had not vanquished the foul Goddess faith of the pagans, or their vile notion that women were free to offer the friendship of their thighs to any man they chose. But since King Arthur had turned towards the true light of Christian faith, the old battles were almost won. So the zest had gone out of the struggle, the glory no longer shone from the mountain tops, and the Almighty had left the high places He stalked in days of yore.

And now, God bless us, she hardly knew her own nuns! No matter how often she scolded or reached for the whip, they scooted in and out of her failing eyesight before she could see who they were. Sometimes, unable to catch the faces hidden by the great white wings of their headdresses, she did not know who came and went. But never would she admit she did not know. Other aged sisters might confuse the new nuns with those who had passed on years ago, but she never did.

No, she was the Mother still, she reminded herself. Because of her, the greatest Christians of these isles had found their way to her house. Brother John was their chief warrior for Christ, a monk who fearlessly challenged the Goddess-worshippers in their sacred retreats. And the leader of the Christians themselves, the Father Abbot of London, had visited too, he who had lent his own churchyard to the pagans when they gathered to make Arthur king.

Jesu Maria, what a stroke of genius that was! the Abbess marvelled. If the Christians backed Arthur when no one else would do so, the Father Abbot had said, then as king, Arthur would have to support them in return. And so it had turned out. Step by step the Christians had won the King's permission to build more churches, and bring more and more pagans to the light of God.

And then God had delivered Arthur's soul into Christian hands. The Lord in His wisdom had taken the life of Arthur's young son, and the King had turned to his monks when his hope had failed. They had taught him to see that he was an instrument of God's will, and now Arthur was a Christian king indeed.

The Lord be praised! The Abbess clasped her hands, and her slack lips moved in thanks. For now he was here, the High King himself, unless that fool of a Sister Gate-keeper had made the biggest mistake of her life. The Abbess threw up her fat white hands, and closed her eyes. *Salve Regina*, hail, Mary, Queen of Heaven for this blessing on our house –

'This way, my lords.'

The sound of boots and spurs in the outer hall brought the Abbess heaving to her feet. The door opened and three or four nuns came flapping into her apartment, with two men behind.

A spasm of anger shot through her fleshy frame. Why had the sisters not brought the candles, when it was so dim in the chamber that she could hardly see? Jesus and Mary, all she could make out were two great shapes in the gloom. Which of them was the King, and which his knight?

Yet the bigger of the two, the lofty, broad-shouldered figure had to be the King, even without the gold coronet round the brim of the helmet he carried in the crook of his arm. Breathing heavily, she settled her bulk inside her flowing robes, and prepared to curtsy to the ground.

'No ceremony, good Mother, do not kneel,' the newcomer said gently. 'I am Arthur Pendragon, and this is Sir Accolon, a knight of King Ursien of Gore. We hear you keep a house of welcome for travellers far from home. We have come to seek shelter for the night. '

The Abbess bowed her head. 'In the Lord's name, we do,' she responded stoutly, 'and in the name of the Holy Mother, the Blessed Virgin Mary, who rules the heavens for her Son. We take in the lost, we comfort the forlorn, we heal the sick.'

The sick . . .

She peered through the gloom of the low chamber at the knight at Arthur's side. He was handsome enough, with his sharp features, wiry body and well-made limbs. He was clad like a knight in a mantle of fine black wool, and he wore a tunic and hose of shining silver mail. But the pale blue eyes had an unfathomable sheen, and his face wore a sickly film of sweat. As he felt her scrutiny, he gave a sudden twitch, and a dim foreboding seized the Abbess's heart. Was it the falling sickness, St Vitus's dance, or what?

'Are you ill?' she demanded abruptly, forgetting the presence of the King.

But the young man only shook his head and hissed furiously, 'No, madam, I am not!'

'Let us beg a chamber for tonight, Mother, and we will be on our way,' King Arthur resumed, in his kindly tones. 'There are three of us out hunting, and we hope for a short chase at least before night falls. We have left our companion in the forest, and plan to rejoin him now. After that, with your permission, we shall all return to you.'

'My permission, sire?' the Abbess said, almost beside herself at the kindness shining from the King's quiet grey eyes, his courteous manner and sweet smile. 'It is an honour to serve you,' she trumpeted, as the two men bowed themselves out. 'Return when you will, King Arthur, we shall be here.'

'Thank you. Farewell.'

What a king, what a man! The Abbess lowered herself into a lumbering curtsy as the visitors left. At once the nuns all around swooped down to help her up. Once on her feet, she waved them harshly away. 'Get on with your work or prayers, all of you, be off!'

They scattered like frightened birds. The Mother Abbess nodded. She liked them that way. Ponderously she made her way back to her chair, the chair in which she now spent all her days, and cursed her nuns again. Why didn't the dimwits bring in the candles now, when an early nightfall had plunged the place into dusk? She reached for the handle of her familiar whip. One of them would feel her displeasure when they returned.

Oh, it was cold! A dank chill stirred the air, like the mist off a graveyard, and a sudden movement in the shadows caught her eye. 'Who's there?' she called, and turned. In the far corner of the chamber, a nun appeared from nowhere and emerged from the gloom. Head down, white wimple flaring around a white face, she glided past the Abbess and left the room.

'Sister?' called the Abbess furiously, heaving herself up. No nun ignored her presence, or left the room without a word! Who was it anyway? Not one of her chamber assistants, her trusted nuns. She caught her breath. It was almost like –

No!

A shudder shook her unimaginative frame.

Mother of God, if it were not impossible, she could swear it was Sister Ann.

Sister Ann –

The very name brought a fine cold breath of fear. Resolutely the Abbess hefted her great body to the door. She would call the nun back, she would punish her soundly, she would –

She threw open the door. But she hastened outside in vain. For peer as she might up and down the long corridor, she could not blame her poor eyesight for the fact that there was nothing on earth to be seen.

Behind them the white convent buildings lay in a westering light snug on their low green hill. The peaceable sound of the angelus followed them down the hill.

Arthur half turned to Accolon, riding in the rear. 'Now we're sure of a bed for the night, we can hunt to our heart's content,' he said heartily. 'There won't be much game to put up at this hour of the day. And Ursien's horse wasn't sound, so it may go lame. But we'll try for a gallop, and we may be in luck.'

Accolon nodded, and silently looked away.

Arthur stared at his young companion with sudden concern. What was giving Accolon's face that sickly tinge? Yet was it so strange? Accolon had been Morgan's knight for years, ordered to keep guard over her to his last breath. Any young man would be sick at betraying a charge like that. Accolon was not to know that Morgan had got the better of older and wiser men.

Men like himself, for instance.

Sombrely Arthur turned his horse's head into the wood. Strange how dark it was now under the roof of the trees, when a June day should last into the night. The air was growing thicker, and colder too. It must be the dew, he thought absently, falling before its time. Where was the feel of the forest in midsummer, the silky kiss of the breeze on sun-warmed skin, the rich loamy smell of the living earth, the sweet fragrance of fern? The rising mist made the place smell like a crypt.

God spare us, Arthur prayed, enough of these wretched thoughts! He turned to Accolon, riding behind.

'Let's have a gallop to make up for lost time. A challenge to see who can reach King Ursien first, before he dies of boredom waiting for us.'

As he gathered up his reins, a movement at the side of the track caught his eye. A doe hare crouched weeping in the grass, her huge brown eyes turned up to him as he passed. An unwelcome sensation swept him from head to foot. What's the creature doing there? he thought irritably. If she was ill, why didn't she crawl to her hollow to die?

'Hold on, my lord,' came a sharp cry from behind. 'No racing for me, my saddle-girth's giving way.'

Arthur looked back to see Accolon vault from his horse and lead it forward into a clearing under the trees.

'God bless us, Accolon, you're fated to ruin our sport today,' he said ruefully. 'First your mount goes lame, and now this.' Still grumbling, he eased himself out of his saddle and dropped to the ground. 'Here, let me give you a hand.'

Accolon was standing on the far side of his horse, lifting the saddle-flap to inspect the girth. Arthur walked his mount forward, and tied it to a tree. The air was colder now, and the mist lay thickly on the grass. Arthur sighed. It did not look as if there would be much hunting tonight. 'Accolon!' he called.

'My lord?'

The voice was right in his ear. Arthur whirled round. Accolon stood behind him, a sickly grin plastering his face. His sword was raised over his head, poised to strike.

'God in heaven, no!' Arthur cried, leaping back as the sword carved past his neck. 'Accolon, I command you – I am your king –'

But Accolon was impervious. With a blind stare, he swung again. As his arm went up, Arthur caught a metallic glint at his side. Hanging from Accolon's sword-belt was a scabbard made of plaited silver and gold, inlaid with crystals and moonstones gleaming in the dusk. Down the length of the shaft, letters of white quartz spelled out the runic charm, '𝔉or the Queen of the

Summer Country from the King of the Fair Ones, to keep safe my love.'

But Arthur did not need to read the words of power. He had known them and the scabbard for ten years and more. Once it had been the finest thing he had. Then he had lost it, and he was justly punished now.

Grief overwhelmed him.

'Oh, Guenevere!' he groaned.

For a moment he bent his head. Then he looked up to see Accolon leaping towards him with the killing grace of a cat. The young knight was grinning, and his pale eyes had turned to blood. Arthur read his fate in their vermilion depths, and did not move.

CHAPTER 11

Goddess, Mother, what had got into the Queen?

With her eyes fixed firmly on Guenevere, Ina urged on her unwilling horse, and stifled a sigh. After all her years with the Queen, her mistress could still surprise her as she had today.

But what a day, the little maid groaned to herself. First of all the Queen of the Orkneys had come flaunting her lover, and painfully reminding Queen Guenevere of her love that had gone. Then a dirty tavern-maid had dragged herself in off the road, half dead from travelling, pleading to see the Queen. The guards had only brought her in because she said she came from Sir Lancelot.

'From Lancelot?' the Queen had asked, in a voice half-way between music and tears. The girl had stood there swaying, on the verge of passing out. Her eyes were bruised with exhaustion, and runnels of dried blood were soaking the filthy rags she wore round her feet.

The girl nodded, joy spreading like water over her plain face. 'Sir Lancelot.'

'He sent you to me?' Guenevere persisted. 'All the way from your village by the coast?'

'He told me to come to the Queen,' the girl fumbled out. Her voice had the soft round sound of the deep shires. 'He said you were the best lady in the world.'

'He said that?' There was a long pause before Guenevere spoke again. 'How was he?'

The girl groped for words, her forehead knitted with effort like a child's. 'Pale, like you are, lady. And just as sickly and sad.'

A small sound escaped Guenevere, and she turned away.

Whatever made the wretched girl say that? Ina frowned crossly at the memory. She might have known it would upset the Queen. Of course a village girl could have no knowledge of court ways. And it was the first word the Queen had had from Sir Lancelot, so of course she would take it hard. But when Guenevere suffered like this, who was it who had to revive her and comfort her? Ina could have strung the girl up by her thumbs for giving the Queen such pain.

Yet after reducing the Queen to helpless tears, Ina marvelled, see if the girl hadn't redeemed herself, after all. Reaching into the soiled bosom of her dress, she had drawn out a gold coin.

'He gave me this,' she pronounced in her slow country burr, 'to pay my way here. But I thought he meant it for you. So I walked here, an' begged all the way, so's not to break into it.'

She reached out, and pressed it in Guenevere's hand. 'Here, lady. From Sir Lancelot. May the Mother in Her mercy bring him safe back to you.'

Was it really a love token, Lancelot, that you could not send me any other way? I want to think it was. I have so little of you that I can keep.

Standing in her chamber, Guenevere did not try to check the flowing tears. She had held on while the tavern-maid was handed over to the women of the bedchamber to be washed and tended and clothed, and tried to take pleasure in the knowledge that the poor wretch would sleep in a bed for the first time in her life. Tomorrow she would be a maid in the Queen's service, and start life anew.

Whereas I –
I am a bleeding hollow, resounding to the cry of 'Lancelot'.
Goddess, Mother, enough!

'Ina, the rose-water, if you please?'

Guenevere roamed into the window, dabbing at her inflamed eyes and face. She had to compose herself before she could go out riding to meet up with Arthur, Ursien and Accolon.

But the three men might already have left the rendezvous. And she did not want to see anyone now. She turned her head. 'Send to the stables, Ina, tell them we won't go. The men won't miss us.' She gave an unhappy laugh. 'They'll probably have a better time alone.'

But as she spoke, a cloud of dusky images came beating round like bats inside her head. She saw a hare in a dark wood beside a narrow track. Black trees overhead were hanging their branches down, their twigs dripping blood like severed fingers' ends. A thick haze hung over the grass, casting a pall of gloom. And in the heart of the forest was something she could not see, a yawning blackness, an evil stench.

'What?' she cried.

Faintly she heard Arthur's voice calling, 'Guenevere –'

She came to herself with a shuddering start. 'Ina, Ina!' she called. 'Send for the horses, we ride at once.'

She knew they had to reach Arthur without delay. But when they came to the wood, there was no sign of the men at the appointed meeting-place. They forged on under the canopy of the trees as the evening drew in. Before long it would be night, and they would have to turn back.

Ahead of them, a movement caught her eye. A dark cloud of flies was hovering to the side of the path. Beneath it in the grass lay a long dark shape, like the trunk of a tree. As they drew nearer, the whole surface seemed to move, rippling as if it were alive. But the life belonged only to the maggots on the body beneath. The dead thing was a man.

'Ina, come!' Guenevere cried hoarsely. 'Quick, hold my horse!' She threw the reins to her maid, and vaulted to the ground. A few steps brought her to the figure lying face down in the grass. *Not Arthur, Goddess, Mother, I beg you –*

Frenziedly she pushed and tugged at the heavy weight. The dead man rolled over with a flaccid thud. His body looked as if it had been mauled by a great cat. His leather hunting garments had been slashed from neck to hem, and a gaping hole marked the place where his throat had been. The grey hair was plastered to the head with blood, and the face was disfigured with long open scars.

Moved by a sorrow beyond words, Guenevere touched the ruined face and tried to close the staring eyes. But there was no escaping the message in their frozen depths. King Ursien had seen the thing at the heart of the wood. He had met the darkness made flesh, and it had eaten him alive.

*

'Traitor!'

Arthur gasped for breath. Instinctively he sidestepped
Accolon's attack, and the upraised sword swept past him without
harm. But the young knight turned on him again with the same
pallid lips and eyes of blood, the look of death.

'Think, Accolon, and stop, while I can still forgive!' Arthur
cried, raising his hand. Anger pulsed through his veins. 'Some
madness has seized you, to attack your lord and offer treachery to
your king. But throw down your sword, and I need not take your
life.'

Accolon did not hear. He began to move towards Arthur
again, smiling like a man in a pleasant dream. Once more he
swung the great sword round his head.

'Accolon!' Arthur cried in anguish. 'Stop, or I must kill you –
there is no middle way.'

'No middle way,' the young knight repeated, with the same
glassy grin. 'No indeed, my lord, for you must die!'

His weapon was poised at the mid-point of its swing. Arthur
leaped back towards his horse, and ducked under its neck. In one
desperate move he plucked his sword from its sheath, and
snatched his shield from his horse's flank. Excalibur sang in his
hand like a bird released from a cage.

'Come, then, my one true friend,' Arthur whispered under
his breath.

Armoured, he turned to face his enemy. 'Lay on, traitor,' he
snarled, 'and prepare to die! You have thrown away all hope of
mercy now.'

Accolon responded with a crashing blow. Fury lent Arthur
strength as he counter-attacked, parrying its fall and turning its
force back on Accolon. His blood rose to the challenge, as it had
so many times before. He was stronger than his opponent and
harder too, blooded in battles that the younger man could not
know.

But Accolon had the scabbard, and only one hand could
have given him that. A burning grief ran through Arthur's
every joint. Was ever a man so betrayed? With it, Accolon had
all the ancient power of the Fair Ones on his side. And either
that, or some poisonous magic of the mind, was lending him

strength beyond his mortal skill. Enraged, Arthur thrust, and drove, and parried with more than his normal force. But Accolon had the advantage at every turn.

The first cut was nothing, a mere nick on the side. Another blow glanced off Arthur's shoulder, doing little harm. But it must have pierced the fine links of his silver chain mail. Soon he could feel the blood running down his arm.

Accolon danced in and out of Arthur's sword-range, grinning like one possessed. He scarcely bothered to ward off Arthur's blows. The heaviest strokes left him unscathed, and drew no blood.

Arthur ground his teeth, and communed with Excalibur again. 'Come!' he whispered. 'Come, my dear, to work.' He turned on his opponent with renewed force. 'Remember the call, *à l'outrance*, to the death!' he threatened Accolon.

But again and again the charm that Accolon bore turned aside Excalibur's shining edge. And all the time Arthur's blood seeped from a dozen cuts, and then a dozen more.

How long they fought, Arthur did not know. But he knew he was losing strength with every step. His grasp on Excalibur was weakening, and his head was beginning to swim. All he had now was the dogged courage of the damned.

'Yield, Arthur!' sang Accolon, with the same deranged glare. 'Bare your neck for my sword, save yourself further pain. One kiss of iron, and your soul will be free! You will walk with the Shining Ones on the plain of delight.'

Arthur turned up his eyes, and looked into his soul. He knew he was bleeding from a hundred wounds. Is this the end? he wondered, then dismissed the thought. He propelled himself forward with the last of his flagging force, Excalibur cutting a silver swathe in his hand.

'Defend yourself, devil!' he bellowed at Accolon. 'And may God have mercy on your spotted soul!'

Bless you, Ursien. May the Mother take your soul –

Guenevere rose to her feet and stepped back to the woodland track. Ina sat on her horse clutching Guenevere's reins, her fist to her mouth, her eyes round with dread.

'Do not fear, Ina,' Guenevere said steadily. 'King Ursien is beyond pain and sorrow now. We have to find the King.' She swung herself up into the saddle. 'They can't be far.'

As she spoke, the mist seeping from the ground began to weave its way towards them between the trees. She could feel its clammy fingers stroking her flesh. And there, shrouded in its depths, she could feel the seething hatred she had known from so long ago, the stirring of evil from the time before time.

'Arthur!' she screamed. 'Arthur, where are you?'

She thought she heard something deep in the forest, far off the track. From Ina's face, the maid had heard it too.

'Over there, madam!' she cried.

'Where?' Guenevere felt the mist choking her throat. 'Arthur!' she cried.

There was no reply. She called again, putting her heart and soul into her voice. The silence deepened. For all they could hear, they might have been underground.

Guenevere closed her eyes, and summoned all her strength. *Arthur*, she called silently, *I can help you, but you must tell me how. Send me a sign, to show me the way. Send your spirit forth to bring me to your aid.*

Furiously she poured her spirit into the void.

Goddess, Mother, help me, speed my prayer!

She opened her eyes.

Nothing.

Not a creature was stirring in the darkening depths. The rolling, oncoming fog ignored her appeal. Mockingly the white wisps wrapped themselves round her, and she felt herself yielding to their soft embrace. *To sleep now*, came the drowsy, sensual thought, *to give myself to the arms of this sweet white sleep, how pleasant that would be.*

Her eyelids, her body were very heavy now. At the edge of her vision she could see Ina drooping too, her small head hanging down like a wild violet. *To sleep, to forget sorrow and pain – to leave this world and go to walk the stars – Goddess, Mother, be with me now as I die –*

Her fading gaze dropped down to the ground. Crouched by the wayside hovered a hare, its large brown eyes turned urgently up to hers. With a shock she saw that the creature was weeping great tears, and its anguish reached her through her fatal lethargy. As she struggled to sit up in the saddle, the hare hopped away. 'Ina, follow!' she said thickly. 'The hare knows the way!'

Unbidden, the horses began to follow the hare. Slowly they tracked it off the woodland ride, pressing into the forest by paths almost too narrow to pass. They stumbled over the rough going in the gloom, and the dense undergrowth tore at their clothes and flesh. And all the time the mist never left them alone. Ebbing and flowing, writhing and hissing, it mocked and tormented their every step.

Yet all the time, Guenevere knew they were drawing near. At last they saw a clearing through the haze ahead. With a last look the hare vanished into the long grass. Guenevere and Ina spurred forward into the dusk.

The clash of arms came to meet them as they drew near. In the centre of the clearing staggered Arthur, covered in blood. Guenevere's own blood rose, and her power sang in her ears.

She reached for the short sword slung by her horse's neck. *Goddess, Mother, grant me this revenge!*

'Accolon!' she cried. 'Beware the battle raven who comes to drink your blood! Beware! Beware!'

Howling the ancient war-cry of the queens of the Summer Country, she drove her horse into a charge. Accolon turned and tensed in terror, but made no attempt to turn his weapon against the huge beast now thundering towards him across the grass. Gripped with a mortal dread, he stood motionless as Guenevere rode him down.

Her sword caught Accolon full on the head. Neighing with fury, the great charger knocked him flying, and trampled him as it passed. Guenevere dragged in the reins, heaved the horse around, and stood ready for another charge.

'Surrender, Sir Accolon!' she cried.

Accolon was slowly pushing himself up on his hands and knees. He staggered to his feet, his eyes glazed with pain. A great slicing wound lay open on his forehead, and he clutched his side, as if nursing broken ribs. As he stood reeling, Arthur lunged forward, and tore the scabbard from Accolon's side. At once the bright blood spurted from his wound and ran down his face.

Arthur cried out in triumph. 'So, Accolon, the odds are even now!' Excalibur floated eagerly in his hand. 'Turn and defend yourself,' he growled. *'A l'outrance!* On guard! To the death!'

He struck straight and true. Accolon raised his sword in a feeble attempt at defence, but Excalibur found its aim. Accolon took the blow deep in his left side, staggered, and fell bleeding to one knee. His face was a mask of sick bewilderment. 'How?' he roared.

Arthur approached him, leaning on his sword. 'Oh, Accolon,' he said heavily, 'prepare your soul for your maker, for you must die.' He brushed the clammy hair out of his eyes, and shook the blood from his head. 'That was your death wound. I will not strike again. '

Accolon clutched his sword in both hands, and struggled to fight back. But his strength was failing, and the sharp point trailed down to the ground. Without the scabbard, the wound on his head was flowing freely, covering his face.

He raised his eyes to Arthur, blind with blood.

'My lord,' he begged. 'Let me crave one last favour at your hands?'

'Of course.'

Painfully Arthur bent to lay down his sword, and set the scabbard beside it in the grass. Then he moved across to face the fallen knight. His face deeply marked with sorrow, he stood before Accolon, and leaning forward, laid his hand on his head.

'What is it, Accolon?' he said gently.

'This! Take this for my lady, Queen Morgan, to avenge her wrongs!'

With a violent effort, Accolon hefted the great broadsword and brought the blade up hard between Arthur's legs. The knight's sharp grunt of pain was drowned by Arthur's scream as he fell to the earth, clasping his groin with both hands.

Guenevere leaped from her horse, and ran to Arthur's side. Blood was pouring from between his legs, bright red against the glittering silver mail. She knelt beside him, and tried to staunch it with the edge of her gown. 'The scabbard, Ina!' she screamed. 'Get the scabbard, bring it here!'

Ina jumped from her horse, and raced to obey. Fumbling, Guenevere tried to thrust it in Arthur's girdle to staunch his bleeding wounds.

But Arthur raised his head from the grass and waved her away. Blood bubbled in his throat as he tried in vain to speak.

'Let me die, Guenevere!' he gasped. 'But find her and kill her! Find Morgan Le Fay!'

CHAPTER 12

How long, O Lord, how long?

The Abbess Placida sat in her inner sanctum turning the pages of the great Bible on her knee, but not seeing one of the large black-lettered words. Where was the King? Why did he not return? And how long must she endure the torment of these thoughts?

There were no such things as ghosts, she told herself. Devils, yes, but they could never enter a house of holy women such as hers. And she had no fear of 'fetches', as the pagans called them, spirit shapes who could walk in human form. So the nun she had seen in her chamber, the woman who had vanished in the corridor as soon as she walked through the door, could not have been Sister Ann. That thing of evil was a bad memory now, no more.

Yet why was she sweating and shaking all the time? We have worked so hard to put all that away, her furious soul complained, how can it return? Yet in spite of herself her mind kept drifting back, Sister Ann, Sister Ann –

The bitter refrain was broken by a knock on the door. A white-gowned novice came tumbling into the room. 'Word from the Sister Gate-keeper, Reverend Mother!' she gasped. 'Will you come at once?

The Sister Gate-keeper had been watching the toiling figures from afar. So the Abbess was called outside in time to see a tall queenly woman in a bloodstained riding-robe entering the courtyard on foot, leading a horse. Tied to the saddle, barely conscious but still upright, swayed the heavy body of a man covered in wounds. An empty scabbard was thrust through his sword-belt, and his sword hung from his side. Behind them came a smaller woman leading another horse with a wounded knight. Face down across the saddle, he was bleeding heavily, his life-blood leaving a tell-tale trail of red.

Already the nuns were streaming out of their cloisters to cluster round the newcomers like a flock of crows. The Abbess saw the gold coronet round the helmet of the rider on the leading horse, and let out a piercing cry. 'The King has had a hunting accident,' she declaimed, rolling her eyes skywards. 'Jesus preserve him, let us pray God for his life!'

Goddess, Mother, preserve me from this!

'No indeed,' Guenevere said furiously, gesturing to the unconscious figure behind. 'This treacherous knight attacked the King in the forest, and gravely wounded him. We followed the sound of your bell to seek your help.'

The Abbess gaped. 'His own knight attacked the King? What happened? Did he –'

'No, not his own knight. King Ursien's knight.'

Goddess, Mother, give me patience with this!

Guenevere clenched her fists. 'Forgive me, but these men are dying while we stand here. Will you order them some help?'

'Of course!' The Abbess swelled with rage at the implied rebuke. 'Sisters!' she shrilled. 'Two litters at once, to carry these men to the infirmary. Send to warn the Sister Almoner that they are on their way.'

Guenevere turned to her maid. 'Ina, ride back to Camelot as fast as you can,' she said urgently. 'Bring the best of the Druid healers, whoever is versed in sword-wounds such as this.'

A white-faced Ina nodded and swung herself up on her horse. 'Rely on me, lady. And may the Gods be with the King!'

'And with you!' Guenevere raised a hand in farewell as horse and rider clattered out through the gate.

'Come, sisters.'

The Sister Gate-keeper moved forward to take charge. Under her direction, two groups of nuns struggled to lift the men down from their horses, lay them on stretchers, and carry them to the nearby infirmary. Guenevere followed with the rest of the sisterhood. As they entered the low, cool building, the tall, spare figure of the Sister Almoner came forward to greet them.

'Take the King to the private chamber at the end,' she commanded, waving them on down the room. 'And for the other, let me have him here.'

'No!' Arthur groaned. 'Set me down with him!' He struggled to sit up. 'Where is Accolon? I must speak with the traitor. Let me see his face!'

Guenevere flew to his side. 'Dismiss these women!' she commanded the Sister Almoner. 'The King must have some privacy now.'

'Come, sisters!' The Sister Almoner shooed the nuns away.

'Guenevere!' Arthur rasped.

'Here.' Guenevere leaned in to help him, and gave him her arm. With a superhuman effort he swung his feet to the ground, and staggered up. Two paces brought them to the stretcher where Accolon lay.

'So, Accolon!' For a moment Arthur stood in angry contemplation of the man at his feet. Accolon's face was a grey mask of pain, and his nose and lips wore the bluish hue of death. His hand was on his side, where the bright ooze of arterial blood pulsed through his fingers with every beat of his heart. His eyes were closed and sunken in his head.

'Why, Accolon?' cried Arthur. There was no reply. Leaning heavily on Guenevere, Arthur drew back his boot, and kicked the motionless figure violently. 'Why, man? Why did you want to kill me? Tell me that if nothing else with your last breath on earth.'

Guenevere drew back shuddering. 'Arthur,' she moaned, 'you know why.'

'Yes, I do!' Arthur clenched his teeth, and once more drove his boot into Accolon's ribs. 'But I want to hear it from him.'

Accolon opened his eyes. The blood-lust had ebbed away, and now his gaze was washed clean of anything but impending death. He tried for a shrug, but the effort was too great.

'I meant to kill you, Arthur,' he breathed out, 'for my lady Morgan's sake. She hated you more than life itself.'

Arthur nodded, and bared his teeth. 'Morgan Le Fay.'

A shaft of joy warmed Accolon's pale face. 'Queen Morgan

of Gore. My lady and my love.'

'You poor fool!' Arthur ground out. 'Morgan never loved anyone but herself.'

His words reached Guenevere through a haze of pain. She shook her head. *No, Arthur. She loved you. She loved you too much.*

But Accolon was unperturbed. 'She loved me,' he said, with an unnatural calm. 'She took me for her Champion and Chosen One. She gave me the scabbard to keep me safe from you. She was going to make me her king.'

Arthur gasped. 'What?'

'She planned to kill you and King Ursien, so that we could rule.'

'Kill Ursien?' said Arthur wildly. 'But Ursien lives!'

Guenevere reached for his hand. 'No, Arthur,' she said sorrowfully. The torn body in the grass rose again before her eyes. 'Morgan waylaid him in the shape of a great cat. But he's beyond her malice now.'

'And I married him to her – to that death!' Arthur threw back his head in pain, and closed his eyes. 'Forgive me, Ursien!'

Accolon gave a wan smile. 'I can take word of your remorse to him myself, King Arthur. Soon I shall meet him in the Otherworld.' His gaze drifted off to another time and place. 'Yet she loved me. Queen Morgan loved me, and took me for her knight.'

Guenevere could have cried aloud with pain. *As I loved Lancelot, and took him for my knight.* A terrible envy of Accolon gripped her heart. *At least this knight was able to enjoy his love.*

'And I loved her when all men hated her.' A flicker of fierce pride shone in the dying face. 'You took her, Arthur, but you cast her off. King Ursien never loved her, he only wanted to marry the sister of the King. She bore your child with never a word from you, and I was the only man in the world who cared if she lived or died.'

He paused, gasping for breath. 'I loved her then and watched her without hope. But when the child was born, she regained her power. One day I saw her look at me and smile. The next day she touched my hand, and took me to her bed.' A look of transcendent joy spread across his face. 'And I knew then that the love she gave me would be worth my life, and more.'

His breath escaped him in a long-drawn-out sigh. His eyelids fluttered and closed, and his face relaxed.

'Die, then, traitor!' Arthur spat in fury, clutching Guenevere as he reeled away. 'Oh, Guenevere, bring me to my bed, for I fear that like Accolon, I shall never rise again!'

'Arthur, don't say that!' Guenevere cried in anguish, 'I'll take care of you. As long as you're wearing the scabbard you won't lose any more blood. Just let me call the sisters to take care of Accolon.'

'No need, my lady. We are here.'

A nun materialised behind them on silent feet, her hands in her sleeves, her face hidden by her wimple as she bent over Accolon.

'Thank you, sister,' Guenevere said distractedly. Adjusting herself once more to Arthur's weight, she gave all her attention to helping him down the room.

At last they gained the sanctuary of the small private apartment at the end. The last of the sun was filling the air with gold, but the whitewashed cell was cool and welcoming. Arthur collapsed on the bed with a groan, and Guenevere straightened his limbs and loosened his bloodstained clothes. His body was cut in too many places to count, and all his wounds were gaping like hungry mouths.

But one, she could see, was worse than all the rest. Below his tunic, there was a deep slash to his groin. It was still bleeding freely, and his legs, and even the insides of his boots were sticky with fresh blood. Carefully Guenevere lifted his sword from his side, and laid it on his chest, clasping both hands around the massive hilt. Then she tightened the belt holding the scabbard against his torn body, and prayed that help had not come too late. Arthur slipped into unconsciousness as she worked.

Goddess, Mother, save him, don't let him die.

Through the door to the outer chamber she could see the black-clad nun on her knees beside Accolon's body, her face no more than a shadow inside her wimple, her hands joined in prayer. Out of the corner of her eye she saw the sister cross herself, rise to her feet, and make her way down the long room towards her to hover outside the door of Arthur's cell.

'The Mother Abbess begs a word with you, my lady,' she

called softly, dipping her head. 'Will you go?'

Guenevere glanced distractedly in the direction of the voice. The Mother Abbess? Gods above, what could that woman want? Irritation seized her as she looked at the nun waiting humbly in the shadows outside the door. What kind of religion forced women to bend their heads like this, be ashamed to show their faces, even their hands?

'Tell the Mother Abbess that I can't leave the King.'

'The Sister Almoner is coming to take care of the King. I will stay with him till she arrives.'

Guenevere gave a heartfelt inner groan. *That dreadful woman now? But maybe it's best to get it over with. I needn't be long, I can hurry back.*

She turned back to the bed. Arthur was deeply unconscious, sleeping peacefully. She bent over the figure on the bed.

'I have to leave you for a while, Arthur,' she said softly. 'This good nun will look after you till I return.'

She dropped a kiss on his forehead, and left the room.

'I shall not be gone long,' she threw over her shoulder as she hastened away. 'I beg you, take your best care of the King.'

The nun bobbed a curtsy and bowed her head. 'I shall, my lady.' The heavy wimple turned as she watched Guenevere's every step down the length of the room. At last the tall, hurrying form passed through the door, and disappeared from sight.

Silently the nun entered the cell where Arthur slept. With skilful hands she straightened the pillow under his head. Tenderly she brushed the hair back from his forehead, and lightly touched his hurts. Her long thin fingers wandered down over his body till they reached the scabbard at his waist. With great care she unbuckled the broad leather belt, and lifted the scabbard away.

At once all Arthur's wounds began to bleed, weeping great tears of blood. Intently the nun stood watching every one. Her hands were shaking as she clutched the scabbard to her chest, and her eyes burned like mulberries in her white face.

'So, brother!' she whispered savagely. 'Where is your safety now?'

A silent prayer poured through the anguish of her mind.

Hear me, Accolon, wherever your spirit walks! And wait a while, my love, in the world between the worlds. Wait, and I shall send you Arthur's soul. I swear by all the powers, he will not last the night!

CHAPTER 13

The Abbess Placida was at prayer, giving thanks to the glory of God. Her fleshy lips rolled with satisfaction as she counted her joys. Praise the Lord who had sent the King here with such terrible injuries into Christian hands. With the High King himself recovering under their roof, the fame of the House of the Holy Mother would spread throughout the land!

Despite the pain in her knees, the Abbess prayed on. Having the King here would bring all manner of great men to her door. Lords and kings and high princes of the Church would visit him. The Father Abbot of London, the King's spiritual father, would be the first of many, she was sure. And one of them must surely notice her, and translate her to a higher place. With all the new bishoprics and archbishoprics now being decreed from Rome, one of them must have room for a woman like her.

And if the King did not live, think what that could be! King Arthur, the knight of the sword in the stone, the hero of countless wars and the first Christian High King, what it would be to have him buried here!

No, not buried, she corrected herself at once. King Arthur would draw as many worshippers in a casket as he would underground. His bones should be placed in a jewelled reliquary, so that she could take him with her wherever she went, when she was elevated to York, say, or Canterbury –

'Holy Mother!'

The Abbess let out a sound between a curse and a groan as an urgent young novice came tumbling through the door. 'What is it now?'

The nun bobbed her head. 'Queen Guenevere is here to see you.'

The Abbess frowned. The pagan queen, who still clung to the Mother-right, by which a woman would give her body to a man as freely as she gave him her hand? What did she want? She waved a ring-laden hand. 'Show her in.'

The smell inside the chamber reached Guenevere as soon as the nun opened the door. 'Please go in, lady,' she said, 'the Mother Abbess is expecting you.' Guenevere stepped inside, holding her breath.

The Abbess sat facing the door, enthroned in a stout chair of ebony with carved arms and a high polished back. Her feet rested on an embroidered hassock, her whip rested against her chair within easy reach, and a low stool for penitents stood nearby. Behind her, a small altar against the wall bore two fat candles smouldering in the gloom. Above the altar a burning censer breathed out the stink of incense, glowing like an angry eye. Overlaying it all was the unclean smell of stale habitation, like that of an animal in its lair. Guenevere swallowed hard.

'Greetings,' she said.

Greetings? Was that all the rude creature had to say? The Abbess let out her breath, and forced a smile. 'You are welcome to our house, the house of God,' she said with emphasis. She pointed to the low stool at her feet. 'Take a seat.'

But for this place, Arthur might be dead. Guenevere forced herself to stay calm, and even made her voice polite. 'Thank you, madam, I would rather stand. I must not leave the King for long. We were truly blessed to find your convent here. It was chance alone that brought us to your door.'

A complacent smile passed over the Abbess's face. 'We are glad to be of use to the King. God moves in mysterious ways His wonders to perform. And only He has the power to heal our sins.'

Her voice was like the buzzing of a gnat. Guenevere felt a sickness she could not name. These wretched Christians with their everlasting talk of sin! What about the joy of life, the love the Goddess gives? She thought of Lancelot, and could have wept. Waves of desire were racking her to the bone. The next second *I must get back to Arthur* floated through her mind.

The Abbess was in full flood now, her face flushed with self-praise. 'Of course, the King has forgiven us for the past. He knew it was not our fault, what had happened here. Why, we saw nothing, she was far too cunning for that. I had no idea when she came, none of us did –'

A shaft of fear struck Guenevere like a knife. 'Forgive me, Mother – when who came?'

The Abbess turned an ugly shade of pale, and her face contorted with old bitterness. 'That daughter of evil. Satan's hand-maiden herself.'

Guenevere sat very still. 'The King's sister? She was here? Morgan Le Fay?'

The Abbess nodded. 'The very same. She called herself Sister Ann.' A whine of self-justification entered her voice. 'God knows I whipped her, as I did them all. She was beaten enough to drive the Devil out.'

But you drove the evil in.

Guenevere hardly knew the sound of her own voice. 'You said the King has forgiven you for the past. But King Arthur never knew his sister was here. When he found out that his father had had her shut up in a nunnery, he refused to hear any more.'

The Abbess gaped. 'But when he came – I thought –'

You thought wrong. 'If he had known this was the home of Morgan Le Fay, he would never have darkened your door. He tried to avoid any contact with her at all. Even when her crimes against us came to light, he sent his knights here to investigate, he never came himself. All he ever knew was the name of the place.'

The Abbess assumed a virtuous, indignant air. 'Well, of course we changed that! The holy Father Abbot came from London, and exorcised the house. Every sister was examined, and all her coven rooted out, and put to death. Then instead of the House of the Holy Mother, we were called the House of the Little Sisters of Mercy, though the Blessed Virgin is still the centre of our prayers.'

Guenevere held up her hand. A tide of foreboding was chilling her to the bone. *This was the convent where Morgan grew up. Where she lived and worked all her life as a nun. Perhaps even a nun in the Infirmary, taking care of the sick –*

The words came from her mouth in a strangled gasp. 'Did you send for me?'

The Abbess's mouth fell open. 'What?'

'Just now!' Guenevere cried, in an ecstasy of fear. 'Did you send one of the sisters to ask me to come to you?'

The Abbess bristled. 'Certainly not!' she said frostily. 'Of course, when you came to me, I had to receive you, pagan though you are –'

'Gods above, save him! Save the King!'

With a howl of distress, Guenevere burst from the room, leaving the Mother Abbess without a backward glance.

'Holy Mother of God!' The Abbess's eyes bulged with rage. Was there no end to the rudeness of these godless ones?

She reached for her whip, and slapped it against her thigh. The pagan was beyond her chastisement, of course. But there were other sinners close at hand, and one of them would have to pay for this. The next through the door, she thought viciously, novice or nun, would feel the weight of her rod.

Slowly she savoured the pleasure of the coming revenge. With every stroke she could imagine the proud pagan queen crouched at her feet, smarting under the lingering punishment. There was a muffled knock at the door, and she closed her eyes.

'Come in!'

Her fingers were itching in anticipation of what was to come. Only when she opened her eyes did she see how wrong she had been. And as she felt the whip torn from her nerveless grasp, she knew for sure that the promised vengeance lay in other hands.

Guenevere coursed though the corridors like one possessed.

This is the house where Morgan was confined.

This is the place where she grew from a tortured child to a black force of nature, hungering for revenge.

Morgan whose cleverness is beyond mortal skill.

Morgan who knows this place like the back of her hand.

Morgan, Morgan, whose malice never sleeps.

Outside the infirmary the Sister Almoner stood waiting with her assistants, armed with bowls of rose-water and clean cloths to minister to Arthur's wounds. Her eyes widened as she saw Guenevere. 'We thought you were inside with the King, Lady Guenevere. We were waiting to come in.' She broke off in alarm.

'Who was with him, then? We heard a voice, we heard you talking to him –'

Guenevere brushed past them into the empty room. In the small chamber at the far end, a dark shape hovered over Arthur's unconscious form, sucking out his life.

'*Morgan!*' she screamed.

The shape quivered, broke away from Arthur, and rose unsteadily in the air, sagging under the weight of Arthur's blood. Guenevere covered the length of the room in a couple of strides. Arthur lay spread-eagled on the bed, his every wound weeping his life away. He was clutching Excalibur to his chest in the grip of death, and his face and hands like Ursien's were torn and clawed. Cold filled the chamber, and a graveyard dew clung to his clammy skin.

'Morgan!' Guenevere howled again.

The dark miasma hovered in the air above her head. Guenevere leaped over to Arthur, and snatched at the sword.

'Arthur, give it me!' she breathed in his ear. 'Give me Excalibur!'

Frantically she prised the weapon from his grip, lifted it with both hands, and furiously slashed the air. The blade whined in her hand, demanding blood.

'Avenge your master!' Guenevere panted as she swung. 'Give me her life for his!'

The air in the little room eddied to and fro. Indolent, taunting, the dark shape parted and re-formed around the slashing blade, its heavy yet weightless body always out of reach. With a mocking hiss it wafted out of range, and floated out through the window into the open air. For a moment it darkened the pink and gold face of the sky, eclipsing the early stars. Then with a whisper of a cruel laugh, it was gone.

Guenevere threw Excalibur to the floor. Beside the bed lay a crumpled black habit, discarded in the heat of flight. A white headdress lay beside it, soiled and askew. The putrid scent of death hung in the air. Arthur sprawled on the bed bleeding his heart out, and the scabbard that could save him was nowhere to be seen.

CHAPTER 14

The setting sun dipped down towards the horizon, gilding the buildings outlined against the sky. Soon it would kiss the water, and lose itself in the broad bosom of the Thames. But even at night, London had a haunting power. The solitary figure in the shadow of the church looked out over the city he had come to love, and felt the gnawing tooth of sharp regret.

Pacing the familiar churchyard where his sandalled feet knew every step, the Father Abbot clasped his hands in prayer and wrestled with his soul. Must I leave London, Lord, is that Your will? And go to York? From there, it is only one step to Canterbury itself. And I do not seek these great offices, I have been happy enough doing Your will here.

He raised unseeing eyes to the evening sky. Lord, Lord! he cried in silence, You sent me to these islands when the pagans still loved their Goddess with a passion that put all Christian lives at risk. We were a handful of young brothers, armed with nothing but our faith in Christ. With Your love, we built a church here in London, and now we have a foot in many towns. In time You made me the Father of our Abbey here, and I have toiled night and day in Your name.

And now this!

His long lean face knotted as he strode round and round the well-trodden square. In the heat of summer, the rough wool of his habit fretted his skin, and he tugged unhappily at the fastening at his neck. Yet this torment too, he had found the way to turn to the love of God. Always draughty and cold in winter and hot in summer, the coarse black gown was the perfect garment for mortifying the flesh. And with the emissary from Rome waiting for him in the Abbey guest-house, the sooner he mastered his own desires and submitted himself to the will of God, the better it would be.

He paused in his pacing, and raised his eyes to the sky. Overhead small clouds rode like ships at anchor in a perfect watery blue. The Abbot's tensions relaxed as he took it in. He had detested London for a long time, both the place itself, and the people who called it theirs. His bones would never forget the heat and light of Rome, his beloved birthplace and spiritual home. Yet now he found much to be enjoyed in these sea-girt islands, with their sweet springtimes and soft summer days.

Of course, it was not Rome. There was nowhere in the world like Mother Rome, no place so fitted to be the centre of the Faith. A young monk in the City of God truly understood the fight against sin, with Rome's feast of flesh available every day. Full-bodied girls with eyes like the backs of beetles, lissom pouting youths half-way between boy and girl, tanned and sweating bodies of either sex, endowed with the swell and bloom of peaches and the cleft of ripe plums, yes, Lord, any one of these was temptation enough for a saint.

Rome.

Oh, that glorious, riotous carnival of the flesh!

Enough.

With a reflex self-discipline, the Father Abbot put away sensual thoughts, and returned to the matter in hand. His soul sank into something like despair. Lord God, Father of Mankind, is this Your trial of me? On this summer evening, myself lost to the world working peacefully in my study, and the message comes that a legate from Rome has arrived?

But he was not surprised. As the Holy See advanced its forward march, old hands like himself were vital in building the faith. Where once their task was simply to spread the Word, now they were called on to be architects of the Church Triumphant throughout the isles. The great See of Canterbury was the cornerstone of the faith. York was its younger brother, and men of strength and vision were needed to shape them into what they had to be.

'So you were thought of, Father, even as far as Rome.'

The Abbot suppressed a dry smile. He might have known

that an embassy from Rome would not wait tamely in the guest
lodgings for the summons to meet. Well, he was as ready as he
would ever be. He turned to greet his interlocutor.

He saw a small man of indeterminate age standing in the
sunset, wearing an innocent smile. He was dressed in the habit of
a simple monk, but the rope round his waist was of silk, and his
sandals were made of fine leather, intricately tooled. The pitiless
sun of Rome had wrinkled his face like a walnut, and his short
body was somewhat stooped, though he held himself like a much
taller man. His tonsured head sported a sparse fringe of hair, and
the hands protruding from his black habit were sun-shrivelled
too. Only his eyes had stood the test of time. As clear as the sky,
they conveyed both wisdom and wit, and a hint of something else
behind it all.

'Forgive me if I intrude on your prayers,' said the little man.
'I am Domenico of Tuscany at your service, the emissary from
Rome.'

The Father Abbot bowed deeply. 'The service and the
honour are both mine.' He gestured towards the Abbey guest-
house across the open space. 'They made you comfortable, I trust?
Is there anything I can get for you now?'

The old man's laugh reminded the Abbot of a fountain
playing in a Roman square. 'I am not here for my comfort, brother
in Christ. Like our Lord himself, I am a fisher of souls.' He fixed
the Abbot with his innocent blue eyes. 'And in Rome they are
asking of you, what bait, what hook?'

The Father Abbot closed his eyes. Dear Lord, he prayed
steadily, You who made the supreme sacrifice, show me the
way. He opened his eyes to see Domenico still regarding him
closely.

'I have done much here,' he said abruptly, staring back.

'You have, you have,' Domenico agreed amiably, spreading
his hands. 'Above all in bringing Arthur Pendragon to Christ. The
Holy Father himself took note of that.' He cocked his head on one
side, and looked around. 'Here in this very churchyard, was it
not?'

'Even here.' The Father Abbot's heart swelled with what he
knew was the sin of pride. But he pointed firmly straight ahead.
To the side of the path just inside the churchyard gates squatted a

huge block of stone covered in moss. A trail of green lichen sprouted from an aperture in the top.

The Abbot nodded. 'The old Druid Merlin came to ask if he could use our churchyard to proclaim Arthur king. Not only as the heir to the Middle Kingdom, but High King of all the Britons, no less.' He gave an embarrassed laugh. 'I did not know the old fraud was planning to fake a miracle. I only thought that if we helped Arthur, he'd be bound to support us in return.'

'And you were right,' Domenico chirped. 'Arthur was proclaimed, he won back the Middle Kingdom, and he has favoured our faith ever since.' He nodded approvingly. 'You did well, brother.' Then his impish twinkle broke out again. 'Tell me, how did they do it? The sword in the stone, I mean.'

The Abbot shook his head. 'The young men here do it all the time. It's their way of testing their swords for battle, to try them on stones, trees, anything. The strongest can find the vein of weakness in a stone, to drive the sword in. Then, because they alone know how they put it in, only they can pull it out. Merlin had Arthur practise the trick in Gore before he brought him here. The lad did it for his prowess many times.'

The little man lit up with mirth. 'No miracle, then?' he chortled almost to himself.

'Not unless you think a broad body and a powerful right arm are a miracle, rather than a simple gift of God. And Arthur has those in abundance, as well as a true heart and a trusting soul.'

There was a pause. 'So, brother?' Domenico resumed gently after a while. 'I think we all know that you have done well here.'

'But there is more, much more!' The Abbot was startled to hear the passion in his own tone. 'I have been nurturing a house of holy women, but its future is far from secure. The Mother Abbess . . .'

He paused. How to do justice to the Abbess Placida's puffed-up pride, her joy in cruelty, her meagre soul? 'Sadly, she is not one of the gifted of God. A great evil grew up there in her time, when one of the sisters proved to be in league with the powers of darkness, and the Mother Abbess was blind to it till too late. I am considering how to relieve her of her post. And I have to oversee the progress of her successor, whenever that may be.'

From the understanding silence, he knew that the legate

must have read the reports that he had sent to Rome. Emboldened, he pressed on. 'There are many such projects I have in hand. But the greatest has hardly begun. And for that I am ready to lay down my life here.'

'Avalon.'

The word dropped between them like a stone. The old bile rose again in the Father Abbot's throat.

'Avalon, yes,' he forced out with unconstrained disgust. 'The so-called Sacred Island, source and site of Goddess worship in this land. And the home of that great whore who calls herself the Lady of the Lake, and encourages other women to spurn the control of men.'

All the light had left Domenico's eyes, and the blue gaze now held nothing but ice.

'The Great Mother,' he said nodding slowly, weighing every word. 'Yes, the great enemy. We have hunted her down from the fringes of the frozen wastes to the Holy Land itself. Country by country, shrine by shrine, we have destroyed her worship to bring these pagans to the love of the one true God. Yet still they hold out.'

'Yes!' cried the Abbot furiously. 'And if we can root out their so-called Lady of the Lake from the haunt of the Great Mother, we can set Christian worship in its place!' His eyes misted, and his voice took on a sacral tone. 'I see a church rising on Avalon. I see the Cross of Christ surmounting the very Tor. I pray for the time when our rituals have so supplanted theirs throughout the world, when no man remembers that the great Goddess Whore ever reigned there, ever existed at all!'

Domenico could see the Abbot's purpose flaming in his eyes. 'You reported that the assault had begun. You sent two monks, I think, to treat with the whore of Avalon. How are your soldiers faring against the foe?'

'Boniface and Giorgio, yes.' The Abbot drew a deep breath. 'As well as two untried young monks can do. For our first overture, it was vital to send the gentlest souls we had.' And the best looking too, he could have added, to play upon the old whore's weakness for male flesh. But he did not have to say this to a man from Rome. 'We sent them to ask if they could stay on the isle, and add to the worship there with their own prayers.'

Domenico raised his eyebrows admiringly. 'Such a simple thing. How could she refuse?'

'She could not. They were accepted. And living there on the island, along with the Goddess followers and worshippers, they have learned much.' He paused. 'Much that will be vital in our struggle to wrest their rituals and relics to Christian use.'

'Their relics, yes.' The eyes of the visitor darkened with desire. 'The objects of their worship are fine, I hear.'

The Abbot gave a bitter smile. 'Finer than anything we could dream of. They have a great loving-cup, a massive plate, a sword of power, and a spear of defence. And all are made of solid gold, studded with jewels and gemstones too. I have made a vow to turn them to the service of Our Lord.'

'Yes,' murmured Domenico thoughtfully. 'We need gold, to dazzle and win the pagan soul. And we need regalia too, to celebrate the high moments of our faith.'

The Abbot fixed him in his gaze. 'From the cup, the pagans claim, their Goddess succours all who come to her. At the Last Supper, Our Lord also succoured the disciples from His own cup.'

Domenico looked at him enquiringly. 'The blessed Holy Grail?'

'The very same. How if –'

He broke off, and steadied his soul for the great leap.

'How if God in His mystery has sent us the Grail here, in this pagan form? How would it be for our Faith, if we could get these vessels from the pagans, and make them our own?'

The setting sun flushed all the sky with red. The silence lengthened between the two men. 'It would be very good,' Domenico said softly at last. 'It would break the power of the Goddess, and draw countless new believers to our side.' A look of naked calculation filled his eyes. 'Can you do it?'

'I can if I stay here. Translated to York or Canterbury, I am in another country, another world.'

'Yes, I see that. The fight against the Great Whore is here.'

'And Avalon is not the only battle I have to fight.' The Abbot sighed. 'For all our efforts, I still have not won Arthur's soul. And our dearest enemy lies nearest to his heart.'

'His Druid Merlin?'

The Abbot shook his head. 'No, the old madman is no real threat. He comes and goes with the seasons, he wanders with the wind. Our foe is one who whispers in Arthur's ear, and sways his mind. One who cares for his body, and sleeps in his bed.' A spasm of raw anger knotted his veins. 'Guenevere the Queen.'

'Ah, yes.'

'Queen, Arthur calls her! She's no more than his concubine, the pagan daughter of a line of pagan queens. Sent to Avalon by her mother as a child, to sit at the feet of the Lady and learn her whoreish ways. The mother herself was a warrior and a whore. She led her own troops in battle, then pleasured herself with the finest of her knights.' He gave a sardonic laugh. 'Their Goddess teaches them that women have the right of thigh-freedom with any man.'

'So the Goddess worship supports the rule of queens,' mused Domenico. His eyes narrowed. 'Root out the one, then, and the other must go.'

'And then we know we are doing the will of God,' the Abbot burst out triumphantly, 'who does not permit women to rule over men!' He paused, breathing heavily, and his voice took on a deep, imploring tone. 'In the name of Christ, let me renew the assault on Avalon.'

'So be it, Father.' The little envoy hitched up his robe. 'You have persuaded me. And I shall persuade Rome. You shall stay here.' He smiled, but there was a warning in his stare. 'For the time being, at least. There are great changes afoot. If Arthur dies –'

'What?'

Domenico broke off, watching the Abbot's shocked face. 'You did not know?' he went on. 'No, I suppose news travels slowly in these watery isles. It happened deep in the forest, near that convent of yours. Arthur was attacked by one of his own knights. He killed the rogue, but he's hovering between life and death himself.'

'A knight of the Round Table?' the Abbot interrupted furiously. 'That cannot be! They are all sworn to defend the King to the death. I myself drew up their order of knighthood, when I persuaded Arthur to regulate his old band of war-companions in the Christian way.'

The little man shrugged. 'Whoever he was, the rogue knight

almost cost Arthur his life. And for sure he's deprived him of the enjoyment of life, if he survives.' His smile grew even thinner. 'Our Lord is with you in your fight against the pagan Queen, it seems.'

'Queen Guenevere? What has she to do with this?'

'They are giving it out that he was wounded in the thigh.' Domenico's grin was frankly cruel now. 'But rumour and gossip tell another tale, one to make all men wince. If the Queen does delight in man's flesh as you say, she may be left with half a man, or less. They were nursing him at the convent, but he demanded to die in Caerleon, his kingdom and his home. They'll be moving him now, if he's not already gone.'

The Abbot could have wept. Curse that fool of an Abbess Placida, King Arthur dying under her roof and she had not sent him word? His anger against her hardened like stone. This was the end. Her rule was over, he would send to the convent tonight. No, he would wait till Domenico had departed, and go there himself. Then he would press on to Caerleon, if the King was still alive. That way he would see Arthur, offer him spiritual comfort, renew the bond –

Domenico was still speaking. 'Of course, a man so badly injured should never have been moved. But they had to leave the convent after the evil there.'

The Abbot caught his breath. 'What?'

'A horror beyond words. Another topic you and I must discuss. And one we shall not solve as easily, I fear, as we have agreed that you will stay on here.'

CHAPTER 15

The group of riders galloped into the courtyard at a furious speed. The leader vaulted impetuously from his horse, and tossed the reins to a startled groom. Behind him the second knight dragged his mount to a halt, and leaped off to confront the first.

'Gods above, what possessed you, Agravain?' he burst out. 'Setting a pace like that, with night coming down? If I hadn't given orders that our band should stick together, I'd have let you go on alone, and break your damned neck!'

'Don't preach to me, Gawain!' glowered Agravain. 'You accepted this damn-fool assignment from the Queen. "Ride out and search around, make sure no evil is lurking to harm the King."' He laughed scornfully. 'As if he's not already on the point of death. The Queen's insane!'

Gawain gasped. 'Agravain, guard your tongue!' He threw a hasty glance over his shoulder in the gathering dusk. To his right his younger brother Gaheris was clambering stiffly down from his exhausted horse, while Gareth, the youngest of the four, was already checking his mount's legs for any hurts sustained in the furious ride.

Beyond them were two others the Queen had singled out for her special care, the brothers Mador and Patrise. Gawain sighed to himself. He had been only too happy to obey the Queen's request to take an interest in the two young fatherless knights, thinking that Agravain would find it harder to challenge him with other knights around. Well, he'd been wrong about that!

He took Agravain by the arm and dragged him roughly

aside. Taller than his brother, Gawain also had the advantage of bulk. 'Have a care, Agravain,' he growled. 'Insulting the Queen like that, a man could lose his head, even if you're a nephew of the King.'

He jerked his head at Mador and Patrise. The two brothers were standing side by side, taking care of their sweating horses and talking softly between themselves. But there was no mistaking the concern in Mador's watchful gaze.

Not much gets past that one, Gawain thought grimly. He'd never understand why the four of us can't get on as devotedly as he and young Patrise do. He turned back to Agravain with renewed rage. 'Where's your family pride? D'you want young knights like these to say that the Orkney brothers fight among themselves, and can't obey a command?'

'Command?' scoffed Agravain. 'What command? All the world knows that the King's a dying man. And if Queen Morgan wanted to come back, a hundred knights would not keep her away. Yet you took Guenevere's command without a word. You led us all on this fool's errand until I called a halt!'

'Listen, Agravain,' Gawain muttered, struggling to keep his fist out of his brother's face, 'we're the King's knights, and the least we can do is to keep watch for him. We're knights of the Table, damn you, it's our faith, our oath! Who knows what wickedness we keep at bay when we're out and about?'

Agravain shook his head disbelievingly. 'Not this time, Gawain. What d'you think put the force behind Accolon's sword?' He gave a scornful laugh. 'And who do you think believes this tale of "a wound in the thigh"?' He thrust his face into Gawain's with a savage leer. 'If the King lives, he'll be worse than dead, he'll be a eunuch, man! And where's our knighthood then? Who in the world will want to follow that?'

'Guenevere?'

Guenevere rose from her seat beside the great bed, and pushed aside the hangings to look in. 'I'm here, Arthur.'

'What time is it?'

Guenevere glanced through the window at the fading sky. Below her, Caerleon lay spread out on all sides. On the far horizon, the love star was beginning to bloom. *Time to light* – She put the thought away. 'It's getting towards evening. Another warm, clear night.'

Arthur gave a pale smile. 'How long have I been asleep?'

She forced a warm glance in return. 'Only an hour this time. I wish you could sleep more.'

Arthur gave a weak laugh. 'Oh, my love, you say that when you hardly sleep at all!'

Guenevere straightened up and passed the back of her hand over her forehead, wishing it were not true. She felt grey and worn and ugly and sick with fatigue. *Thank the Gods that Lancelot cannot see me now,* floated through her mind. *Yet if he were here, I might not look so bad.*

She forced her mind back to the man lying in the bed. Since the fight in the wood, she had not left Arthur's side. From time to time she had snatched an hour of sleep, but the dreams she suffered made her fear to sleep again. Time after time she saw Arthur under the sword, and felt in her own body Accolon's last cruel blow.

Yet wounded as he was, Arthur had lived. Though horrified by the kind of injuries she had never seen before, the Sister Almoner had doggedly searched and cleaned and sewn up the mouth-like wounds, one by one. She had supervised the long days and nights of care, when Arthur had refused any draught to take away the pain, and chosen to bear the worst. She balked only at the great slash between his legs, having no knowledge, she said, of the hurts of men.

Meanwhile a flurry of knights from Camelot had descended on the convent at a gallop, a brilliant troop of glittering lances and flying banners, with Ina at their head. They had scoured the forest, and discovered no trace of what had killed King Ursien, human or animal. But they brought in his body for the last dignities. All night they had honoured him with a vigil, then at dawn a party had set off with the hearse to Gore. The rest had formed a royal guard to bring Arthur back to Caerleon, and home.

The journey had been long and terrible. Yet, despite his suffering, Arthur had hung on. Rage with Accolon and hatred for Morgan had put fire in his veins, even as his blood ebbed out. But then the fire had turned to a fever, which ran like quicksilver through his frame. Now Guenevere had the bitter task of starving his fever by withholding food, yet forcing red wine down his throat to replace his blood. She had had to watch him raging with grief and remorse, till every one of his wounds burst open, and wept with him too. 'Only get me to Caerleon,' he kept chattering out in his fever again and again, 'and let me die.'

'Arthur, you are in your kingdom,' she repeated to him time after time. 'You're in Caerleon, and you will not die.'

She could see he did not believe her. As the fever waxed and waned, he lay helpless in the great bed, brooding on his loss.

'Why did she take the scabbard, Guenevere?' he ground out, through rattling teeth. 'To hurt me, or you?'

Oh Arthur, Arthur, to hurt both of us.

She forced herself to respond. 'Arthur, that wasn't it, don't you see?' she said dully. 'She wants it for her son.'

Her son and yours, Arthur.

She wants her young prince to have the scabbard of a king.

Say rather of a queen.

My mother's scabbard that she took from you.

Guenevere pressed her fingers to the sides of her throbbing head. In time, all this would fade. But one memory, she knew, would not yield so easily to the passage of time.

It was the image of the Abbess Placida as Guenevere had last seen her, her ample body filling her ebony chair. But now her head was tilted back at a vicious angle, and her wimple lay behind her on the floor. Her plump cheeks were scored with deep downward scratches, and her bulging eyes stared at the ceiling, glazed for ever in a last desperate glare. From her gaping mouth protruded her beloved whip, thrust down her throat to choke her to death.

'Guenevere?'

She came to herself with a start. 'Yes, Arthur, I'm still here.'

'Did I fall asleep again?' His voice tailed off.

'I don't know.'

She shook her head. Arthur was asleep again as she said the words.

There was a soft knock on the door and Ina padded in, the lamp in her hand golden in the silver dusk. 'Sir Gawain is here with his brothers, my lady. He is asking to see the King.'

Guenevere threw a look at the still figure in the bed, and shook her head. 'Tell them the King is asleep. I will send at once if he wakes and asks for them.'

Ina nodded. 'And the doctor is here, to see to the King again.'

Guenevere hesitated. 'Are the King's monks still outside?'

Ina nodded, hardly bothering to conceal a smile. 'They're out there mumbling their prayers around the clock. They want to know when they'll be admitted to the King.'

'Tell them when the time comes,' Guenevere said. 'And show my Druid in.'

If Arthur lived, it would be due to him, Guenevere thought, as the white-gowned figure made his way in. A sturdy, cold-eyed man of middle height, he looked more like a wrestler than the healer he was. Like all Druids, he had been a warrior before he gave his life to the service of the Gods, so his knowledge of war wounds was unrivalled, and his skill with the mind was as great. With a murmured greeting, Guenevere led him to the bed, and stood beside him as he lightly touched Arthur's hand, then his forehead, and turned back the sheets.

The smell of blood and pus rose from the bed. Arthur stirred, grumbling anxiously in his sleep.

'How has he been?' the Druid asked quietly, his broad hands peeling back the dressings on Arthur's sides.

'Much the same.'

'Just as this is.' He gestured angrily at Arthur's wound. Dull inflamed blotches of infected flesh marked the wasted stomach and legs. 'The same – or worse. We're making no headway here, none at all.'

Guenevere followed the line of his troubled gaze. At the top of Arthur's leg, a long sword-slash cut deep into his groin, severing tendon and bone. Around the wound, the mangled flesh throbbed purple-red, oozing with decay. Below, the swollen and inflated genitals could have been those of one of the Old Ones, the gigantic creatures who had made the world. Only Arthur's sex lying sleepily to one side, as pale and delicate as a snail without its shell, was a reminder that this was a man.

Arthur, Arthur, oh –

The voice of the Druid broke into her thoughts. 'The blade of the sword must have been treated with venom, to poison the organs of generation like this.' As the healer spoke, his spade-like hands went brutally to work. 'It should have been stitched when it happened,' he said, almost to himself. 'Then we should not have –' he paused, and the unspoken words hung heavily in the air '– the fears that we have now.' The doctor gave a grim smile. 'But it's hard to imagine such expertise in a convent of nuns. Indeed, none of us has seen such a wound since the days of the Sacred King.'

'The Sacred King?' Guenevere struggled to collect her thoughts.

'Yes, when a queen would change her consort every year. The man she discarded was given to the Druids, and they gave him to the Gods. They hung him on a tree for three days and nights, and took his manhood with a golden sickle so that his blood and seed would give the earth new life.'

'Sir –'

'Harsh, eh?' Abstractedly he cleaned, scoured, and dressed the raw tissue as he spoke. Arthur whimpered in his sleep under the merciless hands. 'Then it became three years, and then seven, before the King had to die. Then queens like your mother, lady, spared their consorts to live on in their warrior band. Your mother made her former Chosen Ones into a peerless band of knights.'

Guenevere saw again her mother's face, lit by her undying smile. Her voice broke. 'They all loved her, to the grave and beyond.'

'Because she loved them.'

The Druid pressed the last dressing into place, then laid two heavy fingers on Arthur's eyelids till the low cries ceased. Reaching for a cloth, he wiped his hands with great deliberation, and turned to face Guenevere. 'She loved them, madam, more than she loved herself. She changed her consorts when they failed, for the good of the land.'

His pale eyes held Guenevere in a hypnotic grip. 'The law of the Goddess is that a queen must be championed by the worthiest knight. In the Summer Country, the Queen must obey that law.' His gaze flickered over Arthur, then back to Guenevere again. 'We are all praying that the King will recover himself again. But if he does not, you must be faithful to the Great One who gave you life. A woman wounds herself when she clings to a mate who cannot love her as a man. When a queen does so, she wounds the land too.'

His voice wove a light rhythmic spell around her head. 'Lady, I speak as your Druid father, not as the King's healer now. Arthur's spirit is moving in pathways of its own. But whether he lives or dies, you must never forget your duty to yourself.'

My duty to myself –

'Oh, it's you, Ina, I didn't hear you come in.'

The maid smiled. 'You drowsed off, lady, when the doctor went. You've sat by the bed for so long that you've tired yourself out.' Her eyes were soft. 'Take some fresh air, madam, I'll keep watch here.'

Guenevere lifted her head. 'Thank you, Ina. But I can't leave the King.'

'As you wish, lady.' Ina shook her head, and withdrew.

Guenevere leaned forward to rest her weary body on the bed. The only sound was of Arthur's gasping breath. A shaft of memory stabbed at her wandering brain. *Lancelot caught his breath like that when I asked him to go.*

Lancelot –

Her sight faded, and she saw him standing as he had once long ago, bathed in morning sunlight as his page strapped on his armour and prepared him for a joust. As she surprised him in his pavilion, he had turned to face her, a man clothed all in gold with a gaze of burning fire. 'Madame?'

The lilt of his accent lingered in her ear. She heard it again as she saw him standing in her chamber on the day he went away.

Let us make a good farewell, my queen. We shall have a long time to remember it.

Lancelot, my love, my life, don't go –

She came to herself with a racking start. Her head was pounding, and a strangled sorrow throbbed through every vein.

Lancelot –

With trembling fingers she threw off her veil, gasping for breath. Then she dropped her head on her arms in a grief too deep for tears.

She did not hear the door opening and the sound of footsteps across the floor. The first she knew was a touch on her hand, and a light, accented voice.

'Madame?'

CHAPTER 16

*G*oddess, Mother, don't torment me so – don't bring him to me in a dream, then take him away again –

She sat up slowly, struggling to stay calm. Her eyes were burning, but she could not weep. 'Lancelot?'

His breeches and boots were covered with the dust of the roads, and his shadowed gaze showed he had travelled hard. His face was pale, and he looked troubled to his soul. His travelling clothes hung off his tall frame, and he seemed thinner than when he had gone away.

Oh, Lancelot –

His jaw and chin were covered in the soft stubble her fingers loved. His tangled hair seemed to cry out for her touch. But all this was behind them. Calmness and courtesy were the watchwords now.

'Lancelot.'

She extended her hand, and he raised it to his lips.

'My lady,' he murmured stiffly. His kiss on her hand was cold. 'How is the King?'

'The King?' *Is it Arthur you love, or me?* 'What are you doing here?'

He nodded to the figure in the bed. 'I saw the King attacked. I was far away, but I came at once.'

'You saw it? How?'

'A lady showed it to me. She can cast figures in a wall of falling water, and I saw the King there.'

'What lady?' She tried to keep the jealousy out of her voice. 'Who was she?'

His brown eyes flashed. 'A great seer, and wise beyond her

years. She keeps the Sacred Lake in my own country.'

'Is she beautiful?' Guenevere could not help herself. 'How old is she?'

She could feel his anger rising like a tide. 'She is my foster-mother! She reared me, she taught me to be a knight. My duty to you, Madame, took me away. But when the King was in danger, I had to be here.'

And all I can do is chide like a fish-wife, and show my jealousy –

'Forgive me, Lancelot.' Slowly she got to her feet. 'The King is very ill, have you heard?'

He gave a curt nod. 'We saw the King in danger of his life. So my cousins and I rode back at once to the coast.'

'Bors and Lionel, yes. I forgot they were travelling with you.'

'We came as fast as we could to the aid of the King.'

'Of course.' *So you love Arthur more than me. You honour your fellowship of men more than our love.* She turned back towards the bed. 'Well, there he is. Speak to him if you like, but he won't know you, he doesn't recognise anyone except me.'

She gestured towards the bed. Arthur lay on his back in a red robe emblazoned with the arms of Pendragon, and a white shirt embroidered with gold thread. His coronet lay beside him on the pillow, and his sword Excalibur was in reach of his hand.

Lancelot's heart lurched. Ill as Arthur was, he realised, Guenevere still dressed him like a king, and refused to treat him like an invalid. Tears started to his eyes, and an impulse of wonder shook him like a dog. What a woman, his soul mourned, what a queen!

Her nerves clamouring, Guenevere stared at Lancelot's unyielding back.

Why is he so cold?

Why not?

You chose to kill the fire of love you shared. Can you complain now that he is cold?

She made her voice sound firm and matter-of-fact. 'Why don't you speak to the King? Who knows, he may hear you, wherever his spirit walks.'

Lancelot turned and bowed. 'Thank you, Madame.' Awkwardly he approached the figure in the bed. 'Greetings, sire,' he said loudly to the slumbering form.

At once the words sounded hollow in his ear. Feeling like a fool, he tried again. 'My lord, it's Lancelot. I've come to renew my service now you've been struck down. Command me in anything, I shall obey.'

There was no response. They waited, afraid to speak.

Guenevere fixed her gaze on Lancelot again. 'I'm sorry that the King doesn't seem to hear,' she said stiffly. 'It seems that you have returned from France in vain.'

The stillness in the chamber was as grim as the grave. Yet neither wanted to move and break the spell. At last Lancelot clenched his fists, passed a hand across his face, and turned away.

As he did so, Arthur stirred, and opened his eyes. His wasted face cracked in a broken smile.

'Lancelot?'

Lancelot, Lancelot, what are we doing here?

From his vantage point at the door to the King's Apartments, Bors gazed stonily at the wall of the antechamber, avoiding every questioning gaze and curious eye. It was enough to bear the weariness in his limbs, without having to endure the rest of the crowd waiting here too.

Who were all these people? And why were they hanging around, when two guards barred the door, and the Queen's maid kept repeating that the King could see no one?

Bors glanced around in something like disgust. To his right a group of monks chattered like starlings in a corner, every now and then breaking into high, giggling laughter, quickly suppressed. Nearer to the door to the inner chamber stood Sir Gawain and his brothers, four mighty figures talking among themselves.

Both the monks and the Orkney princes had been annoyed when Lancelot was admitted ahead of them all. But none, Bors noted, had resented it more than Agravain. He had watched with eyes like poison as Lancelot was singled out by the Queen's maid, and ushered in. Then his audible jibe hung tauntingly in the air. 'So, brothers, we see who the King values, not his own kin!'

But Bors was too troubled to care about Agravain now. Wearily he tried to subdue the murmuring of his soul. Why did we return, Lancelot. Why? You had broken away from the Queen, we had crossed the sea, and were safely back in our own land. Only half a day's ride separated us from a great home-coming feast with our fathers, in the place we love and can truly call our own. Yet all because of the vision you had at the Lake, we find ourselves back here. Why, Lancelot?

Standing uneasily by his brother's side, Lionel read Bors's turmoil in the set of his shoulders and the stillness of his gaze.

'Not much longer now, brother,' he said quietly. 'He must come out soon.'

He had not reckoned with Agravain standing by. 'How much longer do we wait, brother?' he said loudly to Sir Gawain. 'Why do we wait at all, when the King's sister's sons are of less account than those who come and go?'

Gawain scowled. 'Of course the King will see us, Agravain,' Gawain said roughly, 'but Lancelot is newly back from France.'

Agravain's face darkened. 'And what are we to tell the King, when we get in? "We searched for your evil spirit, sire, and couldn't find a trace? Your Queen made fools of us, but we did our best?"'

'Forgive me, sirs, did I hear you say that the King has an evil spirit?' It was the leader of the monks, a round-faced youngish man of middle height. With his smooth, full cheeks, owlish gaze, and pale fringe of hair flopping down his forehead from his shaven tonsure, he had a solemn schoolboy look as he spoke to Gawain. 'We know, of course, of the evil that befell the King. But is there more?'

His followers were clustering anxiously round as Gawain considered his request. 'No, no,' he said at last. 'We were keeping watch over the King, no more.'

The monk beamed. 'As we watch over him here.' He gestured to the huddle of black habits in the corner of the room. 'We have maintained a constant vigil, day and night, since the King was struck down,' he said proudly. 'Please God, we shall heal him with the power of our prayer!'

Curiously Gawain noted the ardent faith, the shining eyes. The black-clad brethren looked grey with fatigue, yet still they were bubbling with cheerful energy. 'What's the secret?' he said abruptly. 'How d'you keep it up?'

'Bless you, sir!' The monk let out a peal of laughter before breaking off to cover his mouth with his hand. 'It is no hardship to witness for our Lord! It's a privilege to join the struggle for King Arthur's soul. We hear he's so badly injured that they fear for his life.' The joy drained from his face. 'So we have joined the fight to save the King!'

He blinked short-sightedly and turned back to his monks. 'Come, brothers.' He raised his arms, and they all gathered round. 'Let me see. "*In te, Domine, speravi,*" I think, "In Thee, O Lord". Brother Mark?' At the sign of his upraised hand, a lone voice gave out a single note. Then a dozen voices combined in a low chant.

The pure, rich sound of the psalm flowed round the low room. 'In Thee, O Lord, have I put my trust: cast me not away in this time of trial: forsake me not when my strength forsaketh me –'

Gawain felt a breath on the back of his neck.

'Perhaps we should try the power of prayer.' Agravain's voice dripped its poison into his ear. 'When an upstart knight of the roads means more to the King than his own sister's sons –'

'Agravain, no!' blurted Gareth, the youngest of the clan. His eyes were alight with hero-worship, and his fresh face coloured as he spoke. 'You can't say that about Lancelot! He loves the King as much as we do ourselves.'

Gaheris, the next in line, was more reserved. But his rebuke was unmistakable. 'Lancelot's no upstart, he's the son of a king. He'll be a king himself one day, which neither you nor I will ever be.'

In spite of himself Agravain's eyes flickered across to Gawain, standing in all the unconscious assurance of the eldest son. 'Thank you for reminding me, brother dear,' he breathed, his eyes glittering. 'But if you think –'

Gawain's patience snapped. 'Out!' He jerked his head. 'Get out, Agravain. You're not going in to the King, acting like this.'

Agravain widened his eyes. 'Why, Gawain, I only –'

'Understand this, or you understand nothing at all!' hissed Gawain, his flushed face only inches from Agravain's. 'If we brothers can't hold together, we're nothing, don't you see? There's only the four of us against the world. Orkney should die for Orkney, not fight like cats. You say the King does not honour his kin. Try honouring your own, if you expect honour in your turn! Let me tell you . . .' His voice faded as he drove Agravain before him towards the door.

The monks sang on. 'Deliver me, O my God, out of the hand of the ungodly, out of the clutch of the unrighteous and cruel man –'

So Agravain was getting a dressing-down, Bors observed. Well, he did not envy Gawain the task of keeping that restless, malicious spirit under control. As well preach brotherhood to a hornet, or family loyalty to a bee-wolf on the kill.

But kin still meant something in this wicked world. Bors's heart moved at the sight of Lionel, standing patiently at his side. Ruefully he surveyed his brother's tousled hair and dust-stained face. He could taste the grit of the roads in his own dry mouth, and knew how Lionel must be longing for a bowl of clean scented water, a leg of chicken, a goblet of wine. Yet we dangle foolishly here, he fretted, while Lancelot dances attendance on the Queen.

The Queen.

And Lancelot.

Bors almost moaned aloud in misery. What could they say to him? Of course she was the finest lady in the land. But Guenevere possessed all the danger of her beauty, and the power of an irresistible will. Whatever she wanted was second nature to her. Gods above, she was a force of nature in herself! If she wanted Lancelot away, what else could he do? Yet when she called him again, he was drawn back by a force beyond his command.

Lancelot.

Bors felt an overwhelming spurt of rage. Why did he have to love Guenevere? I could find you a dozen other lovely girls, Bors mourned in his honest soul, and every one would be grateful to have Lancelot for her love.

But cousin, you have fallen deep into the toils of this enchanting Queen. And so we're all caught like fish in a net.

He closed his eyes.

I'll speak to Lancelot, his thoughts ran on. He's got to understand that the Queen's not like other women, and serving her does damage to his soul. We must persuade him to go away again. Then when we get him back to Little Britain –

The doors to the inner chamber creaked and swung wide. Lancelot came through the arch towards them, his eyes very bright. 'Good news, cousins,' he cried, 'the King is much better than we thought.'

Bors could not help himself. 'And the Queen?'

'The Queen?'

Lancelot paused to collect his thoughts. His smile gave Bors his answer before Lancelot could speak. 'She is what she is,' came the heartfelt reply. 'She is Guenevere.'

'Guenevere?'

'Yes, Arthur, I'm here.'

'Was I dreaming, or did Lancelot come back?'

'He was here. You rallied at the sound of his voice, and you spoke to him. '

Arthur smiled, drowsy but satisfied. 'I thought I did.'

'Then afterwards you fell asleep again. I think his visit must have tired you out.'

Arthur struggled to open his eyes. 'Perhaps. But I'm sure I'll feel better now that he's here.' His hands wandered over the coverlet restlessly. 'I can't remember why he went away. But now he's back – oh, Guenevere . . .'

His eyes filled with the tears of bodily weakness, but a smile of joy blazed through. 'Almighty God has blessed me in you two. A royal wife, and a peerless, loyal knight – truly the Great Ones have favoured me more than I deserve.'

Guenevere turned her head away. 'If you say so.'

Arthur's face brightened with a sudden thought. 'Guenevere, we must find Lancelot a wife. If he had a love like you, he'd never leave the court.' He gave a conscious laugh. 'Forgive me, dear, of course there's no one like you. But if he were married, he'd know the happiness we have.'

A flush mounted his pale cheeks as he warmed to his idea. 'Shall we do that, Guenevere? Find Lancelot a love of his own? After all, we both want him to be happy too.'

Guenevere tried to smile. 'Yes, of course we do. But you're talking too much, I'm afraid he's over-excited you. Try to sleep again.'

'Very well.' Arthur's tone was fretful, like a child. 'But I shan't forget this when I'm strong again. A love for Lancelot! We'll do it together, won't we, Guenevere?'

CHAPTER 17

After so long on the road, it felt strange to be indoors. Irritably adjusting his body to fit the contours of the oddly shaped chair, Merlin sat weaving a cats' cradle in his mind and allowed himself to dream. So what if the boy had slipped through his hands at the coast? Things would be very different here, he was sure. The Queen of the Orkneys must yield up the child to him.

The old enchanter surged restlessly to his feet, and with fretful steps traced out the walls of the chamber where he was confined. With a grudging admiration he scanned the smooth granite walls, each stone so finely dressed that even his eye could not tell where one ended and the other began. The whole palace was made like this, he knew. He smiled derisively. If you could call it a palace, this low building scarcely bigger than the neighbouring dwellings clustered around, all the houses, shelters and barns built in the same unforgiving shade of colourless stone.

But grey stone was the only harvest here, he knew. What else would grow so far north on this skein of sea-girt islands, some scarcely more than clumps of barren rock? Life was hard here, and the simplest things had to suffice. Not a tree to be seen, but only driftwood to make chairs like the pitiful thing he sat in, or a bed. The only sound was the endless sigh of the waves, and the sea-birds' plaintive cry. The only crops were a stunted barley, and a rough kind of wheat.

Yet there was more here than outsiders dreamed. A glint of affection lit Merlin's amber eye. Already he loved the bleached-out Orkney air, the unending pale blond light of a land where the sun never set. In the mild waters here, fat fish would swarm into the nets, and seagulls laid their eggs on every cliff. Then there were the short shaggy cattle of the place, whose milk and flesh kept the people alive even in the harshest times. The Old Ones had deprived these far northern islands of many of the goods of common life. But the gifts they had given them instead made this a sacred place.

But sacred to what? Merlin pondered. Did the wife of King Lot still cling to her dead husband's Gods of blood and bone? Or as a ruling queen, did she proclaim the Mother-right now? And what would she tell Morgan's son as he grew up? Would the boy be raised in the knowledge of his father, or brought up to think the world was ruled by queens?

Queen Morgause, yes. Would she –'

He was dimly aware of a man standing before him. Sharply he raised his head. 'Yes?'

It was a warrior of the Orkneys, from his rough plaid and heavy weaponry. His short sword and dagger were stuck through his straining belt, and a massive broadsword swung by his side. His gnarled brown hands and forearms were silvered with old scars, and a hideous wound had collapsed his nose and destroyed his right eye. But the other eye stared out amiably enough, and his mouth hid a welcoming smile in the tangle of his rough red beard.

'Lord Merlin?' he said.

Absently Merlin noted the high sing-song tones of the far northern tongue. Well, these islands were nearer to the Norselands than they were to Camelot. But why was the hairy brute disturbing him?

'Yes?' he snapped. 'Who are you?'

The Orkneyan grinned. A warm animal smell came from him as he moved, and his ruined face took on a new aspect.

'They call me Leif. I am one of the knight companions of the throne. I serve Sir Lamorak, and he serves the Queen. He sent me to tell you that she cannot receive you now.' He squinted his odd eye in the effort to remember his charge. ' "The Queen is busy on affairs of state," ' he recited solemnly.

Gods above, these clowns! Merlin seethed. Affairs of state? So Queen Morgause chose the fiction that she was detained on tasks of government, rather than speak to a Druid of all-power?

She dared to disdain Merlin the Bard, one of the Lords of Light? Well, he was Merlin still. And Merlin could wait.

He was aware that the Orkneyan was still standing there. 'They say you came from Gore,' the warrior said.

'From Gore, yes, the land of King Ursien,' Merlin said irritably.

'Where our queen's sister was queen.'

'Yes indeed,' Merlin snapped. 'Queen Morgan Le Fay.'

'What news from there?' The working eye creased up interrogatively. 'When Queen Morgan was with child, our queen was overjoyed, and sent us all south with gifts. Then it was said that King Ursien had a cuckoo in his nest.' He gave a coarse chuckle. 'That the child was a wedding present he did not expect.'

'So!' Merlin made his eyes look like wolves' urine in the snow. 'What fool pays heed to rumours?' he breathed savagely.

'Some even said that King Arthur fathered the child,' Leif pressed on, oblivious. 'Then he sent word to kill all the newborns, and Lamorak said no man would kill his own son. And the child was nothing like King Arthur, Lamorak said. Just as dark as King Arthur is fair, and born with a full pelt of hair, like a wolf cub in March.'

Lamorak said, Lamorak said –

Merlin sat very still. 'So Sir Lamorak saw the child?'

'And teeth, he was born with teeth!' Leif chuckled on. 'Sign of the lion, eh? Shows he was born to fight.'

Or of the serpent, Merlin thought distantly, born to strike. Well, a Pendragon who knew how to kill would be no bad thing. 'But your lord, Sir Lamorak?' he resumed with gritted teeth. 'He saw the child, you say?'

'When the boy was born, the rest of us were not sent south. Sir Lamorak was the only one to go.'

Merlin felt a joyful quivering in the depths of his gut. 'And did he travel much between here and Gore?'

Leif nodded angrily. 'For weeks we didn't know where he was. Then suddenly he was back, and not a word could we get out of him.'

'All in secrecy, eh?'

'He didn't trust his own companion knights.' The disgruntled Orkneyan frowned. 'And we're the men of the last circle, all sworn to die before a sword touches him.' He stabbed a finger at his mutilated face. 'I took this for him, to keep him fine for the Queen. But still we don't know what happened when he went to Gore. So when I heard in the courtyard that a traveller had come from there, I –'

'Leave me!' Merlin closed his eyes, and willed the Orkneyan away. So! his soul was hissing. *So!*

So Sir Lamorak was in the confidence of Queen Morgause. He had been with Queen Morgan at the time of the birth of the child, then disappeared afterwards. As the boy had too.

And now Queen Morgause would not see him – too busy on affairs of state?

Well, he could wait. Because now he knew he had come to the right place.

He cackled venomously, and rose to his feet, gathering up his robe around his skinny shanks to resume pacing the granite walls of the chamber again.

The secret lay here with Queen Morgause, Morgan's only sister, her closest living kin.

And here he was, Merlin Pendragon, Merlin the Bard.

And Morgause had to speak to him in the end, if only for fear of the Dark Ones, who punished such breaches of hospitality.

Well, so be it. Sighing, Merlin made his way back to his seat. Mingling curses and sacred prayers, he wriggled himself down in the driftwood throne again, and set himself to wait.

The bedchamber was heavily curtained against the light, the small windows muffled against the night that was always day. Glowing rugs and thick hangings softened the grey stone floor, and brightened the walls. One candle burned on a strange wooden chest, beside a big copper bowl of summer lavender. In the scented darkness of the massive canopied bed, a figure stirred with the question she had asked a dozen times.

'What does he want?'

The man beside her loved her enough to answer as if he had not already heard the question many times. 'He is Merlin,' he said soothingly, stroking her well-fleshed flank. 'Who knows?'

'He has a reason!' Morgause heaved herself up on the

pillows with a furious frown. 'And he means no good. How dare the old villain come here?'

Lamorak reached up and parted the long red-gold hair spilling down over Morgause's breasts. At Arthur's court, he knew, Merlin was the King's enchanter, second father and his dearest friend. Yet to Morgause he would always be the the man who had shattered her life. Once again Lamorak felt her misery touch his heart. As a queen, she was sharp in judgement, fearless, poised. As a woman, she was lover and mother, and any man would rejoice to lose himself between her ample thighs. But the child who had seen Merlin destroy her father and prostitute her mother was still there behind it all.

'Answer me!' she begged.

'How dare he? Well . . .'

Lamorak put his honest brains to work. He swept a thoughtful hand over her breasts. His fingers sought and found the long, feral nipples, as brown as those of a she-wolf lying up with her cubs. Absently he played and pulled, kneading their tough surface as he knew she liked.

'Merlin has only one love in life, himself,' he said at last. 'After that comes Arthur, and then would come Arthur's son. My guess is that he's looking for Morgan's child.' He laughed. 'Of course, we know nothing, but he doesn't know that.'

'Could he truly believe that I would betray my sister to him?'

Lamorak laughed. 'If he does, he's even madder than we think.'

Morgause scowled. 'D'you think Arthur sent him, to find out what we know?'

'Arthur? No.' The words were out before Lamorak could stop his tongue. 'More likely Agravain.'

Morgause's heavy eyebrows rose. 'Why Agravain?'

Lamorak trod down a sigh. 'Because he is the most troublesome of your sons.'

Morgause stiffened resentfully in his arms. 'He was an unhappy child. His father punished him because he could never live up to Gawain. He will be better, now he's been made a knight. We shall have them up here to visit, and then you'll see.'

Lamorak loved her too much to argue. 'When he is, sweetheart,' he said fervently, 'will you think again, and marry me?'

A look of tender pain filled Morgause's eyes. 'Oh, Lamorak,' she murmured, 'how many times? Don't ask me again, I'm too old – it's not right.'

'Your age is nothing,' Lamorak said wearily. 'And I'm a worthy match even for a reigning queen. My father was the first of Arthur's vassal kings.'

She tossed her head wildly, flailing the red-gold ropes of her hair. 'And your father killed my husband at the battle of the Kings! With your help and assistance, Lamorak. D'you think any one of his sons will forget that?'

Lamorak groaned from his heart. 'I was sixteen, my father's squire, and only a boy. Surely time has washed away the blood-guilt after ten years? Let me make you Queen of Listinoise, and everyone will rejoice.'

'No, my love.' She reached for his hand, and brought it to her lips. 'Better I stay Lot's grieving widow and you my knight, bearing my arms at tournaments and jousts. We'll send for the boys, and all will be well, you'll see.'

Lamorak shook his head. He put all his anger and love into one long, hard kiss, and reached out for her again.

'No, Lamorak!' Morgause gasped and grimaced as she pushed him away. 'We haven't decided about Merlin. Oh, if only he were as easy to deal with as you.' Once again her mind was gnawing on its misery like a bone. 'What does he want, Lamorak? What shall I do?'

Lamorak groaned. 'It is for you to make policy here, my queen,' he said roughly, 'and for me to love and adore you as I do.' He pushed back the bedcovers as desire stirred again in his spent and aching loins. Reverently he eyed her spreading form. He ran a hand over her white, moon-like belly, caressing the fleshy mound. 'Look at that!' he whispered. 'All the world's in there!'

He reared up beside her on the bed, and heaved her over to lie upon her face. With both hands he kneaded her muscular back and shoulders, and stroked and pinched the dimpled, capacious rump. Kneeling behind her, he spread her massive thighs and plunged into the warm depths between her legs, lifting her wide hips till he gained admittance to the place he loved.

Morgause moaned with delight as Lamorak dug and thrust.

King Lot had been a brutal lover, taking his pleasure by punishing her soft vulnerable quivering parts, and she still needed rough handling to achieve her release. But Lamorak had the measure of her needs. As she felt his weight, she sighed, and drew his hand forward to tease her nipple till she was almost lost in the pleasure of such sweet pain.

What did Merlin want?

The thought chased through her brain again and was gone.

What did it matter?

Let the old warlock sit in the audience chamber for ever, he would get nothing from her.

High in the cleft of a pine, the spirit stirred. Lazily she stretched and uncoiled her sinuous frame as her eyes pierced the miles between her tree-top and the place she surveyed. Voluptuously she released her vapours, and savoured their stench as she writhed. So Merlin thought Morgause would bow to his will? *Ha!*

She brayed like a donkey, and spat with mirth. And Merlin believed he could lay claim to her son? Well, he would have to be taught to think again. And to learn to respect her will, as was her due.

Her black eyes turned to red. The owl roosting in the nearby tree hooted with fear, and flapped off into the night. She burned on unaware. Had they forgotten, all these earthbound fools, the power she had over all of them when she chose?

She cackled again at the thought of Merlin's quest. He pitted his will against hers?

Had the old man forgotten all the times when his ancient frame was racked with unseemly longings from his younger days? When his slack loins and shrivelled genitals itched and twitched with the hunger for young flesh? And how often she had come to him in the throes of his midnight lust?

The eyes in her nipples caught fire.

Must I teach you again, Merlin?

She laughed, and the mountain creatures ran to their holes.

So Merlin, we know what you will choose.

Now she rode him again in her mind, punishing the quivering old carcass between the spikes of her knees. Enough? No, for the man who killed her father and whored her mother, there would never be vengeance enough. Next time she would rake his eyelids with her claws, goad his sides to blood with the spurs in her heels.

For always there would be another time. Merlin was hers for all time, it was his doom. Lord of light as he was, this was the darkness he carried at the core of himself, and never would he be free of it.

Next time, Merlin and Arthur too.

She panted, and birds dropped poisoned from the trees.

Arthur –

She stopped in her airy dance, and the sky grew dark.

What should she do with Arthur? In the convent, she had gladly sucked his blood. She had wanted him dead, to pay for Accolon. And as the pious Sister Ann, she would joyfully have laid him out and sewn him in his shroud.

But now –

Scalding gusts of delight came hissing from her frame.

It was good to see how Arthur suffered now. Never again would he be free from pain. His body was scarred with a hundred crippling blows, and every puckered weal would remind him of the beauty and strength he had lost.

But more, she rejoiced, how he suffered in his mind! He would never forgive himself for losing the scabbard of the Summer Country's queens. And he would never see that again in all his life. That was for Mordred now, as Arthur must know. It was all he would have from the father he did not know. But what else would he need to found a new line of kings?

Her cry soared to the astral plane, and scattered the stars. King Mordred! Yes, for this alone Arthur must not die. Mordred was too young yet to take his place. The boy had to grow in safety, and learn his destiny. Arthur must live to keep the kingdom for his son.

But while he lived, he must pay every day. Her mind wandered lazily through what she might do. Easy enough to finish what Accolon had begun. The wound he gave Arthur was one that might never heal. Arthur's manhood now was hanging by a thread. Cut that, and he would never be whole again.

Smiling, she started to sharpen her terrible claws. Perhaps she would find another way to castrate him too. It was easy for a man to be noble when his faith was never tried. A clacking like a storm of angry crows began in her head. How noble will you be, brother of mine, when you discover that your friend lies down with your wife?

Her scream came from the bowels of the earth. *'I should be your wife!'*

Next time, she would take Arthur for her own. And not only for her lover, but for her brother, partner, king and Chosen One, to rule together and outshine them all. Next time he would love her as she had loved him. She would not lose him, as she had lost so much before. Time out of mind he was destined to be hers. And only the wretched Guenevere had come between.

She writhed in the air, shedding little burning flakes of flame. But for her, Arthur would have embraced his true destiny. So she must suffer, Guenevere must pay. And Lancelot? He too. He would be a fitting instrument of Guenevere's doom.

And Merlin, of course. No other hand had dealt so much destruction through his blind urge to bring Arthur to the throne.

Merlin, yes!

The spirit grinned, and her sharp teeth sawed the wind. How better to punish a man than by giving him what he craved? Merlin had staked his life on finding Arthur's son. Let him find Mordred, then!

She cackled in triumph, and a pregnant woman miscarried in the valley below.

Merlin would find the boy. But not yet. The search must be long and hard, the road uphill. At last Mordred would be his, as the child Arthur had been his years before. Then Merlin would bring Mordred to his father, Arthur would bring him to Guenevere, and the last act of the fate that bound them all would begin.

So! Nothing to do now but to rest here a little longer, revel in the airy blue, float in this green tree. And then –

She stretched again, and began to insinuate herself out of her eyrie in the cleft of the pine. Where to begin her revenges? In a safe place, the safest she knew.

It was time to return to the convent, time to make them pay.

Pay, every one of them, inch by painful inch. She gurgled in an ecstasy of delight. For twenty years she had suffered in that place. In all her years as a prisoner there, no one had spared her. Now she would not spare them.

No, none of them.

Every soul who had hurt her must pay.

CHAPTER 18

A dull late afternoon crept into the King's Apartments, bathing the white walls and the red-swagged bed of state in a mournful grey. Guenevere stood at the window, her folded arms crossed over her aching breasts, her eyes on the gardens below. Midsummer had passed, and the leaves had lost their tender green. A damp June had passed into a sour July, and day after day, rank clouds had strangled the sun.

Behind her Arthur sat propped up on his pillows marshalling his thoughts. 'We've agreed, then,' he said heartily, 'that Lancelot must be married – and soon?'

She closed her eyes. It was good that Arthur was well enough to think about these things. And it was kind of him to want to reward his loyal knight for returning to his side. She should be pleased that Arthur was better every day, now that his terrible wound had at last begun to heal. But nothing seemed to ease the ache in her body, or the tightness round her heart.

She opened her eyes, and forced herself to attend. We've agreed, Arthur said. Did she agree? She stared at the greenish glass of the window till its flaws and bubbles danced before her eyes. 'Yes.'

'Good!' Arthur cried. 'I want to keep him with us here at court. If we don't, he'll only go back to his own land again. When Lancelot's here, we're all happier, you know that.'

'Yes.'

'You don't sound convinced.'

'I know you think he made you better this time.'

Arthur smiled. 'He reminded me of why I wanted to live.'

And I didn't, Arthur? After all the hours I spent watching and weeping at your bedside, wasn't my love worth living for at all? 'He did? That's good.'

'So if he had a wife, he'd never want to leave.' He chuckled. 'If we find the right woman for him, he won't be able to tear himself out of her arms.'

Guenevere raised her hand to her throbbing head. 'I'm sure you're right.'

There was a pause. 'You don't like the idea, I can tell.'

Guenevere stood still. 'I – I haven't thought about it, that's all.'

'No, don't deny it, Guenevere, I know you.' Arthur gave a meaning laugh. 'You want him to have a fairy-tale romance, meet a beautiful lady as they do in the story-books, and fall in love.' He paused again, his hand absently soothing one of the puckered scars on the side of his neck. 'But dearest, not everyone is as lucky as we were. And you've made it hard enough for Lancelot as it is.'

She turned on him. 'What d'you mean?'

Arthur's laughter was open now. 'Why Guenevere, you know he's already in love with you, like all the young men here at court. It's ridiculous.'

Why is it ridiculous? I'm not old!

'Of course you're quite out òf his reach. But, God knows there must plenty of young girls willing to love him in your place.'

Goddess, Mother, help me to bear this – 'I daresay.'

'But where's the girl who'd be right for a man like him?' He paused, and held out his hand. 'Guenevere? You're not with me. Come and sit here while I talk to you.'

Guenevere moved to the seat at the side of the bed. Arthur took her hand in his two great battle-scarred fists, and stroked it lovingly. 'Remember King Pelles, whom you met at the battle of the Kings?'

'Your old friend King Pellinore's brother? Yes.'

Oh yes, I remember him well.

She only had to close her eyes, and King Pellinore's voice was rumbling once again in her inner ear. 'Greet my brother Pelles, Your Majesty, I beg – the King of Terre Foraine, in the far north-east.'

'Your Majesty?'

Before her had stood a thin and desperate man, whose sunken face and bloodless skin had the clammy pallor of one on the point of death. All the life of his body was concentrated in his eyes. Buried deep in their bony sockets, they blazed with a fanatic's fire.

They were meeting on the eve of the battle that would make Arthur king, or destroy them all. 'May all your Gods go with you,' she had said.

'There is only one God, and Jesus is His name!' the mad old king had shrilled. 'He will give us victory, He will ride on the points of our swords, and His foes shall taste death!

One God, the Lord God of Hosts, enemy of the Mother, Father of hatred and death –

King Pelles, yes, I remember him.

Guenevere came to herself, shivering. 'Yes?'

Arthur sighed. 'You know his wife died young, and left him with an only child, a girl. King Pelles believes that his wife died to punish his sins, but his daughter will redeem his destiny. It has been foretold to him that his grandson will be the noblest knight in all the world.'

He paused, feeling his way with care. 'But only if the girl comes untouched to the bridal bed. The prophecy demands that she must be known to no man. Then the best knight of our time will come to her, and father her Christ-given son. This boy is fated to do the work of God. His name is to be Galahad, the servant of the Lord.'

Guenevere felt a spurt of wild distaste. 'So Pelles refuses his daughter every woman's right to bestow the freedom of her thighs in pursuit of his mad dream?'

Arthur gave a careful smile, watching her. 'They are far from the ways of the Goddess in Terre Foraine. But if she must have the best knight in the world, that must be Lancelot.'

Must be? 'How old is she?'

'Oh, eighteen, twenty – marriageable age.'

Ten years and more younger than I am, then. 'What's she called.'

'Elaine.'

'I do not like her name.'

Arthur dared not let his inner smile reach his mouth. 'It does not compare with Guenevere,' he solemnly agreed.

Guenevere shifted unhappily in her chair. 'Where is she now, this Elaine?' she said, watching Arthur with mounting unease.

'Oh, she lives like a princess in a golden tower, up a flight of silver stairs, Pelles said, behind a door of bronze. The tower is secured by three separate locks, each with a different key, each in the care of a different lord of the court, until the knight comes who is fated to father her child.'

'What?' Guenevere repressed a shudder of anger and shock. 'The girl's kept a prisoner? And all for the sake of her wretched virginity? Oh, Arthur –' She leaned forward and pressed his hand. 'That's what comes when the rule of the Mother is over-thrown, don't you see?'

'No, I don't,' Arthur said quietly. 'I've heard that she's pious and virtuous, and she chooses to live this way. She is simply waiting for her knight who is to come.'

Guenevere turned away. A sickness took hold of her gut. 'The best knight in the world?'

'So her father believes.' Arthur was watching her closely now.

'And you? What do you believe?'

'She's young, she's lovely, she's pure, and she's the daughter of a king. I think she'd make a perfect bride for Lancelot.' He cleared his throat. 'You're good at these things, Guenevere. Why don't you put it to him? I want to know what he thinks.'

Agravain made for the tilting yard through the fading light. His legs and arms jerked as he hurried along, and his lips twitched with the curses raging inside his head. Sores, sword-strokes, sharp wounds and foul diseases light upon you, Gawain!

'Get out!' he'd said, in the antechamber of the King. 'You're not going in, Agravain, after saying things like that!'

Thank you, dear brother! Agravain emptied his heart, then began the stream of invective over again. May plagues blister your tongue, and cleave to the roof of your mouth. May tooth-aches and bone-aches, liver-poison and a flux of the gut come upon you, may your toenails rot –

Agravain's head spun. Somewhere there must be a sword that would rid him of this. One blow that would put him at the head of the Orkney clan. But not a hired blade. Rogue knights and men of the road were only good for the kill. Once the knife was in, the wagging tongues were out, and the killer blabbing in the nearest alehouse, telling his tale.

No, Agravain brooded, as he strode along. What he needed was another second son. A younger brother who stood to gain as he did if an unknown hand cut off his brother's life. They could come to an understanding to relieve each other of his difficulty –

He was at the tilting yard before he knew it. The whole place was still alive, though it was getting late. Knights and young hopefuls were all busy here, practising their skill at arms. Agravain pushed his way through the throng around the gates and stood looking about. He knew they would be here.

To his right, a knight on a charger was thundering down a long fenced alley on one side of the field, his lance aimed at a straw opponent at the other end. On the opposite side, a second alleyway held those jousting at shields set up on poles, or aiming to spear small rings dangling from ropes. Lining the edges of the field, hanging from the fences to cheer their own knights on, were the pages and squires. All around, the waiting horses pranced and sweated and frothed, depositing great piles of steaming droppings on the ground.

'A hit! A hit!'

A huge roar rose from the crowd as the mounted knight caught his straw opponent on the point of his lance, and sent him spinning from his hobby-horse. Agravain reeled for a moment at the noise and stench. Then the next cry sent him hastening forward again.

'Sir Mador! Sir Mador of the Meads!'

At the top of the arena, the next heavily armed knight on a restive horse waited his turn to charge. He was flourishing a grass-green banner, and bearing a shield emblazoned with Mador's arms. Agravain grinned like a dog. Mador, good! Where Mador was, Patrise would not be far behind.

Agravain found him at the far end of the lists, where the attendants were struggling to replace the straw target on his wooden horse for Mador's charge. Seeing Agravain coming, Patrise turned and smiled. 'Sir Agravain.'

He nodded curtly. 'Your brother is trying a few passes today?'

'Today and every day.' Patrise's fresh young face broke into a tender smile. 'Though everyone says he's already one of the best. But we must do better for our mother's sake, Mador tells me all the time.'

Agravain paused. 'Your mother?'

'I shouldn't have said that.' Patrise gave a small embarrassed laugh. 'Mador says we mustn't speak of it.'

Mador says, Mador says – Agravain bit back the jibe he wanted to make, and gave a frank and manly smile. 'You can talk of it to me. The fellowship of the Round Table is a brotherhood of blood.'

Patrise bit his lip. 'I suppose so.'

'What does your father say?'

'Our father's dead.' Patrise glanced away to the end of the arena, where Mador was still waiting for the tilt.

So only Mador stands between Patrise and the estate. Agravain's soul crowed. 'How so?'

'He took a bad fall at a tournament. After that, my mother swore that her sons would never tread the path of chivalry. But before he died, he made her change her mind and promise him that she would make us knights. Still, the cost of it has made her very poor, and our land is under threat. So we must restore her fortunes, Mador says.' His attention switched back to the action at the top of the field. 'There he goes!'

The knight in armour charged furiously down the lists. In one smooth motion he set his lance in its rest, struck the straw target on its red paper heart, and tossed the dummy spinning in the air.

The field resounded with cheers at Mador's *tour de force*. Patrise flushed with pride. 'Mador says I'll be as good as he is one day.' He laughed. 'I don't believe him. But he knows I'll try.'

Mador says, Mador says –

Coldly Agravain put aside his irritation and pressed on. 'This land of yours –'

'It's above the Severn Water, where the Welshlands meet the Middle Kingdom, right on the borders there,' Patrise obliged. 'It's good land, green and fertile,' he laughed self-consciously, 'and it's the country of my heart.'

He gestured around at the shouting bystanders, and the

horses and riders gaudy in red, green and blue. 'My heart is in the hills, not with all this. I want to persuade my brother to stay here at court, winning the favour of the King and Queen, while I go back to the Meads to run the estate for him.'

'For him?' Agravain kept his eyes on the distant figure of Sir Mador, lining up for another charge. 'Why not for yourself?'

Patrise stared at him. 'What do you mean?'

Agravain counted to three. 'You are your brother's heir, are you not?'

'No!' Patrise coloured hotly. 'Oh, I suppose if he – yes, it's true there are only the two of us. But Mador will marry and have children, of course he will. He's only twenty, there's plenty of time.' His colour changed again. 'Except –'

Agravain stiffened imperceptibly. 'What?'

Patrise lifted his shoulders in an embarrassed laugh. 'He loves the Queen.' He shook his head, bemused. 'Loves? He adores her, he can see no woman else. He dreams of Guenevere, he talks of her in his sleep. For him, she is the woman of the dream.' He glanced sideways at Agravain with a doubting look. 'I shouldn't be telling you this.'

Agravain made his voice as smooth as silk. 'All men seek the woman of the dream. Sir Mador is no different from all the knights at court. We all worship Guenevere, she's divine.'

Patrise gave a relieved grin. 'But my brother will find a love of his own in time. He'll have a great brood of children, girls and boys. And when he does, there'll be room at the Meads for us all.'

Agravain's voice was cool. 'Did you never think of owning the land yourself?'

Patrise shook his head. 'It's Mador's,' he said simply. 'He was born to it.'

And he could die for it too, Agravain thought, if you weren't such a great fool. Born to it? He wanted to squeeze Patrise by the throat till his eyes burst. He looked away. 'I read once that the first born were not always the rightful possessors of land,' he said casually. 'That if the second son had more vigour and the will to rule, he should put himself in his older brother's place.'

Patrise laughed in disbelief. 'Why should he do that?'

'To give the line more strength. To weed out the weaker for

the stronger, and prune the family tree till only the best and hardiest shoots survived.'

'But my brother is strong. And he's young.'

Agravain looked him deep in the eye. 'And young men never die?'

'Die? I don't understand. Why are you telling me this?' Patrise's high colour had ebbed, leaving him grim-faced and grey. 'Excuse me, sir,' he said, with stiff formality, 'I have much enjoyed the pleasure of this conversation with you, but now I must attend my brother in the lists.' He cleared his throat, and looked back at Agravain. 'I am truly fortunate in having him for my kin. All I want is to be at his side.'

'As you should!' Agravain cried, and clapped him on the shoulder heartily. 'And may the Gods above grant your desire. I, too, am blessed in my brothers, it's a bond thicker than any in the world.' He raised his eyes as Mador came hurtling past, and watched him hit the target once again.

Cheers split the air. 'I must let you go to your brother,' Agravain exclaimed, with a flashing smile. 'Farewell, till we speak again.'

But even as he left, he felt he had failed. As he stalked away, a new grievance clamoured in his heart. That bumpkin Patrise had dared to patronise him? Both the brothers from the Meads must be numbered among his enemies now.

Yet the trip to the tilting yard had not all been in vain. He had learned something that no one else could possibly know. And who'd have thought it – Mador and the Queen? What a card to play when the moment came! It was highly likely that the Queen must love him too. A woman like Guenevere would never live without love, and all the court knew that Arthur had been gelded for months.

Agravain's soul soared. Yes, he must watch the Queen, and Mador too. He'd get the better of all of them in the end. The rigid figure receded into the night with one idea whirling through his brain. The Queen and Mador. Mador and the Queen.

No, Patrise decided, before Agravain had taken three steps away, it's no good, I just don't understand these people, and I never will. Sir Agravain, the brother of Gawain, the nephew of the King, to talk of killing our brothers, and taking their place? I must have got it wrong, it's impossible, it just can't be. I'll look a complete idiot if I breathe a word. It's nothing to bother Mador with, that's for sure.

His honest heart eased. That's it, not a word to a soul.

Which is why Patrise wiped the frown from his troubled face before he went back to his brother in the lists. And why, when the panting Mador demanded to know what had kept him and Sir Agravain talking for so long, Patrise responded stoutly, 'Mere chit-chat, dear brother, nothing at all.'

CHAPTER 19

The door to the chamber banged as Ina came in. 'Sir Lancelot has had your message, my lady. He's coming at once.'

'Thank you, Ina.'

Ina dropped a cold curtsy, and was gone. A baffled annoyance was written in every line of her retreating back. Why would the Queen do this? Gods above, tell me why?

The little maid could not have put it into words. But she always knew when the Queen was grieving for Sir Lancelot. Ina's watchful, wide-spaced eyes never missed the moment when Guenevere began turning her head in distress, when she seemed to lose her way in wandering thoughts.

When the King was ill, the Queen had been all clarity. Then it was 'Call for the doctor, Ina!' or 'Send for the bards, some music would soothe the King now.' And she had saved his life, all the court knew that. But now he was better, she would sit for hours without moving, her head on her hand, till her eyes were pinpoints and her face looked grey and old. Then she would shudder and shake, and come to herself with a start. In those moods she would snap off Ina's head, or reach for the nearest thing and hurl it at the wall. Most often, though, she would take it out on herself. And to Ina's way of thinking, that was the worst.

And now –

Ina relieved her exasperation by clopping her wooden heels noisily down every hollow step of the Queen's tower. She knew exactly what was vexing Guenevere now. Good as he was, what had possessed the King to decide that Sir Lancelot must have a wife? Worst of all, that the Queen must tell him so?

Ina scowled. Dear Gods, was there no end to the blind

folly of men? But for the Queen to agree to do what the King asked – Gods above, what cruel madness was that? After all that had passed between her and Sir Lancelot, it was against the law of the Goddess – against nature, against love, against life itself.

So what to do? Ina's face took on its Otherworldly look. The answer had clenched her face as tight as a fist before she had reached the bottom of the stairs. *My lady must not do this. Sir Lancelot must not give his love elsewhere. The Old Ones themselves will reach down to stop them both.*

Stiffly Guenevere struggled to her feet. She felt like an old woman, clumsy from sitting and dreaming of the past. The sharp slam of the door echoed in her ears. Ina hated all this, she knew. Well, so did she.

She moved into the window. A light summer mist still hung over the early-morning meadow far below. The daisies were turning their golden eyes to the sun, and joyfully opening their pink and white petals on another blameless day.

Whereas here –

Goddess, Mother, is this my punishment? Will nothing take this cup of bitterness away?

She stood at the window, feeling the fingers of the sun touch her cold face and hands in vain. Frozen longings racked her body, but when she wrapped her arms around herself to try to catch the warmth, her skin felt grey and shrivelled and old.

Old –

Yes, old. To a man in his thirties, a woman ten years older is old, old, old!

Yet all that was true when he fell in love with me.

Standing in the kiss of the sun, she drifted back into the past. Her senses faded as the memories came, and in spite of herself, she allowed herself to dream.

The first thing she noticed was the power of his gaze, his bright brown eyes burning with their Otherworldly air. Other men had his height, his hands, his hair, but none his intensity, his special grace. The first time they met, he touched her hand to his lips, and fell to one knee.

'You are the lady of Camelot, Queen Guenevere. I have come to offer you my sword.'

He sighed, and she heard herself sighing too. His voice kissed her ears like the wild wind in the trees. His hand on hers promised days of beauty, and long nights of bliss.

'Hush –' she had said then.

Even then, that first time, it was all she could do not to say, *'Hush, my love.'*

She had seen him coming, it seemed, from the time before time. First a shadowy figure moving towards her in the dusk, shining through gold and silver light, then the lean shape she loved. Then the swing of his cloak, the glint of the gold torque of knighthood round his neck. And then the chestnut sheen of his hair and his long, strong, wonderful face.

Far away on the horizon a horned moon was shining, and all the heavens were burning with pale fire.

Come –

From the airy mansions of the moon, and the far regions of the world between the worlds, she had heard the soft insistent whisper of life itself.

Come –

His eyes were hazel and gold that fateful night, and bright with unshed tears. They held a question, and she had answered without words.

Welcome, love.

May we be granted the peace of loving and not losing, of giving and not resenting, may this newborn thing grow and flourish between us, and become what it can be.

His eyes had a woodland gleam, and to her gaze, no soul on earth ever looked more beautiful. The hollows of his face had been waiting for her touch, and she wanted to trace his cheekbones till the day she died.

When they came together, the moon shone down on groves of white blossom, and trees with silver leaves, making their branches sing. The pale fragrance of apples hung in the air. They kissed, and felt their hunger rise to meet them like a tide.

He gasped and stepped back, only to crush her to him more forcefully than before.

'You are the woman of the dream, you are the love I have

longed for all my life,' he moaned. 'But you're the wife of the King. Oh, lady, lady, what does it mean?'

'Hush,' she said. 'Hush, my love.'

And she kissed the tears from his eyes, and led him towards the bed.

But then the time came when she stood before him, and he knew what she would say. He reached for her hand, and brought it to his lips. 'So, lady,' he said huskily, 'we must part?'

Her senses spun. 'You know I do not choose this for myself?'

'The Gods command our lives. We must obey.' He tossed back his hair, and his eyes were very bright. 'My queen, let us make a good farewell. We shall have a long time to remember it.'

'With you, I lived and loved for the first time.'

He took her in his arms. 'My soul will be with you till we meet in the Otherworld.'

'Oh, my love, my love –'

'One kiss, and then we part.'

One kiss –

The clack of the door-latch brought her shuddering to herself. 'Sir Lancelot is here, my lady.'

'Show him in.'

She tried not to look at his face as he came through the door. His lips, his hands, his every graceful move, all mocked her cold, tormented body aching for his touch. The burnt-umber colour of his tunic scorched her gaze, and the swing of his cloak was almost more than she could bear. She found herself smoothing down her dull chamber gown, and wishing she had dressed better for him today. Yet why? He was nothing to her now, and could not be.

Ina closed the door, and the two of them were alone. A painful tension hovered in the air. He bowed stiffly, and brushed her fingertips with his lips.

'You sent for me?'

So cold, so cold.

She took a deep breath as she moved away. 'The King asked me to see you.'

His face showed interest for the first time. 'How is His Majesty?'

'His doctors say he's doing very well. He's walking again, and talks of riding soon.'

A smile warmed Lancelot's face. 'We'll have him in arms again before too long. Riding out at the tournaments at the head of all his knights.'

'So Gawain says.' She tried to smile back. 'But Kay insists there's no shame in sitting out. He says he and the King will make a good pair of old cripples sitting on the side, running down all the contestants for poor horsemanship.'

Gods above, Lancelot thought, as Arthur gets better, she gets worse. His body tensed with the urge to take her in his arms. Never did she look so pale with suffering, so beautiful, so unloved. He could not bear it, and he turned away.

Guenevere watched him move away from her.

So cold, so cold –

Why does he hate me now?

She lifted her head. 'The King wanted me to speak to you, Lancelot,' she said steadily. 'He is concerned for your future happiness.'

'I do not understand.' The handsome face closed off.

'He wants you to think about taking a wife.'

'A *wife*?' He laughed in disbelief. 'I never think of it.' He shook his head. 'I trained for knighthood since I was a boy. If I married, I would have to leave tournaments and jousts and adventures and travelling where I will. I would have to be with my lady, and stay at court with her.'

Guenevere drew a breath, and forced herself to go on. 'That's what the King desires. He hopes to keep you here.'

He gave her a strange look, and did not reply.

She tried a light laugh. 'The King has found the very wife for you.'

His eyes bulged. *'What?'*

'A pure virgin named Elaine, a very Christian girl. She's the daughter of a king, and fated to fulfil a famous destiny.'

Lancelot stood transfixed. 'May the God of the Christians be with her if she is,' he burst out, 'but her destiny will never lie with me!'

Her nerves could take no more. 'Oh, Lancelot, you'll have to marry, all men do! Even Gawain would leave the life he leads for the right woman, if he came across her. Even Kay will find one who can bear his bitter tongue.'

'You must forgive me, Madame,' he said levelly. 'I cannot marry this lady. And I cannot court her, knowing that is so.'

'Why can't you marry?' she cried. She was in agony. *And why am I trying to persuade you, when it would kill me if you touched another girl?*

He made a dismissive gesture, and refused to reply.

A terrible thought possessed her. 'You have a mistress!'

He turned pale. 'No!'

'You must have!'

'Madame, I tell you it's not true!'

She broke away in a frenzy. 'Admit it, Lancelot! I know what knights expect when they go to the aid of maidens in distress. And I know the stories that go round in the knights' hall.'

'Not between me and those I call my friends.'

'Are you so different from all other men?'

'I do not turn to whores!'

'So any woman who loves you must be a whore?'

'*No!*' He clenched his fists and fought to master himself. His brown eyes were alive with reproach. 'The Gods alone know what drives you to speak like this. But I will not stay while you insult me so. By your leave, my lady.'

With a hasty bow, he turned and strode towards the door. For a moment Guenevere stood still, unable to speak. Then she ran after him, reaching for his sleeve.

'Oh, Lancelot, don't go – I didn't mean –'

He started at her touch, and turned on her. 'You are so cruel, to talk of this to me.' He stared at her in bitter reproof. 'How can I marry, when my heart is given to you?'

'I had to – Arthur said –' She was flooding with sudden tears.

'Why do you weep?'

'Why do you think? I don't want you to marry, I –'

She could not go on.

A moment later he was weeping too. 'You knew I loved you, how could you forget? We lay together, I swore my soul to you!'

'Then you went away –'

'You sent me away!'

'And the King wanted me to speak to you –'

'You are the Queen! You can do what you please.'

'But a queen can't always choose to please herself.'

'You can choose to keep my service for yourself. A queen like you will always have her knights.'

A hollow echo sounded in Guenevere's ear. Her sight shivered, and she saw her mother shining like a flower in the forest, surrounded by tall men. *A queen will always have her knights,* she used to say with her glowing smile. Yet always among them was the one true love, the Chosen One –

She came to herself in tears. 'Oh, Lancelot, forgive me, I didn't mean to wrong you so.' Her body was throbbing from head to foot. 'I know that what happened between us is all in the past –'

'Hear me, Madame.' His voice was raw with pain. 'The past is the present, it is with us now. And together they decide the world to be.' He took her hand, and brought it to his face. 'You are my lady. I am always your knight.'

Her body and soul dissolved. She took his face between her hands, and drew his head down for a trembling kiss. 'Come to me in private,' she whispered. 'As soon as you can.'

CHAPTER 20

'What a woman, eh?' Arthur sighed, leaning heavily on Kay's shoulder. 'What a queen!' He gasped with the effort of speaking as he walked. 'She's kept me alive, Kay, d'you know that? So I owe it to her to get better as fast as I can.'

'As you say, sire,' Kay breathed. His own glistening face and strange colour showed what it was costing him to bear Arthur's weight. Stabbed to the bone of the thigh as a young knight, Kay had never been without pain since that day. But when Bedivere and Gawain had tried to offer their shoulders for the King's first outdoor walk, they were waved away. Only Kay would do, the foster-brother Arthur had trusted from his earliest days.

'Kay can manage, can't you, brother?' he had demanded, half heartily, half in a fretful tone. And Kay, a slender man of no great strength even before his injury, had sharply answered, 'Yes!'

Yet it was long, the broad gravel path round the castle walls, where the knights and their ladies liked to court and stroll and play. The heat of the day had passed, and the mild evening air had encouraged Arthur to try his strength. As the word spread, all the court had turned out to greet the king they had given up for dead. Gathered in excited clusters or solemn ones and twos, they stared and bowed and curtsied as Arthur passed. Moving gamely on from group to group, Arthur was visibly revived by the sight of their love.

But walking behind them, Gawain and Bedivere could see what the effort of supporting Arthur was costing Kay. 'Allow me, sire!' Bedivere said lightly, as he slipped between them and shouldered Arthur's weight, setting Kay free.

'What?' spluttered Kay furiously

'So that's the game!' hooted Gawain. 'Look out Bedivere, I'll be next!'

What a fool Gawain is, Agravain thought, with cold contempt, pacing behind. He thinks like a schoolboy, all japes and pranks. But they're all only trying to weasel their way in with the King, and curry favour with him, whatever the cost. Fools, all of them. He spat on the side of the path.

Gawain heard him and turned. What was souring Agravain now? Well, let him get on with it, whatever it was. The important thing was that Arthur was on his feet. The next thing would be to see him out in the field on a horse again.

A horse, yes. Gawain shifted his legs uneasily as he walked, and rejoiced in the comforting weight of what hung there. He could see that Arthur was moving gingerly, and afraid to stride out. Would the King ever recover himself again?

Gawain sighed. Who knew? Throughout the land, the King's wound had been the subject of countless delicate debates. All Arthur's subjects wondered what it might mean, and no one could say. The oldsters swore that such a thing had never happened before. A knight could take a hundred sword-cuts in his life, and never a one so near the site of manhood and knighthood and so much else.

But how could a man be a knight if he couldn't sit a horse? They had to get Arthur back in the saddle as soon as could be. Gawain waved his arms jovially at the King. 'And when shall we see you on horseback again, my lord?'

Arthur's forehead was creased with pain and glistening with sweat, but a smile of triumph marked every step he took.

'Soon, Gawain, soon!' he rasped. A pale gleam lit his upward-lifted face. 'And as soon as we can we'll have a tournament.'

'My lord!' Gawain burst out into a joyful guffaw. 'A tournament at Camelot?'

'Yes, yes,' Arthur insisted. 'It's been too long since the last one we held.'

Bedivere gestured ahead. 'These young men will be glad to hear of it.'

Arthur looked up to see two young knights waiting in the shadow of the wall.

'It's Mador, isn't it?' Arthur grunted into Bedivere's ear. 'And his brother Patrise?'

'The pair from the Welsh borders, sire, yes,' Bedivere replied.

Mador stepped forward, and fell to his knees. 'The Gods recover you, sire,' he cried passionately, 'and bless you and keep you, you and your beloved queen!'

At which Arthur wept, Agravain noted dispassionately, and gave the young upstart his own hand to kiss. Meanwhile, any other man would have seen the real meaning behind Mador's words. Beloved queen, eh? Agravain's dark eye lightened, and the hair on the back of his neck began to rise. So Mador did love the Queen, just as little brother Patrise had said.

The sleeping evil in Agravain stirred like snake, and his eyes raked Mador up and down. Yes, young Mador was a handsome youth, pale and passionate. How far had he got with the Queen? How much had he dared? No man in love with a married woman could have hoped for a better time. With her husband as good as gelded, would Guenevere live without love? Agravain sighed with satisfaction. No, not the Queen. Not a woman of the Summer Country, where women lived through their thighs. The Queen would take a lover, and Mador it would be. Keep a close eye on Mador then, Mador and the Queen.

Ahead of them the path reached an old moss-oak, with a rustic bench built round its base. Woodland honeysuckle and ivy formed a fragrant canopy overhead. Struggling with Arthur's heavy, weakened frame, Bedivere helped him into the wooded arbour to rest

Breathing heavily, Arthur sat and composed himself, giving humble thanks. Surrounding him were the men he loved most in the world. May God be blessed, he prayed silently. There's Kay, dear Bedivere, and all my nearest kin, Gawain and his three brothers, Agravain, Gaheris, Gareth, and of course –

Arthur lifted his head and looked around. 'Where's Lancelot?' he asked.

Goddess, Mother, bring him safe to me.

Guenevere stood in her window, her eyes on the ground below. Past sunset, and the moon still hid its head. The overcast night would help Lancelot make his way unseen. But a man who had to scale a tower might be grateful for more light.

Lancelot –

She clenched her fists, grinding her nails into the palms of her hands.

Why had she told him *come to me tonight?*

And why had he agreed?

When she said it, in her mind a full white moon would be sailing over the seas of heaven to bring him to her arms. He would climb the old ivy mantling the walls to the window where she would be waiting to let him in.

But now the gloomy night, the darkness, the danger – *what if he falls?*

Goddess Mother, forgive me, save Lancelot –

Seated at her embroidery frame beside the hearth, Ina suspended her busy needle, and watched the Queen's rigid back. Always punishing herself, she thought sadly, never pleased, not even when her lover is almost here.

Guenevere whirled round. 'Ina, I was wrong to ask him. Say he won't come tonight?'

Ina nodded to herself as she raised her head. 'He'll be on his way now, my lady.'

'Surely not! Why would he come here?'

Ina damped down her mischievous Otherworldly thoughts, and dropped her eyes. 'I don't know, lady.'

'He'll have to climb in the dark.' Guenevere turned away and roamed off, clasping her hands.

'He won't fall.'

'It's so dangerous!' moaned Guenevere.

'Well, he can hardly walk in here past the guards to spend the night with the Queen!' Ina cried.

For a moment she thought she had gone too far. But Guenevere had not heard. A new fear had risen to torment her.

'I think the King knows,' she said slowly at last.

'Gods above, knows what?' Ina's mouth was agape.

'Tonight, when I was putting Arthur to bed, he was asking me if I knew where Lancelot was. He said they'd all been walking in the garden, and Lancelot wasn't there.'

'Well, he wasn't here!'

'Of course he wasn't!' Guenevere burst out. 'He was out riding with his cousins, as he so often is. But Arthur missed him, and noticed he was gone.'

Slowly, deliberately, Ina laid aside her work. 'Lady, all it means is that the King wanted him. After all, he's his knight, the King loves him too.'

'I know!' Guenevere bit her lip and turned away. *Oh, Goddess, Mother, tell me what to do –*

Ina saw the torment, and turned back to her work. 'In the country of the Goddess, lady, this is no sin,' she said firmly, as she plied her needle and thread. 'In the olden days, you know the queens changed their consorts every year. Your mother's knights did battle once a year, for the right to call themselves her Champion.'

'But she kept her Chosen Ones for seven years,' Guenevere protested.

'She did,' agreed Ina stolidly. 'And you have been with the King for ten years now. And now he can't be a husband to you, as things are.'

'That won't be for ever,' Guenevere cried. But the thought took shape between them, *Perhaps it might.*

A silence fell that Ina dared not break. When Guenevere spoke, her voice was pale with pain. 'Arthur – I must think of Arthur. Oh, Ina, let's pray that Lancelot doesn't come.'

A soft noise sounded outside. Guenevere ran to the window and looked out. At the foot of the wall, a muffled figure was gripping the ivy and beginning the ascent. 'Ohhh –'

Ina was on her feet before Guenevere turned round. 'Good night, my lady.' She beamed, dropped an excited curtsy, and was gone.

Guenevere paced madly back into the room. He was here, Lancelot was here! Her heart was thundering in the cavern of her ribs. *Goddess, Mother, what have I done?*

She raced round the chamber, dousing all the lights. One surviving candle flickered on its stand as she surveyed the richly-coloured hangings, the thick rugs, the great bed. Then she ran back into the window to look out.

The muffled figure had almost reached the top. Moving

steadily, he found the last few footholds and grasping the frame of the window, heaved himself in. Impatiently he threw off the woollen wrap.

'Lancelot!'

In the dimly-lit chamber, he burned like a flame. The candlelight glowed on the copper-red glints in his hair, and lit a thousand tiny flames in his brown eyes. His eyes held an age-old look that she could not read. But there was no mistaking the troubled face and unsmiling mouth.

She reached out her arms to him, then fell back afraid. Tears rushed to her eyes. 'Oh, my love –'

'What are we doing?' he said hoarsely.

She moved towards him and took him in her arms, drawing down his head to meet her lips. 'Hush now', she said, and kissed him. 'Hush, my love.'

CHAPTER 21

Guenevere my lady, Guenevere the Queen –

Mador dropped his visor and settled himself in the saddle as he drew up his horse to stand at the head of the lists. Absently, he acknowledged the cheering crowds. Walking beside his brother, Patrise waved away Mador's squire and page, and methodically ran through all the last checks himself.

'Girth, stirrups, breast-plate, martingale, crupper – all well, Mador.' He raised his head to look up, shading his eyes with his hand as he squinted into the sun. 'God go with you, brother,' he said quietly.

'Thanks, brother,' Mador returned with feeling, as Patrise backed away. He turned his eyes to the field. Before him lay the long corridor of the lists, with their stout wooden palings down the middle to keep the combatants apart. At the far end, on his own side of the fence, Mador's opponent was likewise preparing for the charge.

'Lord God, merciful God, that takest away the sins of the world, have mercy on me, a miserable sinner,' Mador breathed lightly, and gave his soul to God. After his father's mortal fall at a tournament, Mador had sworn never to die unprepared.

He raised his eyes to the viewing gallery. There, enthroned in the wide wooden tower at the side of the field, the Queen sat among her ladies, glowing in white and gold. Seen through the black slits of his visor, her radiance made Mador catch his breath. From the first, he had worshipped her without reserve. But now she looked even lovelier, he thought, softer, happier and more luminous, like a woman in love. It must be the King, Mador thought. Any wife, any queen, would rejoice to bring her husband back from the edge of death, and have him beside her, smiling and full of health, as the King was now.

A king like Arthur, and a queen like Guenevere, the sun in the sky and the green field ahead – what more could a man want? Today he would do well, Mador felt it in his bones. He would win for the Queen, and cast his victory in triumph at her feet. Then one day he would be the best knight in the world, chosen to wear the Queen's favour and to fight for her. His spirit soared. To fight? To die for her! His blood thrummed in his veins, and the familiar chant sang in his ears, Guenevere my lady, Guenevere the Queen –

Even seen from far away, Mador's rapt pose facing the gallery left no doubt as to the focus of his thoughts. Sir Gaheris struggled with Agravain's girth strap, and jerked his head with grim amusement down the lists.

'Let's hope Mador's mind's not on jousting today,' he grunted to his brother as he tightened the stubborn leather and thrust the tongue of the buckle firmly into place. 'He'll be hard enough to beat, even if you didn't have the sun in your eyes.' He adjusted the flap, and watched as Agravain settled himself in the saddle, making sure it was firm. Well, Agravain looked fine enough in a new suit of black armour, gleaming from head to foot. 'May the Gods be with you today.'

Agravain gathered up his reins, and wheeled away from Gaheris without a word. At the head of the lists, he closed his visor with a snap, and let out a contemptuous breath. Sheer weight and bulk always won the day at the joust. It would take more than young Mador's incessant practice in the yard to unseat him.

'Sir Agravain!' bayed the crowd all around. Agravain ignored them all. Through the slits of his helmet he watched the herald's flag fall, and heard the cry, 'Set on!' At this distance, his opponent looked a mere stripling, too young to fight. No reason to spare him for that, Agravain told himself, as he teased his horse's sides with his spurs, and broke into a trot.

And Gaheris thought that he might take a fall? Agravain grinned, and pushed his horse into a steady canter down the lists. Lads like Mador were too weak to unseat an Orkneyman, a son of Lot. Only Lancelot was good enough to make skill take the place of weight, was the thought that came to him with the final charge.

It was still drifting aimlessly through his head as he took Mador's lance low and hard on his chest, and felt himself tossed backwards out of the saddle to crash heavily to the ground.

The fall knocked the breath from his body, and his head sang. As he staggered to his feet, he could hear the thud of Mador's hoofs coming back down the lists even above the ringing in his ears. His heart was pounding violently, though with fury or with shock, he could not tell. He groped for the shield strapped on his back, and fumbled for his sword in an ecstasy of haste. And all the time his mind was blackly forming the vow, Not me, Mador – no man does this to me!

'Sir Mador! Sir Mador!' screamed the crowd in delight.

Rot you, Mador, cursed Agravain, may you perish from your centre, wounded in your core like the King –

Then Mador was on him again, and Agravain found himself flailing the air. The sun overhead blinded him, and all he could see was the huge shape of horse and rider darkening the sky. The fear of defeat ran like a fever through his veins. Mounted, Mador had an advantage no man could lose. He had only to play with his grounded opponent by the old tactics of strike and retreat, till Agravain was beaten by pain and loss of blood.

A cry from Mador cut through the air. 'Here, sir!' Mador raised his arm, and brandished his sword in the air.

Agravain gripped his sword and shield, and braced himself for the blow. Already he could feel the pain, hear the clash of metal as Mador's heavy weapon caught him unprepared. Then he saw Mador vaulting from his horse to throw the reins to a waiting page. The boy heaved round the head of the great charger, and led it away at a run.

The crowd released its breath in one approving roar.

'Mador! Sir Mador! He's given the vantage away!'

Vomit rose in Agravain's throat, and filled his mouth. Mador despised him so much that he meant to beat him on the ground? Unhorsing him was not enough, he had to humiliate him too?

A red mist filled Agravain's eyes, and he threw away his shield.

Die, Mador.

Prepare to die.

Gripping his broad sword with both hands, he made for Mador with murder in his heart.

'Have at you, Mador!'' he screamed.

'Come on, then!'

Mador stood his ground as Agravain charged, then neatly dodged the weight of the Orkneyan's bulk. Through the thin black slits before his eyes, Agravain hardly saw Mador's sword swinging round behind. But the stinging blow across his shoulders pitched him forward on to the ground.

The crowd was in ecstasy. 'Sir Mador!' they sang. 'Mador of the Meads!'

Mador –

Raging out of his mind, Agravain pushed himself up to his knees. As he scrambled for his sword, all he could see was one iron-clad boot. Mador was standing with his foot on the blade, his own pointing straight at his kneeling opponent's throat.

'D'you yield?' cried the crowd, in delirious anticipation of the ritual demand. But Mador stepped back from the sword, bowed to his opponent where he knelt like a dog on all fours, and opened both his arms in the gesture that said, 'Begin again.'

May every pain, every pox wither your vitals, Mador, and blast your dearest hope –

'You are gracious, sir!' Agravain bellowed falsely, as he picked up his sword, and slowly regained his feet. He took a moment to settle his seething soul. 'Well, then – set on!'

Mador came at him with a speed he could not have believed. A blinding pain shot through his head as a swinging blow caught his helmet on the side. As he reeled from that, Mador slipped to the side, and struck him hard across the shoulders, sending him once again sprawling on to his knees.

Agravain stumbled and sweated, wrong-footed at every turn. *May the Gods deform your progeny, blight your life –*

He could not prevail. Mador darted and danced round his taller, more ungainly opponent, beating him down.

Watching from the side, Gaheris shared a furious glance with his brother Gareth.

'The sun was in Agravain's eyes, he never had a chance!' he cried angrily. 'If he'd drawn the other end of the lists, that country clod would never have had him down!'

In the viewing gallery, Sir Gawain was not so partisan.

'Agravain asked for that,' he remarked to Arthur, leaning over the King's throne. He laughed cheerfully, relishing his brother's drubbing at Mador's hands. 'They'll be good knights to you, sire, Mador and his brother Patrise.'

'True.' A shadow crossed Arthur's face. 'But I'd rather be down there on the field myself.'

'Oh, Arthur, you will.' Seated at his side, Guenevere reached out a protective hand. 'Don't think about it – you're doing so well.'

'True again, dearest.' Arthur gave a crooked smile. 'I'm even sitting a horse, though I can't yet manage a charger in the field. But that'll come.'

A roar from the crowd rose above the clash of arms.

'Look at that!' Gawain guffawed, his eyes on the scene down below. Mador was beating Agravain to his knees. With a final stroke, he swept his opponent's sword from his hand. The tall Orkneyan knelt, defeated and unarmed.

'Yield, knight!' cried Mador, in a voice that carried round the field.

Yield to you, coxcomb? A prince of the Orkneys yield to a yokel from the Meads? Never in the world. The armoured head shook slowly from side to side.

'Yield!' called Mador again. 'You are at my mercy, beaten in a fair fight. You have no choice. Yield!'

Again the great black shape shook its head.

'Yield!' shrilled Mador, a note of panic in his voice. Nothing in the tilting yard had prepared him for this. 'Yield, knight, or die!'

In answer, Agravain threw off his gauntlets, then fumbled with the laces at his neck. A moment later he tore his helmet from his head, and cast it spinning through the air. Stunned into silence, the crowd watched its flight till it crashed to the ground. Then all attention switched back to the glaring Agravain, grinning in mad defiance as he swept his hair off his face, and taunted Mador to deliver the fatal blow.

'Strike, knight!' he howled. 'I do not yield!'

A terrible silence gripped all the field. Mador stood rooted to the ground, riven with fear. Standing on the side, Patrise groaned for Mador. His brother had never killed a man in his life, still less a beaten man kneeling at his feet – still less the King's nephew, a fellow knight of the Table, and the son of a king. Oh, Mador, Mador, God help you now.

In the lists, Mador braced himself, and gripped his sword. Then he seized the blade, turned the hilt towards the gallery, and fell to one knee. He bowed his head as he offered up his sword. I give this knight to the King, the gesture said. Shall he live or die?

'Sire!' Gawain gripped the arm of King Arthur's throne, and knelt at his side. His great beefy face dissolved, and he wept like a boy. 'Sire!' he cried, 'I beg you, spare my brother's life!'

Arthur, hear me.

At Arthur's side, Guenevere sat unmoving in her chair. *The laws of chivalry demand Agravain's death. Three times he has refused quarter at Mador's hands. He has chosen to die.*

In the deep silence, a mist rose before her eyes. *And you should let him, if the truth be told. Agravain is nothing but blackness to us all. Blackness and fire, darkness and burning death –*

She came to herself with a sick taste in her mouth. *What is this? Gods, above, no man should die for war games like these.* She pulled herself together. 'Arthur –'

But Arthur was already on his feet. He raised his right arm, and his voice swept the field. 'Arise, Sir Agravain, we spare your life,' he cried. 'And approach the dais, Sir Mador, for your chivalry today.'

At Arthur's side, Gawain grabbed his hand and kissed it, his great shoulders heaving with relief. Lovingly Arthur raised him to his feet. 'Your brother's a brave man, Gawain,' he said. 'There aren't many knights so unafraid to die. For that alone, he deserves to live. And I don't doubt we'll make him a credit to us after all!'

'Bless you, my lord.'

Gawain turned away to hide his tears. On the grass below, Mador was approaching the gallery with his helmet in the crook of his arm. His face was scored with the dirt of the field, and his young eyes were full of dismay.

Arthur smiled at Guenevere. 'He doesn't know yet whether he's won or lost,' he said gently. 'Tell him, Guenevere.'

Guenevere nodded. She moved to the edge of the gallery, where the waist-high wooden wall was already crowded with lords and ladies craning for a glimpse of the new young knight.

'Sir knight,' she called. 'The King honours you for your chivalry, to spare a fallen knight. And the Queen hails you for your victory.'

The whole of the crowd erupted in wild applause. Mador looked around in dawning wonderment.

Above him, Guenevere was leaning down again. 'Sir Mador,' she called to him huskily, out of hearing of the crowd, 'you are well worthy to bear the name of knight. Take this as recompense for your goodness today.'

From the balcony, a scrap of white lawn came fluttering down. Tears rushed to Mador's eyes as he caught it with both hands. Far off he heard faint music from the spheres. *My lady Guenevere, I shall wear this for your honour in the lists.*

He brought the square of cambric to his lips, and felt its flowery fragrance feed his soul. *A queen is everything,* he thought humbly, *and I am nothing at all. But I will be among her knights one day.* He raised his face to the gallery, blind with love. *Guenevere my lady, Guenevere the Queen.*

Arthur looked down, and smiled. 'He loves you, Guenevere,' he said wryly. 'They all do.' He reached for her hand, and smiled into her eyes. 'How can they help it?'

Guenevere felt fear rising in her soul.

Lancelot.

Did he suspect? 'Arthur –'

He stilled her protests with an upraised hand. 'Guenevere, I was the man who loved you first of all. I understand.' He signalled to the Chamberlain, and looked around. 'On with the tournament, sir. Now, where's Lancelot?'

At dinner that night, the great Hall rang with Sir Lancelot's name. All there marvelled at his chivalry, how he had come in after the others to give the new knights a chance, and then swept all before him, wearing Guenevere's favour on his sleeve. Now he sat huge-eyed and silent, watching the dais where Guenevere dined with the King. As the compliments flowed, he accepted them as well as he could, picking at his food, and drawing sparely on his wine.

One by one, the great candles burned down. At last all the guests had been wined and dined, and all the knights and ladies had gone brimful of cheer to their beds. The last of the servants had finally been sent away, and Guenevere was attending Arthur to bed.

'Lancelot won't change, will he?' Arthur said fondly as he climbed into bed.

Goddess, Mother, let him just sleep now, I don't want to talk.

'What do you mean?'

'What we talked about.' Arthur patted the side of the bed. 'Sit down a minute, will you? I know you must have spoken to him by now, and told him what we wanted for him.'

Guenevere perched herself on the side of the bed. 'I told him you wanted him to have a wife.'

'And?'

'It's still the life of arms he loves best of all.'

'Is that what he said?' Arthur chuckled regretfully. 'Well, maybe he's right.' His voiced warmed as he spoke. 'Look at what he did today at the tournament. Last into the lists, when the light was at its worst, for the sake of the younger men.'

Guenevere clenched her teeth. 'He's not so old.'

Arthur gave a mild, reproving laugh. 'He must be thirty now, Guenevere. And young Mador, for instance, hasn't seen twenty-one. No, Lancelot's an old man at the sport.'

Old man? Old man? What does that make me?

'He still does well.'

'The best.' Arthur smiled. 'He really is the foremost knight in the world. Today we had kings and champions from as far as you could name.' He raised his fingers, mentally checking off the contestants one by one. 'And he beat them all!' He chuckled with delight. 'It must have been your favour on his arm,' he said teasingly. 'A tribute to the power of white and gold. But I warn you, Guenevere, when I'm back in harness, I'll be wearing your rosette again.' His voice thickened, and he reached for her hand. 'Lancelot can be your knight, I know a queen must have her knights. But I will be your champion in the field.'

Guenevere looked at him in dread. His eyes had darkened, and he was kneading her hand, crushing the flesh. 'God has been good to me,' he said thoughtfully. 'With a knight like Lancelot, and a wife like you . . .'

He looked deep into her eyes, breathing heavily. 'You know,

I've been feeling so much better, I think I might –' He pulled her down on the bed. 'I mean if you'll help me, Guenevere, I think we could –'

He broke off and chuckled low in his throat. 'You know what I mean.' His hand reached for her breast. 'Come here, Guenevere.'

CHAPTER 22

Dawn over Avalon – was there anything more beautiful on the face of God's good earth?

His soul swelling with bliss, Brother Boniface gave humble thanks to the Creator, who had placed him here. He loved Avalon more than a good Christian should, and the dawn walk with his fellow monk was the glory of the day. From its smooth rounded top to the green flanks sloping away below, it was easy to see why the pagans saw the island as the shape of their Goddess asleep.

Ahead of them the upward swell of the great Tor gleamed with the first rays of the rising sun. On all sides, surrounding the grassy isle, the still waters of the lake shone like glass. Boniface filled his young lungs with the soft summer air, and glowed with content. He had thought himself happy enough in London, God only knew, serving his order there with work and prayer. He loved the slow, sad rhythm of the monastic hours, vespers, prime, nones all chiming with majestic certainty night and day. With the confidence of his twenty-odd years, he had looked forward to living and dying in the abbey to which God had called him as a boy.

But then the Father Abbot had heard the voice of the Lord, summoning His servant to another task. Boniface was to bring Christ to a place where the Devil had ruled before. He was to go to Avalon, and beg the pagans there to allow him to join his prayers to theirs. So he would be a bridgehead for the Lord, allowing His soldiers entry when the time came.

What a glory, what a terror, what a challenge, what a call! Boniface knew he would have a brother-in-arms for his task, and a young monk from Rome had joined him as soon as he began. But this work would always be the greatest thing he had done. His fair cheeks still flushed every time he thought of it. How long was it now since he had come to the Sacred Island? And still he loved the place more every day.

And today would bring a new turn to their task. At last they would meet the ruler of this place.

'They worship a Great Goddess,' the Abbot had said, 'in plain defiance of God's ordinance that women are subject to men.' Boniface could still remember the pale fire of anger in the Father's eyes. 'They believe that women have the right of thigh-freedom, and may choose the men they summon to their beds. A priestess of the Goddess holds sway there as the Lady of the Isle. She keeps young women around her, and trains them up in these whoreish ways.'

He leaned forward, one jabbing finger lending weight to every word. 'Get to know her,' he said intently. 'Win her confidence, show her you mean no harm. Treat her maidens like the Mother of Our Lord and, in God's time, we may give them back the dignity of pure womanhood they have lost.'

'Yes, Father.'

Boniface had embraced his task with all his soul. Season after season, he had laboured to win an audience with the Lady, without success. But now at last she sent word that they might meet. One of her maidens would bring them to her house. And Giorgio and he were going to the meeting now.

Boniface turned to his companion, brimming with joy. But before he could speak, his fellow-monk cut him off.

'And this they call summer?' the other said, looking heavily around. 'Pia Maria!' He groaned. 'When we see the sun?'

Boniface looked at Giorgio with concern. All these months of sharing a cell had made the young Italian more than a brother to him, more than a friend. He knew how Giorgio suffered for their cause, translated from his native land for this cold and remote place of pagans, whose tongue he did not speak. These days Giorgio's fine aquiline features were haunted with a look of loss. How long would he keep the bloom of his golden skin, the laughter in his dark eyes, his flashing smile?

Boniface sighed. After Rome, he knew, Giorgio could find

little to admire in the island's apple orchards, her fluttering doves, all too pale and fragile for a young man of the full-blooded south. And Giorgio badly missed his monastery in Rome. When he spoke of his church and the holy brotherhood there, Boniface could see what a fine ideal of the godly life his friend had left behind. Against that, to be living two to a small cell, keeping their own hours of worship and trying to interest the islanders in the love of Christ, must seem a poor thing. Boniface bit his lip, and determinedly squared his chin. He must try harder to make Giorgio happier here. Perhaps when they had seen the Lady, he would see God's will for them revealed.

Boniface's spirits soared. He strode up the Tor, mentally making magic for the Lord. Walking alongside, Giorgio stole a look at Boniface, and shook his head. How little his friend knew or understood!

Of course this innocence, along with his fair good looks, must have been Boniface's passport here. The Abbot in London would have chosen him for that purity of his, that wide-eyed stare. And Boniface could have known nothing of this at all.

His own abbot had been plainer with him from the start. The head of his order had dispatched him from Rome with a smile as old as the hills on which the city stood.

'Remember that a little sin may make a great good for the Lord,' he had said, spreading his wrinkled hands. 'The Father Abbot in London needs a fine young man of ours to win an old whore's heart. The witch of Avalon shows thigh-friendship to any man. If she favours you, sin for the Lord. I grant you absolution in advance.'

'For everything?' Giorgio said hopefully.

The tortoise-lidded eyes had been as cold as stone. 'For all that you may do.'

His superior must have known, Giorgio realised now, that women did not call to him at all. Leaving Rome, bad as it was, was not as hard as leaving the boy his heart doted on, the twelve-year-old who sang in the monastery choir. Never had he known such bliss as the stolen moments behind the choir stalls, the secret sessions in the vestry when he had made the boy his own. Each night when he prayed he thought of the boy's silky lips, the peach-like bloom on his buttocks, and the hardness of his young

hands, and vowed them all to God. The boy and he were both
God's creatures, both given to His service, worshipping Him
together when they joined in love like this. When the heart was
pure, there was no sin in the deed. And now his own Abbot had
blessed him, and said as much.

So if he had to sin for God with the whore of Avalon he
would, Giorgio accepted, though he approached the thought
without enthusiasm, and Boniface, he knew, had never dreamed
of it at all. Yet God had not called either of them to that task. The
Lady had shown no interest in them at all.

Until now. And already Giorgio was convinced that whatever happened, the whore of Avalon would not drop into their
hands. Yet every day God made miracles of a stranger kind. He
brightened. Perhaps it could yet be.

Boniface was striding on. 'God does not blame those who
have never known His love,' he said earnestly. 'These women
have never known God's plan for them.'

They were climbing the side of the Tor, passing through
silvery apple groves and higher up, plunging through dark,
tightly-clustered stands of woody pine. Somewhere near the top
lay the Lady's house, they knew, though they had never before
approached so near. Even now they could not see the hidden
guardians they knew must be there. But ahead of them, the close-
knit pines shimmered and parted, and they saw a woman
between the trees, standing beside the path.

She was robed in shades of green like the living wood, and
her draperies moved with the light breath of the breeze. Her
lean body and taut carriage made her look taller than she was,
and beneath the veil covering her hair, her face had the age-old
detachment of another world. Her neat brown hands were
folded before her like paws, not far, Boniface noted with a
frisson of alarm, from the formidable forked dagger at her waist.
Did she always carry the means of dealing death? And what did
she want from them? But there was nothing to be gleaned from
her small pansy face and dusky, secret eyes. She stared at
them with an indeterminate gaze as she waited for them to draw
near.

'God's plan for women?' Giorgio grinned in an effort to keep
his spirits up. 'God's lesser kind, deserving the curse of Eve?' He

nodded to the figure standing ahead. 'I hope we can explain that to her.'

'Hush, brother!' Boniface hissed in agitation, turning a furious red.

If the woman had caught the whispered exchange, she gave no sign. 'I am Nemue, the chief maiden of the Lady of the Lake,' she murmured in a rough voice unaccustomed to speech. 'The Lady welcomes you into her house.'

She waved her hand. Dissolving and emerging through the trees, they saw a frontage of white stone with a pair of massive doors set into the side of the hill. Nemue waved them forward. At their first uncertain steps, the doors opened of their own accord.

'Enter!'

The force of Nemue's command propelled them forward into the gloom. The doors closed behind them, and Giorgio let out a sharp cry of fear.

'Courage, brother!' urged Boniface in a trembling voice. 'Remember we do God's will.' *Salvum nos fac, Domine,* he began to pray, dear God, make us safe –

Slowly their eyes grew accustomed to the gloom. They stood in a darkened chamber lit only by flickering dragon-lamps, tiny pinpoints of flame crouched in niches in the walls. The loam-washed space was low, and domed like the inside of the earth, and the little lights shone all around like stars. Above them they could feel the earthy mass of the great Tor, but here in the Lady's palace the air was warm and sweet. Beyond sweet – Boniface snuffled at the living fragrance half in delight, half in dread. Already he knew that once he let it into his lungs, his soul would crave it for the rest of his life.

They waited, growing more fearful every moment. Now they could see a tall throne against the wall, with a sprawl of dogs scattered at its foot. Their sleek red fur and long limbs revealed them for a pack of water-hounds, and each wore a collar of jewelled gold carved with runes. Reared up on guard, they kept their eyes on the visitors, and did not move. But the glint of their white teeth was enough to make the bowels of both young men almost dissolve. Boniface renewed his prayers. How long, O Lord, how long?

It started as a whisper, hardly a breeze. Then the earth

shivered, and there she was at the far end of the lamp-walled chamber, a tall female figure veiled in filmy draperies from head to foot. She wore a crystal diadem in the shape of the moon, and held another moon of rock crystal in her hand. Without movement she grew until she filled the room, and the space around her echoed with the soundless cries of creatures overhead, and the soft insistent murmur of lake water below.

'Lady?' ventured Boniface, almost weeping with fear.

The muffled figure slowly turned her head.

'I am here. What is your will?'

To Boniface it was the voice of his childhood nurse, to Giorgio the kiss of his beloved grandmother, long dead.

'Lady, we have come to offer our thanks,' Boniface began. Already he felt heartened, though he did not know why.

'For what?'

Giorgio felt his spirits revive a little. If he had not known she was a witch, he could have sworn he heard both humour and humanity in her tone.

Boniface ploughed on. 'When we came here, you graciously granted us the welcome of your isle.'

The veiled figure nodded. 'You asked if you could join your prayers to ours. And truly, you have shown yourselves men of faith.'

Boniface threw a delighted glance at Giorgio. 'We are strong in our love of God!' he beamed. 'We only came to share that love with you.'

'Is that all?'

Suddenly the voice from within the fluttering gauze was as cold now as it had been warm before.

'All?' Boniface started. 'Yes, in God's truth, that is all that brought us here.'

The chill indictment went on. 'But we hear that your Christian Fathers have another aim. They plan to take our Hallows for their own.'

Boniface raised his head. 'How could that be?' he said in wonderment. 'They are the articles of your faith, not ours.' His face was translucent with sincerity. 'Believe me, Lady, all we seek is a union of holy truth.'

The Lady inclined her head. 'You perhaps,' she murmured,

'yes indeed.' She turned her head towards Giorgio, and raised her hand. 'But you?'

The air in the chamber dropped, and an unseen force seized Giorgio in its grip. The fluttering finger seemed to probe into his heart.

Giorgio felt faint. 'Lady, I –' he stuttered.

Sin for the Lord.

The voice of his Father Superior came tolling like a knell.

Our Father –

Giorgio reached for his flashing smile, and threw back his head. Swiftly he ran through the phrases he had ready in mind.

'Lady, we hear of you far away in Rome,' he said winningly. 'I am here to see you, and you alone. We beg to learn from you, we would sit at your feet. We pray we know you better in days to come. Any man would be glad to be admitted to your sight.' He tried for a respectful, yet roguish smile. 'Perhaps one day we see your face unveiled. For me, that would be a fair sight above all.' He composed his handsome face in a flattering gaze, and just in time remembered not to wink.

'Well said, brother!' Boniface glowed approvingly.

There was an endless pause. It stretched out to the edge of endurance and beyond. In the silence, Giorgio suddenly came to know that the Lady had heard his thoughts, and seen into his mind. Shame flooded him. He felt naked, humiliated, cruelly exposed, like the whores in Rome stripped to receive the lash.

'Is it so, Brother Giorgio?' came the soft query.

Giorgio felt his soul slipping out of his grasp. God in heaven, could the witch suck the life out of him too?

Nonplussed, Boniface was looking at him, anxiety on his face. A new dread burst upon Giorgio's disordered mind. The Lady might forbid them to continue here. If they were ordered to leave the Sacred Island because of him, what punishments would be waiting for him in Rome?

'We beg you, allow us to continue our worship here,' he burst out, made frantic by the silence, and his fear. 'For the love of God!'

The still figure on the throne inclined her head. As she moved, the crystals in her moon-shaped diadem flashed with pale fire. 'Love, yes,' came a slow voice like music. 'Religion should be kindness. Faith should be love.'

'Lady –'

Alarmed, Boniface threw himself into restoring the goodwill he had felt when they began. After a while, a chastened Giorgio seconded his attempts. In the whispering dark, the great muffled shape listened patiently to their stumbling pleas.

At last she held up her hand. 'Enough,' she said heavily. 'What will be, will be. Even the Mother cannot turn back the tide.'

Her sigh held all the sadness of the world. 'Very well, then. You and your brothers may continue here.'

CHAPTER 23

The audience chamber was full, and stifling. At the far end, the twin thrones and their heavy canopies glowed red in the August heat. Her hand clasped in Arthur's, Guenevere processed beside him down the long room. The lofty space was crowded with knights and ladies, courtiers, lords, all rubbing shoulders with countless petitioners who had travelled to Camelot to seek justice from the King and Queen. A sea of faces met Guenevere on all sides. She smiled back warmly, schooling herself not to look for Lancelot.

From the dais, she could see the petitioners already in place. On the left, a block of armed warriors stood glowering protectively around their king. On the right, a fierce huddle of monks offered their leader the same mute support. And between them, Guenevere saw bleakly as she took her seat, lay nothing but hatred and the lust for blood.

'Silence for the King of Gore!' cried the Chamberlain.

But the young knight who stepped forward shook his head. 'Call me Sir Yvain, as I was before,' he cried bitterly. 'I never wanted to inherit my father's crown. But now I must, I want vengeance for his blood!'

Arthur leaned forward, resting his hands on his knees. 'King Ursien died in the forest, by means unknown. Who can you call to account for this wicked deed?'

A flurry of tension ran through the monks standing across from Sir Yvain on the other side of the aisle. Their leader drew a breath. Jesu grant me patience, who indeed? thought the Father Abbot furiously. The spirit of darkness does not stand and fight.

Sir Yvain's clear young voice rang round the room. 'Who but

Queen Morgan of Gore? My cursed stepmother. Your sister, sire.'

Guenevere closed her eyes. *Morgan, Morgan – will we never be free of her?*

No – not while she can invade our marriage bed.

Her mind twisted and turned with last night's pain.

'Come here, Guenevere,' Arthur had said. And 'Kiss me', and 'Help me!' and a hundred other things. So she had kissed him and stroked him and caressed his poor body, and tried to help him in any way she could. But every one of his wounds was still tender to her touch. And the dread of his greatest wound hung over them both.

So she had unlaced her gown for his eager hands, slipping off her shift to let him adore her body by candlelight as he used to do. She could feel the blood coursing through him, see the veins pulsing at his temples, hear his breath coming short and fast. But again and again as she reached out for him, he held back and pulled away.

At last he rolled away with a desperate laugh.

'It's no good, Guenevere. I can't make love to you.' His face was gleaming with a sickly light, and his body convulsed with a sudden shuddering fear. 'Dear God, you don't think she's used her power to destroy me for life?' His teeth were chattering. 'It can't be, can it, Guenevere? Say it isn't her!'

Then he wept, and she had held him, and kissed him, and promised him it was nothing, it would pass. At last he had slept, and she lay in his arms all night, thinking of Lancelot.

And of Morgan. For surely she was with us in bed last night.

'Queen Morgan, yes!' Sir Yvain was insisting furiously. 'She should pay for this!'

Only Guenevere saw Arthur's hands tighten on the arms of his throne. 'Queen Morgan?' he asked calmly. 'Why do you blame her?'

'Why?' Sir Yvain's fair skin took on a livid flush. 'Because she hated my father, ever since you forced her to marry him. And I demand vengeance, vengeance for his blood!'

Arthur's voice hardened. 'And I ask again, what vengeance can you seek?'

Sir Yvain took a step forward and gestured towards his knights, twenty or so solid, ferocious men clustered at his back.

Each glared out balefully through a tangle of coarse, thick hair, and gripped their short stabbing swords, hungry for blood.

'They will not rest till they have blood for blood. They have taken an oath to hunt down this treacherous queen. Let them take the nunnery she lived in, and root out the witch's coven with fire and the sword!' He gave a tormented laugh. 'Let all who helped her feel the rule of war!'

There was a harsh rumble of agreement from the knights. In the stifling heat of the packed chamber, Guenevere felt herself grow cold. In every one of their dull, stone-like eyes she could see nuns hacked and bleeding, the white of their collars and headdresses drenched with red. She saw the convent in flames, bodies heaped up for the fire, and women stripped and screaming as blood-soaked blades prised their thighs apart.

No. Whatever happened there, no!

She touched Arthur's arm. 'Arthur –' she began softly in his ear. But a shout from the body of the hall cut her off.

'Arthur Pendragon, you are a Christian king!'

The Father Abbot was surging forward with fire in his eyes. 'In the name of God, will you permit torture, murder, rape? Will you allow blood vengeance against His will? Armed knights against old women, and brute soldiers against pure virgins who never saw a man?'

Sir Yvain threw both arms into the air. 'Your innocent virgins took my father's life!'

God be in my mouth –

The Abbot turned to Arthur, folding his hands inside his black sleeves. 'Sire, hear the truth. One spirit of evil dwelt there for a while. But since she left, the convent has been purged. The nuns are already paying for what she has done.' His forefinger stabbed the wilting air. 'We have set a new regime of spiritual discipline. Their hours of prayer have been increased, as have the penitential services they offer to the Lord. And on four days of the week, they live on bread alone. '

His austere features eased into a smile. 'No female will ever hold sway there again. I have installed a father confessor in the Mother Abbess's place. He has orders to confine all unruly spirits, and bring them to the knowledge of their faults. He has the power to wall them up for life in solitary contemplation, if need be.' He spread his hands, and essayed a confident laugh. 'We shall bring down these women so completely, sire, that there will be no call to take their lives.'

Spiritual discipline, sin and punishment – Guenevere's stomach turned. *A violent death, or a death in life? What hope for these women, caught between men like this?*

'Arthur –'

Arthur's upraised hand was brushing her aside. 'Sir Yvain,' he said harshly, 'whatever killed King Ursien, there is no proof that Queen Morgan took your father's life. Your vengeance must lie elsewhere. I forbid the destruction of the nunnery.'

The Abbot closed his eyes. *A thousand praises on Your name, O God.*

Yvain smashed the hilt of his sword against his forehead, and screamed as the bright blood flowed. 'My father's spirit wanders in the Otherworld. He can have no peace till his murder is avenged. Do not deny my right!'

Arthur shook his head. 'No slaughter, sir. No blood. That is my word. But your father must be honoured with his due.' He raised his hand. 'If you please!' he called out.

Four servants struggled down the hall with a massive chest, and threw back the lid. In its dark wooden depths heavy plates and goblets of gold and a king's ransom in gold coins, rings and chains burned in the afternoon sun.

Arthur extended his hand. 'Yours, sir,' he said.

Sir Yvain drew back, and turned white. 'Blood-gelt!'

'No.' Arthur's face was calm. 'There is no gold to buy your father's life. Take this in his memory, and do good with it. Then King Ursien will not have died in vain.'

Sir Yvain turned in silent question to his knights. The eldest of them gave a long, appraising stare before his hairy head dropped down in a grudging nod. Sir Yvain bowed to Arthur, and sheathed his sword.

'So!' Arthur raised a smile. 'We are all reconciled, it seems.'

The Abbot bowed. Resolutely he kept his eyes on the ground, to hold back the seething triumph in his soul.

'And let me hear no more,' Arthur went on, 'no more of –' His colour turned, and he closed his eyes. A line of tears began to form between the lids.

Arthur, Arthur, not here.

Guenevere rose to her feet and addressed the silent court. 'The King is still recovering from his wounds. Forgive him, this great heat has been too much. I beg your indulgence to excuse us now.'

She raised her hand to bring the audience to an end. Knights, lords and ladies took a hurried leave.

The Chamberlain bustled forward with concern in his eyes. 'Your Majesty, there are other petitioners, some in urgent need.'

'Tell them I shall see them all later on.'

The group at the rear of the hall brightened at her words, and bowed themselves out. Standing rigid on the dais, Guenevere bade a slow and careful farewell to each one.

She could not bring herself to look at Arthur, still huddled on the throne at her side. *I want to hear no more of Morgan*, had he said? She could have laughed out loud.

Impossible, Arthur.

For she has not left us, and she never will.

Three sisters now on water only, bread withdrawn. Two ordered to stand all night, and chant the hours. And one, God forgive us, walled up in her cell, to receive only bread and water and confession till the day she died.

Lord, Lord, is this Your will?

The Father Confessor of the Convent of the Little Sisters of Mercy finished his report to the Father Abbot, and sealed it with his tears. Then he turned away from his desk, and fell to his knees. The Abbot had told him he had been called to a fine, a noble task, to return a convent of women to the love of God. He had not told him how hard it would be.

He clasped his hands in prayer and grief combined. Lord God, shine Your light upon me, show me the way. So much pain to bring these women down. You have taught us that women were ordained to be subject to men, O Lord, so why do they resist? Help their stubborn souls to the light of understanding, and soon, Lord, let it be soon.

Yet there were some here who were purely good. Young Sister Ganmor, now, the tall thin nun who tried so hard to please. The Father Confessor gave a watery smile. Sister Ganmor, yes. At first he had been unnerved by her long pale face, and watchful sloe-black eyes. But now her devotion delighted him, her true humility, her simple faith in God.

There was a knock at the door. 'Who's there?' he called.

'It's Sister Ganmor, sir,' came a soft voice as, head bent and eyes fixed devoutly on the ground, Morgan Le Fay stepped quietly into the room.

CHAPTER 24

The plaintive toll of the bidding bell cut through the evening air. Moving at the same mournful pace, Arthur and his train entered the chapel at the head of a line of monks. Behind them, the latecomers to evensong quickened their steps across the cobbled square. The three cousins came into the courtyard in time to see the last of the stragglers follow the King through the low oak door.

So! Sir Bors rolled his eyes. Lancelot shrugged. He still found it strange to see Christians in Camelot. But if the Queen could endure for the King's sake, who was he to complain?

The Queen.

A rush of joy seized Lancelot, and he felt the tears rising behind to his eyes. That she should love him – choose him – out of all the world –

And love him truly, all this length of time. Summer had mellowed into autumn, followed by winter, and now it was spring, and still she loved him, Guenevere loved him!

He gulped down deep breaths of the sharp April air, and stifled a sigh as they hastened across the court. Loved him too much at times. Always he had had to watch out for both of them: he left the court when the other knights rode out, accepting every adventure for fear of giving the gossips reason to say, 'See, the Queen's knight cannot leave the Queen.'

So he was often on the wrong side of her temper, when he left and she wanted him to stay. Other times he would fall foul of her anger too, if he would not come every time she called. Then she would reproach him in storms of tears, and threaten to send him away. He did not love her, she would never see him again!

But soon she would relent, and send for him. And always she loved him enough to take him to her bed. Gods above, her bed! His breath caught in his throat, and his hard young body stirred at the memory.

Guenevere –

And soon he would see her, any moment now.

He entered the palace with a bounding step. Now that glorious body would be his again, as he had dreamed. Soon he would stand in an agony of impatience as her white fingers struggled to unbuckle his sword, then he would sweep her into his arms and carry her to bed.

He sighed hungrily.

Guenevere.

What a woman!

What a Queen!

Walking at Lancelot's side, Bors glanced at him in bitter exasperation, and had to look away. Would they ever be free of this queen who had stolen Lancelot's soul?

Behind them the call of the bidding bell faded into the dusk. Bors nodded. Christian worship was not famous for its brevity. Arthur was out of the way till sunset and beyond.

But why did they have to think like this at all? Why this deceit, this evasion, this sneaking around? The Queen was wonderful, Lancelot said. Yes indeed, Bors had no doubt of that. Wonderfully bad for Lancelot, for all of them.

'Sir!'

As they entered the palace, the guards on the door leaped to attention and their eyes followed Lancelot with rapt regard. Bors ground his teeth. Did Lancelot know, did he care, how much he meant to these men? And not only to the men, to every woman and child? Only babes in arms and hopeless imbeciles did not know Lancelot. He was a byword for honour far and near. And to risk all this for a handful of nights with the Queen?

Walking behind Bors and Lancelot, Sir Lionel's gaze switched from one to the other with anxious love. Bors, Bors, he mourned, don't torment yourself. A love like this is beyond us to understand. And Lancelot is our kin. We have no choice but to honour and follow him.

Inside the palace, the long white passage-ways were quiet and chill. Above their heads the high vaulted arches vanished in the blue-grey dusk. Farther in, the walls grew lower and thicker, the stones more rough. The Queen's tower rose above the battlements, and looked out over the countryside for miles around. But her private apartments lay at the heart of ancient Camelot, carved out of the fortified hill before the rest of palace rose above the ground.

As they went deeper, the air grew warmer, and a faint scent beckoned them, musky and obscure. Patchouli had been the chosen fragrance of the queens of the Summer Country since the first trader had sailed from the East up the Severn Water, and into the inland sea. Lancelot's senses quickened as he picked up the familiar scent. The deepest part of him beat with one yearning, *Guenevere*.

The outer doors to the Queen's Apartments were under double guard. At the inner door, more guards bowed them through. In the dusk of the antechamber, Ina waited alone. At the sight of Sir Lancelot, her small face lit with its cat-like gleam.

'My lords!' she said loudly. 'The Queen will be glad to see you all.' Then as the guards bowed out and the double doors closed, she turned to Sir Lancelot. 'This way, sir,' she breathed.

Silently she led him forward through the silvery gloom. At the door to the Queen's Chamber she stood aside.

Guenevere –

Lancelot's heart almost failed with the weight of his love. He stood on the threshold, powerless to move. Then a voice from within filled every region of his heart.

'Lancelot?'

Lovers never parted never know love's highest bliss. In tears and soft tremblings, mute caresses and simple murmurings, they consoled themselves for their hours of loneliness, and renewed their faith. Gripping her furiously to his chest, feeling again the sweet roundness of her head beneath his chin, Lancelot stroked her shining hair and held her until her tears of joy subsided, and she was his again. Holding him as tightly as she could, Guenevere stood fast until his body stopped shaking, and he was hers again.

'Oh, my love!'

'My love!'

He kissed her deeply, weeping as he had when they parted, turning it into a kiss of farewell, not reunion.

She laughed in her throat. 'No, no.' She reached up and threw her arms lightly round his neck. 'Come here.'

He started at her touch, and pulled away. 'Here, love,' she said softly, and drew his head down again. This time they kissed like lovers, as they were.

Already now his hand was at her breast. She turned aside and unlaced her overgown. He slid his hand down the softness of her neck, his fingers gently parting her shift to stroke the tender flesh. Her skin gleamed like mother-of-pearl in the candlelight, and her nakedness made him catch his breath.

'So beautiful,' he murmured through broken tears.

The music of his light, accented voice destroyed her last reserve. She folded him to her body, and felt his desire. Yearning possessed her, she could not let him go. She closed her eyes and saw what she desired, his long brown length stretched out for her delight.

Stepping back, she shed her overgown. Tears stood in his eyes, and a low sound echoed in his throat. 'Lady –'

She kissed his fingertips and brought them to her lips. 'Hush – hush, my love.' Taking his hand, she drew him towards the bed.

'From the sins of the flesh, from the evil that besets us on all sides, good Lord deliver us.'

'Amen.' Crossing himself, Arthur got to his feet.

The King still moved awkwardly, noted the priest, as he stood at the altar watching his flock. Perhaps it was true what they said, that his great wound had not healed.

Dear Lord, he prayed with all the fervour of a simple heart, restore the King. And bless the Queen, and reward Sir Lancelot and all the King's knights for their unswerving love. He bowed at the King's approach.

'God be with you, sire,' he said fervently.

Arthur was walking stiffly towards the door. 'A fine sermon,

Father. My warmest thanks.'

The priest bobbed his head. 'Our thanks to you, sire.'

Arthur turned away. 'Kay?'

'Here!' Kay said. 'And all the rest of us.'

'Good.'

With his knights on his heels, Arthur led the way out of the little church. Outside the April night was thick with stars, and the raw scent of spring was in the air. Another season, Kay mourned, limping along behind, and still the King not himself. It doesn't matter about me, I can bear to be the court cripple, but God! he prayed fiercely, let the King get back his strength!

Some good had come of his illness, Kay had to admit. All the knights of the Round Table had rallied round their king. Even those oafs from the Orkneys had learned to bow the knee. Young Mador of the Meads and his brother Patrise hardly reached the Orkneyans' shoulders, but their devotion had been as great. And Lucan, and Sagramore and Ladinas, Dinant and Tor and all of them, they had been there for their lord.

Kay paused, and felt the old stab of pain in his leg.

Except –

Kay shook his head to escape the sour taste of his thoughts. Oh, Guenevere had devoted herself to Arthur, but when did she last look at him with true pleasure, or any sign of love? And what about the constant, veiled and smouldering reserve in Lancelot, who used to be like his father, the French King Ban, bright-eyed and frank? Bors and Lionel too had turned dour and cold. In court, none of their smiles ever reached their eyes.

Kay shook his head. Put it out of your mind, he told himself. Arthur loves her, and that's all you need to know.

Unless what Kay suspected ever came to light.

Gods above, he cursed himself, don't even think of it! Why, it would be the very end of the world.

He could feel his heart almost cracking in his breast. Ahead of him Arthur was laughing among knights.

'We'll have a feast tonight,' he proclaimed ebulliently. He punched Gawain's shoulder, then turned back towards Kay. 'Gawain, chase up Lancelot, will you? And Kay, send to the Queen.'

*

Gods above, what was wrong with the pair of them?

Bors ground his teeth to choke back a wild reproach. Were they mad? After all the dangerous hours they had already spent, a whole afternoon together in the Queen's Chamber under the very noses of the guards, what had possessed the Queen to want Lancelot back tonight?

But there was no mistake, he heard it with his own ears. Emerging from the inner chamber, Lancelot gave a strange, luminous smile. A lingering scent of patchouli hung about him still.

'The Queen wants me to come again tonight.'

Ina gave a gasp. 'Sir?'

'Gods above!' stuttered Bors. 'This is madness, man!' He swept a disbelieving hand over his face. 'It's one thing to come calling at this time of day. But we all agreed the nights were too dangerous. Lancelot, I beg you, think again!'

Urgently Lionel seconded him. 'You'll have to climb the tower, cousin, it's a dreadful risk. And if anyone came, you'd be trapped there, you'd be caught!'

Lancelot favoured them with his Otherworldly smile. 'It is the Queen's desire.'

The –? Bors could have yelped with rage. The Queen's desire will cost us all our heads, he thought vengefully.

Ina drew a breath. 'What time are you sent for, sir?'

'Midnight.'

'Midnight.' Bors forced himself to nod. As good a time as any to risk our lives. 'At midnight, then, we'll guard your way here. And at dawn we'll come back to see you safe away.'

The night was dark, and the sky was thick with mist. From the bell-tower came the owls' lamenting cry. In the King's bedchamber a fire still burned on the hearth, ordered by Arthur when the feast had left him reluctant to end the day, and settle down to sleep.

Guenevere moved round the chamber like a woman in a dream.

'You look tired, Guenevere.' Arthur gave a rueful, boyish laugh. 'You must be longing for your bed.'

Go to sleep, Arthur, sleep.

Guenevere busied herself with the candles. 'No, no.'

'It's selfish of me to keep you up like this.'

She approached the bed. 'Let me make you comfortable, then you can drop off.' Deftly she removed the pillows from behind his head. 'That's the way to get better, you know that.'

'Get better?' He laughed unhappily. 'D'you think I'll ever be a husband to you again?'

Immediately she regretted her brisk tone. 'Oh, Arthur . . .'

'Come here.' He reached out for her hand.

She could see the longing leaping up in his eyes, and her soul recoiled. *Goddess, Mother, forgive me, I can't* –

Lightly she disengaged herself, and pulled the sheets up over his arms. 'Don't worry, you're getting better all the time. You'll soon be your old self again.'

And what happens then? she thought, with an inner groan. *Don't ask, don't even think. Do your duty now, that's all you can do, and go.*

Go!

Get out, get away from him, while you still can.

In one continuous move she straightened the bedclothes, dropped a kiss on his forehead, and left the room. 'Try to sleep. You'll be yourself again before you know.'

Sleep, Arthur, sleep.

High above the palace, the spirit of Morgan hung quivering in the air. How rich to see Guenevere playing the dutiful wife, when only hours before she had been naked on the bed with Sir Lancelot, moaning with passion and waving her long legs in the air! A gale of silent laughter shivered her frame. Yes, sleep, Arthur, sleep.

Slowly she filtered down into the royal apartments, and down into the great bedchamber of the King. Arthur lay on his back, his great body dwarfed by the massive bed's heavy hangings and deep canopy. Morgan shuddered with desire. In another life, he had taken her in this bed. They had acted out the true roles of royal brother and sister here, as the old Gods had decreed since time began. The Egyptians, the Etruscans, the earliest Chinese, all these had honoured the union of siblings to preserve the blood royal in its purity.

But Arthur –

He lay on his back on the bed, his eyes closed, but still awake, she knew. His hands, his lips, the soft skin of his temples pricked at her heart. She wanted to slit his eyeballs, and drop poison into his mouth. He had failed, and like the wretches at the convent, he must pay.

But not with a simple, easy, little death. No, he must suffer what she'd undergone when they called her a whore in the face of all the court. To know that his wife had betrayed him with his dearest friend, to be known as a cuckold the length and breadth of the isles, there was grief and shame in abundance for any man.

Morgan spat, blistering the oak of the bedpost as she hovered above.

And the white-and-gold Guenevere would be scalded in her own shame too. Seen as loose in the loins, a betrayer, an adulteress, she would lose her flower-like fragrance in all men's eyes. And nothing she suffered could ever be too much.

She had broken the charm that had bound Arthur to Morgan's desire. A woman so blessed in a husband, lover, son had taken from Morgan the one love she had ever had. The spirit sharpened her claws, and rubbed her scaly hands. Time to make them pay.

Softly she approached the bed, and laid her fingers on Arthur's lids.

Sleep, Arthur, sleep.

She slipped into the bed.

Sleep, sleep, my dear.

And then prepare to dream.

Arthur lay on his back, breathing easily. He dreamed that he was suddenly whole again, his body enjoying the tender shape of a female body lying next to his. His mind explored the soft planes and shapely contours, and his hands knew at once the long limbs, full breasts and rounded hips.

'Guenevere!' he murmured, and laughed, and wept.

'Yes, Arthur.'

She reached out for him, and this time he did not resist. Her hands fluttered lightly around the site of his great wound, weaving a web of light touches and caresses on his skin. In disbelief he felt the familiar, joyous throb, felt himself lengthen and thicken without pain.

'Guenevere!' he moaned, praying the dream would last.

'I want you, Arthur,' hissed the spirit in his ear. 'I'm all alone in my bed, weeping for you. Come to me, dearest one, come tomorrow before dawn. Call your knights together, as you did when we first met. Spring is here, the green shoots are on the bough. Call on me to go with you for a dawn ride. Come and take me in my bed, as you always did.'

Arthur wept with joy. 'Tomorrow at dawn, Guenevere? In your bedchamber in the tower? Trust me, my love, I'll be there!'

CHAPTER 25

'Wake up, sleepy-head!'

The servant awoke to a boisterous box on the ears. Standing over him was the head chamberer with a grin on his face, and a candle in his hand.

'What is it?'

'Look lively, it's the King. He's calling for all his knights to make a dawn party to greet the Queen. He wants to go maying, as they always did.'

'But the blossom's not out yet.'

'I know that, clot-poll, it's still in the bud! But who cares what chamber-servants think? Our orders are to attend the King.'

The boy stumbled to his feet. 'And wake up the knights?'

'Yes, he won't go without them, call them all, Sir Lancelot, Sir Gawain, you know who.'

'And send to the Queen?'

'Gods above, man, not the Queen! The King wants to take her by surprise.'

'She'll be surprised all right.'

'You're right there, lad. There won't be a more startled woman in Camelot when the King walks through the door!'

'Sir!'

Bors came to himself, in the throes of a bad dream. Someone had been beating on the chamber door, demanding Lancelot. And Lancelot was not there, he was with the Queen. In another second he knew the nightmare was true. There was no imagining the pounding fist, the echoing cry.

'Sir! Sir Lancelot!'

Across the chamber he could see Lionel, still half asleep, dazed and terrified. As always, the sight of his younger brother brought out the best in Bors.

'Lay off that noise, and wait!' he shouted, in commanding tones. 'Allow your betters to cover themselves before they open the door.' He leaped up off his rough pallet, reached for a robe and threw open the door. In the corridor outside stood a servant of the King.

'So, dimwit,' Bors began dangerously, 'what's the news that disturbs Sir Lancelot in his bed?'

The servant hung his head. 'No offence, sir,' he mumbled nervously, 'but the King has a fancy to go dawn courting of the Queen, and surprise her in her bed. All his knights must attend him before the cock crows. He specially called for Sir Lancelot. Oh, and you too, sir, of course.'

Bors did not move. His mind stood still. Arthur wanting Lancelot, who was with Guenevere. Arthur calling on Guenevere, who was with Lancelot. He forced himself to speak. 'When the cock crows, you say, we must meet the King?'

'Yes, sir.'

'And what's the time now?'

'The monks are singing matins.'

Bors nodded. They had half an hour, maybe more. 'Tell the King that Sir Lancelot sends his loyal greetings, and we'll attend him as soon as may be.'

He turned back into the chamber, and slammed the door with unaccustomed force. 'Goddess, Mother, what are we to do?'

Across the room Lionel was wide awake and trembling. 'The Queen,' he said wildly. 'Lancelot's with the Queen.'

'As the King will be.' Bors gave a bitter laugh. 'Within the hour.'

Lionel's face collapsed. 'We're lost, brother,' he said frantically, 'there's nothing we can do. We can't get word to them in there, past the guards. Lancelot will be caught with the Queen, and it'll all come out.' His eyes widened as a new horror came into his mind. 'The Christians call it sin, and their wretched monks are all round the King now. She'll go to the fire, and we'll all burn for it too!'

He let out his breath in a low wail of despair.

Bors brought his fingers to his temples. 'What did you say?'

'I said we'll all die! They're both trapped in her chamber when he should be here. We can't get word –'

'No – after that.'

'It's a sin! The Christians call it sin! They burn women for –'

'That's it.'

Bors cut him off. He dropped his sweating head between his hands, and when he lifted it again, his face had a marble calm.

'Thank you, brother, for your helpful words,' he murmured, through a sick half-smile. 'It's good to have a brother. And the spirit of brotherhood is our only hope, I think.'

'My lady! My lady!'

The low voice was like a wave on Avalon's shore. Guenevere swam up to consciousness from a deep pool of sleep. Her hand moved sleepily to the body by her side. Lancelot here, loving her, again and again all night, what could be wrong in this best of all wonderful worlds?

'My lady!' Ina's voice throbbed with panic now. 'Lady, wake up, I beg of you!'

Guenevere opened her eyes. The flame of a candle danced before her sight. By its faint light she could see Ina hovering at the bedside, holding out her chamber gown. She glanced down at the sleeping figure in the bed. Lancelot slept like a boy, tangled up in the sheets, spreading his lordly length. She gazed at him, and almost lost herself in love.

'Lady –'

'Hush! Don't wake Sir Lancelot.'

She slipped naked from the bed. Ina wrapped the gown round her, and wept softly, like a child.

'Oh, my lady!' she whimpered. 'The King's coming, he'll soon be here!'

'What?'

'I overheard a message brought to the guard. They were laughing and joking outside the door, and noise woke me up. "The King's coming," they were saying, "to surprise the Queen. Just as –" '

'– just as he did when we were sweethearts in May.' Guenevere nodded dully. Whatever had put this idea into his head? What did it matter? He was on his way.

Her mind surged on. So, no hope of Lancelot leaving through the window, the way he had come. If the King was on a May adventure and about before dawn, all the castle would be awake. They were trapped in the tower like the guilty souls they were.

'Madame?'

She had not heard him wake. He sat up in bed, saw Ina, and fumbled to draw the sheet across his waist.

'What is it?' he said in confusion, his eyes wide with sleep. 'Why is she here?'

'Arthur is coming to surprise me in my bed.'

Lancelot's eyes flared.

'He knows?' he cried.

'No. He –' The words choked her, but they had to be said. 'He's coming for love. To take me maying, as we used to do.'

Lancelot caught his breath. 'With his knights?'

'Yes. He always used to come with his chosen knights.'

'So the King will have sent for me.' Suddenly he was unnaturally calm. 'Bors will have dealt with that,' he said evenly. 'But when his knights meet, I will not be there.'

'And he'll find you here.'

She glanced round the great chamber hopelessly. Chairs, tables, and a comfortable couch, but not a cupboard, not a chest where a man might hide.

She looked at Lancelot, and terror bloomed. 'Gawain'll kill you, my love, or Agravain, one of them will.'

He swung his legs from the bed, winding the sheet round his hips, and reached for his sword. 'We shall see.'

'You can't kill them all!'

He shook his head. 'Madame, I hope and pray I shan't have to kill any of them. But neither shall they kill me.' He gazed at her with a sudden dark regard. 'Or you.'

She ran to him and threw herself in his arms. 'Don't talk of killing, I can't bear it!' she wept.

He pushed her away. 'We must.'

'Lancelot –' She tore her hair. 'Listen to me!' she howled.

'Lady! My lady!' Ina ran to her weeping, and seized her hand. 'Lady, don't take on so, the King will forgive –'

'Never! He can't, his monks won't permit –'

'Listen!'

Lancelot started like a stag, and turned towards the door. 'What's that?'

'Goddess, Mother, save us!' Ina wept.

'No, do not ask for that.' Lancelot raised his hand with a terrible smile. 'The Great Ones do with us as they will.' He sighed. 'Ours is not the first love to end in fire and blood. Let us prepare ourselves. To the antechamber, Ina, if you will.'

'Lancelot –'

'No, lady, no more tears.' He moved towards Guenevere with a look of mingled love and death, gripping his sword and hefting it in his hand. 'One kiss, my queen, for I hear them. They are here.'

CHAPTER 26

E ven at dead of night, some creatures never slept, and the strangest things were at large between dusk and dawn. The Captain of the Guard had never seen the Fair Ones walk. But keeping up with human prowlers was more than enough for him.

Especially when the night-wanderer was the King. Gods above, who'd have expected that? the Captain asked himself, as he moved down the Queen's corridor at a rapid pace. Well, time to worry about that later, the King would be here any minute now.

Striding up to the door of the Queen's apartments, he frowned at the guards' rough clothing and tousled hair.

'Smarten yourself up, lads,' he growled. 'No time to lose!' They stumbled to obey.

At the entrance to the Queen's Apartments, a lone torch burned above the door. Ahead, the long, low passage was smoky with its guttering flame. An uneasy silence settled on the little group. Then, in the darkness at the end of the corridor, the shadows stirred.

The Captain drew his sword. 'Who's there?'

Slowly the blackness formed itself into shapes, two shuffling figures darker than the night outside. Monks, the Captain noted, with a silent curse. What were they doing here? Well, their black habits were everywhere now, thanks to the King.

Grimly he watched the two hooded figures approach, their heads bent, their faces hidden in the all-concealing cloth, their arms and even their hands tucked up in their sleeves.

'Your business, sirs?' he challenged the newcomers.

The two monks came to halt in front of him, refusing to lift their heads. A low voice issued from beneath the first of the thick woollen hoods.

'We have come to see the Queen.'

'The Queen?' The Captain paused. The smell of sweat and incense choked his throat. Great Gods, they were vile, these Christ-followers with their claptrap from the East. Why would the Queen want them? She followed the Goddess, everyone knew that. She only bore with these stinking monks for Arthur's sake. Nothing on earth would make a Christian of her.

He frowned suspiciously. 'You want to see the Queen?' he temporised.

'She sent for us,' hissed the short, black-hooded form.

The Captain stared. 'Now why would she do that?'

'Ask her yourself!'

The Captain shook his head. 'The King's expected any minute now,' he said commandingly. 'On your way, sirs, you won't be admitted today.'

There was a frozen silence. Then the shorter of the two came forward menacingly. Despite himself, the Captain felt a qualm. Why couldn't he hold his head up and threaten like a man?

'We are monks of the King,' the monk muttered in violent tones, 'and you defy His Majesty if you keep us out today. He'll have you stripped and whipped before all your men. Let us through, numbskull, if you value your hide!'

He stepped forward aggressively, with the second monk close behind.

'Sir!' The younger of the guards plucked at the Captain's sleeve.

He shook the youth off, intent on the monks. 'Now, you two, look here –'

'Stand aside!' They shouldered past him, and stood before the door.

'Sir?' the young guard tried again.

'Hold your tongue, soldier!' said the Captain dangerously.

The taller of the monks pounded on the door. There was only the echo of silence from within.

The Captain collected himself and returned to the attack. 'Woe betide you, sirs!' he threatened the black-clad backs.

'Hush!' The shorter monk raised his hand. From within came the sound of bolts being drawn back.

A moment later the Queen's maid looked out. 'What?' Ina cried.

The Captain gestured to the monks with an angry laugh. 'These two are saying that the Queen's expecting them. Just say the word, lady, and they'll be out of here before their feet can touch the ground!'

'One moment, lady.' The shorter of the monks stepped forward, and lifted his hood.

Ina's eyes grew wide as she saw his face. A small, hysterical sound, quickly suppressed, fell from her mouth. She nodded to the guard.

'Why yes,' she said, in a strained, unnatural tone, 'Her Majesty will be glad to see these monks.' She stepped back and opened the door. 'Welcome, good brothers, I beg you, come in.'

'By all the Gods . . . !'

The Captain turned in fury from the door. 'Monks in the Queen's apartments now, is it? Well, she's welcome to the whole lousy pack of them!'

'Sir,' the young guard tried for the third time, 'something odd, sir –'

'Odd, soldier?' the Captain burst out, 'there's nothing odder than Christians in Camelot, believe you me! Gods above, what's the world coming to?' He gave the guard a nasty look. 'Don't answer, or I'll have you on a charge.'

He stalked away with a ferocious frown. The young guard was relieved to see him go. What he'd seen couldn't have been important, not with the Captain in a mood like this. After all, did it matter that instead of the usual sandals on their raw, bare feet, both the monks tonight had been wearing boots?

The dank vapours of night still clung round the walls, but by the faint lightening in the east, dawn was on its way. Striding through the courtyard among his knights, Arthur grinned with boyish delight. He knew he was moving more easily, despite the biting air. He looked around.

'You know, there's nothing like an adventure to make me feel young again!'

Kay, struggling not to jar his bad leg on the cobblestones, was not impressed. 'That's not a feeling, sire, it's a fact. We're not old. We're still in our thirties, for a while at least.'

'Young?' Gawain let out a guffaw, punching Kay on the arm. 'The King, maybe. But you were born old, Kay!'

Kay's eyes flared. 'Well, I was certainly born wiser than you, Gawain.' He paused. 'Which was not hard!'

Behind him, Gaheris and Gareth suppressed snorts of schoolboy glee. Bringing up the rear, Agravain took a fleeting comfort in the jibe at Gawain's expense. Well used to Kay's badinage, Bedivere and Lucan shared a smile with the rest of the knights.

They passed through the courtyard to see the chapel doors opening for the end of matins, and the monks come flooding out. They pressed past the hooded shapes, gained the wide cloistered walkway, and made their way into the inner court. At the entrance to the Queen's corridor, Arthur called a sudden halt.

'Wasn't Lancelot going to meet us here?' He turned to Kay. 'What did Bors say?'

Kay's sallow face changed imperceptibly. 'He said that Lancelot had gone out hunting, and that he and Lionel would find him and bring him here as soon as they could.'

'Don't worry, my lord,' Gawain urged. 'He'll be here.'

Bedivere nodded. 'Lancelot will never let you down.'

In the far distance, a cock began to crow. On the other side of the courtyard, two monks hastened by.

'Cock-crow,' Arthur smiled, 'it's dawn.' He nodded amiably. 'Well, we won't wait any longer. Let's go on.'

Outside the Queen's apartments, the guards stood to attention to greet the King.

'Knock on the door, Gawain,' Arthur cried.

The old oak almost split under Gawain's fist. The door opened to reveal Ina's flushed face. 'My lord!' she cried with a curtsy, her eyes wide. 'What a surprise to see Your Majesty!'

She did not look so surprised, Kay thought, as they all trooped in. And her cream silk chamber-gown did not look as if she had been disturbed from sleep. But perhaps it was all his suspicious mind. For nothing looked as if it had disturbed the peace of the inner chamber where the Queen lay.

All the windows were muffled against the light. The heavy hangings and thick carpets made the low whitewashed space unnaturally quiet and calm. Against the wall, the Queen's bed loomed like a ship of state, its heavy billowing draperies tightly closed. One tall candle burned on a stand beside the bed.

The musky scent of patchouli teased the air. The knights lingered on the threshold as Arthur bounded into the room.

'Guenevere!' he called.

A sleepy voice came from the depths of the bed.

'My lord?'

She knew she had done well. As she sat up slowly in the bed, she could see herself as Arthur would see her now, heavy-eyed and dazed, looking full of sleep. As she waited for his hand on the hangings, she rehearsed her surprise. *Oh, Arthur, this is lovely, what is it? A dawn ride?*

To show a natural delight was not too hard. *What a wonderful idea to go maying as we always did. Yes, of course it's wonderful, I said so, to see you here with your knights.*

And then she had arrayed herself in her best chamber-gown, and sallied out to the antechamber where Ina had summoned refreshments for the knights. Sir Gawain had led the demand for something hot and strong, and now the room was filled with the rich, spiced odour of mulled wine, despite the early hour. Moving around the group, she had greeted each knight and taken him by the hand, and they were all jovial, even the dark Agravain. And Arthur himself had watched her every move, laughing and smiling, full of joy. In body and spirit he seemed his old self again.

Yes, she had done well.

But the cost, Gods above, the cost.

Lies and deceit, a picture of false innocence.

A show of wifely devotion from a woman who had just spirited her lover from her bed.

Goddess, Mother, forgive the woman I have become.

'Farewell, sirs!'

'Our thanks to Your Majesty.'

One by one the knights trooped out through the oak door.

Ahead of them Arthur was swinging down the corridor to the courtyard like a man reborn. He turned to Gawain.

'We must do this again!'

'Sire!' Gawain let out a bellow, pointing ahead. 'There they are!'

In the distance three figures had turned into the courtyard and were hurrying their way.

'Lancelot!' Arthur cried in delight.

'Apologies, sire,' muttered Lancelot. He was very pale.

'And Bors and Lionel,' Arthur went on. 'So you found him then?'

'Yes, sire,' Bors returned stiffly, 'and brought him back as quickly as we could.'

'Where were you, Lancelot? What took you from your bed at that raw hour?' Arthur demanded, throwing a companionable arm round Lancelot's shoulders.

'I was – out hunting, sire. For the exercise.'

'Hunting?' hooted Gawain, rolling his eyes, 'On a foul day like this? Ye Gods, Lancelot, you're an example to us all!'

Hunting, eh? Agravain moved up to hold the three newcomers in his gaze. Thoughtfully he assessed Lancelot's heavy eyes, his pallid sheen. 'Catch anything?' he asked easily.

Only shame and dishonour, Lancelot mourned in his soul. He turned away in misery. 'No.'

CHAPTER 27

'So you're leaving the Orkneys, sir?'

Merlin ground his teeth. The cry of the sea-birds filled the echoing air. A fat pink sun bloomed on the horizon, promising a cloudless day. Warm breezes whispered, and the white road wandered away over the hilltops, calling him into the blue. His heart revived to be on the road again, after so many bitter, barren moons wasted here. And only this foul hairy creature darkening the day.

'Leaving?' Merlin favoured the Orkneyan with a yellow glare. 'I thank the great Gods, yes.'

'Well, we'll look forward to your speedy return,' the man continued with a gap-toothed grin, giving the mule's girth a heavy-handed tug. He moved round to the far side of Merlin's mount, checking the saddlebags, bridle and bit. 'Those who come here always return one day. Even our princes, they'll be coming back.'

Merlin gave a mirthless smile. Princes, indeed, those great Orkney louts? Still, they were Arthur's kin. A spark of interest stirred. 'When are they coming back?'

'Soon,' said the man confidently. 'The Queen wants to see them, that's for sure. As any woman would, who'd mothered four such fine sons.' He gave the mule a final slap, and raised his hand. 'Farewell.'

Maybe, maybe not, Merlin thought, as he pulled the mule's head round and made for the open road. He chuckled lecherously. If he knew women, Queen Morgause would not be in a hurry to have Gawain, Agravain, Gaheris and Gareth back with her at court. Would any woman want four grown-up sons breathing down her neck as she took her handsome lover to her bed? Would any son want to see his mother mounted by a man of his own age, a lusty young knight?

Let alone a man guilty of spilling their blood. They would not forgive Morgause that her lover and his father were the killers of King Lot.

Merlin's sight darkened, and a thin lamentation rattled in his throat. Suddenly he smelt death, raw blood, and bursting flesh. It was true that Lamorak had been only a boy when he fought with his father at the Battle of the Kings. And like Lamorak, King Pellinore had had no choice but to fight against Lot: he was bound to support Arthur by his loyal oath. But fate had made them the instrument of Lot's death.

Merlin dropped the white mule's reins, trusting the patient beast to find the way. Wrapping both arms round his thin body, he rocked to and fro in the saddle, pregnant with a burden of foreboding, struggling with a seeing he could not yet see. Arthur had meant to heal that blood feud when he sent Sir Lamorak to serve the Queen. But he had not known that Morgause would take Lamorak to her bed.

And there was a price to be paid for careless rapture, always a price. For all her fleshly wisdom, this was a truth that Morgause did not seem to know. She had loved him, yes, this was no random tale of an older woman's lust for a fine young man. She loved him still, rarely were two people so in love, and to Morgause, that cancelled out her husband's death. But to her sons, their father's corpse must still be walking the earth, crying for vengeance.

And so?

Merlin groaned. And so there would be blood. Above the Queen's slow-eyed smiles of satisfaction and the smell of sex that hung in the palace walls, Merlin could not free himself of the rich ripe stink of blood.

So be it, then.

On, you old fool, he told himself, get on.

The white mule settled into a slow, swaying walk. In the coarse grass by the roadside, dragonflies buzzed to and fro. The rising sun warmed Merlin's hawk-like head, massaged his old shoulders and played on down his back.

The golden fire warmed his withered body to the root, and a fleshly relish crept into his soul, mingled with a rancorous anger too. A fine woman, Morgause, with her fair acres of fat white flesh. But she had played with him for weeks and months, disclaiming all knowledge of Morgan, then sending for him at strange times of the night, to feed him scraps of information that were nothing in the light of day. Whole seasons had rolled by while he played her game. He grinned savagely. And still he had no more knowledge of Mordred than when he came.

So the amorous Queen had amused herself by tweaking his nose. And one day he would have vengeance on Morgause, if her sons did not punish her first.

He grinned again, and felt the familiar stirring in his loins. For Arthur he had wanted a submissive wife, bud-breasted and undeveloped in her mind. But all his life, all his many lives, he had sought a woman of power, a woman worth taming, and a woman who would tame him. She rode him hard, the dark spirit, and she changed shape every time. Yet it was always the same woman, at least he knew that now.

He had a sudden vision of Queen Morgause tied naked to a post, her hands above her head, her full white body flinching from his attentions as she awaited the unhurried unfolding of his revenge. His sight dimmed, and his old flanks strained as his flesh rose with each imagined hurt. The pink and gold Orkney noon faded into night. Then a voice came to him, singing down the wind.

'You called me, Merlin. See, I am here.'

He was not surprised. She always came to him out of the darkness of his lust and despair. Indeed she brought the darkness, she was the despair, and it was always worse when she had gone.

He greeted her with a groan. Already he could feel the hot stink of her breath. No use to cry for mercy, he knew. She gloried in goading him to bursting point, then condemning him to bear the painful standing of his juddering flesh for hours, days, weeks.

'Morgan!'

He groaned and fought, his thighs and belly covered in blood. Her white talons tore his flesh, and the glare of her red nipples was scorching to his eyes. But she tired of the game before it was half begun, and he felt himself tossed aside. Was she gone?

Yet she wanted something from him, he knew. He could feel her will reaching out to envelop him, coaxing, cajoling, *look here, see* –

He closed his eyes to see better through the dark. 'See what?'

Just out of his view, Morgan nerved herself for what she had to do. Must I help my enemy? her spirit moaned. But her will overrode her resistance with its one all-encompassing urge: *Mordred, Mordred, see, Merlin, see* –

Merlin strained his inner vision to the point of pain. A moment later the air around him thinned, and there he was.

A sturdy boy, walking in the world between the worlds. A boy with Morgan's thick cap of blue-black hair, and Arthur's shapely frame. He was with a group of other boys, all dressed as pages of a noble house. Behind them Merlin could see a homely castle, low and welcoming. Two round fat towers stood athwart an open gate, and the boy stood framed in the archway like a little king.

'Mordred!'

Merlin cried out for joy to see again the well-shaped, strong-sinewed body he had loved in Arthur as a child. As the boy turned his head, he had Arthur's frank, open gaze. But as he gazed, he had Morgan in his eyes. In their age-old depths, Merlin saw hyacinths bruised and bleeding under foot. Then his sight ruptured, pain split his heart and he feared for his mind.

He threw his skinny old arms high in the air. 'Merlin calls you, Mordred!' he screeched. 'Come!'

He thought the child heard him, but he could not be sure.

'*Merlin* –'

She had returned to play with him again. Yet even as the familiar agony gripped his frame and gnawed at his gut, Merlin felt himself smile.

I have you now, Morgan, was his last conscious thought. You have shown me your son, and as good as told me where he can be found. Even you cannot stand against the child's fate. He is Arthur's son as well as your own, and sooner or later you will give him to his father, because you love them both.

High overhead, Morgan tossed and writhed as she rode the clouds.

'Love Arthur?' she screamed, 'I hate him! And his bastard brat is nothing to me.' Her wail died away between the echoing spheres. 'Morgan Le Fay loves no one but Morgan Le Fay!'

Merlin shook his head, and let loose a mocking laugh. 'The threads of your three lives were woven into one before time began. Arthur was mine, you have been mine, and now I know that Mordred will be mine too. Hear me, Morgan! However long it takes, you will give your son to me!'

CHAPTER 28

'And then to see the King coming towards us, with Kay and all the others on his heels!' Lionel laughed, his bright young face creased with delight. 'How we got past them, I swear I'll never know!'

'Hush,' Bors said uneasily, glancing around. Even in the heart of the forest, he feared trees had ears. He looked up the track to the Queen and Lancelot riding ahead. Who could tell if they might not overhear, however absorbed in each other they looked now?

He drew a deep breath. What was he fretting about? It was not as if Lionel was laughing at the lovers' desperate plight. Ina, too, was out of earshot, trailing behind in a world of her own. And it had all been weeks, no, months ago now. He summoned up a laugh. 'It was a rare adventure, without a doubt.'

Lionel looked at him with a younger brother's love. 'How you came up with the idea of getting Lancelot out of the Queen's chamber dressed as a monk, I'll never know.'

Bors shrugged. 'It came to me as soon as you said, "The King listens to his monks." Those robes of theirs make a perfect disguise. The King himself wouldn't be recognised in one of them.'

'And then you said, "The spirit of brotherhood is our only hope,"' Lionel exulted, 'but I still didn't understand what you meant.'

Bors smiled. 'Well, I knew if two Christian brothers could get in to see the Queen, two could come out. The rest fell into place. '

Lionel nodded, his smile fading away. 'The Gods were with us,' he said soberly.

'They were.'

Silently the two shared the grim memory of that night, beginning with the raid on the monks' quarters to purloin the robes. Then there was the fearsome business of getting past the Captain guarding the Queen's door. The final scare when the guard had noticed their most un-Christian boots beneath their monkish robes still made Bors sweat.

And even when they gained the safety of the Queen's chamber, two monks entering meant that only two could come out. So while Lancelot donned the monkish habit that Bors had brought in concealed under his own robe, Lionel, habit and all, had climbed out of the window to make his escape. The risk he had taken was the greatest of all three, since all the court was likely to be awake with the King. But Lionel was known as a blameless youth, who meant no more to the Queen than any other knight. If he had been caught slipping round the Queen's tower dressed as a monk, he would have been taken for a Maytime prankster, nothing more. His name, his presence would never compromise Guenevere.

But Lancelot –

Bors gritted his teeth. The horses were picking their way softly through the shining shadows on the path, and the midday sun trickled lazily through the trees. The autumnal smell of the forest enveloped them in the rich, sad scent of nature in decay. In other company, in another place, his soul would be revelling in beauty such as this.

But now –

Painfully Bors acknowledged that he did not understand his cousin any more. Even trapped in the Queen's chamber with the King on the way, Lancelot had laughed at the danger, and kissed the Queen like a man who would choose to die in her arms rather than save all their lives. Since then, Lancelot had not seen the Queen at all. For safety's sake, the lovers had kept apart.

Then at dawn today, Lancelot had called Bors and Lionel to leave Camelot with him, and take the road north. Three hours after that, the Queen and Ina had ridden south. At a certain point, both parties had turned west to meet in the forest, in the heart of the deep green shade.

But for what? Bors felt his helplessness rising like bile. For the Queen to do nothing but weep, and heap angry reproaches on Lancelot's silent head? Don't listen to her, Lancelot, Bors prayed silently, put an end to this, tell her you must go.

Tell her, Lancelot.

The low sound of Guenevere's voice wove in and out of the branches overhead. Lancelot listened in moody silence till it died away. Then he looked at her, wild-eyed with disbelief. 'You're telling me I have to go away?'

'Yes.'

'And not see you again?'

Never again.

Guenevere turned her head. Beside the track grew a tree laden with ivy, its pale berries sprouting balefully beneath the glossy leaves. For the rest of her life she could never look at ivy without the memory of that pain.

'You must go, Lancelot,' she said stiffly. 'We both know that.'

'You are angry with me because I left you alone all this time.' Strong emotion made his accent more pronounced 'But we had to be careful, we were nearly caught –'

'No.'

Why did she feel so bleak, so cold, *so old*? 'No, I was not angry that you did not come. It was for the best.'

'Agravain,' he said suddenly.

She turned to him with a start. 'What?'

'That morning, when I came late to meet the King, he spoke to me.'

'What did he say?'

'He asked me if I had good hunting, nothing more.'

'Agravain?' *Gods above, no, not enmity from him?*

Unexpectedly she felt her eyes stinging, and the furious grief starting up again. She straightened her back. *No tears.* 'You think he suspects?'

'I thought he had noticed something. He was trying to test me out.'

'Ha!' She gave a short unhappy laugh. 'All the more reason then for you to go.'

He shook his head. 'You blame me, Madame,' he persisted. 'I do not want to leave because of that.'

'I told you no.' *Can't you see that I blame myself? That I can't bear this guilt, this grief, this pain?* 'We can't go on like this. We have to think of Arthur, not of ourselves.'

'Gods above, yes!' he groaned, covering his eyes with his hand. 'I swore an oath to love and honour the King. And instead I take his wife behind his back, and dishonour him.'

'It's not dishonour! Our love is above the honour code of men!'

'But that's all I have, don't you see?' he ground out. 'Since I was fifteen, I have lived that life. To serve King Arthur is every young knight's dream, and it was mine.'

'So you love Arthur more than you love me?'

He gasped with rage. 'All this time, I have broken my vows for you. I have waited and endured, lived without hope. And still you reproach me with my lack of love.' He shook his head. 'You were right, Madame,' he said harshly under his breath. 'It is time for me to go.'

She could not bear it. 'Where?'

The look he turned on her was cold and blank. 'Does it matter, as long as I am not here?'

'Of course it matters!' Gods above, what was wrong with him? *'I want to know what you'll do, where you'll be . . .'* And who will love you, when I am not there.

He threw her a glance. 'You do not trust me,' he said, with a savage laugh. 'Already you see lovers in my bed!'

'I do not!'

'No matter.' His face was like marble now. 'I must go, and I will. We must part.'

There was a silence in the forest, as if all life had fled. Lancelot drew a ragged breath, and lifted his head with unconscious authority. 'I am the son of a king, and I would have made you my queen. As it is, we can have less than the shepherd and the milkmaid in the fields. I have loved you more than anything in the world. But I was not born to love a married woman who will never be free.'

'Lancelot, I –'

'No more words. I go, Madame, as soon as I speak to the King.'

He looked up. On either side of the track the trees were

thinning as the path wound uphill towards a crossroads ahead. From left to right across the skyline ran the broad highway leading back to Camelot.

Lancelot reached for her hand, and pressed it to his lips. 'Farewell, Madame.'

She could not speak. He gave a broken smile, then swung his riding whip, pointing down the hill. 'To Camelot, my queen. There lies your way.'

CHAPTER 29

The ride back was as wretched as anything she had ever known. The air of the forest seemed laden with grief and decay. When Camelot's white towers came into view, the golden turrets and bright banners in the autumn haze seemed like a mocking memory of another life.

They turned their horses down to the valley below.

'So, Ina, he's going,' Guenevere said dully. 'Well, I suppose it is all for the best.'

Ina bit her lip. "You'll see him again, my lady, I know you will. Sir Lancelot won't leave you for ever without a word. He loves you too much.'

Guenevere shivered. 'Perhaps.' She turned away with another chilling thought, *I am quite alone. For sure, Ina has some skills of the Otherworld. But she never had a lover in her life.*

Camelot rose up to meet them, glaring in the afternoon sun. As they rode into the lower court, the Chamberlain hurried up. 'The King has been asking for you, my lady. He wants to hold an audience this afternoon. One of the petitioners has been pressing for help, and must be answered now.'

Guenevere held her hand to her aching head. 'Forgive me, sir. Please tell the King I shall be ready as soon as I can.'

In the crowded audience chamber, the girl at the front was already on her knees. Her moist dark eyes settled on Guenevere like sticky flies, and her round red mouth was open and ready to speak.

As soon as Arthur and Guenevere were seated, she rose to her feet. Her breasts, her whole body moved invitingly under her light gown. Guenevere looked at her with distaste. This petitioner would have no difficulty in finding a champion, whatever trials she faced.

The chamber was crowded with knights and their ladies, lords and lookers-on. There was no sign of Lancelot. Guenevere glanced around in pretended calm. Which of the knights would Arthur send out on this quest?

'The petitioner may approach!' the Chamberlain cried.

The girl dropped her eyes, and curtsied low before the throne. Her long dark hair swung down seductively over her breasts as she tossed her head, and launched into her tale. In spite of herself, Guenevere found her attention caught by the story of the girl's older sister, left sole heir to their father's estate.

It seemed the lady had fallen prey to a rogue knight of the road, swept away by his rough wooing, his white grin, his swaggering laugh. Foolishly she had promised herself to him, and taken him to her bed. Then she had come to her senses, and found out what a brute he was. But now he had turned on her, claiming her as his wife. He was keeping her prisoner in her own castle, to force her to marry him and make him her lord.

The girl ended in tears, on her knees. Would the King send the best knight of the Round Table to do battle with the rogue, and save her sister's life?

Arthur listened avidly to every word. 'Never fear for your sister, maiden!' he breathed, entranced. 'We shall find you a knight worthy of this great task.'

Guenevere looked around. With an ugly start she saw that Lancelot had slipped in at the back. He stood at the entrance to the chamber, plainly dressed and ready for the road. Beside him stood Bors and Lionel, similarly equipped. His eyes were fixed on the girl, and he was watching intently all that went on. Her heart lurched. *Goddess, Mother, not Lancelot. Not with this woman.*

'Guenevere?' It was Arthur, murmuring quietly at her side. 'Who shall we send?'

She forced herself to scan the body of the hall. Already Gawain was grinning coarsely at his brothers, lusting for the girl, it was clear, not for the quest, whatever rewards it may bring. Agravain's glowering face and jutting chin showed that he longed to challenge Gawain's bid to defend this maiden in distress. But the girl would have to be protected from them both.

She leaned across to Arthur, and touched his arm.

'Not Gawain,' she murmured. 'Nor Agravain.'

'No,' Arthur said softly, and she knew he shared her fears. She knew too that she could trust him to do right. He was a good man, and a good king. The thought made her feel worse.

'Who, then?' Arthur wondered quietly in her ear.

Anyone but Lancelot.

Through a rising mist Guenevere could see the young woman's staring, bold black eyes, her glistening mouth, her bulging breasts beneath her low-cut gown. The memory of Lancelot's long lean brown nakedness came to her with a sharp catch of pain. The girl must want him, every woman did. He would rescue the sister, and both of them would be duly grateful afterwards. They'd do anything for him, he could count on that.

Enough.

She shook her head in disgust. No need for thoughts like these. There were other knights. Her eyes roved over the group nearest the dais. Kay and Bedivere were waiting patiently, secure in the knowledge that they would not be sent. Sir Lucan was holding his handsome face impassive, making sure that he did not catch the King's eye. With his long red-gold hair and lithe body, Guenevere reflected, Lucan could not help but be a ladies' man.

But much as Sir Lucan loved women, this knight liked to choose his mistresses for himself. Being chosen to help a damsel in distress was not what Lucan had in mind. Yet perhaps he was still the man. She turned to Arthur. As she touched his arm, he leaned forward and she heard him call out, 'Sir Lancelot?'

'Arthur –' she said thickly. But she knew it was too late.

Lancelot broke from the ranks, and came forward down the hall. The girl turned towards him, eyes and mouth open with joy.

'Yes, Guenevere?' Arthur said fondly, as he watched him approach. 'What did you say?'

She was trembling. 'You could have chosen anyone else.'

Arthur laughed. 'Lancelot's the man to make short work of this rogue.'

'Yes, but –' She broke off. What was there to say? Her mind twisted and turned to find a drop of comfort in the desert of her hopes. She and Lancelot had been almost caught in her bed. If he favoured a beautiful young girl, that would still any gossiping tongues. It could save both their names, and even their lives. It must be for the best.

I don't care! her heart wept. *Not her! He shouldn't go with her!*

She looked at him, and put all her sorrow and foreboding into her eyes. He looked back with a strangeness that felt like a blow.

I cannot put my life into your hands, said his cold gaze. *I must be free to choose.*

A mad impulse seized her, and a torrent of bitter reproach poured through her mind. *So, Lancelot, was that what you wanted, the right to have your freedom at all costs? Is that why you made love to me, and chose me for your lady above the rest, to keep other women at bay, because you never wanted to marry and settle down?*

She gasped, and fought to put away these poisonous thoughts. How could she question his freedom, when she did not have her own? No power on earth could free her from Arthur now. And while Arthur lived, Lancelot could not be hers.

With a leaden heart she watched Lancelot move steadily down the hall, drawing near. But as he came up to the dais, there was a flurry among the knights, and a slight figure stepped out before the throne.

'Sir Mador of the Meads!'

A buzz of excitement ran through the crowded hall. The whispering died away as Mador approached, his face shining with the light of love. A sudden shadow of fear gripped Guenevere's heart. On the day of his knight-making, Mador had glowed with that same ardour, that radiant flame. How could he sustain that devotion? How could she?

Mador threw her a glance of adoration, and fell to his knees. He bowed to Arthur. 'Sire, send me!'

Lancelot gave a half-smile, and fell back.

'What do you think?' Arthur leaned towards Guenevere. 'He's a good knight,' he added quietly.

'One of the best,' she murmured, struggling to stay calm. 'Remember when he defeated Agravain, and showed such chivalry?'

Arthur nodded. 'You're right. And it's important to give him a chance. Lancelot won't mind. He's the first to bring on the younger men.'

He waved his hand, and summoned the girl to the throne. 'Lady, we grant you Sir Mador of the Meads to take up your cause.'

'Sire –'

It was almost a wail of dismay. The petitioner was looking from Lancelot to Mador with undisguised disgust. Her eyes roamed up and down his short, slight frame, his long fair hair and almost girlish face. Well, he's not Lancelot, Guenevere found herself thinking savagely, but like it or not, madam, he's your knight now!

'Sire!'

There was a flurry among the ladies as Sir Gawain stepped forward to challenge the decree. His eyes played over the young woman lasciviously. 'If Lancelot is not to go, send me, my lord!' he implored.

Arthur smiled fondly. 'You want an adventure, Gawain? Then you shall go too. Not with this young lady, for Sir Mador is her champion now. But I give you leave to ride out on your own. A knight errant can do much good in the world. See that you do so, Gawain, and come back safe.'

He raised his voice, and spoke to the open court. 'Do any other of my knights wish to go out adventuring?' He chuckled. 'The rewards are rich, when the ladies are so fair.'

'Sire?'

Lancelot had moved unnoticed to the foot of the throne. Bors and Lionel were standing quietly at his side. He bowed, and threw back the cloak of his travelling dress. Already she could see the woodland greens and browns melting into the landscape, and felt she was losing him, watching him fade away.

He moved towards Arthur, and avoided her eye. 'I would have told you this, sire, if you had picked me for the quest. My cousins and I have been called back to Little Britain, where an attack threatens from our overlord of France. We must go at once, and cannot say when we will be free to return. May we have your permission to leave, my lord?'

CHAPTER 30

The dying garden was dotted with scattered groups enjoying the last fleeting rays of the winter sun. Agravain stuck out his chin, and lengthened his stride to widen the gap between himself and his two brothers following behind. How slowly those idiots walked! Didn't they know who they answered to now?

Their leader, yes. Agravain grimaced with satisfaction to find himself at the head of the clan. Of course Gawain would be away only for as long as it took to find a damsel in distress, take advantage of her, and then return. Still, even for a short while, this was his true place. He turned to glower triumphantly at Gaheris and Gareth bringing up the rear.

Yet his twisted soul was still far from peace. Every mouldering leaf, every withered rose, and the all-pervasive smell of death and decay seemed to echo his black mood. Why should the sons of Orkney attend on the Queen? They were knights of the King, and nothing but the King's orders would have brought them here today.

But there it was, a command they could not ignore. 'With Gawain away, and Lancelot too,' Arthur had told him solemnly, 'make sure that the Queen is attended, Agravain.' Agravain laughed darkly to himself. He had not been surprised. Both the King and Guenevere, he knew, still clung to the belief that a queen must always have her knights. He had had no choice but to obey.

So every day at dawn, Agravain sent his page to see how the Queen had slept, as Sir Lancelot used to do. And at night, in another mocking echo of Lancelot's chivalry, the same boy was sent to ask if the Queen had taken peacefully to her bed, and could her servant now retire?

What nonsense it all was! Agravain's patience shrivelled in the fire of his contempt. What woman would believe such hollow protestations, such a false parade of love? And what man who called himself a man would even play at such pretence?

But there it was, he told himself again. Willy-nilly he had taken on the mantle of Lancelot's make-believe love. Yet perhaps he, too, could win Arthur's favour by courting the Queen. And it was no bad thing, Agravain brooded as he walked, to keep an eye on Guenevere.

For there was much here that he did not understand. That night of the King's May jaunt, when Lancelot finally appeared, he could have sworn there was something in the knight's demeanour, some consciousness, some guilt. Yet leaving court like that, with no plan to return, was not the action of the lover of a woman like Guenevere. And when Mador had pushed forward to claim the quest of the young woman's sister, it was clear that his love for the Queen was very much alive.

Agravain's brow cleared. So that was it, he concluded. If the Queen had a lover, Mador was the man. All he had to do was to watch her closely to turn the 'if' into knowledge he could use.

And there she was now, a sudden pale wisp of colour up ahead, drifting through the garden in her eternal white and gold, though summer had long gone. Agravain's frown deepened, and he drew to a halt. Gaheris and Gareth drew up to his side.

'The Queen is sad.'

It was Gareth, the baby giant of the brothers and youngest of the four, his freckled face contorted in sympathy.

Agravain gave an unkind laugh. 'She has lost her knight. There is no one left to adore her now.'

Gaheris looked at him thoughtfully. 'But Lancelot has always come and gone.'

'Not Lancelot, you idiot!' Agravain scoffed. His desire to crow over his brothers overcame his innate secrecy. 'I say her lover has gone.'

'Gods above, Agravain, don't say that!' Gareth gaped at Agravain, moon-eyed. 'Not about the Queen.'

'The King was ill for a long while,' Agravain said

unpleasantly, 'and would a woman like Guenevere live without love?'

The question hung in the air. Each of the brothers struggled to answer it.

'But even if it's true, you said not Lancelot,' Gareth mumbled, his mouth trembling. 'You can't mean Gawain?'

'Gawain?' Agravain was enjoying this. Making mischief, he thought with glee, is something I do well. 'Gods above, the pair of you are even bigger fools than I thought! Gawain? Lancelot? Am I the only one with eyes in my head?'

Gaheris's milky skin flushed, but he did not rise to the bait. 'Tell us what you mean,' he said evenly.

'I mean a certain young knight of the shires,' said Agravain, lingering on each word. 'One who loves the Queen so much that he tries to win her favour by undertaking this young petitioner's impossible quest. One knight on his own will never free a lady held in a castle, under lock and key. But a love-struck boy would be fool enough to try.'

Gareth gasped. 'Mador?'

'Well done, little brother!'

'You think he's the Queen's lover?' scowled Gaheris.

'It can't be true!' Gareth had turned an angry shade of red.

Gaheris nodded. 'I don't believe it either,' he said flatly, shaking his head. 'Gods above, not after being married to the King – the Queen wouldn't betray Arthur for a beardless boy!'

Agravain stroked his nose with a knowing air. 'I have it out of the side of his own mouth.'

'Meaning his brother?' Gaheris frowned. 'Well, Patrise could be wrong. And if Mador's in love with the Queen, why should he volunteer for this quest, going off with a woman who has "whore" written all over her for any man to see? I can't see the Queen being very pleased with that.'

'Easy, brother, easy,' Agravain sneered. 'He did it to throw the gossips off the scent.'

Gareth's eyes had settled into a permanent stare. 'How?'

'That girl is ripe for love. Against the promise of tumbling her into bed, why would any man look twice at Guenevere?'

Agravain paused. Some called the Queen a beauty, he well knew, but the eyes that they called cornflowers were nothing to him. And, Gods, she was old, well into her thirties now! To her, Mador could be little more than a boy.

Yet not such a boy.

The raw memory of his defeat at Mador's hands flooded Agravain. Again he felt the anguish of that day, the pains in his body, and the insult to his soul. Once again he renewed his vow to be revenged. The boy would live to regret his chivalry. Whose honour would be at the stake when he caught Mador in the arms of the Queen, exposed their adultery, and had them killed?

Agravain paused as another thought slipped gently into his mind. He could always deal with Mador in a quieter way. There were many silent means to end a life. Not all plants were wholesome and good to eat. Purple nightshade, wolf's bane, all-sleep, every town had its shadowy vendor of such things.

Or hemlock. He bared his teeth in an animal grin. That cup of forgetfulness was old when the world was young. It must have claimed a thousand Madors in its time. What difference would another young life make?

Or two?

A muscle jumped for joy in Agravain's neck. If Gawain sickened, how fine that would be. The thought of poison fed his poisoned soul. Yes, he would search it out. Brother Gawain, is your soul prepared?

'What's wrong with Agravain?' he heard Gareth demand. 'Why is he looking like that?'

Gaheris gave a harsh laugh. 'All this talk of adultery must have gone to his head.'

Gareth giggled like the boy he was. 'Perhaps he thinks he should be the lover of the Queen.'

Gaheris nodded grimly. 'Well, I'd say he's got as much chance with her as Mador has. But the whole thing's nonsense, he must have made it up.'

'Well, any woman would have to be desperate to take Agravain to bed,' Gareth chortled disrespectfully. 'Just wait till Gawain gets back and we tell him this!'

Agravain turned back towards them, rage boiling in his soul. 'Take care, brothers,' he said calmly, and turned away. Unless you want to meet me tomorrow in the ring, said his menacing back. Where you know I will beat you both bloody, because I can beat you, and only Gawain can beat me.

A wild laugh swelled inside him, and he fought it down. Yes, Gaheris and Gareth had better learn to show respect. Once he had the poison, who could tell? They would all have to reckon with him then. A cold glint lit his eye. Even his mother, even Queen Morgause.

For why did she love a man young enough to be her son? Surely it should have been enough that she had four fine sons as her pride and joy, her reason to live? Yet still she had had Lamorak as her secret lover for years. Thinking that no one knew made it all worse.

The wayward spasm in Agravain's neck had reached his face. He felt the muscle flickering underneath his eye. Morgause and Guenevere, loose, lustful women, unworthy to be queens. Monsters of self, hardly fit to live.

Black bile pulsed through his soul.

Vengeance on all who crossed Agravain!

Let them die, along with Mador his mortal enemy, and Gawain, the oaf of an older brother who stood in his way.

Faithless wives, wicked women, evil men deserved all they got.

He fixed his eye on Guenevere's back, and lurked after her down the path, stalking like a wolf.

All along the garden walls, the last roses hung down their heads. The path was strewn with tumbled petals, red and white, their edges crinkled like the fallen leaves. Guenevere wandered among them and let her thoughts drift with the petals, one by one. Where had the summer gone?

With Lancelot.

Far, far away.

Behind her she could hear the soft rustle of Ina's gown, and further off, the light talk of knights and ladies sounding through the air. She had always taken pleasure in the life of the court before. Any one of the courtiers would be honoured to speak to her now. But the best of them could not cheer her wintry thoughts.

The air was growing cold. Guenevere reached out and picked a rose. It glowed in her hands like the dark red heart of love, mocking her hollow, pale and passionless life. The damask petals were silky to her touch, and her fingers remembered the sweetness of Lancelot's skin. When would she feel such happiness again?

Lancelot, Lancelot –

Her yearning for him was a constant ache. Chill longings came by day, and pangs of hot desire gripped her at night.

Morgause can have her handsome lover by her throne all day, and take him to her bed when the sun goes down.

And why am I alone, when he will not be?

For Lancelot would not, could not be faithful to her, she knew. Some innocent young maiden in distress would need to be consoled, leaving him in all chivalry unable to refuse. Or a lady of a castle would offer him shelter for the night, and he would find out too late which bed she had in mind. Such things happened constantly to a knight on the road. Sooner or later the weakness of the flesh, his or another's, would catch him out.

And how could she complain? Viciously she crushed the red rose in her in hand. Could she protest if Lancelot went to another woman's bed, when Arthur came to hers as of right?

Arthur.

Every thought of Arthur was a burning pain. She longed to purge her heart of its hidden load. But Arthur must never know.

Especially now he was himself again, and restored to full health. Often now she felt his pressure on her hand at dinner, and saw the invitation in his eyes as they left the hall.

The Queen has joined the King in his apartments for the night – when it happened, the whole court shared the joyful news. The word ran like wildfire through the whole palace, from the guards on the battlements down to the ancient custodian of the treasury, drowsing deep in the heart of the living rock.

How then could she reproach Lancelot? Yet how could she not? *I love Arthur, but I do not choose to have his love,* her soul complained aloud. *If you betray me, Lancelot, it is your choice.*

And he would betray. She could see it with open eyes. Another body would soon tremble beneath his hands, other arms would enfold him, other legs open to admit him to their bliss.

No.

Yes.

A spasm gripped her, and the garden around her darkened and faded from sight. She saw the outline of a young woman half turning away, the curve of a rounded flank, the bloom of a pink and white cheek. Like her, the girl held a drooping rose in her hand. As Guenevere watched, the rose died, and one by one the petals dropped to the ground.

Is this my rival, Lancelot?

She came to herself with a sick, shuddering start. *How many women will waylay him now? How many will he yield to, and break my heart?*

She wanted to howl, to weep, to tear her hair. But a cold and dry-eyed certainty seized her heart. *I have been given a sight of what will be. I must betray him with Arthur, and he must betray me.*

CHAPTER 31

From the path below, they were part of the forest itself. Even seen close up, on the top of the ridge where they lay, the six or eight leafy mounds gave nothing away. All creatures of the woodland know how to make themselves invisible when they choose. Those lying in ambush were a part of the greenwood now.

But they were men too, and all men have to live. At the sound of hoofs, the foremost mound stirred and raised a watchful head. Travellers on the remote woodland track so late on a winter's day spelled plunder for the outlaw band, and nothing but ill fortune for themselves.

The leader swivelled his one good eye through the pile of leaf mould, and grinned at what he saw. Two young knights, richly clad, brothers by the look of them, always easy pickings, these soft sons of old lords. Brought up with every indulgence, equipped with the finest weapons, they never knew what real fighting was. But this pair of milksops would soon find out what their swords were for.

The leader prepared to give the signal for the attack. At his side his second-in-command lay poised to strike, and the men were all eager for the coming kill, snuffling for the taste of blood like winter wolves. It would be hard, he knew, to make them act cleanly, take the plunder, and get away. They were starting to show a dangerous preference for dragging out unlucky wayfarers' deaths.

The leader bared a mouthful of blackened stumps. No one but a madman enjoyed the work of death. And only one who truly wanted to die would linger in the place where he had killed.

His deputy stirred, and lightly touched his arm. The two young knights were almost below them now. Both were riding unguardedly on a loose rein, swinging their mailed feet to ease their tired legs. They had ridden long and hard, that was plain. All the easier to make short work of them.

He signalled, and the attackers slid down the slope as swift as snow in March. The knights were given no time to cry out before each was dragged from his horse, beaten and disarmed. Then they were brought before the leader with their hands bound, one bleeding freely from a cut above his eye, the other dazed and trembling from a cudgelling to the head.

'So, lads,' the leader sneered, 'and who are you?'

The two knights shared a glance before the taller replied. 'Sons of Sir Bernard of Astolat, lord of the manor by the marsh.'

'Names?'

'My brother is called Tirre, and my name is Lavain.'

'Knights, both of you.'

'Of course.'

' "Of course," ' mimicked the outlaw, with an ugly emphasis. He jerked his head at Tirre. 'And what's the matter with him? Can't he speak?'

The younger of the two answered with a trembling start, 'Believe me, you villain, I can and I will –'

'Hold on, brother.' Lavain kept his eye firmly on the leader as he spoke. 'We are in your hands, it seems. Let us discuss what can be done.'

'So!'

The leader advanced towards the horses that stood snorting and shying in the outlaws' hands. 'Good nags you've got here.' He grinned. 'Or did have, I should say. They're ours now.'

'Take them,' said Lavain, with an unconscious toss of the head. He looked at the outlaws' loamy rags, their wild eyes, pinched faces and starved mouths. 'Take the saddle-bags too. There's clothes and blankets, and some food in there. It's yours.'

He had spoken more out of charity than fear. But he had not calculated the effect of his careless chivalry on the desperate and deprived creatures all around.

'Who do you think you are?'

The deputy gripped his sword in his hands, moved forward,

and with great deliberation, spat in Lavain's face. A hoarse cheer broke from a handful of the men, and excitement sparked between them, one by one.

The leader felt a tightening round his heart. He had to exert his authority, and soon. Or else he, too, could face the fate that awaited the two young captives, a knife in the guts or the long, slow dance in the air.

Around them the night was gathering through the trees.

'What are we waiting for?' hissed the deputy. 'Let's kill them now!'

Tirre's eyes flared. 'Kill us? Why?'

Lavain lifted his head. 'Kill me, if you must,' he said quietly, 'but let my brother live. It will kill my father to lose his youngest son.'

'Then you'll all be together pretty soon.' The leader gave a coarse guffaw. 'Because you're dead men, you and your brother both. We're condemned already, so it's nothing to us how many more we kill. But we never leave a soul to tell the tale.' He nodded to his deputy. 'Get on with it, then. Hang them.'

'Hang yourself!'

With a wild scream, Tirre burst the rope that secured his hands, and twisted from his attackers' grasp. In an instant Lavain followed his brother's lead, though the ropes around his wrists held fast. Yet still he plunged and reared and kicked and fought, ducking out of the grasp of his captors like an eel.

In one inspired move, he succeeded in getting his back against Tirre's. Back to back, the two brothers fought nobly, but not for long. Both wounded, and one still bound, they were no matches for half a dozen brutes hungry for the kill. Within minutes a rain of furious blows had driven Lavain to his knees. Tirre was brought down by a cudgel in the stomach, and lay on the ground coughing blood.

You fools, thought the leader, with something like despair. I'd already given you the chance of a good clean death. Now the men will make your dying last for hours. Well, so be it. There's nothing can save you now.

Still, he'd give the order just the same. 'Hang them!' he said.

The deputy looked at him. 'They've had their fun,' he said. 'It's our turn now.'

The leader turned away. 'Hang them!' he shouted to the men.

All stared impassively. None moved to obey.

'You see?' said the deputy with interest, waving at the grinning ranks.

A dull fear fastened on the leader's heart. He had felt this moment coming for far too long. He rounded on his deputy, feeling for the cold comfort of his sword.

'Do you challenge me?' he barked.

The deputy stepped towards him, his arms hanging down, his own sword and dagger swinging lightly by his side.

'No,' he said easily.

'Good.' The leader felt an inward spurt of relief. He stuck his face into the deputy's as he approached, then glanced round the band. 'Let's hear it, then. Am I the leader here, or you?'

'I am.'

The unseen dagger flashed. The leader's eyes came to a pinpoint of pain, and blood frothed from his mouth. The deputy pulled the blade from his leader's heart, and watched the dark red stream as the dead man crumpled slowly to the ground. Nothing moved.

The deputy stirred the heap of rags on the ground with the toe of his boot. Then he advanced on Tirre and Lavain, his hands still dripping blood. His grin was terrible. 'Now then,' he said. 'Who's first?'

On the edge of the forest, thick pools of darkness gathered under every tree. Lancelot drew his horse to a halt and felt the beginnings of despair. Parting from Guenevere had surely been enough. Did he have to send Bors and Lionel away as well?

He shook his head. He knew only that travelling with his cousins had been more than he could bear. Each day he faced the growing sense that his love for Guenevere had blighted their lives too. And he did not know whether Bors's grim incomprehension, or Lionel's ready sympathy had been hardest to bear. In the end he had sent them away. They had left without protest, a clear sign that they, too, felt the misery they were in.

And now –

He drew a deep breath, and looked round without hope. Not

an inn or a castle for miles, nowhere for a stranger to rest his weary head. It was not wise, he knew, for a lone traveller to venture by night in the wood, but he did not care. There would be shelter under the trees, and some rest for his aching heart. He closed his heels on his horse's sides, and the willing beast moved off. 'Onward!' he whispered. 'On!'

The first he knew of the disturbance ahead was a faint sound or two reaching him through the dark. He slowed his pace, and eased his horse in the direction of the noise. In a clearing ahead he could see two young knights tied half-naked to a tree, their bodies covered in blood. Blood puddled around their feet from countless knife cuts to their chests and arms. Surrounding them were a pack of their tormentors, and even from a distance Lancelot could see their savage glee.

Keeping close to the side of the track, he progressed as silently as he could. The horse's hoofs made little sound on the grass above the raucous shouts and laughter of the men. Their attention was divided between their sport with the two young knights, and the spoil they had seized from the saddlebags. One cavorted in a shirt of silver mail taken from Lavain's back. Another was drawing Tirre's mailed gauntlets on and off with the delight of a child. But none of them noticed Lancelot in the gloaming till the great white horse came down on them with the force of an avenging ghost.

'Benoic! *A moi*, Benoic!'

Chanting the ancient battle cry of his house, Lancelot put the heavy horse into a gallop, and drew his sword. He swept into the clearing, swinging his sword like an axe, then using the point to stab this way and that. One outlaw fell like a stone, transfixed through the throat. A second dropped where he stood, his head almost severed from his neck.

'Every man for himself!' The outlaw band scattered screaming to the winds, with Lancelot in pursuit. Two of the fleeing band were brought down with blows to the head. Another crawled off into the undergrowth to die, a torrent of red spouting from his chest.

'God bless you, stranger!' croaked Tirre, his lips black with blood. Lancelot pulled his horse's head round in furious haste, and renewed his attack.

At last only the former deputy remained, standing his ground.

'Surrender, wretch!' cried Lancelot, from his horse. 'You are defeated, throw down your sword.'

'Not so, lord,' the outlaw replied, his eyes bright. 'There's no honour to you to kill a man on the ground. I challenge you to single combat, man to man.'

Lancelot nodded.

'Agreed.' He sheathed his sword, and prepared to dismount.

Lavain found his voice. 'Beware him, knight!' he called weakly, through a mouthful of blood. 'He killed his own leader treacherously without a fight. He'll do the same to you!'

As Lavain spoke, the outlaw sprang at Lancelot and stabbed him in the thigh. Then he threw both arms round Lancelot's waist, and dragged him to the ground. As he felt himself falling, Lancelot grabbed for his dagger, and struck straight and true. The blade found his attacker's throat, and severed the main artery in the neck. The outlaw died as his leader had, surprised by death.

Lancelot lay on the ground entangled in his dead adversary's limbs. Above him, the white flank of his horse was dark with the blood from his leg. Lancelot heaved himself up, and limped over to the tree to release Tirre and Lavain. Bloody and deathly cold, they stumbled out of their bonds.

'We owe you our lives,' said Tirre, weak with wonderment.

Lancelot waved his trembling thanks away. 'Any knight would have done the same.'

Lavain took his hand. 'What may we call you, sir?'

Lancelot hesitated. 'My name is nothing. And the life I led by that name is nothing but sadness to me now.' He frowned at them anxiously. 'Will you allow me to withhold it from you?'

The brothers exchanged a bruised smile of disbelief.

'Sir, we will deny you nothing in the world,' Lavain said earnestly. 'But you must not deny us this. Our father's house lies on the far side of the forest, not an hour from here. I beg you, be our guest for as long as you please to stay.'

Lancelot looked away. He did not know what to say.

'You must, sir,' Tirre ground out, between chattering teeth. He gestured towards Lancelot's bleeding thigh. 'If nothing else, you'll need treatment for that wound.'

Lavain looked at Lancelot with concern. 'The wretch who attacked you cut deeper than he knew.'

Lancelot nodded bleakly. The outlaw's knife had struck through to the bone. Infection would follow from the rusty blade, he was sure. Grimly he took the girdle from round his waist, pressed together the two edges of raw flesh, and bound up the wound.

'You'll come, sir, say you will?' Tirre's young face was full of hope. 'Our father will want to see the saviour of his sons.'

Lavain smiled. 'And our little sister will never forgive us if we let the hero who saved her brothers get away. Like all girls, she dreams of the knights of King Arthur's court, as I guess you must be. I beg you sir, to come.'

Lancelot bowed his head. The pain in his leg made it hard for him to speak. 'I must accept. But first let me get you some covering from the night air. You are sorely wounded too.'

Hastily they assembled their belongings, and retrieved what they needed from the forest floor. Concealing his own pain, Lancelot assisted the two injured knights to mount. With an effort that made him sweat in the bitter cold, he heaved himself on to his horse. Already he could feel the fever invading his bones.

'So, sirs!' he said, summoning up a cheerful smile. 'To your father's house, then?'

'We call it Astolat,' returned Lavain, with an answering smile.

'To Astolat,' beamed Tirre. 'Our father and sister will rejoice to see you, sir.'

The night settled on them like a sleeping thing. Slowly they picked their way down the forest path. All the light snufflings of the woodland soothed Lancelot as if he, too, were a forest creature going to his lair.

Ah, Guenevere, he mourned deep in his soul, you fear my adventuring will bring me other women, who will want me in their beds. But tonight I have saved two lives, and my only reward is to tell tales of knighthood to beguile a child. Lavain's little sister, the young maid of Astolat, will not let me off lightly, I know. But my faith to you will not be threatened by her.

Watching Lancelot carefully, Lavain took up his reins. His heart overflowed with joy. Wait, sister, see who's here, look who we've brought for you!

It was worth it, he decided, the outlaws' beating, the knife wounds, the attack. For years he had wanted to bring home a knight for Elaine. At last he could make her childhood wish come true.

And though he called her his little sister, she was a woman grown, and a fair one too. Perhaps this handsome knight might care for her? Weaving a gossamer tissue of hopes, Lavain allowed himself to dream.

CHAPTER 32

The two hooded figures trod carefully down the hill. The first snow of winter had clothed the island in white, and a mantle of ice had all but locked up the frozen waters of its inland sea. Brother Boniface raised his head and savoured the biting air. Ahead of them the sky was showing the first late signs of dawn, as the days ran down to the very depths of the year.

'Christmas on Avalon,' he breathed ecstatically. 'And this year for the first time we may celebrate in full. Could there be any greater blessing on our faith?'

'Perhaps.' The voice of his brother monk was dubious. To Giorgio, there was only one city in the world where Christ's day could properly be kept. Rome! The very thought was a stabbing pain. When would he see the City of God again?

'But we do good work here, brother, do we not?' Boniface asked anxiously, watching his companion's sallow face. 'We have done as we were ordered, won the Lady's favour, and gained permission for Christian worship on the Sacred Island. With each month we have made some small advance. Surely we fulfil God's will?'

'Perhaps,' Giorgio said again, indifferently. The warm olive bloom he had had when he arrived had left him, and his handsome face looked lifeless and grey. From October onwards, his hands and bare sandalled feet had been inflamed with chilblains, now cracked and bleeding painfully into the snow.

Onward, thought Boniface, onward in the name of the Lord. Aloud he said, 'The first Christmas on Avalon is a cause for joy in heaven. How many centuries has this been a pagan shrine? And now we can celebrate the birth of Our Lord in this place.'

He lifted his head and threw back his hood, careless of the cold gnawing at his ears.

'By next Christmas, brother,' he said jovially, 'we shall have a true congregation here, I do not doubt. A small one, to be sure, and mainly composed of women, for we can only work with what we have to hand. But St Paul himself did not disdain to work with females, even though they are God's lesser kind. He used them widely in the founding of the Church. So may we use these benighted women, and help them redeem the lower nature that God ordained for them. God's purpose will prevail.'

He looked around him with an expansive sigh. On all sides, a million tiny glimmers of the rising dawn had set the snow on fire. In the apple groves of the hillside below, the frost had made a delicate tracery on every branch, and the trees held up silvery fingers to the sky. Yet even now the faint scent of blossom lingered on the hill, and the white doves called from the shelter of the pines. This was a place of magic, Boniface acknowledged humbly, his soul aglow. And he and Giorgio were bringing it to the Lord.

Giorgio watched moodily out of the corner of his eye. Living in close confinement with the fair-faced, open-souled Boniface had taught the Italian to read his fellow-monk's every thought. He loves this place, and he feels the joy of the Lord, thought Giorgio. Whereas I pine for Rome, and the warm darkness behind the altar where Tomaso waits with his kisses like nectarines . . .

At once he felt ashamed. Resolutely he put away all his resentment of the burning cold, the torture of his poor bare sandalled feet, the deadness of the fingers huddled in his sleeves, and forced a smile. 'How shall we keep Christ's feast?'

'A fast on the eve, I think,' Boniface replied seriously, 'and a vigil all night, to remember the Virgin's pains. After that we should hold a High Mass for all who come.'

Giorgio could not keep the sourness from his soul. 'Who will come to Christ's Mass on Avalon?'

'One or two of the young maidens, to be sure,' said Boniface confidently. 'Those who have visited us for spiritual counsel over time. And a few of the Lake villagers too, that is my hope. Some of them seem ready to move out of their darkness into the light of God's day.'

'You think so?'

Giorgio had yet to see in the young maidens who visited their cell any signs of spiritual growth. He knew, even if Boniface did not, that the fair, blue-eyed youth and his dark companion with tawny skin were an intriguing challenge to these girls. To Goddess worshippers, men vowed to celibacy were merely men who had never known the love their Great One gave. The spirit, he feared, had little to do with it. It was their bodies these women were interested in.

As the so-called Great Whore herself was most definitely not, Giorgio mused. Since the hard-won audience with the Lady of the Lake, neither of them had seen her again. If their two holy fathers, plotting from London and Rome, had expected the Lady to take either of them to her bed, they had never been more wrong. Yet the old always love to blame the young. In the eyes of London and Rome, Giorgio knew that he and Boniface had failed.

And Giorgio saw, too, that Boniface had no idea of this. His hopes for the Sacred Island did not end with Christ's Mass. He saw himself on Avalon till the end of his life, winning souls for God. Plans for the coming feast and for the years ahead tumbled from his lips as they walked along. Giorgio had to nudge him to draw his attention to a figure coming down the path.

Stepping firmly towards them through the snow was Nemue, the chief maiden of Avalon and the Lady's closest aide. Like her mistress, she wore only light drifting robes, and though her head was covered, her arms were bare. She must have some enchantment against the cold. And how old was she? Giorgio wondered, for the thousandth time. He would go on wondering, he knew, for Nemue's small, secret face gave nothing away.

'Greetings,' she said shortly. Her voice was like the croak of the night-fowl on the marsh. 'You go to the jetty too?'

They looked at her in surprise. 'No, lady, why?' said Boniface, with sudden concern.

In reply she pointed to the edge of the lake below. At the foot of the Tor, the grass sloped down to a stone-built causeway protruding out into the frozen water like a monster of the deep, drowsing half-submerged. Tying up at the jetty as Nemue spoke was one of the shallow Lake boats that plied to and fro between the island and the countryside around. Today, only the goodwill of the boatmen had brought it through the frozen mere. In a matter of hours, Avalon would be locked in ice.

Disembarking from the boat were two men in black gowns. 'Monks of our order?' Boniface gasped.

'You did not know?' The sound of Nemue's voice at his elbow was half a laugh, half a sigh.

'What are they doing here?' cried Boniface.

His pale skin had taken on a flush of distress. He set off running down to the jetty as he spoke.

Giorgio followed him as fast as he dared. Could it be – ? He wanted to laugh and cheer, to do cartwheels in the snow. But getting safely down the frozen slope was the main task now.

'Hail, brothers!' Boniface cried as he approached, raising his hand. There was no answering salutation from the dock. Instead they met the hard-faced stare of two older men.

'You're Boniface? We're here to take your place,' said the taller one abruptly, as they came up. His lean, unpleasant face was set in an attitude of cold disregard, and his small pale eyes looked out of a deep well of contempt within. Reaching into his baggage, he retrieved a scroll, and pressed it into Boniface's hand.

'Orders from the Father Abbot in London. You're relieved of the mission here, and sent back right away. You,' he nodded to Giorgio, and gestured to the boat, 'you're to go with him back to London, then on to your church in Rome. The Lake's freezing, but you'll get out today.'

Rome! Giorgio burst into floods of ecstatic tears. Now he would see Tomaso and the city of his heart once again. There was nothing here to hold them back. They would be packed and gone within an hour.

'Joy to you!' he wept.

Beside him Boniface stood dry-eyed, numb with shock. 'Who are you?' he mouthed.

The tall monk moved his mouth into a smile. 'I'm Brother Sylvester, and this is Iachimo.'

The monk beside him nodded with an empty grin. Short and squat, he had a coarse, hostile air, and a deep scar marked his bare tonsured head. He pointed to his colleague. 'Syl-vester,' he said. He turned the mocking finger towards himself. 'Ia-chi-mo,' he repeated, lingering on each sound.

Boniface flushed, but tried to smile. 'Well, brothers, we surely do not need to leave today. If you're coming to join us, you'll need our help and guidance here. We have done much –'

'But alas, not enough.' Sylvester's cold voice cut through the desperate plea. 'Read your orders, friend.' He widened his eyes unpleasantly. 'They do not come from me. Like you, I am only God's messenger in this place. And the message is – you leave.'

Boniface gasped. Grief overwhelmed him, and he could not speak.

'Say no more,' came Nemue's voice from behind. 'The Lady has seen it written in the stars. Your time here is at an end.'

Her sigh sounded through Avalon and beyond. Its echo reached the two young monks through the glistening air. Boniface stood still. Before him stretched the white expanse of the frozen Lake, its surface broken with ragged clumps of frost-encrusted reeds. High overhead the starving marsh-fowl mourned in the thin air, while a few searched hopelessly for food along the ice. And suddenly Boniface knew that he, too, was doomed to fly away from Avalon, and starve for ever like the birds, eternally grieving for what he had lost.

CHAPTER 33

'Not far now, sir. Hold on, if you can.'

The night was very dark under the trees. The air was thick with mist, and the weary horses stumbled over every stone. At the start of the ride, the fresh wet stink of his blood rose up to choke Lancelot with every breath he took. Before long he lost all feeling in his leg. Then as time went by, the jolting of his horse opened up the wound, and the pain and the blood both began again.

At least it stopped him thinking of Guenevere. He took off the blood-soaked girdle binding his thigh, and made it into a tourniquet, twisting his dagger in the knot to tighten it. But the blood ran again despite the ligature, and he could feel his life ebbing away.

'Not far now to our father's house, good sir, hold on.'

'Look out for a lantern shining through the trees. Our sister will be waiting to light our way home.'

Sir Lancelot sighed. Who were these voices? Not men he knew. Was that a lamp ahead, or a will-o'-the-wisp?

He thought he saw the dark shape of a dwelling through the mist. The horses drew up at the door of a rambling grange. Beneath a mossy stone porch, a low door stood open, and a warm light spilled out from within. But the pain in his leg had now invaded his brain. And with the fever beginning to burn its way through his bones, he hardly believed what he saw by the light of the lamp.

A soft face, pink and white, with trusting eyes and smooth round girlish cheeks. A heartfelt smile of welcome, shadowing at once to shock. Quick tears of anger as she saw her brothers bleeding and in distress. A fall of thick fair hair as she turned her head at the sight of him.

He caught his breath. 'You are – ?'

She brushed past his stirrup in her haste to get to Sir Lavain. 'Elaine of Astolat, sir.'

Lancelot did not move. This was Elaine? The little sister he had thought must be a child? She was a woman grown. Her body was small but shapely, and her rounded breasts moved freely beneath her gown as she reached up to Lavain. Lancelot looked away. His fading mind struggled with a new pain. Would he have come if he had known she was a young woman, and lovely too? Would Guenevere hear of this, and think he had betrayed her as soon as he left court?

He groaned with pain. Guenevere doubted him, he knew for sure. He knew, too, that he must never give her cause, or her green-eyed jealousy would eat them both alive. Yet now they had parted, was he condemned to be faithful to a memory, exiled for ever from the joy of women's love? The sight of the girl's shining hair tormented him, the movements of her body cut him to the quick. The thought came before he could check himself: If this were Guenevere now, warm, loving, *free* . . .

'Sons!'

Behind the young woman came an old man, white-haired and richly dressed. He hastened forward to embrace his sons in tears of grief and joy. A moment later he was standing at Lancelot's stirrup, his hand on his arm.

'Sir, you are dearly welcome here in Astolat. I am Sir Bernard of the Grange, and this is my daughter Elaine. My sons tell me that you saved their lives. Allow us to welcome you to our hearth and home.'

The old man bowed to the ground.

'No, no, sir.'

Sir Lancelot shook his head. The young should salute the old, not the other way round. He must dismount to return the courtesy. But as he threw back his injured leg to vault off, he fell forward over the horse's neck, and crumpled to the ground.

Then came a long time of sleep, and waking sleep. For a time he thought he had died, and felt no grief. His spirit left his body and roamed at will, riding the winds and walking among the stars.

Guenevere came to him there, clad all in starlight, shining in white and gold. The stars leaped up to greet her in flaming bursts of fire and ice. But nothing in that vast, glittering void was as bright as her eyes, and her smile lit the cold vault of the sky. He stood holding his soul in his hands, and she stretched out her arms and folded him in her embrace. Her lips touched his face, and her kiss soothed all his grief. Her fingertips brushed his eyelids as she said, 'No tears, my love.'

When he awoke, he could taste salt on his lips, and knew he had been weeping for hours. He knew, too, that he had not been alone. A presence, a faint scent still lingered in the air. His unknown guardian had withdrawn as soon as he stirred to allow him to recover himself unobserved. Whoever it was, he blessed her thoughtfulness. And he found himself wishing that the rosy presence would return.

Slowly he turned his head. He lay in a well-sized room with a vaulted ceiling and whitewashed walls. From the distant noises of life below, he judged his sick-room was at the top of the house. When he had first arrived and seen the low, rambling, ivy-covered front, he had taken the old grange for a place of peace, never meant to be defended in time of war. But this high, stone-built round chamber could withstand a siege. The thought gave him deep comfort, even though he knew there was no fear of attack. Puzzling over conundrums like these ate up his days.

He was at peace then, though he knew he was very ill. The infection he feared came soon, and gripped him hard. His body was jerked by strong internal strings, and his head rang with the chattering of his teeth. Grey heads and long beards came into his vision and departed again, grave voices debated when they thought he could not hear.

'The wound is festering. Could the rogues in the forest have envenomed their blades?'

'What venom would they need, doctor, living like rats in their own poisoned dung?'

'True, but the fever he suffers is more than a rat-borne plague.'

'We'll bleed him, of course, to bring the fever down.'

'You leech-men have no other remedy! With what he's lost, his veins must be empty now.'

'Wine, then, to renew his blood. And more blankets, tell the Lady Elaine. He must not get cold.'

And then a young woman's voice, soft and sad. 'But he's burning, sir, scorching all over his skin. And his wits are wandering enough without giving him wine.'

'Madam, are we the doctors here, or you? More wine and more coverings, straight away.'

Every time he felt better, they came and bled him again and made him as weak as a girl. They searched his wound too, scouring deep into the suffering flesh whenever he thought it was beginning to heal. And every time they came, there was her hand in his hand, her voice at his elbow, low and controlled, but feeling with him pain for pain.

'Hold on, sir, hold on –'

Time passed without reckoning as he lay and watched the sun's fading scrawl on the plain white walls. One by one the days dwindled down to the shortest day, the dead heart of the year. Down in the house he could hear the celebrations for the mid-winter feast, and the men from the fields laughing and shouting as they dragged the Yule log in. On the night the year turned, his spirit left his body, and drifted through the grange when all the merry revellers were asleep.

He saw the old hall hung with ivy and holly, the evergreen symbols of the Mother with Her promise of new life. He remembered the great balls of mistletoe swinging from every beam in Camelot at this time of the year, and saw Guenevere standing beneath one of them alone, her head bowed, her face veiled. Then he thought of the girl who was tending him here at the grange, and wondered who her lover was, who would press her body to his beneath the golden mistletoe ball. A fair rose like her must be the pride of some lusty young lord. A wisp of longing passed into his wandering brain: how sweet it would be to walk with her in a summer garden under the kiss of the sun. Then he thought of Guenevere, and turned his face to the wall.

All through January, he felt his strength return, step by step with the lengthening days. At Imbolc, the storms of February battered his tower room, and he feared the Dark Mother had come to take him home. But his nurse and guardian filled his room with light, to drive the dark away. All night she sat with him, tending the candles, not letting one burn out. After that, he knew that he would live.

'So, sir, are you feeling better now?' she said to him one day, on a rising note of hope, as a leaden dawn broke through a pewter sky. For no reason that he knew, her round apple cheeks, her innocent gaze, the catch in her throat filled him with unimagined pain.

'How old are you?' he said.

'Almost twenty, sir,' she said with the sweet importance of a child.

He turned his head away. Had he or Guenevere ever been that young?

'So, sir, our sister tells us you are doing well.'

Lavain and Tirre came to see him every day, at first with sad faces like the doctors', then with increasing hope. Their own wounds kept them tied to the grange until midwinter and beyond, and even when they could ride out again and hunt, not a day passed but they remembered him.

But it was Elaine who cared for him hour by hour. She was a stranger to his body, since the doctors dressed his wound and her brothers' menservants washed and tended him. Yet her hands arranged his pillows and turned down his lamp, her devotion coaxed down the sour red wine needed for his blood. Her voice read to him, talked to him, prayed for him, and at last rejoiced with him as his strength returned.

'I think he might take the air,' pronounced the oldest of the doctors one sweet day in May. With glowing eyes, Elaine oversaw her brothers as they carried him outside, and settled him in a chair. Almost bursting with pride, she spread her small plump hands and gestured around.

'Well, sir?' she dimpled.

At the back of the grange, a green lawn ran down to a broad river rolling by. As far as the eye could see, great oaks and willows traced its winding course. Buttercups and daisies rioted over the fields beyond, and the scent of new-mown grass hung in the air. At the water's edge, a large, flat-bottomed barge floated in the sun, tied up to a wooden pier.

'Astolat is beautiful,' Lancelot said.

'Thank you, sir!'

Lavain, Elaine and Tirre hung around him, laughing and excited like children at play. The air warmed his wasted limbs, and the breeze off the river felt like a lover's kiss. I should be happy now, Lancelot told himself. Then the next thought was, *Guenevere* –

'Sir?'

He forced himself to follow Tirre's pointing hand.

'We call that Elaine's river,' said Tirre with a mischievous glance. He gestured towards the dark waters flowing by. 'Since she was a child, she always said she would take the barge, and float down the river one day.'

'Why so?' asked Lancelot politely.

'Oh, Tirre!' protested Elaine. The pink and white had risen to her face, and she was laughing and confused.

'Because it goes down to Camelot, where the knights and ladies are.' Tirre gave a wicked laugh. 'And she always wanted a knight of her very own.'

'As do all fair ladies,' said Lancelot courteously. 'And one of the fairest, as your sister is, may expect one of the finest knights.'

Too late he saw the brothers exchange a glance, and Elaine's confusion deepen to a rosy blush. A shaft of guilt and distress went through his heart. He had not meant – surely she could not think –

A moment later she was bright-eyed and fluttering as her father drew near.

'News, sons!' cried Sir Bernard, brandishing a scroll as he approached. 'There's to be a great tournament in the Humberlands, on the far side of the wolds.' He smiled at Sir Lancelot. 'And if our guest continues to recover his strength, you might all make up a party to ride there for the sport.'

Elaine smiled, and blushed, and smiled again. 'You will, sir, won't you?' she murmured earnestly. 'A tournament will be fine exercise when you're well.'

'Lady . . .' he murmured, at a loss.

'At least you'll stay until you're better again.'

Lancelot bowed his head in mute acknowledgement. 'If you say so,' he said at last.

She looked at him, huge-eyed, and laid her hand on his arm.

'You can't leave us now,' she said happily. And once more he was pierced with a sadness he could not explain.

He knew then that she loved him, and realised too that he had known it all along. Yet how could she love a knight who had no name? Her father, her brothers too, would never countenance a man from nowhere, a soul in flight. A man who would not, could not say who he was, perhaps a wastrel, an outlaw, or worse. Sir Bernard would never throw away his cherished only daughter on a passing fancy for a knight of the road.

And he knew in his heart that he had not encouraged her. True, he had noticed the gleaming curtain of fair hair, and the trusting, blue-eyed gaze, as sweet as a child's. He admired her lissom body as she moved, saw the woman in her calling out to him, and smelt the petal fragrance of her skin. Her innocent freshness revived his battered heart, and she made him feel both wise and young again.

Yet none of it meant anything to him. She was not Guenevere.

Guenevere –

The thought of her raged worse than any fever, and cut deeper than his pain. They had been so dear to one another, dearer than life. Did she hate him for his love, then, to cast him off like this and send him away?

Yet perhaps she was right, to try to avoid more pain. She wanted to live in honour, and make sure that he could live so too.

How true she is, his thoughts tormented him.

How loyal to Arthur, how loving –

– to him, but not to me –

He forced the thought away.

Guenevere.

She was his lady.

He was her knight.

Whatever she did, nothing could alter that. He could not love Elaine. His heart, his mind, his soul were all elsewhere, given to Guenevere before time began. He had made no advances to Elaine, and he would make none. The girl and her family must see that now.

So when she came and asked him for a favour, he was quite unprepared.

'Whatever lies in my power, lady,' he answered absently.

Too late he saw the pearl-encrusted gauze crushed in her hands. She looked him in the eye as she passed him the scarf.

'Wear my favour at the tournament, sir, when you go to the Humberlands,' she said steadily. 'Then all the world will know you fight for Elaine of Astolat.'

CHAPTER 34

With the sun at his back, Merlin watched his shadow moving ahead of him along the narrow way. Idly he played with it, amusing himself by making it swell up like a puff-adder, then rear and sting. In the long journey south from the Orkneys, he had needed many diversions such as this. He paused. Of course, he must never forget that Madam Morgan was no mean shape-shifter too. And there was nothing to compare with the venom of her sting.

Morgan.

His silver-gilt eyes flared and turned the colour of blood. Morgan was playing with him, he knew that now. Now, if ever, he needed to be Merlin the hawk, and fly above the game. For he could not abandon the hunt for the child.

Child no longer, old fool, Merlin reminded himself with scorn. Old enough now to be a page in a noble house. Without that boyhood training in chivalry, he could never become a squire, and then a knight. And Morgan must want that for a boy born to be king.

Merlin groaned, feeling his thoughts begin to run like rats in their tracks. Many great houses took in young boys as pages. After leaving the court of Queen Morgause, he had moved down the map like a mole, working through them one by one. Why did he still not know where Mordred could be?

He bunched his fist, and shook it at the sky. When he had had to place Arthur for his knighthood training, he had known all the lords and all their lands and estates, the length and breadth of the isles. That was thirty years ago, he admitted grudgingly, so most of them would be dead and gone by now. But some of them kept going, these knight-masters of young lads. Old Sir Ector, Arthur's foster-father, was still training knights the last time he had sent greetings to Arthur's court.

Sir Ector – Merlin's scowl softened into a frown. There was none like him for bringing up a boy. Most lords took pages, or squires, or young knights for training at that one stage. Only Sir Ector could steer a boy's course through all three.

Merlin snarled. Not that Madam Morgan would place her son with him. Arthur's foster-father would be the last man she would choose. No, she would try to keep Mordred as far away from Arthur as she could. Which was why Merlin had renewed hopes of the place he was coming to now.

For the Castle Fils de Dame was, indeed, far away. Buried as it was in the heart of Listinoise, Merlin might have overlooked it on his journey south. But passing through the neighbouring kingdom of Gore, he had heard of a Sir Dorward and his mother who lived there. They kept a school for pages which, although small, was admired for miles around.

So he had skirted the land of Terre Foraine, Listinoise's neighbour to the north. With a glad heart, it had to be said, for there was nothing for a Lord of All-Power there. A spasm of disgust clenched Merlin's gut. Who would have thought that King Pelles, the King of Terre Foraine, was blood brother to the good old King Pellinore, Arthur's truest friend? While he lived, Pellinore had ruled Listinoise in the love of all faiths, while the fanatical Pelles insisted his subjects follow only one. Terre Foraine was indeed foreign terrain to those who did not cleave to the God from the east. Merlin shuddered. The Christians had their hooks in King Pelles, body and soul.

But at least he knew for sure that Mordred would not be there. Morgan would never allow a Christian to rear her son. On to Listinoise, then, and the Castle Fils de Dame.

Fils de Dame, yes –

A little wintry cheer crept round Merlin's heart. It was foolish to place any meaning on the name, he knew. Many places were called after ladies, and Morgan was far from being the only lady with a son. But one thing did kindle a fragile flame of hope. The knight of the castle, Sir Dorward, he was told, had been born in these parts. But his mother, who cared for the boys, was from far away. Once, long ago, she came from Tintagel on the kingdom of Cornwall's wild north-western shore. As did Arthur's mother Queen Igraine, and Igraine's daughter Dame Morgan herself.

The mule plodded on. The sun sank through the trees, and the forest prepared for night. Those caught within its shelter would have warm leaf-mould for their bed, and countless bright-eyed companions if they chose. Merlin had no fear as he unpacked his bedroll, and lay down to sleep. On the road like this, he slept outdoors more often than in, when he ran out of time in the unforgiving day.

But the lady on horseback emerging from the skirts of the forest miles ahead had no trouble reaching the castle before darkness fell. Veiled all in black, and riding a sure-footed black horse, she pressed on steadily through the failing light. At last she came down to the clearing where the castle stood, and was spotted at once by the guard. The gates opened for her in the glimmering dusk, and she vanished within.

The next morning Merlin arose in high content. A night in the woodland raised his spirits like nothing else. With slow deliberation he donned his gold rings and earrings, his crown of power, and his finest gown. He must be Merlin the royal bard to meet Mordred, not the mad old man of the road who travelled unnoticed elsewhere. His careful grooming took a little time. Then refreshed with a handful of acorns and a few draughts from a nearby spring, he was on his way as dawn suffused the sky.

Above the trees, blue-black and grey gave way to red and pink in bursts of colour washing across the sky. Admiring the Goddess's flaming artistry brought Merlin many miles along his path. The day wore on. At last he could see the castle through the trees. Low and welcoming, with two short round towers on either side of the gate, the Castle Fils de Dame stood in its clearing exactly as Morgan had shown it to him so many moons ago.

And now, as then, a clutch of small boys stood in the gateway under the central arch. Was he there? Merlin craned forward frantically in the hopes of catching a blue-black head, an Otherworldly glance. But as he watched, the boys were herded away under the care of a maid. A tall knight stood and fondly watched them go.

'Sir! Good sir!'

Merlin spurred his mule into a furious trot.

The knight turned to greet him across the clearing in the wood. 'Good day to you, stranger,' he called.

'And to you,' Merlin called back, hurrying on. As he drew near, he saw the knight take note of his coronet, his rich garb, and the wand in his hand, and watched recognition dawning on the stranger's face.

'You are Merlin, sir,' he said respectfully. He bowed. 'Our house is honoured to have your presence here.'

'Many thanks, many thanks,' cried Merlin, struggling to keep his impatience within bounds. 'I am glad to be here, sir.' He jumped down from his mule. 'And you are – ?'

The knight gave a rueful smile. He was a rumpled soul of thirty-odd years, with a manner both boyish and schoolmasterly by turns. Tall and thin, he had an engaging unawareness of the hair sticking up at the back of his head, and the ink-stains on his hands. His blue tunic had seen better days, and his sword and dagger were well made but archaic, the fine weapons of a former time. But he came forward with great courtesy, and his smile had a rare sweetness and honesty combined. Yes, Merlin thought with rising excitement, this is just the man Morgan would choose to rear her son.

'I am Dorward, sir,' the knight said gently. 'My mother and I keep a small college here.'

'To train boys as pages?'

Sir Dorward smiled. 'If their parents wish. We try to balance the skills of sword and pen, in the hope that some will go on to be poets and scholars too. Then they learn horsemanship, and all the skills of the ring. And my mother is a harpist, as many Cornish-women are. So the boys learn music and singing at her knee.'

He broke off with a laugh. 'But you must meet her yourself,' he said eagerly. 'Come in, Lord Merlin, and take some refreshment here. You'll dine with us, of course. How long can we persuade you to stay?'

He was ushering Merlin in through the gates as he spoke, and through the nearest archway within the court. A short flight of steps led up to a low wooden door, and Sir Dorward knocked, calling a greeting, and plunged in.

As he opened the door, Merlin caught the plangent strains of a harp dying away. They entered a sunny apartment bright with fires and flowers. In the low but well-sized room, a lady sat at a great golden harp, with a number of small boys clustering close around. She wore a rich but old-fashioned gown of silvery velvet with a train of gold, and a tall headdress graced her finely shaped head. But Merlin scarcely threw a glance her way. His eyes fastened hungrily on the boys with one silent cry: *Are you here, Mordred, are you here?*

Alarmed at the interruption, the boys stood wide-eyed and open-mouthed, like fledglings in a nest. They were all dressed alike in Sir Dorward's royal blue, and all had the same round heads, chubby cheeks, and downy skin. Merlin's eyes swivelled madly from face to face, then he turned away. Turnip-heads, dimwits, every one, not a prince to be seen – *yet he must be here!*

Dimly he was aware that Sir Dorward was performing introductions with all the chivalry of a royal court.

'So, madam, I trust you will forgive our interrupting now. Lord Merlin, this is my mother, the Lady Clariva.'

Merlin forced himself to bow and kiss the proffered hand. Its owner was Cornish through and through, he noted silently, taking in the blue-grey eyes, the dark hair and delicate skin, and the tall, poised body so like Queen Igraine's. When she spoke, her voice had the same sea-washed sound as the surf round Tintagel rock.

'So, Lord Merlin, what brings you here?'

He could not dissimulate before her clear-eyed stare. 'A boy,' he said abruptly.

Lady Clariva laughed happily. 'We have many here, around twenty at a time. Of course, they come and go.'

Dorward reached out to pat the nearest curly head. 'We keep them till they're seven or eight as a rule. Then they go from here to train to be young squires.'

Seven or eight. Merlin heaved a sigh of joy. Mordred would still be here.

'So which of our boys do you seek?' probed Lady Clariva, in gentle puzzlement.

Merlin took his heart into his hands. 'A child called Mordred.'

'Ah, Mordred!' Sir Dorward's face was aglow. 'If only all our boys were like Mordred! He's a most unusual child.'

Hungrily Merlin pounced on Dorward's praise. 'Good, is he?'

'At everything.' Sir Dorward turned to Lady Clariva. 'Remember when he knew all his letters as soon as we taught him to read? And how every pony he had would always go for him, mile after mile, even if it wasn't the best of the bunch?' He gave a wistful smile. 'He was the best boy we ever had.'

Lady Clariva returned her son's smile. 'He could sing any note I played when he'd heard it once. His ear for a melody was remarkable –'

'Madam, you say "was".' Cold shafts of fear were piercing Merlin to the root. '*Is he no more?*'

A burst of laughter answered his demand. 'Mordred lives and thrives!' Sir Dorward chuckled. 'Why should he not?'

Merlin shook his head, wild with relief. 'No reason. Only the fears of his kinsman, who's an old fool!'

'Oh, so?' queried Lady Clariva with interest.

'He and I are both Pendragon born,' Merlin proclaimed, with fierce pride. 'He's destined for great things.'

Sir Dorward beamed. 'Then you'll rejoice to know that his mother thinks so too. It's a great shame you missed them both, good sir. He's progressed so fast that she came to take him away. They only left a few hours ago – just before you arrived.'

CHAPTER 35

Patrise hurried down to the courtyard, his soul on fire.
'Your brother's back, sir,' the wide-eyed page had gasped, breathless with running from the outer gate. 'Back safe, not a mark on him, and in triumph too!'

Mador back? Patrise leaped for joy, punching the air as he ran along. The sun was on his face, and the ripe tang of late summer scented the air. The lower court was thronged with horses, men and wagons, as the servants laboured to get the harvest in. Never had a day seemed more beautiful.

'Patrise!'

'Mador!'

And there he was, vaulting lightly from his horse, looking thinner and taller, Patrise thought, with a pang, than when he went away. He was wearing a fine russet cloak Patrise had not seen before, and his gleaming gauntlets looked new and costly, like a lady's gift. His face, his whole body had hardened, and there was a light of wary appraisal in his eyes. Still, some changes were only to be expected, Patrise told himself loyally, after so long.

'Welcome back, brother!' he cried, folding Mador in his arms. He closed his eyes and blinked away the rising tears. 'Gods above! It's good to see you again!'

'It's been too long, brother,' Mador breathed joyfully, hugging Patrise hard. He stepped back and took a breath to compose himself. 'But I have not wasted my time on this quest. The lady I rescued was lavish in her reward. This winter our mother will live like a lady again, without fear of cold and want.'

Patrise gasped with delight. 'She gave you gold?'

Mador laughed with an assurance Patrise had not seen before. 'And more.' He cocked his head to one side, and gave a knowing smile. 'You remember her sister, who came to the King for help? The girl who wanted Sir Lancelot for her knight?'

'Of course.' The memory of the girl's open disappointment with Mador annoyed Patrise even now.

'Well, by the end, she had quite changed her mind,' said Mador, with an unconscious lift of the head. 'And when I dispatched the rogue knight and released her sister from her castle, she liked me even more. But the lady of the castle had first claim on me.' He grinned broadly, and flourished the chestnut-coloured leather gauntlets. 'She loaded me with gifts. She even wanted to marry me. I could be lord of all her lands by now. A fertile estate, it was, and she's a fine lady too.'

'Brother!' Patrise gazed at him, almost speechless with delight. 'You didn't –?'

'No, I didn't.' Mador's aplomb fell away from him like a cloud. He sighed. 'She was lovely, truly she was. But . . .'

He bit his lip and turned his head away.

But she was not Guenevere, thought Patrise, with a shaft of burning love. There is only one Guenevere, and she is here.

'Come, brother,' he said fondly, 'let me bring you to the Queen.'

All through the castle, servants scurried to keep pace with their knights and lords.

'He's back, Sir Mador's back!'

'And Sir Gawain, he's returned from his quest too. The King's called the whole court into the Great Hall to hear their tales. Gods and Great Ones, what a fuss!'

'The Queen wants fires in there, I dunno why. It's only September, it's not cold at all.'

'Just you run and light those fires, my lad. The Queen doesn't have to ask you what you think!'

In the knights' quarters, Gaheris and Gareth tumbled through the door of the chamber they shared with Agravain, both talking at once.

'He's back, Gawain's back!'

Lying on his bed, where he had been deep in his own dark

thoughts, Agravain froze. 'What are you talking about?'

Gareth laughed. 'Don't look so black, Agravain, it's the truth!'

'He's right,' Gaheris put in eagerly. 'We heard it at the stables, now, as we rode in. We're going to his quarters to greet him. Want to come?'

Gareth's baby-blue eyes were beaming with delight. 'And then the King and Queen have commanded us all to the Great Hall.'

Agravain's mouth seemed to be stuffed with cloth. 'I don't – I won't –'

Two brotherly voices laughed in unison. 'No excuses, Agravain. Face it, you couldn't lord it over us for ever. Gawain had to come back one day. And now he's here!'

High on her throne, Guenevere watched the fire in the hall, and counted the dancing flames. *Red and gold,* she thought, *the colours of love. How long have I lived without love, since Lancelot went away?*

No, not without love.

He still loves me, wherever he is. I know.

And she did not need to look at the man at her side to know that Arthur loved her too. She had found it in her heart to feel for him in return, and there had been times of gentle care and warmth. Arthur's tears of joy when he found himself once more a man had made her weep as she never wept before. In these healing waters, something was restored.

Now Arthur had recovered, and the land and the kingdom were safe. Guenevere nodded with a distant sense of a hard task done. She had learned to survive without Lancelot, without sight or hope of him, or even the mention of his name. She had lived with dignity, and kept her sufferings in the silence of her soul.

As she must do now. With an effort she switched her mind back to Sir Mador as he stood before the dais, his brother Patrise glowing proudly by his side.

Mador had changed, that was plain. The young knight still bore the dust and grime of the road, but a new nobility hung on him like a cloak. To his left stood Sir Gawain, with his three massive brothers, their great legs straddling the flagstones, forming a guard of honour as the King's kin. Nearby Sir Kay, Sir

Bedivere and Sir Lucan waited beside Arthur's throne. On all sides, smiling ladies nodded and whispered to their knights, while old lords, monks and courtiers looked on. Guenevere nodded. Yes, it was well. A full court had turned out to welcome the heroes home.

'So you triumphed, Mador?' Arthur leaned forward eagerly, absorbed in Mador's tale. 'You set the lady free? And the rogue knight is dead?'

'He is, my lord.' Mador was very pale. 'I would have spared his life, if he had agreed to trouble her no more. But he challenged me to the death. I had no choice.'

Arthur waved his hand. 'Think no more of it,' he ordered. 'Ravishing a lady carries pain of death. His life was already forfeit to the law. And this knight had many other crimes to answer for, it seems.'

He paused. 'Sir Mador, you did well.'

The sun glinted on his coronet, and turned his hair to gold. He turned to Guenevere, and took her hand. 'As I am sure my Queen will say.'

The Queen.

Mador fixed eyes of adoration on Guenevere, and reverently drank her in. That gown, the very colour of a summer night – did she know how it deepened the twilight in her eyes, and brought out the starshine in her hair? And that wisp of gossamer round her head and neck, as soft as her skin, as fragile as her smile –

Guenevere –

He shook his head, and marvelled to himself. Every night he was away he had prayed to her image before he slept, calling up every detail of her face with the eye of love. How could he have forgotten the quick toss of her head, the full-lidded, shadowy gaze, the thousand tiny movements of her mouth?

So full, so red her lips, so white her skin – why did she look so forlorn? His soul yearned for her, and his spirit almost left his body as she spoke.

'Sir Mador, you have upheld the honour of a knight, and of your fellowship too. The Round Table is proud to call you one of its own.'

What rot she spoke, what lying rot it was!

Festering with fury, Agravain kept his face expressionless and did his best to drown out Guenevere's voice. How dared she stand there in that dismal gown, torturing men's ears?

Slowly, furiously, he reviled his Gods. Why do you cast me down, his soul wailed in torment, and glorify these great fools over me? Mador back in triumph, and Gawain too? His every muscle knotted in revolt. I must act! he howled in silence. Gods above, I must fight for myself, if you will not fight for me!

Agravain looks sick, Guenevere noticed, with unease. *How ugly that yellow flush is on his dark face.* Was it the heat in the hall? Restlessly she loosened the veil at her neck. Perhaps she should not have ordered the fires to be lit when the afternoon was so warm. But Agravain always made her feel like this. She was burning now, if she let herself look at him.

And Mador, too, was not as he was before. There was a change in him, a harder edge. What was it the old warriors used to say? *The man who has never killed remains a virgin all his life.*

Sadness descended on Guenevere like a cloud. When he beat Agravain at the tournament, Mador could not kill, even though Agravain braved him out and well deserved the sword.

And now –

Guenevere looked into the grey eyes raised to hers, and read their depths. *So, Mador, this quest has cost you your soul's virginity.*

And your body's? Did you lie with a woman too?

She thought of the girl who had come to seek his help, with her wet eyes, her ample, pear-shaped breasts, her bedroom smile. Then she caught herself up in a spasm of disgust. *Goddess, Mother, what is this to me?*

'Sir Mador!' She gave him her hand with a luminous smile. 'Bless you,' she breathed.

'My lady –'

Mador trembled from head to foot. From the core of his being, one name, one sensation pulsed out like the waves of the sea. Guenevere touched me, his soul chanted, the Queen touched me, Guenevere the Queen –

Fools, all sentimental fools! Agravain seethed. How could he bear it? It was more than blood and bone could endure. He watched in mounting despair as Arthur raised his hand, and Gawain stepped forward with a preparatory cough. Gawain's turn now, spare us! Watch him start boasting, and delight the King.

'My lord.'

Gawain moved expansively towards the throne, tossing back his travel-stained cloak. His great chest was emblazoned with the black bull of the Orkneys, and his red tunic and breeches were edged in black and gold. His broad face was wreathed in smiles, and his small blue eyes were lost in the joyful creases of reunion.

'Sir Gawain!' Arthur chuckled knowingly, as the big knight approached the dais. 'Did your quest end like Sir Mador's, with a lovely lady in your debt?'

'Not mine, my lord.' Gawain's beefy face was creased with mischievous delight. He rubbed his massive hands. 'But I have news that you would least expect!'

'Another knight, adventuring with a lady? A knight of mine?' Arthur leaned forward, his eyes alight.

'Aha!' said Gawain, revelling in his tale. 'Sire, you shall hear. When I left court, I wandered far and wide. Midwinter found me in a castle deep in the north. The master of the house used to go hunting every day before dawn. And the lady of the manor –'

Suddenly he felt Guenevere's eye from the dais. No, he thought suddenly, not here. This conquest would be best savoured when the men were alone. He cleared his throat.

'– and the lady would arm me herself, to go out hunting with her lord,' he finished hastily. 'I left there when the snows melted, and spring unlocked the roads. As summer came in, I heard of a tournament up in the Humberlands. When I got there, three knights were triumphing over all the rest. Three in white armour, with golden shields.'

Guenevere's heart constricted. *Knights in white and gold?*

She shivered. Gawain's voice wound on like a bad spell. 'They called themselves the knights of Astolat, sons of old Sir Bernard of the Grange. But it seems that Sir Bernard only had two sons before. And neither of them could fight like Lancelot!'

Gawain let out a mighty guffaw.

Lancelot.

Guenevere fixed her features in an attentive smile. 'A strange

story, no?' she murmured in Arthur's ear. She turned to Gawain.
'And did he win?' she asked pleasantly.

'Win, madam?' Gawain bellowed with delight. 'He trounced
these country clod-hoppers, one by one! They all limped off with
split helmets and broken swords.' He nodded gleefully. 'Oh, he
hid behind plain armour, and a shield without arms. But I've seen
him fight, I've felt the weight of his sword.' He grinned. 'It was
Lancelot, I'm telling you. And he won the day.'

Goddess, Mother, bless my love, praise his name –

'And all because of the favour, the ladies said.'

'A favour?' Lucan, the ladies' man, cut in, twinkling. 'He
wore a lady's favour in the lists?'

Sir Bedivere leaned forward, his eyes alive with curiosity.
'And it brought him luck?'

Gawain nodded importantly. 'Along with his white and
gold.'

Guenevere put up her hand to conceal the sudden colour in
her cheeks.

My favour.

My colours, white and gold.

Mother, Great One, bless him for his faith to me.

Arthur laughed with joy, entranced with Gawain's tale. 'So
Lancelot has a lady-love at last? Who is she, Gawain? Speak out,
man, don't keep us in suspense.'

Guenevere smiled.

Ask what you like, you will never know.

'Sire!' Gawain flexed his great shoulders and grinned
triumphantly. 'The favour he wore was the badge of Astolat. A
silk scarf, pearl-embroidered with the arms of the female line.' He
paused, enjoying the suspense. 'And there's only one female in
Sir Bernard's line.'

Gawain clapped his mighty hands like a conjurer finishing a
trick. 'A daughter, Sir Bernard's darling and with his sons
provided for, his only heir, it seems.' His eyes rolled. 'A real
beauty too, they say. Folks call her the Fair Maid of Astolat.'
Gawain began to laugh. 'And the best of it is, he's going to marry
her!'

CHAPTER 36

The hovel was low, and the roof at the back touched the ground. The newcomer hovered in the shadows outside. As a stranger to the town, and one with evil in his heart, he did not want to ask if this was the place. But even by day there were few passers-by in a foul and secret alley such as this. Only a desperate man would be here on a night so black that even the creatures of the dark had kept their holes.

Darkness and devils, what was the matter with him? Was he a coward now? Furiously the stranger reached for the latch and pushed open the door. The stink that met him would have deterred many men, but he muffled his nose and mouth in the folds of his cloak and plunged in.

The gloom inside was little different from the darkness he had left. One tallow lamp lit up a foetid space, cluttered from floor to low ceiling with boxes and bundles and objects he did not know. Strange-smelling plants and herbs hung drying from the rafters, along with rough pelts, foxes' brushes and hares' feet. One corner held a large vat full of a dark noisome liquid with an oily skin.

'Ho, there!' The stranger made his voice manly and strong. 'Anyone within?'

A chorus of low growls greeted his words. As his eyes grew accustomed to the place, he caught a glint of bright eyes and teeth, more than he could count. He knew then one reason for the stink in the room. Half a dozen cruel-eyed dogs crouched on a bed of rags beside a makeshift hearth. Their growling rose to a fury as he came in.

'Down! Get down, all of you!'

Abruptly the snarling ceased, and the dogs lay down. From the far back of the hovel, a dusty shape crawled out of the darkness and shuffled to its feet.

The meagre lamplight fell on a black-capped head, and a black-gowned body, old before its time. A face sharpened by famine swam into view, and stained hands with nails like claws. A cage of rats was swinging from the newcomer's crooked grip.

'Are you the apothecary?' the stranger demanded roughly.

'If you say so.'

A good answer, the hovel-dweller told himself. He had been an apothecary once, and in time he might be again. He knew at a glance that he still had the skill this young lord would require, and more. Cynically he eyed the stranger's dark hood and all-concealing cloak. Let me guess what has brought you to my door, young sir, he grinned to himself.

He set down the cage, and made a washing motion with his hands.

'What's your will, sir?' he enquired.

The stranger gestured to the rough workbench along the wall, where coloured liquids glowed blood-amber, green and gold.

'How much?' he demanded brusquely.

The hovel-dweller gave a yellow smile. 'Those are all sovereign cordials for the heart. They are guaranteed to bring a dead man back to life. Whereas you, I think –?'

But the stranger had already turned away. 'That, then?' he demanded, pointing to the viscous pottage in the vat.

The hovel-dweller gave a sardonic laugh. 'Not unless you suffer from the spavins or the strangles, or any such diseases of the horse. Of course, if your windgalls are troubling you –'

'Hold your tongue!'

For a moment it seemed that the stranger would strike him down.

'You know what I want,' came the venomous hiss. 'Let me have it, and I'll be gone.' He was fumbling with the purse at his waist as he spoke.

The hovel-dweller bared his ruined teeth. He turned away, and muttered a soft command. At once the dogs left the heap of rags. Without taking his eyes off the stranger, he knelt and rummaged in the filthy bed. 'Here.' He rose to his feet with something clutched in his hand. It was a thin glass phial smaller than a woman's little finger, with a dark brackish liquid swirling inside. 'Three crowns.'

'Three crowns? For that?' The stranger gave an unconvincing laugh. 'There's not enough there to kill a cat!'

'Oh, sir . . .'

With a shake of his head, the hovel-dweller unstoppered the tiny container, crossed to the work-bench, and reached into the cage. His pouncing fingers seized a rat from behind, pinching the jaw to make it open its mouth. Swinging from his hand, the rat wriggled and screamed with a piercing intensity.

The hovel-dweller chuckled unpleasantly. 'Now, now,' he said.

Tipping the phial, he allowed one drop to fall into the creature's mouth. Instantly it gave a scream ten times more agonised than before. Convulsing with a force that broke its back, it twisted out of the hovel-dweller's grip, and was dead before it thudded to the floor.

'Enough!'

The stranger shuddered, and fumbled to pass over his crowns in an ecstasy of haste.

'One drop'll do it, even for a man,' said the hovel-dweller conversationally, kicking the rat away. 'In a drink, maybe, or on food. My mother swore by it dropped into the heart of an apple, in the very core. It soaks through the flesh, and leaves no trace on the outside.'

'Let me go!' muttered the stranger, almost to himself. He seized the black phial with a determined hand.

'Allow me.' Grinning, the hovel-dweller carefully stoppered it, and handed it over wrapped in a filthy rag.

The stranger made a bolt for the door, and he followed him.

'Careful how you use it, now,' he called after the stranger, with graveyard joviality. But his visitor had already vanished into the night. The hovel-dweller withdrew, shaking his head. They had no sense of humour, these young knights.

Ina entered the antechamber as dusk fell, a three-branched candle-holder in her hand. 'Leave me,' the Queen had told her hours ago. 'I have light if I need it, I will tend the fire, leave me, Ina, I shall be all right.' But her distracted air and haunted eyes had told another tale. So Ina was not surprised to find the room in darkness, and the hearth long cold.

'Lights, my lady,' she called cheerfully. 'Evening's drawing in. It's almost time for dinner in the Great Hall.'

There was no reply. Ina set down the candles with a stifled sigh, and looked around. The outer chamber was cold and deserted, with no sign of life. Cautiously she approached the inner door, pushed it open gently, and peered in.

Guenevere lay stretched out on the bed, staring at the canopy overhead. In the gloom her eyes had an eerie wildwood gleam, and her hair spread out around her in tumbled disarray. She looked crazed with pain, like a forest creature caught in a cruel trap, and for a moment Ina flinched from her piteous glare. Then her love for her mistress took over, and she surged across to the bed.

'Lady?'

She reached out and placed her hand on Guenevere's head. The skin was cold and clammy to her touch, as if all human warmth had drained away. But a febrile vein throbbed between the frozen brows, and to Ina's touch it said, *Lancelotlancelotlancelot* –

'My lady,' she said sturdily, trying not to weep. 'See now, I've brought the candles, let me help you to get up.'

The shape on the bed stirred and pulled away. 'No.'

'It's the dinner hour soon. Even if you don't go down to the hall, you must eat.'

'No.'

'Yes, lady,' Ina repeated, as if to a child. 'Let's get up.'

She slipped an arm round Guenevere's neck, and spoke softly and persuasively into her ear. Guenevere sat up obediently, but seemed to have no command over her legs as they swung to the floor.

'He's going to marry her, Ina,' she said dully, her eyes staring.

'Not Sir Lancelot,' Ina replied, in the dogged tone she had used a hundred times.

'You heard Gawain.'

'Sir Gawain?' Ina cried defiantly, 'And what does he know, a great lubbock like him? Why, he knows no more about love or – or anything – than a bull in the fields!'

Guenevere got to her feet and moved into the window, where the evening candle stood in its usual place. In the west, the day was sinking into night in a welter of purple and blue-black. Here and there were faint shafts of golden fire. But great clouds like bruises darkened the rim of the sky, and the star of love was nowhere to be seen.

'He knows something,' Guenevere said faintly. 'He saw –' She broke off. There was no need for words. *You know what it means when a knight wears a lady's favour at a tournament in plain sight of all. Gawain saw Lancelot with the proof of another woman's love.*

Proof of his betrayal of our love and me.

'It's all gossip, lady, hearsay, nothing more,' said Ina, through gritted teeth. 'Sir Lancelot's a better man than that. He wouldn't turn from you to the first girl he saw.'

Guenevere gave a wan and bitter smile. 'Even if she's an heiress, a beauty, and twenty years old?'

'Not even if she's the Goddess herself, decked out in the flowers of May!' Ina burst out in exasperation. 'Not Sir Lancelot!'

Guenevere turned away. 'He's only a man, Ina.' Her voice grew pale and remote. 'And he's free to choose. I set him free. So what can I say if he chooses to marry her?'

Lancelot took a last look round the tower room. The narrow wooden cot took him back to the months of pain, lying there with nothing to do but chart the passing of the seasons by the sun on the whitewashed wall. Here he had heard the Dark Mother draw up to his side, and felt Her breath on his cheek. Here he had braced himself to meet his death, and here he had taken his first steps back to life. Thanks to the Great Ones, all that was behind him now.

Except for the scar. Unconsciously he fingered the puckered welt on his thigh, a hideous thing, still red and inflamed. Well, what did it matter? No one would see it now.

Guenevere –

His loss stabbed him again with the familiar pain, and a restless mournful anger gripped his heart. Gods above, he was only twenty-nine! Must he live like the monks of the Christians for ever more?

He stifled his longing, and moved towards the door. Now all that remained was to make his last farewells.

'You're really leaving us, then.'

Lancelot bowed his head. He had not heard Lavain coming up the stairs. Sir Bernard and his sons had made many attempts to persuade him to stay. There was nothing to be added now.

'You'll come back and see us soon?'

The hope in his face made Lavain look very young.

Lancelot turned away. 'Not soon. And before I leave –' He took a breath, and turned back to the knight.

In his russet breeches and tunic of sky blue, Lavain was the picture of youth and innocence. Lancelot felt defeated before he began, corrupt and old. But he must speak.

'One last thing, sir,' he began in a low voice. 'All this time, I have never told you my name. You and your kin have most nobly honoured my wish to bury myself and my past.'

There was a pause. The morning sun burned on the white-washed walls. Then Lavain's voice dropped into the silence between them, more loudly than he meant. 'I know who you are, sir. We all know.'

Lancelot was astounded. 'How?' he cried. 'I never breathed a word!' A sudden thought struck him, and he ran a distracted hand through his hair. 'Did I talk in my fever? Or when I was asleep?'

'Neither, sir,' Lavain said quietly. 'But you forget one thing. Our sister has watched the river, and dreamed of her knight to come for many years. And for Tirre and myself, Sir Kay and Sir Lucan, Sir Gawain and Sir Bedivere were the heroes of our childhood days.' He smiled with the joy of happy memories. 'And of all their exploits, we knew most of Lancelot.'

Lancelot dropped his head. How strange, how cruel to hear his name again now.

Lavain stepped towards him. 'No other knight of the road would have challenged that outlaw gang, one man against eight, even though you were on horseback. We thought there was something then.' He gave a gentle laugh. 'But as soon as our sister saw you, as woman do, she knew.'

Lancelot had the sense of hearing something he should have known for many weary months. But his pride still drove him to speak. 'You had no proof.'

Lavain smiled. 'After the tournament, we did.' His smile broadened. 'Did you think anyone there was blind to what they saw in their midst?'

Lancelot heaved a sigh, and tossed back his hair. 'It does not matter now.' He fixed Lavain earnestly in his bright brown gaze. 'I must be gone.'

Lavain paused. 'Hear me, sir. I have to speak to you as the head of our house.'

Lancelot's soul filled with dread. 'Surely that must be Sir Bernard's place?'

Lavain waved a hand. 'I speak with his authority, and my brother's too.'

And your sister's, I dare swear, thought Lancelot desperately. He gathered up his soul. 'Forgive me, sir. I know what you will say. I heard the gossip at the tournament. The whole world had me betrothed to your sister before the day was out.'

'She loves you,' Lavain said simply. He gave an embarrassed smile. 'As we all do.' His head went up in the lordly lift that Lancelot had learned to know. 'And she is worthy of any man's love. She's truthful and brave, and as constant as you could desire. Where her love is given, her heart is set.'

'She is a young woman of great –' Lancelot put in awkwardly.

But Lavain did not hear. 'And I think you know she's our father's only heir. Tirre and I have estates of our own from our mother, so our father has vested Elaine with his holding here. And Astolat is no mean inheritance, as you know.'

'No, indeed.' Lancelot took a deep breath, and tried to check his guilt and distress. 'Your sister is a pearl,' he resumed gently to Lavain, 'and she needs no estate to enhance her worth. Any man would be proud to call her his.'

Lavain's face lit up. 'So you –?'

'I cannot, sir.'

The words fell with a dread finality from Lancelot's mouth. 'I follow one lady, Queen Guenevere. Her love is the lodestar of my imperfect life. I will never marry, never take a paramour.'

'But surely –?' Lavaine had turned pale with the death of hope.

'But all that is courtship, surely, you would say?' Lancelot muttered almost to himself. 'Oh, sir, if only it were.' His sigh cracked his ribs. 'Believe me, if your sister, if any woman could come between me and the love of this queen . . .' Tears rose to his eyes. 'But it is not to be. I love her, and I shall until I die. So you see what cruelty it would be to offer another woman the shadow of a love.'

Lavain shook his head. 'We thought –' he said brokenly. 'My father hoped –'

Lancelot groaned. 'Gods above, Lavaine, she's been goodness itself to me, and she's lovely too! D'you think I'm made of stone?' He could have cried aloud. 'And children.' He could hardly believe he was saying this. 'I shall never have children, Lavain, d'you understand that?' A bright vision shot through him, of laughing children running to meet him, arms reaching up for a kiss, and he brushed it aside. 'That's only one of many things Elaine could offer me. Truly it grieves me that I am not the man of her dreams. But I swear to you, your sister will find another knight, one who will love her as I never could.'

Even if I have to send him here from Camelot myself, he resolved, turning away. There's Sagramore now, or Sir Tor, both fine knights, and good-looking too. Or there's Dinant, or –

'Never.'

She stood in the doorway as Lavain had, but her wide eyes and mouth were badges of sorrow, not hope.

'I begged your favour once, Sir Lancelot,' she said clearly, 'and I have come to beg you once again.'

'God bless you, my dear sister,' murmured Lavain. He pressed a kiss on her temple, and left the room.

Lancelot felt a chill around his heart.

'You are welcome, lady,' he ventured, as cheerily as he could. 'If it is in my power, what you ask is yours.'

'Oh, it is in your power!' Her eyes were very bright. She gave a brittle laugh. 'You are too good to let me die for your love.'

'Die?' Lancelot gasped. 'What do you want of me?'

She came towards him quivering, and took him by the hand.

Her soft body was as sweet as dawn in spring, and her scent of pink and white petals filled the air.

But Guenevere smells of roses as red as blood, the blooms of high midsummer, moody and strong. She breathes honeysuckle and wine, the hot scent of Beltain fires, as well as the fragile hope of bluebells in the spring.

Elaine had not taken her eyes off his face. 'Sir Lancelot, I want you for my husband,' she said.

'You honour me, lady.' Lancelot cast around him in despair. 'But truly, I never saw myself as a married man.'

She nodded doggedly, as if she knew what he would say. 'Then will you be my paramour?'

Lancelot wanted to weep. 'Oh, lady,' he said hopelessly, 'I beg you, think what you are asking of me. You are a maiden of the highest hope. You saved my life, and your father and brothers have treated me like their own flesh and blood. How could I reward all your goodness that way?'

Her eyes flared. 'Then you are saying I must die for your love.'

'No, no!' he cried. 'No, you must live! Live and love, lady, and marry a good knight.' He did not know what to say. 'I will dance at your wedding, I will stand godfather to your sons, I will champion you until the day I die –'

'But you will not love me!' She let out an agonised shriek. 'And my life is over if you won't care for me.'

'Maiden, I cannot!' Lancelot bowed his head.

'Then Sir Lancelot, my good days are done!' Her great gasping screams filled the air. 'I shall die!'

CHAPTER 37

Thank the Gods, the eternal summer was drawing to an end. Now at last the days of endless pale blond light would shorten to give the land a few hours of sleep. Only in these winter months did this skein of scattered northerly islands ever see the dark, but then it was all the more welcome when it came. Sir Lamorak sighed, and drew the crisp air deep into his lungs. Though born in the south, he loved this place like his life.

And he could not leave it now.

He clutched the letter, and looked with unseeing eyes around the room. How many times had his fingers traced these granite walls, and never found a joint? He loved this palace, this world of endless grey.

And he loved the Queen of these islands more than she loved herself. That was hard to believe of a strong, self-loving queen, a proud and wilful woman brought up in the ways of the Goddess since she was a child. But he saw Morgause's subtle mind at work as she ruled her land. He watched her tireless efforts for her people, and read the love in their eyes whenever she passed. He never tired of her deep, smoky voice, her stone-pale face, her russet hair. And for all that and more he loved her, there was nothing else to say.

So how could he leave her now, after all these years? He slapped the stiff parchment furiously against his thigh. How could he live in a place where the Christians ruled?

The Christians! His sturdy frame shuddered at the thought. Men who refused all the goodness the Great Ones gave, and chose cold, pain, starvation and self-punishment? Who denied the love of women for the love of their God? He thought of

Morgause, and her wonderful, ample flesh. Live without that? Goddess, Mother, no!

Yet what else could he do? He stared at the letter again. If Morgause persisted with this, how could he stay?

He stalked round the Queen's chamber racked by thought, oblivious to the witnesses of his reverie. Waiting in loose formation round the walls stood a dozen Orkney warriors, their coarse plaids belted with bronze weaponry. Not a man among them still boasted the natural complement of bodily parts with which the Old Ones had sent him into the world. But give or take the odd hand, eye or nose, every one knew his value, and his role. They were the Knight Companions of the Throne. Their task was to die for the Chosen One of the Queen, as his fate, when it came, was to die for her. There was nothing else. So they waited patiently as Sir Lamorak wrestled in his soul. It would all be settled when the Queen appeared.

With a rustle of silks she came sweeping in.

'Lamorak?'

'Your Majesty.'

Lamorak bowed low, and kissed her hand. He could tell she felt happy today, sensual and young. But he could not pretend to be in tune with her mood.

'I have written the letter you ordered,' he said, without delay. 'And tell me, lady, when must I leave for Camelot?'

Her mouth opened in dismay. 'Leave for Camelot?' she said stupidly. 'What do you mean?'

He looked at her, grim-faced, and put the parchment into her hand. 'You asked me to write to Camelot, and send for your sons. Sign the letter, lady, and I'll take it straight away. I'll stay with King Arthur as long as they are all here. After that, when you command me, I shall return.'

She stared at him. 'But Lamorak, I cannot spare you now. I must have you with me when my sons come.'

'Madam –'

'No, Lamorak,' she said simply. She bunched her fists. Her bosom was heaving beneath her velvet gown. 'I need you here. Another knight can take the letter south.' She nodded to herself. 'Now, who shall go?'

She whirled round to survey the men along the wall. At the

head of the knight companions, their leader grinned, and arranged his ruined face in its best aspect. It was hard to look charming with only one eye, Leif knew. But for the court of King Arthur, nothing else would do.

One circuit of the hacked noses, scarred faces and missing teeth, and Morgause had made up her mind.

'Leif shall go,' she pronounced. 'He'll be there and back before we know he's gone.' Her face softened as she turned back to Lamorak. 'Let you go?' she said tenderly. 'How could I do that?'

'My Queen –' The words burst from Lamorak before he was aware. 'Why do your sons have to come?'

Morgause caught her breath, eyes wide. 'Why? Because this is their land, their ancestral home, and they are strangers here. One day it will be their kingdom when I die, and none of them may want to take that burden on. Because –'

Lamorak let her voice wind on unheard, and listened instead to what she did not say. I understand, my love, his battered heart acknowledged wearily. They are your sons, your babes, your flesh and blood, and your mother's heart is yearning for her brood. He bowed his head. So be it.

Morgause came to an end.

Lamorak drew a breath and spoke with all the emphasis he could. 'If this has to be, I beg you, think what it will mean. Your sons have not seen their home for full ten years. They will have to know how you and I live here.' He paused. 'For your sake, and for mine, this must be the time.'

'Oh, Lamorak!'

Morgause reached up her hand, and laid a finger on his lips. Lamorak took it and covered it in kisses, then cradled it gently between his hands as he spoke. 'The time has come,' he repeated patiently. 'The time to marry.'

'Lamorak, don't torture me!' Morgause moaned.

Lamorak stroked her hand. 'When I loved you first, your sons were only boys. Their father had just been killed. It was not the time for them to learn that their mother had taken a Chosen One.'

'Lamorak –'

'Now they are men. More than men, they are Orkney men,

princes, knights of the fellowship. In the years since King Lot died, they've grown in pride, and learned their status and their place in the world.' His face grew hard. 'They will resent me now. My father killed your husband, and the blood debt is still unavenged.'

'That was –'

'But if I am your husband, no man can challenge me. Your sons could never say that I dishonoured you, using your body but refusing to marry you. If you marry me, you will be Queen of Listinoise. Then they will see our two kingdoms joined in one, just as King Arthur did with Queen Guenevere.'

He crushed her hand to his lips, and put his heart into his plea. 'Marry me, lady!'

But as he spoke, he knew his cause was lost.

'I am their mother.' Morgause wept. 'How can I tell them of the love we share?' She broke away and roamed weeping round the room. 'I'm too old for you, Lamorak! This and all else, my sons will not forgive.'

She swept up and down the long chamber, wringing her hands and beating her breast, crying to herself. He was still waiting as she returned to his arms.

'Let us send the letter, then,' he said bleakly as she nestled into him, 'and prepare to take what comes. Your sons are men of the world. Perhaps they will see that you have need of me.'

'Of course.' Suddenly at peace, Morgause smiled into his eyes. 'I need my knight. They will all know that. A queen must have her knights.'

The Great Hall was alive with dancing light. Every table was laden with gold and silver candlesticks, every candlestick studded with jewels reflecting the candles' flickering flames. At the far end of the room, the tall bronze doors threw back the reflection of laughing faces, of goblets raised in greeting, of silks and velvets flashing white and red, green, purple, and sloe-black. Outside, the rain beat down on the roof, and the first storm of winter howled about the hall. But at the round table in the center of the bright, warm space, spirits were high. A week after Sir Gawain had come back to court, the knights were still relishing his startling news.

'Lancelot getting married!' cried Sir Sagramore ebulliently, waving up a servant to bring more wine. His full face was flushed, and in the heat of the room, an old scar on his forehead took on a silvery sheen. 'And after all the times he told us he'd never be a married man! But it must be true. There's no smoke without fire.'

Sir Dinant chuckled. Lean and keen, he enjoyed the life of court and camp alike, and no lady appealed for his help in vain. 'Ah, the fire of love!' he declaimed rhetorically. 'Or is it lust at last for Lancelot?'

A volley of sniggers and cackles followed his words.

Lionel shot a glance at Bors seated by his side. His brother would hate the knights' boisterous banter, he knew.

Sir Lucan laughed, then pulled a serious face. 'Poor Lancelot doesn't have your luck with the ladies, Sagramore,' he said gravely, 'so he has to take the first woman he can get.'

There was a general burst of merriment among the knights. Too fond of his food and wine, fat-faced and ample in the girth, Sagramore pursued women furiously, without success.

'Yet still she must be a fine lady, this maid of Astolat,' offered Mador, his young face aglow. Not like my lady, Queen Guenevere, he told himself. But the girl who could win Sir Lancelot must be rare indeed.

'More likely a fine estate.' Lucan smiled cynically, and thrust back his thick hair. 'And I'm sure the girl knows every penny of her worth. There's no such thing as an innocent woman, after all. '

He looked round the table, challenging a response. There was a silence among the older knights. Sagramore, who had been planning a loud riposte to Lucan's taunt, lost his taste for revenge. It had been years ago now, the Gods knew, and long buried in the past. But no one had forgotten the woman who broke Lucan's heart.

And not even a beauty, as Sagramore remembered her. Tall and scrawny, when in his opinion women should be small and plump and fair, like dormice waiting to be stroked and uncurled. Yet black-haired and bony as she was, the King's sister Madam Morgan had something special about her, every man knew that. Was it her long, white face, her sullen eyes, her small sharp

breasts, her tight damson mouth? Sagramore shook his head. No
man could say.

And no one knew how she had bewitched Lucan, a man
more versed in women than any knight at court. But they knew
she had practised her black arts on him, and he suffered for it still.
She had stolen his heart and seduced him to her bed, dazzled him
with the future they would share, and then cast him away. And
after her, even the down-to-earth Sagramore could imagine, other
women would be like milk and water to red wine.

A voice untroubled by the past broke in. 'But Sir Lancelot
would never marry for a fine estate, would he?' said Patrise
wonderingly. 'And surely there are good women in the world?
Ladies to be loved for their truth and nobility?'

Of course there are, Bors wanted to cry out, and this maiden
may be one of them, pray God she is! If Lancelot had found
someone honest and true, a girl who could be his, he would weep
with joy. But he knew it could not be.

'It can't be true, this nonsense of Gawain's,' he muttered
furiously to Lionel, under cover of the noise.

Lionel nodded miserably. 'Not as long as he loves the
Queen.'

He loves the Queen.

Bors pushed aside his platter with an inward groan. His
stomach was sick with chewing on nothing but his fears, and the
steaming dish of pork made him want to retch. His mind ran to
and fro in hopeless spurts. Where are you, Lancelot? What's this
marriage nonsense all about? What's to become of you, of all of
us?

A raucous burst of laughter broke in on his thoughts.

'So what's your bet, Lucan? Will he marry her?' Sagramore
guffawed through a mouthful of food, spraying pork and herbs as
he spoke. 'And what'll the Queen say when she loses her
favourite knight?'

'The Queen?' Lucan laughed sardonically. 'The Queen will
not be pleased. And Lancelot may find that his fair young virgin,
even with her fine estate, will cost him dear. He's always been
high in favour with the Queen. But her displeasure will be the
King's too.'

'That's why he's staying away,' Sir Dinant put in. 'He knows he's angered the Queen.' He shook his head. 'Why would he risk it? The Gods alone know why he'd marry the girl.'

Sagramore's eyes took on a lecherous gleam. He filled his mouth again. A trickle of pork fat ran down his chin. 'We haven't seen her yet! What's the betting she's a real –'

Bors turned away in disgust. Gods, they were vile! What he'd give to be away from here!

Suddenly he felt a servant at his elbow, plucking his sleeve. 'There's been a stranger in your quarters, sir, asking for you. A man of Little Britain, so he said, to see the Queen.'

'Thank you.'

Bors rose to his feet. He threw an arm round his brother's shoulders, and breathed in Lionel's ear. 'Come to our lodgings as soon as you can.' He met Lionel's questioning gaze with a slight nod. 'Yes. He's back.'

CHAPTER 38

'Lady, lady, he's back! There's a page from the knight's quarters with a message, a stranger from Little Britain craves your –'

Ina, Ina, do I care?

How many days had she spent living with the constant stabbing thought of Lancelot's betrayal, yet having to smile and talk as if nothing were amiss? How many nights of endlessly prowling the floor, flinching at shadows, snapping at Ina, then weeping in her arms?

And all the time her anger with him grew.

'It can't be, lady,' Ina protested, tight-lipped. Through it all, she believed in her lady's knight as fervently as she loved Guenevere. 'He can't be married, not Sir Lancelot.'

'Why not?' Guenevere snarled. 'Is he the first man to lie and betray? I'm sure she's soft and sweet, and never contradicts a word he says.' She gave a hysterical laugh. 'And she can't be more than nineteen. Why should he be faithful to an old witch like me?'

She knew she was hurting Ina when she spoke like this. But not as much as she hurt herself.

It seemed to her now that her love for Lancelot had been almost alchemically pure before he had polluted it. Now it was poisoned, he had killed her love, and with it her hopes for the future, her reason to live.

And Arthur, too, had wounded her this way, first when his folly had cost Amir his life, and then when he took his sister to his bed. Now Lancelot had betrayed her as Arthur had. She thought she had suffered when Arthur loved Morgan. But nothing before had been as bad as this.

Never more, came to her like the death knell of their love, rolling through the wasteland of her mind. *He'll never come to me again, hold me or kiss me now. He has another love, and he loves her more than me.*

She wrapped her arms across her stomach to hold down the gnawing pain. *Her body won't have the marks of childbearing, she'll be lithe and firm. And a virgin too, so she'll think he's wonderful. Wouldn't any man choose a woman like that, soft and undemanding, easily satisfied, above a partnership of equals, with its constant wrestling of body and soul?*

On her love-finger she still wore the ring he had given her, a pure-water moonstone of mystical silver-blue. But the comfort it gave her had departed now. On her left hand she bore the burden of her wedding ring. The heavy hoop of gold was a torment too.

He's going to marry her, Gawain said. Well, she'll want that, any girl would.

But, Goddess, Mother, married? She was gasping now, tears sprouting with every breath. *Yes, he'll marry her, he'll be with her, and I'll be all alone –*

In the end, her nature could not continue in such pain. She passed from numbness to indifference, then felt nothing at all. So when a glowing Ina slipped up to her in her chamber, moon-eyed and pink-cheeked, she did not care.

'My lady, he's coming!' Ina breathed. Her wide-spaced eyes were gleaming with their Otherworldly light. 'Now we'll know the truth.'

Will we?

Guenevere turned away. The candles had burned down. It was hours since she left Arthur and his knights revelling in the hall, and climbed the steps to seek refuge in her tower. There she had bathed her temples with patchouli, her mother's long-beloved sweet musky scent, and lit fresh candles in bowls of rosewater and lime. Then she had moved in a cloud of soothing fragrance into the window to read the faraway stars. She was at peace in her own domain. Why should she bother now?

'Ina, say it's too late –'

But Ina was already at the door.

'A traveller from Little Britain,' she announced loudly, as she showed him in.

Standing in the window, Guenevere heard the words with a shrug of disregard. Once they had needed to be careful when he came to her chamber alone. But now it no longer mattered what the guards thought.

'This way, sir.' Her heart in her eyes, Ina disappeared behind the closing door.

Lancelot came in, and a chill of fear brushed his heart. Guenevere stood with her back to him across the chamber, looking out into the night. Before, she would have run to meet him and thrown herself into his arms. Now all he could see was a column of blood-red silk, and a veil of pale gauze covering her hair. Her familiar fragrance reached him like a new dimension of pain, and a ring of frozen stars danced round her head. *She has heard it all,* came to him like a curse. *And she believes the worst.*

He shrugged off his travelling cloak and threw it on a chair. 'My lady,' he said.

'Your lady?' She whirled round, pouncing like a snake. Her eyes were glittering. 'Not any more, Lancelot, from what I hear.'

He stiffened. 'Madame, allow me, I can explain –'

She had always loved his lightly accented voice. The girl from Astolat must have loved it too. 'Oh, I'm sure you can, Lancelot,' she said, with savage emphasis. 'You've always been able to speak up for yourself.'

He stared, confused by her hostility. 'Is that wrong? Surely a knight should be able to speak to a lady, even a queen?'

Goddess, Mother, how dare he! Her frail control collapsed. 'Oh, I hear you gave a very good account of yourself while you were away! Sir Gawain says you have a new love. Her brothers call you brother, and you wore her favour at the tournament.'

His heart, his stomach clenched. 'How did you know this?' he managed.

'Gawain saw you! He saw it all.'

'Gawain –' He shook his head. 'I did not know he was there.'

'Evidently!' She took a gulping breath. ' So! Is she as young and lovely as they all say? Is she an heiress, Lancelot? Will she be rich?'

Lancelot shook his head. He had never before seen Guenevere like this. But still it never occurred to him to lie. 'She is the heiress of all Astolat.'

'Ha!' Guenevere drew in her breath with a hiss. 'And a beauty too, they say?' She gave a brittle laugh. 'She must be, or they would not call her "fair".'

She paced away, and covered her eyes with her hands. *Only moments before he came, you thought you did not care. And now?*

Now I hate him! Now I can't bear him, his brown eyes burning in his long, pale face, that body of his that she must have enjoyed too –

She clutched a hand to her head. Her eyes grew dim. She saw Lancelot lying in bed in a quiet, white room. She saw his body stripped and then covered, tended and stripped again by unknown hands. Night fell, and she saw a slender shape steal into the room. Then it was dawn, and she watched the girl slip out. But a fragrance, an aura lingered with pervasive force. Guenevere came to herself choking on pink and white.

'Madame?'

Lancelot was gripping her by the forearms, staring into her eyes. She gasped, and recoiled from him. 'You have, haven't you?' she spat.

'What, Madame?'

'Made love to her! You have, I know, I've seen it!'

His eyes flared. 'You see nothing but your own jealousy!'

'My jealousy? Not your treachery?' she cried

Lancelot stepped back from her, and took a breath. 'This is madness, lady.'

'Tell me the truth! I know you've married her!' A red rage was sweeping her like a storm. 'Wedded her, bedded her, call it what you like. Don't you understand what I'm saying? What's it called in French?'

'Madame.'

At last he felt his anger rising to answer hers. The rhythms of his speech had never been more pronounced. 'I speak your language well enough to speak the truth. I am not married, and not likely to be.'

'Oh, so?' She gave a scornful laugh.

He gritted his teeth and pressed on. 'And I bedded no one. The Maid of Astolat is a pure virgin for me.'

'You say that? When you wore her favour in the tournament? When all the world knew you were pledged to her?'

'She begged a favour before I could refuse. I never gave her my pledge.'

'Why should you owe her a favour?'

'She saved my life. I came to her house with a wound that would not heal. For months she took care of me as I lay in bed, day and night.'

The image of Lancelot in bed with the girl at his side came back to her again with all the force of a blow. 'It must have been good to be ill,' she burst out, 'to be nursed like that!'

'Gods above, enough!' He bounded forward, and gripped her by the wrists. 'Why do you say these things and make us both suffer so? It was you who sent me away, and I left my heart with you. Yet the first gossip you hear, I am a liar, I am untrue!'

She turned her head towards him as if caught in a bad dream. 'Words, words.'

'You are my lady! I am your knight. That means I am pledged to you.' He gave a scornful laugh. 'To you! And you taunt me with being pledged to her, when –?' *When you are married to the King, and sleep in his bed*, he might have said, but could not. He shook his head, and turned towards the door. 'I will leave you, lady. I have no stomach for your jealousy.'

'This girl –' She changed course with brutal suddenness. 'This Elaine – she loved you, yes? Did you know?'

Lancelot gritted his teeth. 'Madame –'

She assumed a lighter tone. 'I want to know.'

He drew a breath. He should tell her the truth, he had nothing to fear. 'When we met, she was very kind to me. I was sick in bed, and she was with me a lot.'

She tensed imperceptibly. *So it was true*. A throbbing pulse picked up on the side of her head.

Lancelot paused, his senses suddenly alert. 'There was nothing in it. There's really nothing to say.'

'No no, go on, it's fine, I want to know.'

He wanted to believe her. 'Then after that, she was always quiet when she saw me, and would sit by my bed and never say a word.'

'She was a quiet girl, then?' Her voice was calm, but the beating in her mind was growing faster as she spoke.

'Quiet and gentle,' he said unwarily.

'And pretty too?'

'Oh, yes. She's a beautiful girl.'

'And kind and loving towards you?'

He did not see the pit his words had dug. 'Always.'

Always?

Guenevere screamed like a mare breaking her leg. 'You did go to her bed!' She trembled in a panic of distress.

He felt an answering impulse of pure terror. 'No, Madame!'

'Or she came to yours!' she howled. 'Did she seduce you? Who made the first move?'

He turned to face her. 'No one! Listen to me!'

But the madness was running unchecked through her body now, drowning out her brain. She saw again the lean frame she had so much loved, and her smiling rival drifting up to his bed.

'No more, Lancelot!' she screamed. All her life's loss and grief were in her cry. 'You have betrayed me, you're a faithless man. You've killed our love, Lancelot. You have to go!'

Fear flooded him. 'Lady, let me speak –'

She was panting so hard that she could hardly breathe. 'Get out.' She pointed a quivering finger towards the door. 'Go!'

She is mad, he thought. He tried to take her hands. 'My queen, we should –'

She broke away and struck him in the face. 'Go!' she screeched. 'Don't you see I hate you for what you've done?'

He drew into himself, hurt beyond thought, beyond speech. 'So, Madame,' he forced out at last, 'if this is your will, I go. Till tomorrow, then, I kiss your hand.'

'Not till tomorrow!' she howled. 'No more tomorrows, no more after today!'

He could not believe her. 'I am not your tame falcon, lady,' he began angrily, 'to be sent away, then whistled back as soon as you change your mind. I am –'

Her heart, her mind were breaking all at once. 'I know who you are. And you're nothing to me now. Get out!'

His face was set like stone. 'Have a care, Madame!'

Her voice dropped to a piercing hiss. 'I mean it, Lancelot. Go, and don't come back. You're banished from the court, from the Summer Country, from my love. Get out, *now!*'

He turned and left the room. Her last words were still ringing round his head as he slammed the door and started down the steps.

'Go! I never want to see you again!'

CHAPTER 39

The antechamber to the King's apartments was dull and devoid of life. The grey light of a late winter afternoon played over the groups of people waiting for the King to return, and lost itself in the shadows of the roof. A few of the bystanders talked quietly among themselves. But where Bors and Lionel waited by the door the silence was almost too deep to break.

Lionel stared at the walls, gazed out of the window, and finally studied his feet. 'We should have gone with the King,' he said at last.

Bors glanced round the room, and found no relief from Lionel's reproach. He knew they should not be idling away here among the grim-faced monks and sad-eyed lords too old for the hunt. They should have joined the laughing, shouting band that had streamed out joyfully in the winter dawn.

He nodded a weary assent.

Lionel pressed on. 'And we should have stopped Lancelot from going straight to the Queen.'

Bors gave a savage laugh. 'Or at least warned him how angry she might be.'

'He thought she would understand if he told her the truth.'

'The truth?' Bors smiled bitterly to himself. 'She's not interested in the truth. She believes whatever she wants to believe. She's out of her mind!'

'Brother, you don't mean –'

'How else to explain her sending him away?' Bors's face darkened at the thought, and he could not contain his rage. 'Think of it! A prince of Benoic to be banished like some evil-doing wretch? A king's son to be discarded like a servant who gives offence?'

Lionel glanced uneasily around. Nearby was a group of earnest monks, further off a cluster of knights and aged lords. Some of their ancient ladies were there too, and mischief-making kept them all alive. Any of them might overhear Bors's complaint. In a royal antechamber, even walls had ears.

He lowered his voice. 'He loved her too well,' he said placatingly.

'D'you call it love?' Bors spat. His eyes narrowed. 'Sometimes I think she must be a witch. How else –?'

Lionel straightened up, stretched his long legs and looked over his brother's head. His clear grey eyes were veiled with a secret thought. He knew why men loved the Queen. He could have told Bors why their cousin was moved to the depths of his soul by the sight of her hand lifting her veil, by the tragic shadows around her mobile mouth, by her ever-youthful ways and her age-old soul. And he knew, too, why Bors, dutiful and precise, could never admire Guenevere.

But Bors did not have to hate her, as he did now. Lionel flinched. Hate was not the word. Bors loathed Guenevere for her treatment of Lancelot.

Their silence now was filled with private pain. Bors cursed himself. He did not want to go out hunting with the King. Yet least of all did he want to be in a dull chamber on a late-winter afternoon, waiting for him.

He raised his head as a cry came at the door.

'The hunt is back. Make way for the King and his knights!'

There was a flurry of cries and commands, and Arthur strode through the doors, tossing his cloak and gauntlets to a servant as he came. 'Thank you, good sir!' he said. 'And come, wine for my knights and guests, give them good cheer!'

He was glowing from his day in the saddle, bright-eyed and welcoming. 'Greetings to you all,' he cried. He smiled on all, and gestured expansively. 'Fill your glasses, come!'

He always did this, brightening a room as soon as he came in, Bors noted with an upsurge of love. When Arthur entered, the flames leaped up on the hearth, and the torches danced in their sconces to keep them company.

'Sir Niamh, you should have been with us – you too, Sir Lovell.'

Arthur moved across to the aged knights, greeting the greybeards tenderly, one by one. A bevy of scribes and councillors entered with the day's missives and papers for him to sign. Behind them the knights tumbled noisily through the door, jostling one another like bullocks in a pen, reliving the day's hunt.

Sir Gawain and his brothers were at the head of the troop. Gawain fetched Agravain a boisterous clout across the back. 'Don't look so bad-tempered, Agravain!' he crowed. 'You missed the boar, but Gaheris got him in the end.'

He gave the grinning Gaheris a push that sent him spinning into Gareth who, for all his bulk was giggling like a girl.

'Lords, lords! Is this good behaviour to show before a king?'

It was one of the clerics waiting to see the King. Gods above! Gawain swore to himself in a fury, how dared he address them like this? He turned to face the source of the rebuke. Clad all in black, with a huddle of monks on his heels, the gowned figure loomed like a column of basalt in the shadowed hall. The stink of stale incense and candle grease wafted ahead of him like a bad prayer, and he exuded an air of great holiness. But behind the lofty gaze and domed forehead lay a brain like a hunting knife, Gawain knew. Not to me, you don't, he seethed in silence, none of your pious Christian lectures to me!

'Away the Orkneys!' he announced abruptly, turning on his heel. Startled, his three brothers followed without a word.

Gawain crossed to Arthur to take his leave. 'My lord, we shall see you at dinner in the hall.'

'Before you go, Gawain . . .'

Arthur was flourishing a letter, wreathed in smiles. 'I have good news for you. Your mother has written to beg a visit from her sons. And I intend to give you leave to go.'

'Sire?' Gawain was stupefied. Behind him Agravain stood in tense silence, while Gareth and Gaheris exchanged glances of surprise and joy.

'Your mother, Queen Morgause,' Arthur repeated, with a smile, 'she wants to see you, and I know you must want to see her.'

'Of course,' Gawain agreed hastily. He had to admit that his mother had been far from his mind, but now a host of cheerful memories flooded in. Long days of hunting through the golden Orkney air. White nights of revelling with the Queen's knight companions, mighty drinkers to a man. A world where his mother was queen, and he was every man and woman's future king.

Gawain felt himself expand and grow. Yes, a return to the Orkneys would do very well. He gave an elaborate bow. 'The Orkneys, eh? You are gracious, sire. My brothers and I will gladly take leave to go. In the meantime, we shall attend you in the hall.'

He bowed himself out, and his brothers followed suit.

There was a moment of silence after they left. The Father Abbot pursed his lips in a cold smile. Gone, were they? So may all heathen shrivel in the fire of truth. And so may I separate the King from all his benighted kin, when they stand between him and the Lord as these Orkney louts do.

And so shall I part them all from the Great Whore. When I speak to the King –

'Father Abbot!'

The monk came to himself with a start. Arthur was standing before him clasping his hand with delight. 'I did not see you there! What, have you come all the way from London without sending word? The Queen and I would have sent out a troop of knights to welcome you, if we had known.'

The Queen? the Abbot mused dispassionately. No, he could never think of the concubine as a queen. God alone knew why Arthur ever took a daughter of these pagans as his wife, when there were Christian princesses to be had. Surely he'd known that the women of the Summer Country gave their bodies like beasts, and offered their so-called thigh-friendship wherever they willed? But he had chosen her, and now he called her his queen. Let him call her what he liked. To a man of God she would never be more than a whore.

And this whore would never welcome him in Camelot. The Father Abbot stiffened along the length of his spine. Had he ever believed that he would find himself here in the stronghold of the Mother Goddess, almost in the arms of the Great Whore herself? No, in truth he had not – but such was the wonder of God's plan. Already His soldiers were taking Avalon. Now Arthur would be apprised of their progress there. When they had succeeded in getting the Holy Grail, only time would be needed to bring down Camelot itself.

Time, Lord. Give me time.

'You are gracious, sire.' The Abbot forced his thin lips into a smile. 'But I need no special welcome to do God's work. A while ago, I begged you to spare the Convent of the Little Sisters of Mercy from the vengeance of Sir Yvain, when his grief at his father's death made him want to put the whole nunnery to the sword. You spared their lives, in the name of Our Lord Jesus Christ. And now you'll rejoice to know that the convent is whole again.'

Arthur paused. 'How can you be sure?' he demanded uneasily.

The Abbot treated him to a confident smile. 'I found a spiritual father, whose loving care has redeemed his tainted flock. And he has been favoured, he tells me, in the help of a new young nun, a true child of God.'

The Abbot paused. Now, what was the nun's name? He laid a bony finger on the side of his sunken cheek. Gaynor, Gannor, what was she called?

A faint chill seized him. Suddenly he knew that he had to tell Arthur the name. Help me, God! he berated his lagging brain. His mind threw up a pair of dark eyes in a long, pale face, a long, thin body, and a long, mulberry-coloured mouth. What was her name?

A growing urgency seized him, for a reason he could not tell. But it came to him with a force he could not deny that Arthur should know, must know of Sister – who?

But Arthur was not disposed for any further discussion on the theme.

'So, then,' he said brusquely, 'the convent prospers? Good! Our brothers and sisters in Christ do well, it seems. I am glad to hear it.'

The Abbot smiled again. 'Thank you, sire. Now I must beg your attention to another matter too. On Avalon –'

'My lord, my lord!'

It was the Chamberlain, hurrying in with a face of sorrow and dread. 'Oh, sire,' he gasped, 'there's a terrible thing come floating down the river. It's at the water's edge. They're calling for you there, sir, will you come?'

*

Hurry, hurry, show that you don't care.

Guenevere lengthened her stride across the courtyard as she hastened through the dusk. She could see her own breath making plume after plume in the frozen, star-lit air. With every breath, she could feel knives of ice in her lungs. But the cold outside was nothing to the chill within.

Lancelot, Lancelot, why did you betray me? Was it her sweet young flesh, her newness to the wonder of love? She shuddered, and feared she might vomit with distress.

'We must get to the Great Hall, Ina, the stewards will be ordering the dining by now.'

'My lady?' Ina struggled to throw a woollen wrap over Guenevere's shoulders as she hurried along.

'Thank you, Ina.' Guenevere shivered, and burrowed into the cloak. 'We're late,' she said forlornly. And it's so cold.'

'Once we're inside the Great Hall, madam, you'll be as warm as your heart could desire.'

But the Great Hall loomed cold and silent as they drew near. The great bronze doors were standing back on their hinges, and not a soul was within. The fires had all died down, and the lofty space was empty of its welcoming throng.

A noise in the corner made Guenevere freeze with fear.

'Lady? came a thick, distorted voice.

'Ina!' The hairs stood up on her neck, but she could not scream.

'It's all right, lady,' she heard Ina's voice, low and calm. She forced herself to turn round.

It was the son of one of the servants, a boy she had always known. A natural, he was one of the simple souls the Fair Ones called their own. His over-large head, coarsely thatched with corn-coloured hair, lolled on his shoulders and his tongue hung from his mouth as he peered out excitedly from behind his hands.

Ina approached him, and took his hands down from his face. He gave her a peg-toothed grin, and crowed like a cock.

'Where are all the people, boy?' Ina asked briskly, patting his hands. 'Where's the King and the court?'

'Haroo!' he chortled in his strange thick tongue. 'Down at the river, where the lady is.'

'What lady?' Guenevere did not know the sound of her own voice. But she could feel the onset of a sick fear.

He wriggled, and scratched himself front and back. 'The lady in the river.' His round eyes swelled. 'Go see! Go see!'

Ina laughed uncertainly. 'He's a simpleton, lady, poor thing. What does he know?'

Guenevere could hardly speak. 'He knows something.'

'The river!' he hooted, 'the river. See! Go see.'

Why were they all at the river? Leaning on Ina's arm, Guenevere hurried down Camelot's winding streets and out through the water meadows towards the crowd clustered at the river's edge. The dense throng of courtiers and townsfolk parted as she drew near. *What were they looking at?* Her nerves were on fire.

A long black barge lay at the water's edge, draped in mourning silks of the same funereal shade. Arthur stood beside it in tears, his hand covering his eyes.

In the barge lay the body of a young woman, in a long gown of black. Her arms were crossed on her breast, and her hands held a parchment in a bold black script. Beneath her black headdress her hair tumbled down, golden like the end of summer sun. Traces of an eglantine beauty still lingered in the fragile pink and white of her face. But she was far beyond her earthly beauty now.

'May I, sire?'

Sir Kay gestured towards the letter on the Lady's breast. As Arthur nodded, he reached forward and drew it out.

'Read,' Arthur said.

Kay unfolded the black-lettered script. His sharp tones filled the hollow evening air. ' "I loved Sir Lancelot, but he would not return my love. I begged his favour, but what I wanted he could not give. Queen Guenevere is the lodestar of his life. My days are done, for I have no wish to live in a world where he is not. While I lived, I was called the Fair Maid of Astolat. But I die as poor Elaine, forlorn for Lancelot's love." '

Kay finished reading, and handed the letter to the King. Guenevere ran forward and took it from his hand, although the sight of it scorched her eyes. Madly she read the words again and again, though already they were branded on her heart.

Guenevere is the lodestar of his life.

As you were of mine, my love, yet I sent you away.
Oh, Lancelot –

The stink of her own betrayal rose to overwhelm her every sense. She gave one agonised scream, and fell to the ground.

CHAPTER 40

'This way, sirs.'

The Chamberlain swept through the door with his attendants on his heels, and paused to take pleasure in what he saw. The panelled space ahead of him was glowing with the warmth of a log fire, and bright with countless candles along the walls. The flagstones were covered in rich rugs from the east, not rushes for the floor of a lady's chamber, thought the Chamberlain with a fastidious shudder, bringing all the flea-ridden dogs of the court to nose through the greasy refuse for the filth that lay beneath. Perhaps in time he might even manage to introduce rugs, not rushes, into the knights' hall? But for tonight, this was a feast for a queen, and all was clean and sweet.

'It looks well,' came a voice from behind.

It was the older of the two chamber attendants, a wrinkled ancient who had served under the King's father, Uther Pendragon, in his time. His shrewd old eyes wandered over the table in the middle of the room, a smooth disc of white damask glowing like the moon, bright with silver plates and golden goblets, autumn leaves and berries, and flagons of wine.

He nodded to his assistant. 'And that will please the Queen.' He pointed to the table, where a centrepiece of sugared lady-apples rose from a silver platter in a perfect, glistening cone.

The Chamberlain smiled. 'She's ordered the best of every-thing, feasting her knights. Sir Mador must be rewarded for the success of his quest, she says, and she wants to give a good send-off, too, to the King's kin.'

'The Orkney clan,' said the old attendant, responding with-out enthusiasm to their name. 'They're going back north, I heard.'

'Tomorrow,' confirmed the Chamberlain, 'at dawn.'

There was a pause. 'The King'll miss them,' said the younger man, 'what with Sir Lancelot gone too.'

'That's why the Queen is bringing on knights like Sir Mador and Sir Patrise,' said the Chamberlain, moving round the table as he spoke. 'She wants Sir Mador seated here in the place of honour, to the right of her throne, and Sir Gawain to her left.'

The two attendants exchanged a surreptitious glance. And Sir Agravain as far from her as possible, they all knew without the need for words.

The Chamberlain moved on, absently checking the candles, the place settings, the fuel for the fire.

'How is the Queen?' queried the old man, with a frown.

'After she fainted at the riverside, you mean? When they found the lady in the barge?' The young servant's eyes misted with memory. The sight of Guenevere being borne back into the castle, unconscious and as pale as a lily, would live with him till he died.

'Yes, well, it must have been a nasty shock, seeing the body and all,' the old man said with relish. 'Perfumed, of course, with all those flower essences and oils. But under all that black silk, dead as a doornail for days –'

'The Queen is well enough,' said the Chamberlain loftily. Servants' gossip should always be nipped in the bud. 'She had a moment of weakness, nothing more. And now the maid's been buried, the Queen means to put all that behind her with this feast. So it's up to you, good sirs, to see that it does.'

He came back to the threshold again, and paused to cast a last glance round the room. At the back, two doors to the right and left led off to the serving pantries behind, and the Chamberlain made a mental note to send to the kitchens and check that all the dishes the Queen had ordered were in hand.

He raised his head and delicately scented the air. 'Just a touch of chamber fragrance to finish off, I think,' he told the attendants. "Lavender or juniper, the Queen favours them both. Then all you need to do is await the knights.'

'We'd better hurry, then,' said the older man. 'They'll soon be here.'

'And don't forget the mulled wine when they arrive. The nights are getting cold.'

Talking among themselves, the three men withdrew. Their voices echoed down the stone corridor, and died away. Inside the chamber the only sounds were the crackling of the fire on the hearth, and the whispering of the candles along the wall.

Nothing stirred. Then the door of one of the serving pantries opened by degrees. Silently a dark figure slipped into the room. It stalked towards the table with a pace as slow as death, and stood for a moment, staring at the centrepiece, the highlight of the meal, when the Queen would present the best of the fruit to the one she chose to make her knight of the feast.

The best of the fruit.

There came a hissing laugh. A hand snaked out and removed the topmost apple from the shining cone. In its place was set another, small, round and perfect, bright with sugared gold.

The intruder took a step back and considered his handiwork. The golden apple glowed on the top of the pile. A secret smile passed over the haunted face. Yes, it was well. The Queen could not help but offer it to her knight of the feast. And for him, for all of them, it would be a memorable meal.

The face in the mirror was luminous with despair. Ina watched Guenevere struggling to compose her expression in the glass, and had to swallow her own feelings before she spoke.

'Almost done, my lady, then you'll be as fine as you ever were.'

Her small fingers worked deftly on Guenevere's hair as she spoke. Now there was something for the Queen to take comfort from. Most women in their thirties were already turning grey, but the Queen had never lost the brightness from her hair. Only her eyes showed what her heart endured, Ina mused grimly, as she plaited, and looped, and pinned. Come, lady, she wanted to say, when will you forgive yourself for mistrusting Lancelot?

Guenevere read the reproof in Ina's gaze, and heard the answer deep inside her soul.

Never, Ina.

Never while I live.

I doubted him, and thought he was untrue. But all along, it was my faith that failed. And for that the Mother has punished me to the death. I have lost my true love, and all that is left is to die.

The face in the mirror stared back at her unblinking, the eyes dilated, the brow and cheekbones carved out of stone. *No, not all,* came slowly back to her. *I have my duty, and I have my knights. And tonight I must feast my knights.*

The thought of Sir Mador made its way briefly into her heart. There was a fleeting comfort to be had from his pure love. He had done well, he deserved his reward. And to be feasted by the Queen in her private chamber would be a reward for him, she knew, above his dearest dreams.

'There you are, my lady.' Ina stepped back, with a sigh of quiet pride. Never had the Queen looked so fine.

'Thank you, Ina.' Guenevere rose to her feet. The crushed velvet of her gown shimmered in the candlelight, its varying shades of old rose calling back the high days of summer in its prime. Her sleeves were shaped like lilies lined with cloth of gold, and a train of fine gold lawn fell from her coronet. In the centre of her forehead she wore the great moonstone of the queens of the Summer Country, and the blue-water stone on her hand gleamed with the same light. Ina looked, and her heart dissolved with sorrow at the sadness of it all. *Sir Lancelot gave her that ring. It's all she has of him now.*

'So, Ina, to the feast.' Guenevere's face was set in a smile, but her eyes were dark.

'Yes, lady,' Ina said loyally as she attended Guenevere to the door. 'And it will be a great feast, I can tell you now. A night to remember, the Chamberlain said. Your knights will be talking of this for years to come.'

In the Queen's private dining chamber, the air was warm with laughter and the heady tang of wine. Clustered around Sir Gawain on the hearth, her chosen knights were waiting for Guenevere. Standing to Gawain's right and left, Gaheris and Gareth were resplendent in tunics of green wool edged with fine blue silk. Even Agravain looked cheerful tonight in his russet silk, Gawain told himself, as he looked round. Yes, it would be a night to recall.

Opposite Gawain, Sir Lucan was cheerful in a tunic of red and gold. Next to him, Sir Bors and Sir Lionel waited quietly, drinking little but following the merriment as it flowed to and fro.

Only Sir Mador stood aloof with Sir Patrise, his face unnaturally pale in the firelight's glow.

Oh, Mador –

Patrise threw his brother a quick glance, and a chill of foreboding crept around his heart. This was the finest night of Mador's life. To be dining in private with the Queen was a joy beyond joy. But the thought came to Patrise without warning: Brother, my dear brother, is the price too high?

Sir Lucan gave a mischievous laugh, and lightly punched Gawain's arm. 'So, Lancelot's not to be married after all?'

Gawain groaned. Since his story of Lancelot's love had been proved to be false, he had suffered unmercifully at the other knights' hands. 'I told you what I'd heard in the Humberlands. How was I to know that he'd change his mind?'

Agravain smiled contemptuously. 'He probably took his pleasure of the girl, then thought again. He knows he can't be married if he wants to keep the favour of the Queen. And if he's looking for advancement, we all know that the Queen is the way to the King's heart.' His eyes were glittering as he grinned around.

Trust Agravain to put a foul complexion on everything, thought Gaheris, listening quietly at Gawain's side. The Gods alone knew why he looked so pleased with himself tonight. Aloud he said, 'Lancelot's not the man to dishonour a woman like that. He can't have promised to marry her at all.' He nodded at Bors and Lionel standing by. 'These two would know if Lancelot was in love. And you heard nothing about it from him, did you?'

'No.'

Bors gripped the stem of his goblet, and stared tensely ahead. He could not think of anything else to say.

Lionel came swiftly to Bors's aid. 'Lancelot has always said that he'll never marry because he serves the Queen.'

Mador stirred out of his trance-like state. 'As we all do,' he said fervently.

'The Queen!'

A flurry of distant shouts came down the corridor and rolled through the open door. 'The Queen! Make way for the Queen!'

The candles on the walls were burning down, and the great fire was slumbering on the hearth. The wine had been passed round again and again, and trenchers of roast boar and pheasant, partridge, pigeon and hare, had come and gone with bowls of salad and herbs and fine white bread. Guenevere settled back on her throne, and composed her face into a smile. The feast had gone well, better than she had hoped.

True, it had not been pleasant to sit opposite Agravain for hours on end, watching him in that state of odd excitement, his dark face twitching for the whole of the meal. But the burning devotion of young Mador had more than made up for it. He had sat by her side all night, eating nothing, scarcely able to breathe. *He loves me*, she thought, with a sad inward smile. *And even a boy's love, a pale echo of Lancelot's, is welcome now.*

A rattle of activity from the serving pantry announced the final course. Bowls of damsons and hazelnuts, plums, quinces and ripe medlars were making their way on to the white damask cloth between the guests. Agravain watched, and his evil spirit leaped in his breast. Not long now, his inner demon rejoiced, not long.

Sssooon –

Ssoon, Agravain, ssssoon.

The golden apple called sweetly to him, in a high, thin whine. Agravain caught the sound, and held his breath. It was the choicest fruit of the feast, without doubt. The Queen either had to present it to Mador, to reward his triumph on his quest, or else to Gawain, to bless his journey home. Gods of all darkness, he raised a frantic prayer, let my brother die.

Or Mador.

He laughed. His eyes were black hollows in his head. In truth, it mattered little now which one, for in time, it would be both.

Yet Gawain should be first.

He fixed his eyes on Guenevere. *Choose Gawain,* he willed her, *now.*

Guenevere felt the force of Agravain's glare, and flinched. His eyes were pools of blackness, and mirrored in each she could see the golden apple of the centrepiece. Yet when she looked again, the apples were gone, and Agravain was smiling at her pleasantly enough.

With an effort she addressed herself to Sir Gawain at her side. 'So you ride for the Orkneys at dawn?'

Gawain laughed. 'Or sooner, madam, if I can get my brothers out of bed! Many miles lie between us and our mother's isle.'

'Then let me wish you and your brothers good speed,' said Guenevere. 'May the Great One watch over you, and cheer every step of your way.'

She reached out her hand for the golden apple on the centrepiece.

It's coming, Agravain triumphed, it's here.

Guenevere favoured Gawain with her most gracious smile. Then she turned to Mador on her other side. 'Sir Gawain has many triumphs to his name. I know he will forgive me if I present the fruit of the feast to you.'

Mador's eyes were moons of rapt delight. Exaltation over-whelmed him. He opened his mouth, and found he could not speak.

Gawain was the first to break the spell. He gave a raucous laugh. 'What's the matter, man? Has the Queen got your tongue?'

Patrise felt an impulse of furious rage. He surged pro-tectively to his feet, and bowed to Guenevere.

'Sir Mador accepts your gift, gracious Majesty,' he said, 'with deepest gratitude.'

Guenevere passed him the apple. 'Thank you, Sir Patrise.'

Patrise cradled the golden apple in his hands. 'No, Majesty, our thanks are due to you,' he said reverently, 'and that of all our house.' With his eyes fixed on the Queen, he bowed again, and brought the glittering fruit to his lips in a ceremonial kiss.

Mador watched Patrise speaking for him, and his heart almost burst. Feeling returned to him in a sudden flood, and he stumbled to his feet.

'By the Great One Herself, my lady' he began chokingly, 'you have honoured me more than I deserve –'

And that at least was true, a disgruntled Sir Gawain complained to his brothers, as they left the Queen's Apartments at the end of the feast, and strode into the night. Of course the golden apple should rightly have been his. Nothing but a woman's perversity could have made the Queen give it to a young upstart like Mador.

So he had little patience with Agravain's seething rage, the baffled fury the dark knight was showing now.

'And what's the matter with you, Agravain?' he demanded aggressively, threatening his brother with a good drubbing in the tilting yard if his humour did not improve.

But try as he might, Gawain could not get to the bottom of Agravain's black mood. Brooding over it kept him awake till almost dawn. Then, bad-tempered and short of sleep, he chivvied his complaining brothers out of their beds and down to the courtyard to be gone.

'To horse, Orkneys! We ride forty miles today.'

Sir Mador lay on his bed in the lodgings he shared with Patrise, heedless of the distant sounds of the four Orkney brothers departing with their horses, their dogs and their men. He had not slept at all since the feast last night, and now his aroused soul floated out into the breaking dawn, soaring into unknown realms of bliss. She gave me the golden apple, sang round inside his head, she has chosen me for her knight. Guenevere my lady, Guenevere the Queen.

Across the narrow cell, Patrise lay unmoving on his bed. In his hand lay the golden apple, which Mador had refused to take from him, unable to touch the evidence of his good fortune in case it disappeared.

'Humour me, brother,' he had breathed to Patrise. 'Tomorrow we shall share and enjoy this great gift.'

Patrise had smiled. 'As you wish, Mador.'

The younger knight had lain down then and there, rejoicing in the knowledge that Mador had been favoured by the Queen. As sleep descended he saw the family home restored to all its grandeur once again, and their widowed mother living in comfort for the rest of her days. He saw a fine lady marrying Mador, once his love for Guenevere had burned down to a soft glow. Then a loving wife of his own was coming towards him with open arms, surrounded by a handful of rosy babes. There would be love for them all in time to come.

Dreaming, Patrise drifted off. In shades of blue and black,

night deepened over Caerleon's high white towers. Still cradling the golden apple, Patrise fell asleep, feeling he was the happiest man in the court. And Mador, too, floated in measureless joy as, inch by inch, his brother's life ebbed away.

CHAPTER 41

The pattern of moonlight was fitful under the trees. A sharp wind tore the ragged clouds to and fro, and the silent watcher on the hilltop was lost in their flickering light. Across the valley, the great castle stared proudly down from its rocky mount on to the woodland below. Newly built, commanding the countryside for miles around, it was a place to inspire confidence in its allies, and terror in its foes.

Not that the lord of this fortress could have many enemies, Merlin reflected as he peered through the falling night. Since Arthur had united all the petty kingdoms under his rule as High King, the whole country lived in peace, where beforehand there had been nothing but war. The only real threat these days came from the Saxons, who might one day grow bold enough to leave their toeholds on the Saxon shore, and strike down the coast and through into the Narrow Sea. But here in the south below London, this castle was assured of strong neighbours near at hand. And it was well placed, too, for Morgan to spirit Mordred away to France or even farther off, to Gaul, if Merlin's pursuit seemed likely to locate her son.

'If-fffff –' an owl hooted mournfully overhead.

'Hold your tongue, fool!' Merlin snapped back, but without ire. He hardly cared now, in any case.

For in truth, by now his hope was almost gone. How many years had he followed the trail in vain? From Camelot to Gore, and back down to the Welshlands, all the way up to the Orkneys, and back again, he had swept the island from north to south, then worked it from east to west like an old mole, burrowing all the way. No castle, no grange, no estate, had escaped his notice as he went along. Terre Foraine, the domain of the fanatical Christian King Pelles, was the only kingdom he had passed by. In Listinoise, he had come closest, but his quarry had fled. And for all he had heard or seen of him since then, the boy called Mordred might as well be dead.

No, not that! Merlin beat at his head, and furiously drove out the ever-present fear. But Morgan had been too clever for him all along. And if she were still against him all the way, Mordred was as good as dead to him.

Yet, the boy had to be somewhere, and he might as well be here. And boy no longer, but a grown youth now. Without enthusiasm, Merlin surveyed the castle on its moonlit rock, gleaming in the glory of its pale golden stone. What did they call it? Castle Bon Espoir? Perhaps it might yet be a place of good hope for him.

Stiffly he peered out from between the trees. He had done all he could to ensure that if Mordred were there he would not escape this time. Arriving before dark, he had taken up his station in the wood to watch as the denizens of the castle returned home. Only when they were all safely locked up for the night did he plan to show himself.

The moon had risen early, and it was not yet fully dark. In the oak tree above, the owl hooted a warning, but Merlin's ears had already caught the sound. From a distance came the drumming of many hoofs, as a troop of riders raced home through the night. Merlin waited in perfect patience for them to appear.

And there they were, sweeping into the narrow valley between the wood where he lay and the castle on its mount. Young riders all, from their breakneck speed and from the exuberant calling and hallooing to one another as they galloped along. Merlin parted the branches, craned forward, and strained to see.

They were twenty or so young squires, dressed for a boar hunt, all equipped with short swords and hunting spears. In the lead, a tall young man stood up in his stirrups to wave the stragglers on. Merlin's heart leaped wildly inside his breast. Surely he had Arthur's strong body and horseman's legs, even the upward sweep of his arm, to the life?

But he could not see his face. Like all his companions, the

young rider was helmeted and lightly armoured too. They passed by in an instant, leaving Merlin groaning aloud. What could he make of a glimpse in the dark?

By the time the young hunters had thundered up to the castle, and clattered inside to the welcoming shouts of the guard, the old man was almost sure that he was deceiving himself. But of one thing at least, he was certain now. The daredevil rider and all the other young men were inside the castle, and the castle had made fast for the night. The drawbridge was up, the heavy portcullis was down, and the postern gate was manned by men-at-arms. Only a bat or a rat would leave there that night.

The evening moon rode higher in the sky, the wind dropped, and a light rain came drifting down from the clouds. Grumbling softly, Merlin eased his old limbs down the hill, reclaimed his mule from the thicket where he had left it hours before, and slowly climbed the castle mound to the top.

At the postern gate, he made short work of the guard.

'Take me to your lord!' he ordered imperiously.

Despite his wild-eyed glare and long grey tangled locks, few would argue, he knew, with a hawk-faced stranger clad in furs and gold. Moments later he was traversing a series of inner courts in the company of a small detachment of the guard, passing a range of fine stables and a well-equipped tilting yard as he went. Another sliver of hope came to warm his heart. Yes, Morgan wanted all this for her son. A young squire would get the best of knighthood training here.

They came to a halt before a pair of wooden doors. A short exchange took place with the guards on the door, and a moment later Merlin was ushered in.

He entered a long, high chamber warmed by roaring fires. Candles round the walls shone on bright new panelling, and lit up the well-fitted private apartment of a lord, with fat, sheepskin-covered couches, tables and chairs. At one end, an array of steaming dishes announced the dinner hour. The sweet tang of tender lamb roasted with sage gave Merlin a sharp reminder that he had not eaten since yesterday. Ruthlessly he thrust the thought aside. Time afterwards to eat and drink his fill.

The knight seated at the long table pushed aside his plate, and rose to his feet as Merlin came in. He was a well-muscled man of middle height, with a body hardened by exercise, and accustomed to command. Close-faced and wary-eyed, he looked older than he was, and the life of arms seemed second nature to him. Even taking his ease over dinner, Merlin saw, he wore his sword and his knife at his belt, and had not donned a loose chamber gown. This warrior would be ready at all times.

The knight's sharp eyes narrowed, and he gave a satisfied nod. 'Lord Merlin,' he said, with a thin-lipped smile, 'I heard you had been sighted hereabouts. I'm glad to know you have not disdained my house.'

He gestured to the food on the long board. 'You find me dining alone, not with my knights in the hall. I know they would gladly entertain you in their midst. But I beg you'll join me here.'

He beckoned Merlin to the seat next to his, and clapped his hands. 'Ho, there!' he called. 'More viands and fresh plates.'

Merlin moved towards him in a fever of haste. 'Forgive this intrusion, Sir – ?'

'Hervis de Rivel is my name. How may I serve you?'

Where to begin? Merlin was gripped by a sudden furious fear he could not explain. Gabbling, he plunged into what he had to say. 'Sir Hervis, a matter of urgency brings me here. You take in squires, and train them as young knights?'

Sir Hervis nodded warily. 'That's no secret, I've been doing it for years. It keeps me in condition for tournaments, and the lads keep me young. And in return,' a look of simple appraisal passed over his eyes, 'they get one of the best knighthood trainings to be had.' He cast a look at Merlin from the corner of his eye. 'Do you have a lad to be placed? Riding, fencing, ground fighting, we do it all.' A smile of faint derision hovered round his lips. 'Oh, and dancing, and singing, and all that fol-de-rol. But I make sure that the life of arms comes first.'

'No, no, I have no boy,' Merlin said faintly. Now the moment had come, he could hardly speak.

'Well, then?'

Merlin forced himself to open his mouth. 'Do you have a youth here called Mordred?' he blurted out.

The knight gave Merlin a suspicious stare. 'Why?'

He does! A mist of joy flooded Merlin's brain. He thrust his skinny wrists under Sir Hervis's nose. The blue tattooed dragons writhed and leaped with glee. 'He is my kinsman,' he cried, 'he's Pendragon born! So he's also kin to the King. He's wanted at court.'

Sir Hervis's eyes widened with new respect. 'To court, eh? Well, I always knew he was destined for great things. He's a rare lad, Mordred, and no mistake.'

Merlin's heart swelled till he thought it would burst. 'He is here?'

'Here right enough, and soundly asleep by now. The squires go to bed after sundown, that's the rule. They were hunting today, so they'll all sleep well tonight.' With a shrewd glance, he read Merlin's face. 'You want to see him?' he demanded abruptly. 'Come with me.'

Taking up a branched candlestick from the table, he led Merlin out into the corridor again. Together they threaded endless stone passageways, making for the centre of the house. With every step, Merlin felt he was on knives of fire. His heart was hammering agonisingly in his chest. *Can it be, can it be?*

Sir Hervis threw a shrewd glance at the old man's tortured face.

'He'll be there, never fear,' he said sharply as they strode along. 'With twenty of them on the brink of manhood, we keep them under lock and key at night. There's no end to what they'd get up to otherwise. We don't want any nonsense with the girls of local houses, or the kitchenmaids. We're trying to teach them chivalry, after all.'

They rounded a corner to see another long corridor ahead. At the end loomed a pair of stout oak doors, guarded by an old custodian nodding over a book. He came to trembling attention as they approached. A large key lay on the table at his side, and Sir Hervis picked it up.

'Don't disturb yourself, Caedric,' he said briskly to the old man, moving to the door. 'We've just come for a quick look at one of our young men. Mordred's in his bed where he should be, is he?'

The old man's rheumy eyes goggled at his lord. 'Yes, sir, I saw him come in,' he said, in bewilderment. 'Where else would he be?'

Sir Hervis nodded, and unlocked the door. Merlin almost

trod on his host's heels as Sir Hervis stepped in, craning his neck till it ached. *Can it be?*

In the darkened room, not a mouse stirred. The only sound was of twenty healthy young sleepers breathing as one. In the faint light of the candles, a long narrow dormitory stretched to the right and the left of the door. Ahead was the chamber's one window, shuttered and barred.

Sir Hervis stood by the door, and shone the candlelight around. At last he saw what he had been seeking, and moved a pace a two. In one of the beds a huddled shape lay submerged in its bedclothes, all but the crown of a head. Against the white sheets and pillowcase, the hair was as dark as the night sky outside.

Sir Hervis pointed. He did not need to speak.

Mordred.

Merlin felt tears like elf-arrows stabbing at his eyes. The longing to touch the boy was almost too much. He wanted to hug him, to crush him to his chest, to shower kisses on the top of his head. He wanted to laugh, to weep, to cry his name.

Mordred.

Sir Hervis raised his hand. Silently he led the way out of the room. He locked the door, handed the key to old Caedric, and led the speechless Merlin back the way they had come.

By the time they reached the apartment, Merlin found that he was more than ready to dine. The servants had kept the food hot, and the old man proceeded to do justice to all that Sir Hervis could provide.

With every mouthful, Merlin's spirits soared. Roast lamb with woody sage, jugged hare, and pigeons in a pot followed hot broth and salads down his hungry throat. In between, he plied Sir Hervis with questions about Mordred, and rewarded the knight's high praise with tales old and new about the Pendragon line. Both men drank deep, draining bottle after bottle of strong wine like water from the well.

Afterwards Sir Hervis was to swear that he never spent a better night in all his life. Merlin, too, retired to bed in highest content. Despite the night's indulgence, both men were up before dawn the next day, when Caedric opened the locked doors of the squire's dormitory to allow Merlin his first sight of the boy. And neither he nor Sir Hervis and least of all the loyal old man on the door could explain why, in the locked room, all the squires were still slumbering peacefully, except one. Where Mordred had lain sound asleep in his bed, there was no one to be seen – only a faint indentation, and a blue-black hair or two on a pillow long grown cold.

CHAPTER 42

Every night now was fitful, and full of fears. By day, Guenevere could often keep her miseries at bay. But as soon as the twilight trailed across the sky, she fell a prey to thoughts she could hardly bear. By midnight she was torn by wild regrets, pangs of sorrows hunting in packs like wolves. And always in the small hours, grief was most alive.

Even the greyest dawn came as a relief. When she woke on the morning after the feast, she even felt pleasure and a little joy. Was it the heart-warming adoration of young Mador? Was it the warmth, the comfort, the fine meal, was it the wine?

Whatever it was, it was not to last. It vanished as soon as she heard Ina fly up to the bed, and tear the bed-curtains back.

'You must come, lady,' the little maid wept. 'It's Sir Patrise.'

The crowd thronging the knights' lodging spilled out into the courtyard and beyond.

'Way there, make way for the Queen,' the guards shouted as they approached. Courtiers, monks and servants drew aside to let them pass.

A strange and fearsome smell came out to meet them as they stepped through the door. Inside the cell, Arthur was standing with his back to her, by the look of his heavy gauntlets and leather attire summoned here on his way to the hunt. Beside him she saw, with a spurt of furious disgust, the long black form of the Father Abbot, craning like Arthur over the bed against the wall.

Both men turned towards her as she came in. Looking at their shocked faces, the greeting died on her lips. Arthur shook his head hopelessly, and gestured behind. Guenevere stepped forward to face what was there.

On the bed lay the thing that had been Sir Patrise. His flesh was black, and already beginning to rot. In his hand he still held the golden apple she had given him last night. Dully she recognised the red silk tunic he had worn, the brown woven woollen breeches, his best leather boots. But his clothes were the only human thing about him now. White bone gleamed through the ruins of his face, and maggots were crawling in the hollows of his eyes.

Guenevere tried to cry out, and found she could not speak. Vomit rose in her throat, and she thrust her hand into her mouth to keep it down.

From behind her came the keening of a soul half mad with grief. 'He's dead!'

On the bed behind the door crouched Mador, plucking compulsively at his skin and hair. Blood flowed from his forehead and stained the rough whitewashed loam where he had beaten his head against the wall.

Guenevere crossed to him, and tried to take his hand. But he stared at her unknowing, gibbering in terror and pointing towards the bed. 'Patrise – Patrise – he's dead!'

'What is this?' Arthur demanded helplessly.

The sonorous reply filled the small cell. 'Witchcraft!'

Guenevere turned. The Father Abbot towered, gesticulating, over the pitiful body on the bed. 'The powers of darkness have taken this knight's life. All that remains is to establish the cause.'

Mador leaped twitching to his feet. 'The apple!' he howled. 'The apple killed Patrise.'

Guenevere gasped. 'Surely not!'

'This?' Arthur pointed to the golden apple in Patrise's hand.

'He took it from the Queen, he kissed it, and held it in his hands.' Mador wept. 'It was meant for me. But he died instead!'

'Mador, no!' Guenevere reached out for him, and again he jumped away.

'The apple, you say?' The Abbot's head swivelled like a hawk finding its prey. He gestured to the golden object in Patrise's hand. 'It must be bewitched, my lord.'

Arthur nodded heavily. Guenevere stared at the gilded fruit

in disbelief. The smooth golden surface had a greenish glint in the early morning sun. And suddenly it seemed an object of evil beyond compare.

'Let me see.'

Arthur took up the apple in his gauntletted hand, reached for the hunting knife at his belt, and sliced it in two. The golden halves parted with a soft hissing sigh, and a stench beyond compare seeped into the room.

'God save us!' With a convulsive twitch, Arthur threw it to the floor.

'As you say, my son.' The Abbot crossed himself, staring at the fruit. Inside its gilded skin, the flesh of the apple was as black and putrid as Patrise himself.

Arthur's gauntlets saved him, came to Guenevere. *Goddess, Mother, tell me what this means –*

The Abbot collected himself. Ignoring Guenevere, he fixed Arthur in his glare. 'And the Queen gave it to him?' he demanded ominously

Mador started and turned towards Guenevere, his face alive with questioning fear. 'The Queen?' He was trembling so violently that he could hardly stand. 'She did – she did –'

The Abbot nodded. The germ of a dazzling plan was coming into his mind. 'And I say to you again, this is witchcraft.' He placed a commanding hand on Mador's arm. 'Believe me, all witches, like whores, are destroyers of good knights.'

Mador was staring at the Abbot with rapt regard, drinking in his every word. Guenevere bowed her head. Had this boy ever loved her? Or had she dreamed it all?

At last Arthur moved to intervene. 'Forgive me, Father,' he said, with an effort to take control, 'I trust you don't speak these words against the Queen?'

'He's dead! Patrise is dead,' Mador wept, 'and his soul will look to me for its revenge.' He threw himself at the feet of the Father Abbot, reaching up to him like a child. 'You'll help me, won't you, Father? Help me hunt down the witch?'

The Abbot leaned down to him. 'I will, my son. All our forces are at your command.' He glanced at Arthur, ignoring Guenevere. 'As yours are too, sire, I dare swear.'

Guenevere gasped with rage. She turned to Arthur. 'Sir –'

But the Abbot already was helping Mador to his feet, a fatherly arm around the slight shoulders, a firm hand on his arm. 'Have no fear, my son,' he said forcefully. 'We in the Christian faith are experts on such things.' He looked straight at Guenevere, and she saw the shadow of a smile. 'Believe me, I shall not shrink from hunting down this witch.'

She had been a fine old beast in her time, no doubt about that. She stood four-square on sturdy, well-shaped limbs, displaying a deep chest and powerful torso with a run of long teats that had suckled many young. Her fur was still a deep umber shaded with black, hardly brindled at all with grey. But age or softness had weakened her grip on her young. Why else would a son of the pack turn on the mother wolf, and pull her down?

And in the courtyard of the palace too, Orkneyans marvelled as the tale spread. And at this time above all, with the Queen's sons due any day. For weeks the whole place had been in a fever as the princes and their entourage made their way up north. The forests had been scoured for miles around to provide enough boar, hare and wood-pigeon for the pot, not to mention every log, every branch and stick to feed the fires, now that winter had come.

It must have been the activity in the forest that had flushed the she-wolf from her lair. But nothing could account for her appearance at the palace gate, with a young wolf on her heels. And as she ran, he had caught up with her, leaped to rip open her flank, and grinned in triumph as she dragged herself away, mortally wounded, back to the woods.

Thank the Old Ones that this unlucky portent had been forgotten in all the excitement when the Queen's sons arrived, Sir Lamorak mused grimly, standing with the knight companions behind the Queen's throne. Sir Gawain had been the first off his horse, and into the Queen's Hall, where Morgause waited on her single throne. She wore a velvet gown the colour of the chains of amethysts covering her full bosom, and plaited into her long flowing hair. The ancient diadem of the Orkneys crowned her head, and the ruby-coloured train of her cloak flowed over the back of her throne and down the steps of the dais like a river of blood. Her long, strong face might have been carved out of stone, and her hair, freshly hennaed in fantastic shades of crimson and plum, fell to her waist like coloured rain.

Morgause rose to her feet, and spread her arms. 'My sons!'

Four mighty figures bounded down the hall and fell to their knees. 'Your Majesty!'

The full pageant of greeting took its lengthy course. Lamorak shifted his weight on his aching feet, and watched with under-standing as others of the knight companions did the same. He glanced at the Queen, aloft in solitary eminence on her bleached driftwood throne. Glowing in all her glory, Morgause filled the grey granite space. Never had she looked more remote, more queenly or more terrible. But Lamorak knew what lay behind the regal façade. He had watched Morgause with eyes of troubled love, as fear and foreboding had grown in her day by day, alongside the joy she felt as her sons drew near.

He felt a sigh grind his innards to pulp. If you had married me, my love, you would not have to fear, he mourned within. I would be seated beside you now, your king and companion, your true partner and protector, never to leave your side. And, instead, I must sneak in darkness to the bed we have shared for ten years, lurking in the shadows like your seedy paramour.

Yet did it have to be so? At their age, did Morgause's sons really care? He turned his eyes to the four princes standing before the throne, and saw with a start Agravain's eyes fixed on him with a terrifying force, their glittering black depths raking his face. Lamorak gritted his teeth. He knew he had an open, unguarded mien. What had he given away?

Again a dark premonition gripped his heart, and he struggled to fight it down. What could he have revealed, after all? Even those who walked the world between the worlds could not read all men's minds, and Agravain was no wanderer from the astral plane.

No, all would be well. Lamorak sighed, and brought his mind back to earth with the thought of his aching feet. Soon the long ritual of welcome would be at an end. Then each of the princes would be escorted to his own palace in the Queen's compound. There they would be attended by the island's fairest maidens, pampered, bathed, perfumed and clad in the finest plaids the islands could provide. Lamorak nodded to himself.

Agravain would be prepared for the Queen's feast like a king. Surely that must improve his temper, and help him to behave like a loving son?

CHAPTER 43

'Oh, my lady, it's Sir Mador – he's petitioned the King!' She had heard of the meeting at once, as soon as Ina hurried back wide-eyed and trembling from the lower court. She went straight to the King's Apartments, sent out a bevy of messengers to track him down, and by the time Arthur returned, she was ready for him.

'Why did you agree to this without consulting me?' she began, without preamble. She could barely speak for rage.

Arthur's head went back. 'I am king in my own kingdom, Guenevere,' he said stiffly. 'I don't need your agreement every time my council meets.'

She ground her nails in her palms. 'If not as my husband, then as king, why?'

Arthur did not want to admit that he had been asking himself that question ever since he had agreed to the Father Abbot's smooth suggestion a few hours ago. 'Sir Mador demanded a hearing about his brother's death,' he said stubbornly. 'It's every subject's right.'

'But you know that the Christians have been working on Mador. They're only using him, he's half mad with grief.'

Arthur essayed a laugh. 'Come now, Guenevere, using him for what? Mador's a grown man. He knows what he thinks.'

If only grown men did, Guenevere thought, with a bitter surge. With a furious effort, she held on to her argument. 'They're using him to push forward this vicious nonsense about witchcraft. You know that isn't true. So that must mean –' she tried to calm herself – 'that we have a murderer among us – someone who wanted one of our knights to die.'

'I can't believe that,' Arthur said with confidence. He cocked his head knowingly to one side. 'There are many forces of evil beyond our ken. Witchcraft is only the name the Christians have for it, after all.'

'But Arthur – if you give in to it, don't you see where it will lead?'

Arthur's honest face showed his bewilderment. 'No, I don't,' he said irritably. 'You mustn't forget that the Christians are men of God. They don't want to hurt you, or anyone.'

If only, Arthur –

She waved a hopeless hand. She wanted to scream.

'Guenevere –' Arthur moved towards her and tried to take her hand. 'You're taking all this too seriously, my dear,' he said, in reassuring tones. 'Can't you see that it's better to let young Mador have his say? It won't be for weeks in any case. I've set the date well ahead so things can cool down. But we have to let him have his moment in court. Then honour will be satisfied, and it'll all die down.'

Arthur, you're wrong.

Guenevere turned away, and began to pace the floor. 'What if he demands the right of challenge for his brother's death?'

Arthur smiled. 'He won't,' he said confidently. 'He only wants this hearing to lay it all to rest.'

Guenevere ground her teeth. 'But if he does, you'll have to agree to it.'

Arthur stared. 'You don't understand, Guenevere. I'm still the King.'

Guenevere could have wept. 'But even as king, if a challenge takes place and I'm found guilty, you won't be able to stop the course of law.'

Arthur burst out laughing. 'You can't be found guilty, you're innocent! So it won't arise.' He gave a contented beam.

How to make him see, to understand?

Her control broke. 'You don't know!' she howled. 'The Christians hate the Mother. They're calling me a witch, and they want me dead.' She flew at him, and beat him on the chest. 'And you won't listen to a word I say!'

Arthur flushed with anger, and drew himself away. 'Guenevere, you're hysterical,' he said coldly. 'This is utter nonsense, and I won't hear any more.'

'Arthur, I beg you –'

'No, Guenevere.' He held up his hand. Never had he looked more self-righteous and more aloof. 'Leave this to me,' he said, with chilling emphasis. 'You'll soon see I'm right. And I think you'll be sorry for this afterwards.'

'Let us honour the Old Ones at our feast tonight! And may the Great Ones in their mercy bless us all!'

Morgause raised her goblet in salute to the crowded hall, and resumed her seat on her throne. All around them now, the granite walls were swagged with deep woven tapestries against the cold. In the body of the long chamber, a forest of trestles had been rigged for all who came. On the dais a long table held the Queen, her knight companions and her kin. She sat with Gawain and Gaheris on her right and Agravain and Gareth on her left, turning from one side to the other in nervous joy. And Lamorak sat with his knights to his right and his left across the table facing her, profoundly wishing that it was not so. I should have been at your side, my love, he mourned, at your side, not here.

The servants were bringing the food into the hall, each struggling with a trencher as big as himself.

'Serve yourselves, my lords!' Morgause cried.

Gawain lifted his head, and savoured the smell of roast boar, roots and wild thyme.

'By the Gods, my lady,' he cried, raising the curious wooden pitcher that held his wine, 'I know I speak for all your sons when I say, a toast to our mother, the Queen, and may the Old Ones bless our return to our native isles!'

Gawain, Gawain, threatened Agravain in his ugly heart, don't speak for me. There are no blessings here for a second son. My Gods have deserted me, or you would not be carousing here, you would not be alive!

Frenziedly he reviewed the night of Guenevere's feast. How could the apple have failed to miss its mark? To waste the precious death-juice at a stroke, and miss both Gawain and Mador too! Gawain should have died, there was no question of that. But failing Gawain, Mador's death would have done. Instead, he raged, I had to watch as that fool Patrise walked away with it unharmed, and who knows if Mador ever tasted it at all? I am cursed, he wailed inside, I am cursed and abandoned, while others live to rejoice.

Seated next to Morgause, he watched moodily as she accepted Gawain's toast. His mother had lost her stony pallor now, and a drowsy flush bathed her face and empurpled her heavy-lidded eyes. She was thickly perfumed in a rich heathery scent, but above it there was something else, high, thin, and sour. With a stab of recognition, he knew it for the tang of a mare in season, overlaid by the sharp trace of mingled bodies, the smell of sex. A sick rage seized him, and he could not look at her. He jerked his head away.

'Thank you, Prince Gawain. And may the Mother herself bless you, my sons.'

Morgause smiled on Gawain, and felt a surge of warm contentment sweep over her. The old year was ending, and the new year would bring joy. Her sons and her lover were at peace, feasting together around a groaning board. Gawain and the others would come to accept Lamorak as her Chosen One. Life was blessed here, they could all live in accord. Whereas at Arthur's court –

'My sons!' She leaned forward. 'You've been on the road so long, you won't have heard.'

'Heard what, madam?' demanded Gawain.

Morgause sighed, and her face grew grave. 'One of Arthur's knights has met a terrible death. His brother blames the Queen. The Christians are crying witchcraft against Guenevere, and demanding a hearing against her, even a trial.'

Agravain twitched as if he had been stung. So Mador had eaten the apple, after all? A flame of joy ignited in his heart. His Gods had not betrayed him. Mador was dead!

'One of the knights?' Gawain gasped. 'Madam, tell us who?'

'Sir Patrise, the brother of Sir Mador.'

Patrise! Agravain started, and could have screamed. So his Gods had been mocking him all along!

'Patrise?' cried Gaheris. 'How did he die?'

Morgause shook her head. 'No one knows. He was found dead on his bed the night after a feast.'

'It was the feast the Queen gave us before we left! We were

all there!' Gawain stuttered. 'And Patrise was on fine form that night. Gods above, what a terrible thing!' He brought his hand to his eyes.

'But how's the Queen to blame?' Gareth cried.

'She gave him an apple with poison inside,' Morgause replied. 'It turned him black, and rotted the flesh off his bones. The Christians are calling it witchcraft. They say Guenevere made him an offering to the Dark Mother.'

There was a general laugh of sharp contempt.

'As if the Great One craves such offerings,' said Gareth hotly.

'But no one there would have wanted to kill Patrise,' Gaheris put in. 'So it can't have been a human hand at work.'

A momentary chill passed between them all. Gawain was the first to recover. 'Whatever it was,' he declared, 'surely they can't call the Queen to account for that?'

'In Camelot, never,' Morgause agreed. 'But they were in Caerleon, where the rule of the Mother passed away long ago.' Her face darkened with old memories. 'Uther Pendragon destroyed the mother-right. And Arthur is influenced by his wretched monks.'

Gaheris groaned. 'Christians see evil everywhere.'

Gawain frowned. 'And they burn witches,' he said grimly. 'It's one of their foul beliefs. So the Queen stands in danger then, it seems?'

Morgause sighed. 'Indeed, she must.'

Lamorak stirred. 'But surely not of her life?' He gestured to the knight companions all around. 'Sir Lancelot must defend her, just as we would fight to the death for our queen.' He bowed his head in homage, and smiled with transparent reverence at Morgause.

He is her lover, came to Agravain like a pain. He felt something tearing and splitting inside his head, but he forced himself to speak. 'So you think a queen is above the law, Sir Lamorak, always beyond reproach?'

Lamorak looked at Morgause again. 'She is,' he said simply.

'Whatever she does?'

Lamorak turned his gaze to stare at Agravain uncomprehendingly. 'She is the Queen.'

'And a queen can do no wrong?'

'I do not follow you.'

Agravain bared his teeth in a dreadful smile. 'What of murder, say, like Queen Guenevere? Or cruelty or lechery, or any foul conduct not fitting for a queen?'

'Sir Agravain.' Lamorak drew a breath. 'You are my lady's son, and a prince of these isles. I am bound to honour you, as I do her. But while I defend her, no other man would sit at the Queen's left hand and question her royal right as you have done.'

'Well said, Sir Lamorak!' Gawain burst out laughing. 'That's one in the eye for you, Agravain.'

There was a general outbreak of mirth at Agravain's expense.

Agravain flushed with rage. 'Let me tell you, Gawain –'

Morgause raised a hand. 'Enough.' She turned to Lamorak. 'I thank you, sir.'

The smile she gave Lamorak scorched Agravain's sight. He saw his mother naked on a bed, her soft white flesh spilling into Lamorak's hands. He saw the young knight's body entering hers, rising and plunging in the act of love. He saw the languid longing in her eyes, the look that she wore now. And it came to him again, the smell of sex.

'What, sulking, Agravain?' cried Gareth boisterously.

Agravain's head was bursting. Great breasts and monstrous nipples, hips splayed wide and open white thighs, blinded his sight. He surged to his feet, and caught up the wooden goblet at his place, sending it smashing into the opposite wall. The red wine trickled down the pale stone like blood. Then the torches on the walls flared up with the wind of his passage as he broke away.

Morgause rose to her feet. 'Agravain!'

Agravain raced on down the room without a pause.

'Agravain!' Morgause howled in fury. 'Return to your seat! No man may leave the royal presence without consent.'

Agravain stormed through the door without a backward glance. In an instant Sir Lamorak was at the Queen's side, the knight companions rallying round him to a man.

'Your son defied you, madam,' he said urgently. 'Shall I pursue him, and force him to return?'

He finished speaking, and looked deep into Morgause's eyes. Charge me with this, he besought her silently, and I will

bring the young whelp to heel. Give me the power to do what
must be done, or he will hurt us all.

There was an aching silence. Lamorak felt his fate hanging
suspended far above his head. He heard a great crying from the
astral plane, where stars and tears are one. Then a blanket of dark
foreboding covered his sight and he knew without knowing the
answer that Morgause would make.

Morgause's anger had drained away like an ebb tide. She
shook her head. Lamorak bowed, and returned to his seat.
Reluctantly the knight companions sheathed their swords, and
silently hushed their weapons' blood-hungry whine.

Morgause composed herself. 'So, my sons, more wine?'

Around the table, the party made valiant efforts to restore
the vanished cheer. After a while, some warmth and comfort
returned to gladden them all, as the love they shared revived and
did its work.

But outside the hall, all was dark and cold. And, ranging
murderously through the chill of a winter night, maddened and
alone, Agravain counted his injuries and dreamed of a great
revenge, something faster and bloodier than even his precious
poison could give him now.

CHAPTER 44

'Understand this, all of you.' Arthur's voice echoed round the low, panelled room. 'There will be no blood shed.'

Sir Mador drew in his breath in a hiss of dismay. A hectic flush rose to his pallid face. 'Sire –'

Arthur leaned forward, his finger jabbing the air. 'Agree to this, Sir Mador, or these proceedings are at an end.'

Mador's eyes were unnaturally bright. 'You are the King. I must agree.'

'Very well, then.' Arthur directed a troubled gaze round the Council board. Already he was beginning to fear that Guenevere was right, and the meeting could prove him wrong. 'We are all here, I think. Let us begin.'

Mador stepped towards the long table, trembling in every limb. His black mourning clothes lent an unnatural pallor to his wasted face. But when he spoke, his voice was clear and cold.

'Your Majesty, lords of the Council, and knights of the King, I come before you to seek justice and my right –'

Arthur held his head. Would nothing stop the boy? In the weeks that had passed since the death of Patrise, nothing had taken the edge off Mador's grief. Time had only hardened his resolve to seek revenge. Mador, Mador, Arthur almost groaned aloud, let it be.

Outside the window, a leaden winter day was slipping into a frozen, windswept night. Icicles clung to the mullions, and flurries of snowflakes lightened the brooding sky. A dull fire sputtered on the hearth, and gave little warmth. Arthur drew his furred gown more tightly around him, and tried to pay attention to Mador's speech.

All round the time-worn green baize, the members of the King's Privy Council were doing the same. To Arthur's right sat his most trusted knights, to his left were Caerleon's wisest and most ancient lords. Further down the table, the Father Abbot formed a single column of black surrounded by black-clad monks. The faint smell of incense seeping from their robes mingled with the stale air of old furs and velvet in the room.

'My lord!' Mador's rising stridency assailed Arthur's ears. 'Twenty knights saw what happened at the feast. The Queen killed my brother. I ask for justice, justice, justice!'

'Sir Mador, you do not know what you ask.' It was old Sir Niamh, a knight who remembered the days of the Mother-right. 'A queen cannot be brought to trial.'

Mador swept the councillors with his glittering gaze. 'Tell me, then, how may I have redress? Or must my brother's death go unpunished here?'

'No evil goes unpunished where Pendragon reigns,' came the quiet voice of old Sir Baudwin, one of King Uther's former councillors, seated at Arthur's side. 'I was your age, young sir, when King Uther restored the rule of law in a kingdom ravaged by lawless men.'

He turned earnestly to Arthur. 'As you did yourself, sire, when you reclaimed your right. Pendragon means justice and truth for all.' He paused, stroking the forks of his iron-grey beard. 'It is true that a great evil has been done. And in the Middle Kingdom, no man must be beyond the reach of the law.'

The Father Abbot leaned forward. 'Or woman, sire.'

Mador's voice rang triumphantly round the room. 'Thank you, Father!'

'Gods above, man!' Sir Niamh's beetle brows swivelled down the table in alarm. 'What d'you mean?'

The Abbot fixed his pale gaze on Arthur, and composed his long face. God speed my words, he prayed. 'With your permission, sire,' he began smoothly, 'there is another issue for us here, not merely the death of Sir Patrise, but the way he died. No human hand brought him to his grave. The apple he ate, the unseen poison inside, the blackening of his flesh, all show the hand of a witch at work.'

Arthur started in horror. 'A witch?' he cried. 'Not Guenevere!'

The Abbot paused. *Lord, Lord, give me the concubine. With Your aid now, her life lies in my hand.* He reached for his softest, most reasonable voice. 'Sire, all women are daughters of Eve. It is their birthright from the Mother of our sin.'

Sir Niamh felt his old blood boil in his veins. 'In your faith, Christian, not in ours!'

The Abbot shrugged his shoulders. 'Eve was the first betrayer of mankind. She was doomed to be the destroyer of men. Likewise her daughters are born to turn men from their destiny, and draw them down to dust. For that reason, Our Lord himself shunned women, and held aloof from their carnal embrace.' He turned to Arthur, and spread his thin white hands. 'Sire, no man on earth would accuse your queen. But we cannot escape the fact that a knight lies dead.'

"Yes!' cried Mador.

'So evil is at work. And we must root it out.'

'Your Majesty.' Mador clenched his fists, and sent his voice ringing round the room. 'I beg no more than the law of this land allows. Let the Queen be brought to the field of trial, to face the challenge I make. Let her champion appear, and meet me, man to man. I will make good my claim against any who comes. Whoever wins, the truth will then be known.'

Arthur closed his eyes. How had it come to this? He shifted his great bulk on his throne. 'I am the Queen's Champion, Mador, do you know that?' he growled. 'And I shall meet your challenge, as you demand.'

'You?' Mador's mouth gaped. 'Oh, sire –'

Sir Baudwin shook his head. 'My lord, you may not fight against our laws. The King must be impartial.'

'And the Queen's knight is Lancelot,' Sir Niamh put in.

'But Lancelot is away,' Arthur ground out. 'And no man knows where he is.'

The Abbot smiled. 'The Queen will not go undefended,' he said confidently. 'And innocence is its own best defence.'

'Give me my right!' Mador cried. 'A trial by combat, *à l'outrance*, to the death!'

'Sir Mador –' Arthur sat torn in an agony of doubt.

Sir Baudwin leaned in to speak into Arthur's ear. 'My lord, you may not refuse Sir Mador's request. Trial by combat is a knight's ancient right. Moreover, your father gave it the force of law when he was ordaining justice in this land. Will you overthrow all this to protect your queen?'

Arthur groaned, and gripped the arms of his throne. 'It seems I must grant you your right, Sir Mador,' he cried at last. 'But the Queen will be defended, if I have to break the law to fight for her myself.' He bunched his fist and pounded on the board, wagging a warning finger at Mador and the Abbot alike. 'And however the verdict goes, remember one thing. You have sworn to shed no blood!'

He rose to his feet, and the Council followed him. The voice of the Abbot fell softly amid the bustle of departure, and none could have said who heard and who did not. But those nearest to Arthur saw what passed over his face.

'Shed no blood?' the Abbot mused conversationally as he gathered up his robes to leave. 'No, indeed. Yet witches may be burned. And if we have such a witch among us, who would spare her from the fire?'

CHAPTER 45

She could hear Arthur's voice, booming and over-confident, outside her chamber door. 'Tell the Queen, I am still her Champion. I will not let her die.'

Hopelessness seized her in an iron grip. When Ina returned with the message, she waved her away. Mador would have his revenge, and Arthur could not overthrow the course of the law. Lancelot was gone, she might as well be dead. What did it matter now?

The night wore on. High overhead a storm howled in from the Welshlands, and the owls in the bell-tower hid their heads in fear. Great blasts of wind beat at the windows, and sleet as sharp as elf-arrows pelted the glass. Again and again she built up the fire on the hearth, but still her blood ran cold. And again and again it came to her like a knife-blow: The Christians are setting the fire to burn me now, and Mador wants me dead.

'In Camelot, no man would dare to think such things.'

On a low table by the wall, a grey mouse sat up on her hind legs, looking at Guenevere. Her age-old eyes were smiling yet sorrowful too, and her plump sleek body was composed in an attitude of watchful love.

Guenevere groaned. 'Tell me, Mother, why does Mador want me to die?'

'He wants you to pay for the life that he thinks is lost. He does not know that his brother has sweetly sailed the sea of unknowing, and reached the isles of joy. That Patrise will be restored to bodily perfection, and come again as a great hero to win love and renown.'

Guenevere gave a bitter laugh. 'But he's turned to the Christians, and they want to kill me too.'

The little creature inclined her shining head. 'Mador takes comfort from the Christians because they flatter his ignorance with their foolish certainties, one way, one truth, one life. Like him, when our spirits leave us, they see only our body's death.'

'And they hate the Mother,' Guenevere said sombrely, 'and want to destroy Her laws.'

The small messenger nodded again. 'In the country of the Great One, all men know that women are the givers of life, and must never be put to death. But here . . .' She twitched her nose, and spread her tiny hands. 'You are in danger, daughter,' she said sadly. 'I have come to warn you to beware.'

Guenevere shuddered. 'Of the Christians?'

'Of the Christians, certainly. Their leader will not rest till he has rooted out the Mother from this land.' Her eyes filled with tears. 'One day soon the Great One will need your help. Soon you will be summoned back to Avalon. But for now, Guenevere, my word to you is, prepare for your fate.'

Guenevere pressed her hands together and brought them to her lips. 'I am ready. Speak.'

A great sigh filled the room, and the voice of the Lady echoed from Avalon. 'The dance of life is the rhythm of rise and fall. When we fall, we must rise to live our dance again.'

She leaned forward, her large luminous eyes searching Guenevere's face. 'Remember, Guenevere, you are not like other women. Fate spins as it will, and even the Mother cannot turn back the wheel.'

Guenevere felt hopelessness drowning her like a wave. 'What can I do?'

The tiny body was changing and dissolving as she spoke. 'Embrace your fate. Farewell.'

'Mother,' cried Guenevere weeping, 'don't leave me, don't go! They are all against me now, and I can't fight alone. If you don't help me, I'm lost, and I shall die!' '

'Remember, Guenevere,' came the low, musical tones, 'all women are blessed with the strength of the Great One Herself. Those who follow the Goddess can always enter the dream. Break free of this night of darkness, and you will become all that you have dreamed.'

The voice died away, and Guenevere was alone. But now the winter-bound midnight chamber was fragrant with apple blossom, and pulsing with the sound of Lake-water lapping over stones. A surge of power passed through Guenevere and brought her leaping to her feet, clapping her hands. 'Ina! Send for Sir Bors and Sir Lionel. Tell them I need them now!'

Bors shook off the snow from his mantle, and handed it to Ina without a word. Beside him, his brother Lionel looked frozen and hopeless too.

'So, my lady,' Bors said, in a voice as cold as the winter night outside, 'you sent for us?'

Guenevere steadied her voice. 'You know that Sir Mador has won the right of trial by combat to challenge me for causing his brother's death?'

'We know,' said Bors shortly.

'So I stand within his danger, the law says. Yet if my knight will fight for me, I may be cleared.'

'Your knight?' Bors burst out. 'Madam, if you mean Lancelot–' He broke off, scarcely able to contain himself. Ye Gods, was there no end to this woman's demands? 'He's not here, madam! You sent him away. Is it your wish to unbanish him now?'

Guenevere nodded. 'It is,' she said simply. 'I want you to find him, and beg him to return.'

Bors laughed in fury, gesturing to Lionel at his side. 'The trial will take place as soon as the hard weather breaks. Can the two of us scour these islands before then?'

'If he's still here.' Lionel shook his head. 'We've had no word from him since he went away.'

'We think he went back to France,' said Bors, with savage relish. 'And he'd never get back from there in time for the trial.'

Guenevere held him in a level stare. *I know you hate me, Bors. But you love Lancelot, and he loves me.* She forced a smile. 'Nevertheless, Sir Bors, I beg you to try.' She passed him a leather bag, whose heavy contents clinked as it changed hands. 'Twenty thousand crowns,' she said evenly. 'You may hire many messengers with that.'

Bors recoiled in hot disgust. 'We do not need your coin! The sons of Benoic do not serve for hire.'

Guenevere waved a hand. 'Then keep it as a gift for Lancelot when he returns.' She stepped towards Bors, and looked him in the eye. 'Understand this, sir, I must have a knight to fight for me at my trial. You are the nearest I have to my lord and love. If Lancelot fails, I call on you, Sir Bors, to champion me.'

Lionel gasped in horror. 'My lady, Sir Mador is one of the foremost fighters of the court! And you must know that my brother is not Sir Lancelot.' And poor Bors is short and not gifted at arms, he wanted to shout, he's no horseman, and not strong. Mador will hack him to pieces, Bors will die – Goddess, Mother, *no!* Gabbling, Lionel rushed on. 'I will defend Your Majesty. Take me as your champion, I'm Lancelot's cousin too.'

'No, Lionel.'

Bors was trembling, and his face had taken on an ashen sheen.

Lionel gripped his arm in a frenzy. 'Bors, listen to me –'

'Brother, this fight is mine.' Bors gently pushed him away, and gave a crooked smile. 'And this death is mine too, if it has to be.'

He turned back to Guenevere with a wooden bow. 'In fourteen days then, lady, I will fight for you.' He paused, and added, almost like a prayer, 'and for Lancelot.'

'Good night, my sons.'

The great bronze moon of the Orkneys looked down and smiled. The palace compound was loud with fond greetings as the night's festivities drew to a close.

'Sweet sleep to Your Majesty.'

'And to you all.'

One by one Morgause embraced her sons.

Gareth bent his head for another kiss. 'Good night, Mother,' he said happily.

'And don't give Agravain another thought,' added Gawain, with a laugh. 'Tomorrow I'll take him down to the tilting yard, and give him the lesson that's been long overdue. Our brother has disgraced us all tonight. Now we're all at home, we'll teach him how to behave.'

'Yes indeed,' Gaheris agreed. Already he could see Gawain thundering down the lists to thwack Agravain soundly to and fro, and Agravain crashing head down from his horse to eat the ground. He gave a wicked grin. 'Leave him to us.'

A look of sorrow and regret shadowed Morgause's face. 'Don't be too hard on him.'

Oh, lady, lady, you never were hard enough. Standing stiffly in the rear, Lamorak felt a chill greater than the winter night. A sense of being watched came to him suddenly, and the hairs rose on his neck. He turned back towards the buildings clustering in the darkness round the edge of the compound, then brushed away the fear. Agravain would not be lurking out here in cold like this. No, he would be sulking in his guest palace, nursing his insults over countless cups of wine.

With a burst of final farewells, the party dispersed.

Morgause turned to Lamorak. 'Good night, Sir Lamorak,' she said, with a glance from her heavy-lidded eyes. Come to me as soon as the palace is asleep, her look said as plainly as any words. And again Lamorak felt a chill breeze on his face like the hostile scrutiny of a watcher in the night.

'Good night, my lady,' he said carefully. He stood for a while watching them all depart. Then, dwelling by dwelling, he began to make the rounds of the outlying buildings huddled in the dark.

He had not gone far before he could feel a silent shadow trailing his every step. He drew into the darkness in the angle of a wall.

'Leif?' he breathed.

A soft chuckle reached him, and the leader of the knight companions emerged from the dark. His one eye caught the faint rays of the moon. His cratered face had a death-washed aspect, and his hunting stoop gave him an animal air. But the short sword and dagger he gripped in each hand gleamed with a reassuring light, and his grin was friendly and even sheepish in the depths of his curly beard.

Leif shrugged, and looked away. 'I was watching for you,' he grunted. 'The dark one means you ill.'

Lamorak drew a breath. 'He hates us all. And most of all, himself.'

Leif bared his teeth. He studied the edge of his sword, then favoured Lamorak with an unblinking stare. 'Such men are better dead.'

Lamorak did not move. A nod, a glance, he knew, and Agravain would be no more. Not a sound would disturb the peace of the sleeping court, but tomorrow the Queen's second son would be gone. And no trace of him would ever be found, even if the searchers turned the world upside down.

Life without Agravain –

The urge to nod was almost irresistible.

Goddess, Mother, Lamorak prayed, show me the way.

He waited. Then slowly the image of Morgause swam into his sight, her maternal body decked out to welcome her sons, her large, lupine eyes alight with a mother's love. Tears started to his eyes, and he stared at the moon. On the pale disc in the sky he saw Morgause's face. From the world beyond the worlds, he heard her voice, calling him through the music of the stars. And it came to him: I cannot kill her son.

'The Queen awaits me,' he said quietly. 'Tomorrow her sons will ride in the tilting yard. We must attend them all at dawn.'

Leif grunted. 'So be it.' The night air moved very slightly, and he was gone. 'Beware the dark one,' floated back to Lamorak through the dank air.

Lamorak stood for a moment, and raised his eyes to the sky. Did I do right? he asked the Old Ones, and waited humbly as the answer came. Above his head the blue-black vault of the heavens blazed with pale fire. The stars danced in their courses, and he heard their soundless cry, *What will be is already written here*. A vast sense of peace possessed his soul. And again he heard the low music of a woman's voice, ripe with the love and desire of a thousand years, *Come, Lamorak, come*.

'I come, my love,' he said softly. With an eager step he strode towards his fate. 'Wait for me, I come.'

Night settled over the compound. One by one Gawain, Gaheris and Gareth, aided by the knight companions who had brought them home, revelled themselves into deep and dreamless sleep. In twos and threes, the knight companions staggered back to the knights' hall, and the hard-pressed servants dropped thankfully into their beds.

High overhead, the moon rode weeping in the sky. Her tears fell to the earth as moonstones, and were taken up by lovers doomed to be parted till the world turns again. And Morgause drowsed in her great bed of state, waiting for Lamorak, who was lying on his back, staring at the moon, with a knife through his heart.

CHAPTER 46

In the woods above Caerleon, the first green shoots were bringing hope of spring. A misty green veiled all the hills and valleys, and a pale sun warmed the raw, damp air. High on its hilly bluff, the old castle rejoiced with the forest at the promise of new life. But there was no joy in Caerleon as Guenevere was led out of the castle and down through the town to her trial on the plain below.

The white and gold figure was dwarfed by marching men. A heavy guard of soldiers accompanied her every step. Stunned and silent, the townsfolk lined the streets to watch them pass. Only one old woman dared to raise her voice. 'The curse of the Mother light on you all for this!' she screeched, shaking her fist. 'May the Dark One come to take you all home!'

Another witch, thought the Father Abbot dispassionately, as he followed with his monks behind the armed guard. Well, we have made a good start with this trial of the concubine. Sir Mador must win the challenge, and prove that witchcraft is rife in the land. Then the stake and faggots lie waiting for Guenevere. And when the Great Whore of Avalon is overthrown too, we shall have all these women under our control. Then the witches among them will learn to fear the fire.

He frowned, and pressed a finger to his aching head. So much to do, Lord God, so much to be done. His thoughts returned to the letter on his desk, whose contents had troubled his sleep since it arrived. 'With the love of God, we struggle on,' the Father Confessor had written in a faltering hand, 'but I fear the sickness will consume us all.'

Now of all the convent, only a handful remain alive. This week I can take no food, and my bowels are melting in a bloody flux. Soon Our Lord will take me to Himself. My death is nothing, but God's work must go on. There must be a new leader here, and a fresh body of young nuns, if the Convent of the Little Sisters of Mercy is to survive.

The letter petered out into a faint scrawl.

But for Sister Ganmor, we should have lost the battle long ago. She has been my right hand throughout, and her piety has been an inspiration to us all. She is a true believer and a child of God. Pray think of her as a worthy successor to me, Abbess in her own right. She has my dying voice.

Sister Ganmor, eh? The Abbot frowned again. That was the name he could not remember when talking to Arthur about the convent before all this came up. What was it about Sister Ganmor that had seemed so important then? Faint wisps of memory chased through his brain, and he recalled a tall, thin, pale-faced nun, humble and devout. She had been young then, but time passed so quickly now. And she might indeed have the spiritual power to become abbess, if the fire in her deep black eyes was any guide. He warmed to the thought. A new leader, a new start. Let us get this witch Guenevere burned and her bones cast away, dear Lord, he prayed, then give me Your guidance on this holy house.

The procession wound on, with the townsfolk trailing behind. At the foot of the hill, the river valley opened out on to a wide green plain. There the stewards had fenced off a jousting arena on the level ground. Another fence ran down the centre of the grassy square, to keep the horses apart as they charged. On either side, at the point where the chargers would meet, were viewing platforms for the King and Queen.

Entering the field, Guenevere felt a vast nothingness suffuse her soul. Till the last moment, Arthur had never ceased to promise her safety, rescue and release. Sir Mador would give up the challenge, he would accept blood-gelt for his brother, he would not fight. Arthur would forbid the contest, he would fight for her himself. The more frantic his protestations, the calmer she grew. Arthur had betrayed her to her enemies. He had to see that now.

Surrounded by her guard, Guenevere was escorted to her place on the high wooden dais. Facing her across the lists with all his knights, Arthur leaped to his feet as she appeared, and saluted her with a deep, extravagant bow. She nodded a cold acknowledgement, and turned her head away. Seating herself, she cursed him in her heart. It was all she could do not to wish him dead.

The heralds were circling attentively round the field, keeping a watchful eye on the people of the town pressing eagerly against the rails. At one end of the lists was Mador, mounted and waiting for the trial to begin. His sombre armour was the same mourning shade he had worn since Patrise died. Decked out in black plumes, black harness and black trappings, his heavy charger seemed in mourning too. Black bells at its neck and knees rang out plaintively as a wind off the river lifted and died.

At the opposite end of the lists, outlined against the sun, armed and mounted, Bors waited too. Behind him stood Lionel with a group of men. Lionel had done all he could to prepare his brother for the fight. But the presence of so many doctors, bone-setters and healers showed how he feared it would end.

Perched on his great charger, Bors had equipped himself in the Queen's colours, and his white and gold armour blazed like spring itself against the greening grass. But nothing could conceal the stiffness of the figure in the saddle, or the tension of dread revealed in his every move. At the other end of the field, Mador seemed to feel little, if any, of the excitement around. He turned a cold eye on Guenevere, and she looked away. *Well, let it end.*

She watched without emotion as the monks of the Father Abbot followed their leader to the far end of the lists. They came to a halt behind Mador, and broke into a chant. The thin wisps of sound came purling up the field. *Dies irae, Domine, dies peccati* – the day of God's anger is here, when all sins shall be revealed, and the wretched shall be cast into misery –

Sin and misery, the eternal cry of the Christians –

But the thought reached Guenevere from another sphere. She was in limbo, floating beyond feeling, without fear, without hope. Bors and Lionel had sent messengers far and wide, and Sir

Lancelot was not to be found. Bors could not beat Mador, everyone knew that. When he lost, her life would lie in Mador's hands. And even Arthur would find it hard to suspend the law.

The wind was rising again, a sharp north-easter with more winter in its kiss than spring. But Guenevere was oblivious to the cold. A vast indifference held her in its grip. *What does it matter? The sooner it ends, the sooner I shall go down to the house of darkness, and there I may find some peace.*

Hovering beside Guenevere, Ina scanned the marble face and wondered anxiously when her mistress would break. Sir Lancelot lost and now a grief like this, the little maid fretted. Why doesn't she howl, break down, run screaming from her fate? Goddess, Mother, she prayed, hear me, be with the Queen.

Across the arena, crows and ravens were circling the viewing platform where the King sat with his knights. Arthur looked over at Guenevere, and clutched his head. He still found it hard to believe that he had not prevailed. How had he been so wrong, when his heart was right?

'Gods above,' he groaned, 'why has it come to this? I am the King! Why couldn't I spare the Queen?'

There was a silence among the knights. Sir Bedivere hesitated. 'You are the King, sire, but not above the law.'

'If it had to happen, why wasn't Gawain here?' Arthur swept on. 'He would have beaten Mador hands down.' He clenched his fists. 'And where's Lancelot?' He turned to Sir Kay. 'Do you know why she sent him away?'

Kay did not move. 'Why, my lord?' The familiar bilious rage curdled his soul. He writhed inside. I could tell you, Arthur, but you do not want to know.

He took a breath. 'Sire –' he began.

'Hear ye!'

A shudder ran through the crowd. The knight marshal was entering the arena, with his heralds and trumpeters marching behind.

Arthur waved a wretched hand at the brightly coloured pageant entering below.

'So,' he sighed, 'events must take their course.' Then the great bear-like body stirred, and the strong fair head went back with unconscious nobility. 'Yet I am king here still. The Queen will not suffer, if I have to take to the lists myself!'

'Draw near!' The heralds were calling the combatants into the field. The cry of trumpets split the noonday air. 'Where is the challenger?'

'Here!' Mador raised his lance, and rode on to the field. 'I accuse Guenevere the Queen of witchcraft and murder, practising to take my poor brother's life. I challenge her knight champion to the death!'

'To the death?' The knight marshal stepped forward. 'No quarter given, Sir Mador?'

'None given, and none taken! To the death.'

The knight marshal coughed. 'The King begs you to be merciful.'

Mador slammed down his visor, and shook his helmeted head from side to side. 'No!' came the howling cry. 'Let the loser die!'

The knight marshal bowed. 'As you will.'

He raised his hand, and the trumpets rang out again. 'Who answers this challenge in the name of the Queen?'

Bors lowered his visor, and rode to the centre of the field. He raised his lance to the marshal, and bowed to Mador.

'I do,' came his voice, muffled and faint.

Sorrow swept Guenevere like a weeping cloud. *You will die, Bors*, she thought, *and so will I. Well, I shall see you in the Otherworld.*

'The contestants will vie for the best of three falls!' the knight marshal proclaimed. 'Then each knight must give battle on the ground. Sir Mador has called for combat *à l'outrance*, battle to the death. Only one man may leave the field alive.'

Among the crowd lining the arena, not a soul moved. The knight marshal raised both arms to the midday sun. 'Let the contest begin!'

The contestants withdrew to either end of the field. Turning, they urged their horses into a canter, and then to the charge. Already Mador had the advantage of speed as he thundered down the lists. Guenevere turned her head away. A joust was often over with the first heavy fall. The first encounter might break Bors's neck outright.

With a hideous crash, Mador's lance met the centre of Bors's armoured breast. The impact tossed him almost contemptuously out of the saddle, and sent him spinning backwards to the ground. Bors crashed to the earth and lay still as Lionel and his helpers ran on to the field.

'He's down! Sir Bors is down!'

Lionel knelt and tried to raise his brother's head. Others pulled off his helmet, and worked frantically to bring him round. But the small figure spread-eagled on the grass showed no signs of life. At the side of the field, the bearers were already preparing the stretcher to lift him away. Mador still held his place at the head of the lists, ready for the second charge. Guenevere shook her head. It was over, as she knew it would be.

'Sir Mador! On guard, on guard!' the knight marshal cried.

A mounted figure was galloping out of the sun, and into the lists.

Instantly Mador put his horse into a charge. 'Have at you!' he cried.

The two knights met in the centre of the field. Mador's lance was aimed straight at the newcomer's breast. But with a lithe twist, the stranger knight evaded the weapon's point, and planted his own squarely on Mador's chest. The whole arena resounded as Mador's heavily-armoured body flew backward out of the saddle, and hit the ground.

Ina pointed to the new knight in the lists, sobbing with relief. 'Who is it, lady?' she wept.

Guenevere stared, unable to move or speak. The stranger knight was armoured from head to foot in red. A red helmet hid his face from sight, and the whole of his torso was sheathed in flame-red mail. He rode a big red roan, cunning and bold, a charger Guenevere had never seen before. Guenevere shook her head. She dared not hope. *Lancelot?*

Mador staggered to his feet, furiously gesticulating to his squire to help him remount. The red knight wheeled away for the second charge. Guenevere felt herself breaking inside. *Lancelot, is it you?*

'Make ready!'

The heralds were trumpeting the second charge. From the set of Mador's lean body, this time he would not miss. He spurred his horse to a gallop at the start of the course. The stranger knight was slower to reach full tilt.

This time as the red knight feinted, Mador did too. His sharp lance tracked his enemy's every move, and its glinting point caught the red breast-plate full on. But the red knight slipped backwards in the saddle, and deflected the lance's thrust. Mador's scream of fury could be heard around the field.

'No fall!' proclaimed the knight marshall. 'Let the combatants prepare for the last charge of the three.'

Once more the two knights charged down the field. Mador rode with all the fury at his command. You are mine now, his vengeful posture said. Try all your tricks, my lance will find you out.

But the red knight anticipated Mador's approach. Almost reluctantly he threw himself forward along his horse's neck, dipped the point of his lance under Mador's guard, and hooked Mador lightly out of the saddle, sparing his opponent the full force of the charge. Guenevere held her breath. *It's Lancelot.* She closed her eyes to hold back a storm of tears. *Oh, my love, speak to me. Give me a sign.*

Mador fell to the ground.

'Prepare to give combat on foot!' the knight marshal cried. 'Sir Mador, you may breathe for a while, if you wish.'

But already Mador was on his feet, and reaching for his sword. The red knight dismounted to face his attack. They circled each other three times, then Mador struck.

'Oh, madam, it's to the death – spare them, Great One, spare the Queen!'

Beside her, Guenevere could hear Ina's muttered prayers.

'Never fear, Ina,' she told her, through dry lips. 'Our fates were all decided long ago. What will be, is written in the stars.'

On the field the two knights struck and parried and struck again. Mador fought with the fury of a cornered boar, and the red knight matched his onslaught step by step. Taller than Mador, and stronger, his skill left Mador baffled at every turn. Yet he seemed reluctant to press his advantage home. Time and again he stepped back from the fray, and withheld the blow that would have had Mador down.

The day wore on. As noon passed, a primrose-coloured sun

danced briefly in the sky, then faded behind banks of cloud. Both knights were tiring now, but Mador's armour was marked with his own blood. Bright red seeped from his helmet, and ran from a wound in his side, staining the grass. The young knight was staggering now every time he swung his sword. Yet still the stranger would not strike him down.

At last Mador stopped dead, swaying in his tracks. Feebly he swung his head from side to side, then shook his fist at Guenevere.

'Lord God of Hosts, ride on the point of my sword!' he howled. 'Grant me vengeance for my brother against this witch!'

Gripping his sword with both hands, he lifted it above his head and ran at the red knight with tottering steps. The red knight stood his ground, then at the last moment, lightly ducked aside. Mador pitched forward on to his face, and did not rise.

'He's down!' A fury of excitement swept the crowd.

'Arise, Sir Mador!' called the knight marshal. 'Arise and give battle, or your opponent wins the day!'

Three times the trumpets echoed his command. There was no response from the motionless figure on the ground. At last the stewards ran on to the field, and dragged the beaten knight to his knees.

Mador swayed in their grasp, as the chief steward pulled his helmet off his head. He was bleeding from his mouth and nose, his face and forehead thick with clotted blood. Black shadows veiled his eyes, and he wore a dull vacant stare.

'I'm coming, brother,' the men beside him heard him mutter thickly. 'Patrise, are you there?'

'Prepare yourself, Sir Mador, to met your end,' the knight marshal cried sombrely. 'As the challenger, you chose combat to the death. And the Queen's Champion has the victory.'

The heralds thrust forward Mador's kneeling body, offering his neck to the red knight's sword.

'Strike, sir!' the knight marshal called.

The stranger stepped forward, raised his sword in both hands, and swung it round his head. Then he brought the blade to his lips in salute of his fallen foe, and sheathed it in his belt. One mailed hand called up the attendant holding his horse. The other hovered briefly over Mador's bent head. 'Live, sir,' those nearest heard him say. 'Your mother still has one son left alive. Go back to your country, and cheer her heart.'

Nothing moved. Stiffly the red knight mounted the red roan. Circling, he pointed its head at Guenevere.

'Madam, he's coming to see us!' Ina thrilled.

Guenevere wrung her hands. *Goddess, Mother, let it be my love –*

The rough roan gathered pace towards the dais. As it drew near, something left the rider's hand in a slow shining arc. It fell from the sky in a glittering curve, and thudded into the rough boards before Guenevere's throne.

It was the sword with which the red knight had defeated Mador, still dripping with his blood. Point down, it stuck in the platform close to her, quivering and bleeding like a living thing. Passing by at speed, its owner swept off at a gallop into the setting sun.

'The Champion!' shouted the people. 'He has saved the Queen!'

'He has come to lay his victory at your feet!' Ina cried.

'The Champion, the Queen's Champion!' The crowd howled its approval again and again.

On the King's platform, Arthur was weeping for joy among his cheering knights. 'Guenevere!' he cried.

Sir Kay signalled urgently to the stewards below. 'Bring the Queen to the King!'

Guenevere said nothing as the knight marshal came to escort her from the dais.

'Guenevere!' Arthur wept as she approached. 'You're safe, thank God!' He clasped his hands in prayer, and raised his eyes. 'God spared you, as we knew He would all along.'

Guenevere dropped a frozen curtsy. 'Thank you, my lord.'

She nodded and even smiled as Arthur crushed her to his chest, then took her hand, still weeping, and led her back up the hill through the ranks of cheering townsfolk to the castle again.

But she knew in her breaking heart what the sword meant. A weapon drawn and thrown down, covered in blood, spelled undying enmity. Lancelot had saved her, but he would not forgive.

*

That night, Arthur and all Caerleon feasted her in the Great Hall. A mood of solemn joy possessed them all. She sat at his side as knights and ladies, courtiers and councillors came to kiss her hand, and call down all the blessings of the Great One on her head. The servants were weeping openly, and the Chamberlain gave up all hope of a normal, orderly service at the table, for tonight at least. Even the Father Abbot bowed before her throne, though she saw his hopes for her death still twitching in his eyes.

'God is with us, Guenevere,' Arthur proclaimed, weeping with delight. 'He has shown that there was no witchcraft, and proved you are free from sin. Sir Mador must accept God's verdict on his brother's death. No man can trouble you now. It all turned out exactly as I planned. Oh, Guenevere!'

At the end of the evening he folded her hand in his arm, and led her to his bed. There he laughed and wept and took her in his arms, expending every ounce of his great bear-like body to give her joy. She held him and let him kiss her and do what he wanted to do. But the sword thrown by the red knight stayed lodged in her heart.

Later, as the moon shed the last dark wreaths of cloud and drifted towards day, she slipped to her chamber and found herself alone.

Huddled in her window, she lit the candle that she knew he would not see. Falling to her knees, she kissed the ice-cold glass. And she wept then as she had never wept before.

Eight hundred miles to the north, another woman was weeping her heart out too. Prostrate over Lamorak's body, Morgause was howling and tearing her hair, while Agravain ran through the palace proclaiming that he had killed a traitor in his mother's defence.

CHAPTER 47

'Whoo-ooo- ooo!'

The warning cry of the owl hung over the mere. 'The messenger of the Goddess,' said the maiden softly. Her voice in the dark was like the plashing of a water-vole.

The sign of a witch, thought Brother Sylvester venomously. But he kept it to himself, and bent all his efforts on following the slim figure ahead flitting forward through the night. The midnight call of the maiden had wakened him and Iachimo from a dead sleep. They needed to keep their wits about them now.

It would help if they knew where they were going, or why. Sylvester grimaced, hating to have his fate in others' hands. He had pressed relentlessly for a meeting with the Lady, determined to tackle the old Jezebel and flush her out of her lair. When the maiden led them towards the water, he knew that they were not going to the Lady's house high under the hill. But it must be a summons to encounter the witch in one of her secret caves, the Lake grottoes he had heard of round the shore.

The going was hard around the edge of the Lake. The water lapped at stones made smooth for a thousand years, and the shoreline came and went beneath their feet. They were floundering in and out of the shallows in the gloom, and already their habits were soaked to the knees and beyond. The thin sliver of moon waning palely overhead gave little or no light, and already they had lost track of where they were. Sylvester gritted his teeth. Be with us, Lord. Help us to give, and not to count the cost, to labour and not to seek for any reward, save that of knowing that we do Thy will.

Behind him he could hear Brother Iachimo's regular

breathing and heavy splashing as he paddled along. His tough, squat companion would not fail, he knew. Iachimo had been a warrior for Christ in far worse places than this. True, he was not one of the spiritually gifted of God. But he wore his scars with pride, and had been a loyal aide in the war against the pagan whores waged here.

And tonight would see another decisive battle in this holy fight. Tonight they would encounter the Great Whore, and put her to flight. They would do what Boniface and Giorgio had failed to do, and prove to her that her days were done. Not by appealing to the devil between her legs – that tactic had been imperfectly conceived at best, and then entrusted to two green boys. No, God's power, man's authority, the right of command, these were the ways to wear down a witch.

Unconsciously Sylvester's hand rose to his tonsure, and he smoothed down the remains of his hair. He was the man to put the so-called Lady in her place. And he would not fail that glorious task tonight.

Ahead of them the maiden stopped and pointed through the dark. 'There,' she said.

Already she had made this announcement twice as she led them round the isle. She did it to confuse them, Sylvester knew. If the Lady refused to see them in her house, she clearly meant to ensure that they could never return to her Lakeside cave again. But in the hours they had spent splashing round the edge of the water, he had begun to wonder if their guide herself really knew where they were. A vague, ghostly presence in wraps of wispy green, she hardly seemed to know anything at all.

But this time she pointed firmly up the shore towards the black mass of the island ahead. A few paces brought them to a broken cliff-face with a cluster of massive rocks tumbled in front. The maiden slipped behind one, then another, till they were hard pressed to keep on her trail. At last a low archway opened in the rock face. A dim light shone from the unseen space within, and the maiden motioned them on.

'Go,' she said, in her soft, watery voice. 'I shall await you here.'

Sylvester paused to settle his habit into place, and adjusted the rough rope binding his waist. He glanced at Iachimo,

standing stolidly at his side. Raising his eyebrows, he received a
simple nod. With a breath and a prayer, Sylvester bent his head,
ducked under the arch, and plunged in.

The passage was dark and slimy, its roof no more than three
feet from the ground, and dripping with icy water from above.
Stumbling forward, crouching in the dark, he knocked his forehead sharply against the overhanging rock, and could feel
constant cold wet trickles down his neck. As he emerged, flushed
and tense, from the passageway and looked around, he knew for
sure that the poised figures awaiting them in the cave had not
come in that way.

One enclosed lantern burned in the hollow space. By its dim
light he saw two female figures veiled from head to foot. Above
their heads, the roof of the cave was lost in darkness, and great
stalactites floated down from the damp void. Underfoot, the wet
stones gave way to firm dry sand. Lurking in the shadows at the
rear of the cave were a group of Lake-dwellers leaning on their
staves. Their bright eyes squinting out from beneath their thick
black mats of long tangled hair, they rustled together quietly
without speech.

'So!' Brother Sylvester coughed, and stepped forward to take
control. He turned interrogatively from one to the other of the
two shrouded forms. 'Which is the Lady here, you, or you?'

The shorter nodded. 'I am the Lady,' came a spare, rusty
voice. 'Address me.'

I wonder, Brother Sylvester thought sourly to himself. Aloud
he said heartily, 'You have done good work, Lady, on this isle.
You have kept a sacred trust for a thousand years.' He nodded
encouragingly to the Lake dwellers standing behind. 'As I'm sure
these good folk would say.'

The muffled figure bowed, and spread her arms.

'You are gracious, monk.'

Brother Sylvester stiffened. Was he mistaken, or had he
caught a rustle of dry amusement from behind the all-enveloping
veil? He drew himself up. 'But change comes to us all. In former
times, God's truth was unrevealed. His plan for His children was
not known.'

There was an echoing silence in the cave. The monk pressed
on. 'That means myself and my brother here. It means all of us. It

means you. For a thousand years, you and your sisters have borne the burden of maintaining sacred worship in this place. Now we are sent to aid you in your task.'

'Aid us? Or replace us?' The hoarse voice from behind the veil was not amused now.

Sylvester summoned up his smoothest smile. 'To share with you the love and care of the great sacred relics you have here. What has been holy to you for so long must command our worship too.' He paused for a little specious flattery. 'Your Hallows are things of matchless beauty, we hear.'

'And value, too.' The short figure nodded. 'Your faith of Christ began among the poor, the slaves, the oppressed. You have no such things. You have no gold.'

'Not as you do,' Sylvester agreed, biting back hot resentment as he spoke. A witch like this to condescend to him? This pagan whore to disdain the men who followed Christ?

A poisoned pang of envy seized his soul. Yes, it was true that the followers of the Goddess honoured their Great One with showers of gold, and every other precious thing they owned. Swords and cauldrons of bronze, plates and urns of silver, jewelled knives and collars, rings, chains, and ropes of gold, all found their way into their sacred lakes. God's curse on them! He cast a hungry glance round the bare cave. Elsewhere on Avalon, he knew, there were grottoes, caverns, hollows in the rock packed with the sacrifices generations had made, cast into the Lake as offerings, and retrieved by the maidens swimming through the deep.

And this great prize, this gold and silver hoard, must be his object now. Swallowing, he made his voice like velvet again. 'True, Lady, we poor Christians have no gold. Yet we love beauty as you do, and see the glory of our Creator in fine things.'

He paused. Behind him he could hear Iachimo's steady breath, and feel his companion urging him on. 'Therefore we beg a boon. Grant us to join our prayers with your sacred worship when you next honour your Goddess and reveal these sacred Hallows of yours.'

'You wish to join our worship?'

The voice was as thin and dry as a leaf in the wind. Beside her the taller woman tensed, and seemed to grow.

Sylvester felt a strange sensation round his heart. But he stiffened his will, and plunged on. 'We wish to see these things with our own eyes. We want to honour their maker with our words and prayers. In time we hope to aid you in the care of them. And through them, working together, we may bring the common folk to the knowledge and love of the One who made us all.'

He finished with the sense of a speech well made. Surely that final flourish must carry the day. So he was not dissatisfied when the Lady bowed, and said that she would consider the request. She could consider all she wished, he assured Iachimo on the way home. It was not as though hers was the final word. God held them all in the hollow of His hand. Sooner or later they would know that truth.

With polite farewells, the two monks were dispatched into the night. The two veiled figures stood and watched them go in a brooding silence that filled the cave. At last the shorter of the two unveiled her face, and cast the flimsy draperies to the ground.

'So, Lady?' Nemue said.

The taller form shuddered, and the slow music of the Lady's voice sounded through the shadows of the void. 'They want the Hallows. And they mean to have them now.'

'Lady, no!' Nemue's lithe frame tensed, and grew cold. At the rear of the cave, the Lake dwellers hissed and murmured in distress.

The Lady nodded. 'True, Nemue,' she said, her lyrical tones finding their deepest note. 'The two monks who came before have failed in their masters' plan. These newcomers are hardier warriors for their God.' She paused. 'And cleverer too. How can we begrudge them sight of our holy things? How can we deny them their right of prayer?'

Nemue's closed-up face flowered with rage. 'They would refuse us if we made the same request! More, they would punish all who dared to ask.'

'But we may not punish too.'

'They are prepared to kill!' Nemue's cry was that of an animal in the snare. 'Lady, remember what happened to Guenevere! They hounded her unjustly as far as the stake!'

'Their evil will not justify our wrong.'

'Where may we draw the line?' Nemue cried. She could feel

her soul filling with thunder as she spoke. 'The island of Avalon is still our sacred place. Forbid them, Lady, refuse them admittance here! Kill them, if need be! Theirs is a faith of death.'

Already her hand was on the hilt of her dagger, and she thought with fierce joy of her stabbing sword. All the other maidens had trained as warriors too, and the Lake-folk would tear to pieces any man the Lady called an enemy.

Kill them, yessss! Nemue's sight swam. She saw the two monks given to the Dark Mother at Imbolc, on the feast of death, their blood pouring out to nourish the good earth. She saw the Lady at the altar wielding the Great One's sword of power and Her spear of defence. The mighty weapons sang their ancient song, and bright gold and jewels flashed before her eyes.

She seized her dagger, and raised it over her head. '*Kill them!*' she cried.

Through the silence fell a sigh from the astral plane, a breath of all the world's defeat and loss.

'No, my dear,' came the low sound of the Lady's voice. 'Even to save ourselves, we may not persecute, deny or kill. We must leave the Christians to their religion of death and hate. Ours is a faith of love.'

Across Avalon, the two monks lay sleepless in their cell.

Sylvester stared unseeing through the dark. In their long discussions since they had returned, he had found more to rejoice in than Iachimo.

'They will not permit it,' the second of the two monks said. 'We will not be admitted to worship with the whores. We will not be granted the sight of their holy things.'

Sylvester smiled. 'But it does not matter, brother, any more. We know now that they will not resist. Indeed, they cannot. If all their force consists of women and girls, and a pack of water-dwellers armed with sticks, they'll be no match for a dozen tough young monks. Hear me, Iachimo. We shall send for a few of the right sort to increase our numbers here. Then, when the moment comes, we shall simply take them away.'

In the darkness his pale eyes passed from water to fire. 'The Holy Grail, brother!' he breathed, entranced. 'It is in our hands! It will be ours!'

CHAPTER 48

Avalon, Avalon, home –
Guenevere came softly to herself in the silver light of dawn. A damp fragrance filled the chamber, and through the last wisps of sleep she saw the beloved landscape once again, the island rising from the dark, still waters, its slopes veiled with apple blossom in the pearly air. Above the birdsong outside her window she could still hear the call of Avalon's doves, and the rustle of white wings in every tree.

Avalon, sacred island home.

Soon you will go back to Avalon again, the little mouse had said. And Guenevere knew that it must be today.

Embrace your fate, the spirit messenger had said too. Yes, this she also had to do. Arthur had betrayed her. And the worst of it was, he did not know what he had done. She had to save herself.

She found him in his chamber, dressing for the hunt. When he saw her, his face burst into smiles and he folded her tenderly in his arms.

'My love,' he said joyfully. 'My little love!' He kissed her on the lips.

She disengaged herself. 'I am going to Avalon,' she said. 'Today.'

Arthur's joy vanished. 'You're going away?'

'To see the Lady.' She paused. 'And to recover from the trial.'

Arthur sighed. 'You were never in any danger, Guenevere, you know that.'

You think so, Arthur? I think you are wrong.

In silence Guenevere pondered what to reply. All through the feast last night, she had felt the Christians' eyes. While all those around her were celebrating her escape, they had kept to themselves, huddling at a table apart. There they had refused the meat and fine dishes, gnawing on their frugal ration of black bread and herbs, and she had seen the hunger for her death on every face.

'The Christians called me a witch,' she said at last.

Arthur gave a confident smile. 'Oh, that's all nonsense, ignorant superstition, nothing more.'

'They do not think so.'

'What they think carries no force in law,' Arthur said, with sudden irritation. 'It was the Council's decision that Mador should have the right of trial.'

'But the Christians sat on the Council. And I'm sure they made their voices heard.'

'Guenevere, listen to me.' Arthur took a breath, and his voice grew hard. 'You may be keeping the Mother-right in the Summer Country, but the Christians have made themselves a force to be reckoned with here. I have to govern for the good of all, regardless of their faith. And that means keeping the balance, don't you see?'

'I know you mean well, Arthur.' *That at least is true.*

He frowned. 'And Mador had a claim upon me too. He'd lost his brother, and we had to acknowledge that. Oh, we could load him with blood-gelt to pay for Patrise's death, and so I did, before he went back to the Meads. But honour demanded he had his day in the field.'

If you say so, Arthur.

He came towards her to take her in his arms. 'And it's over, Guenevere. You're safe with me now.'

Safe? No, not now. I will never trust you again.

She stood unresisting as he smothered her with love.

Do I know this man?

Did I ever love him, share his bed, bear his child?

Oh, Arthur, Arthur, how did we come to this?

All women have to find out some time that their husband is not the man of the dream. But you have broken the dream between us twice.

You took our son from me when he was seven years old. Perhaps I could have forgiven you for Amir's death. But to turn to your sister for comfort in your grief?

Yes, yes, I know, Morgan is your half-sister, not your full blood kin. And the Old Ones themselves called her Morgan Le Fay, so her bewitchments were hard to resist. I know she fed you dreams and potions to enchant you to her bed. But your arms held her, your feet led you there, your body took hers for her pleasure and your delight.

And I forgave that too.

Yet I am a queen, and I come of an ancient line. The first Pendragon limped out of Ulster with his bloody hand only a few generations ago. The first queen in these islands was the Great Mother herself. My foremothers led the Britons into battle, and threw the Romans back to Rome. You should not have thought I was yours to give to the Christians, or save as you wished.

No, Arthur. You have betrayed me again, and I must save myself.

To Avalon, then.

Where the Lady will show me how.

She stepped back, and raised her eyes to his troubled face.

'Arthur, I know you try to do what's right. But you have given power in this land to men who believe that women are witches and vessels of Eve's sin. Perhaps you would have saved me from the fire. But how will you defend all other women against that?'

'I don't understand,' he said in bewilderment. 'You were innocent, Guenevere, and there's no danger any more.' He ran a distracted hand through his hair. 'Not to you, nor to any woman. Why do you have to go?'

On the island, a raw red dawn stained the pale northern sky. The people huddled inside their houses, and did not dare to stir. A terrible deed had been done, and Queen Morgause would take revenge. Any found wandering and busying themselves abroad, obstructing her knights while her justice swept the land, would share the wrong-doer's fate.

In the granite hall, Morgause sat alone on her dais. Before her stood the chief of the knight companions, gripping his sword. The blade writhed in Leif's hands, whining for blood. 'Wait, wait,' he soothed it silently, 'it will come.'

The rest of the knight companions formed a circle round

Agravain. Each held a drawn sword pointed at his heart. Pale and defiant, he stared straight ahead. He did not glance at his brothers standing nearby.

Leif took a step towards the throne. His one eye was red and bloodshot from his night of grief. 'Give me this man,' he said, in a singsong hiss, 'and he will feel what it was to kill your knight.'

On the dais, what had been Morgause stirred and laughed. Her body was still clad in the velvet, gold and amethysts of last night's feast. But all her finery was grey-white with ash from the hearth, heaped on her head in the ecstasy of her grief. Great bleeding weals showed the mark of Lamorak's sword, where she had used it to beat her head and knock out her teeth. Her fingernails had torn at her eyelids and cheeks. Now her fingers scrabbled in the dank locks of hair that had lost its colour overnight.

'My knight,' the bruised lips moaned, 'my Chosen One, the partner of my soul. The man who gave me love I never dreamed. A love that would be living in this dawn, not cold and in his tomb if I had trusted him, trusted and believed – ohhh, Lamorak!'

The high keening wail tore through the air.

Gods above! Gawain turned his eyes away, and met Gaheris's despairing stare. Gaheris was fingering his drawn sword, while Gareth was weeping openly at his side. None of them could bear to look at Morgause. This thing was not their mother, not the Queen of the Isles.

Morgause laughed again, a hideous sound.

'You killed him, why?' she said madly to Agravain. 'Why did you want to take his life from me?'

'Madam, you ask me that?' cried Agravain. 'When I came upon him lurking in the dark? He drew his sword, and I feared for my life. I raised my dagger, and struck a lucky blow. The Great One herself blessed the point of my blade.'

'Lies, black lies,' grunted Leif at the foot of the throne. Agravain had lain in ambush to take Lamorak's life. The leader of the knight companions knew it as surely as if he had been there. Leif had foreseen it, he had felt it in the stars. Yet still he had not saved his dear lord's life.

Morgause nodded owlishly. 'Yes, he lies.'

'Punish him, then,' came Leif's soft demand. 'According to the custom of the isles.'

'Your Majesty, I beg of you, hear me.'

Gawain stepped forward urgently. He knew too well the custom of the isles. In the hands of the knight companions, Agravain would face an eternity of cruel dying, and still be revived for more. He took a breath, and launched into his plea. 'Madam, our brother only meant to –'

But Agravain was blind and deaf to his plight. 'Punish me, lady?' he burst out in self-righteous rage. 'You owe me thanks! Sir Lamorak was an enemy of our house. When I saw him outside your apartments with his sword, what was I to think?'

Gawain forced himself to look at the large lost figure mourning on the throne. 'Your Majesty, Sir Lamorak died through a grievous turn of events. Our brother says he feared the blood-feud from the past. Whatever the truth, let there be no more bloodshed now.'

Leif nodded to the Queen. 'We will not shed his blood.' Around him the knight companions shared a savage grin.

Morgause's voice rang like the sound from a tomb. 'Yessss, no blood – but punissshh him, yessss –'

Gawain fell to his knees. 'Majesty, I beg you, give our brother to us. He has cruelly offended, but his own kin should deal with his offence. Let us take him to King Arthur for trial and judge-ment there. I swear he will never set foot in your kingdom again.'

'Yessss.'

Once again the soft, flaccid bulk shifted on the throne. Morgause smiled, revealing the bleeding stumps of her teeth. 'Take him, then.'

'Give him to your knights, not to them,' barked Leif furiously.

But Gawain was already shouldering Leif aside to take Agravain by the arm. Gripping him like a prisoner, he marched him down the hall, with Gaheris and Gareth striding behind.

Within minutes the sound of their departure floated up to the silent hall from the compound below. The knight companions stood like a ring of stones as the four sons of Morgause rode away, and the Queen herself sat on her throne and howled.

It was only to be expected, that the Queen would set him free, Leif told the knight companions later that night, feasting in the knights' hall when all the princes had gone. A dam will not kill her son. The young whelp may turn on his dam, and tear out her heart. But the Mother will not permit a mother to revenge.

'Whereas we . . .' Leif grinned a mouthful of blood. The tallow lamp played over a table of bleeding entrails, served hot with herbs to feed the knights' revenge. Stray shafts of light lit the depths of their blood-red wine, and threw up the hills and hollows of their scars. 'We are free,' he said softly. 'Free to avenge our lord.'

He cast his one eye around. 'Some of you will stay here to take care of our lady, who will not be with us long. She loved our lord too much, and soon she will join him in the Otherworld. Meanwhile, she has ruined her face. So she cannot have better companions than men as ill-favoured as you.'

The knights laughed gently and companionably. They had lost their faces in a good cause, it seemed.

'But you and you –' Leif pointed, and all knew why the two he chose had been singled out for the task. 'You come south with me. Our lady has given the dark one to her sons. He is dead to her, he will never come back here. So he is ours, to do with as we like.'

He paused, and stretched out, luxuriating in his power, while they hung on his words.

'So,' he grunted at last, 'we shall track the dark one by the smell he leaves behind. He will not see us or hear us, but he will know we are there. When the moment comes, we will take him as the hunter takes the wolf.'

In the silence that followed, all the men round the table shared a single joyful thought.

And then the young whelp will learn what it is to howl.

CHAPTER 49

The Presence Hall was thronged with fur robes and fine cloaks, silks and satins whispering happily together as they waited for the King. Lingering near the door to the audience chamber, the Father Abbot had waited a long while for the privilege of being admitted first. He drew himself up, and hoped that the fool of a Chamberlain had taken note of this. How long, O Lord, how long?

At last there were sounds of action from within, and the great doors swung back.

'Come forward,' the Chamberlain intoned, knocking his staff on the floor. 'All who seek audience with the King may attend him now.'

He glanced around. 'You, sir.' He signalled to the Father Abbot with a lofty upraised hand.

'Thank you.'

The Father Abbot hurried through the door, his eyes darting to the dais ahead. In the stately audience chamber, Arthur sat alone. His knights were well to the fore, but the great bronze throne at his side was empty of the white-and-gold figure usually seen there. The Abbot's mind raced. So the gossip was true, the concubine had taken herself off. If only he could stay here to work on Arthur now, there could be no better opportunity to bring the King firmly to God.

But even he could not be in two places at once. And this sickness in the convent was too grave to ignore. If only he had not wasted so much time on the concubine. All these weeks, and they almost had her in the fire. Then at last she had wriggled away, like the serpent she was.

And if only he had paid more attention to the letters from the convent as they came. The Abbot fought down the fear that things were far worse than he had been ready to believe. The Father Confessor was a man of robust faith, but there was something there that had defeated him.

Well, it would all be dealt with now.

'Your Majesty.' He quickened his step to the throne, and fell to his knees. 'I come to beg your leave to depart. I hope I have been of assistance while I was here. But another grave matter calls me away now.'

'Of help to me, Father?' Arthur replied. 'Oh, you were indeed. All kings have need of counsel, and I more than most. I was lucky to have Merlin to advise me when I began. But it's many years now since I saw my dear old friend.' His eyes filled with tears.

He's coming, the Abbot told himself. One day Arthur will be ours, heart and soul. He almost chuckled aloud. One day we shall rule him and all this kingdom, and its whores and witches too. And then let them beware!

He lowered his eyes. 'You are gracious, sire,' he said.

'How can I help you, Father, as you leave?'

The Abbot frowned. 'I go to a house of our holy women, visited by the plague. The Father Confessor is dying, and a successor must be found. He tells me that there's a candidate already there. A nun called –'

A spasm of pain shot through the Abbot's chest. He tried to speak, and an iron hand crushed his lungs. Why could he not say the sister's name? God be in my mouth, he prayed, and struggled on. 'A Sister Ganmor, sire, a nun of great piety –'

'What?' Arthur screamed, and hurled himself down from the dais, seizing the Abbot in a madman's grip. 'Ganmor? Did you say Ganmor?'

Behind him, the Abbot could see a dawning horror on the faces of Arthur's knights. The warrior Sir Lucan was the first to react, seizing his sword, and leaping to Arthur's side. 'To horse, sire?' he burst out.

Arthur broke away, and reached for his sword, swinging it through the air. 'To horse!' he howled. 'To horse! All men to the convent at once!' He threw back his head in an agony of despair.

'Oh, God, God, why do you punish me? Will I never be free?'

Still weeping, he tore from the room. Led by Sir Lucan, all the knights followed him.

'Sir! Sir! A moment, I beg of you!

Still fighting for breath, the Abbot tried vainly to question them as they ran. But the limping Kay was the only one he could catch. Kay's sallow face was blotched and grey with bile, and his eyes had shrunk to pinpoints in his head.

'Tell me, sir,' the Abbot gasped, 'what –?'

Kay brushed him aside in a rage. 'Gods above, man, don't you see? The King knows who this is! It's a name she's used before when she was up to no good, reversing her real name. This Ganmor of yours is the King's sister. Your pious nun is Morgan Le Fay!'

Lord, let it be soon.

The Father Confessor lay on the hard wooden pallet, and fixed his eyes on eternity. He could feel the morning sun on his face and hands, but his sight was fading, and he was too wasted now to move. Serenely he prepared his soul for its final flight.

Earlier in his sickness it had grieved him terribly that others were suffering too. As disease swept through the convent, he had watched the nuns dying one by one, and shared their pains. Old and young, fearful or steadfast, they had all passed the gates of death, sobbing, praying, or simply closing their eyes. Many, indeed, had been praying to die. After the onset of his own bloody flux, the Father Confessor had been praying too.

Should he have foreseen it all, on the day when the sickness struck? As he went to the chapel that dawn, he had seen a cat lying in the angle of the wall. Sheltered within the curve of her body were five or six kittens, newly delivered and still glistening. She had stared at him with oddly coloured eyes, and he had felt his stomach turn. Then as he watched, she had taken the first blind squirming thing between her teeth, and eaten her entire litter, one by one.

By the end of that day, the first four nuns were dead. At the height of the sickness, those left alive were burying their sisters all day long, and by candlelight too. Soon there were none left with the strength to dig a grave. The sick and dying both went untended as he dragged himself from bed to bed to administer the Last Rites.

Now even that was beyond his failing strength. For days the dead had lain rotting where they fell. He had not had the strength himself to move for a week, and by night he would be dead. The House of the Little Sisters of Mercy, once Convent of the Holy Mother was no more. And on her feast day too. This Candlemas there were none to light candles for Our Lady the Virgin, as they always had before.

His soul darkened with grief.

Salve, Maria, salve Regina –

His cracked lips moved painfully through the words of the great hymn to the Virgin Mary, the Queen of Heaven herself. Save me, Lady, save me, he prayed, and have mercy on my poor showing here. I was sent to this place to cleanse the house of sin. I have failed, or God would not have sent this plague to destroy the holy sisterhood, root and branch.

Yet there is hope, he prayed. One sister has been spared. Her spotless soul must have preserved her flesh. Is it too much to hope that she may yet survive, to lead this dead community to new life?

A footfall in the corridor caught his ear, and his heart lifted with a painful lurch of joy. Here she was now, his right hand and helpmeet through all these troubled years. His task here had been hard, the work even cruel, to purge the place of sin. But her Christian piety had led the way for them all. Whoever had had to be beaten, starved or walled up, it had never been her. And always she had been at his side, urging him on.

And through all the recent plague, he marvelled, she had never faltered once. Indeed she seemed to grow stronger as her sisters wasted away. Her black eyes had grown bigger, her pallid skin warmer, and he even thought she looked taller and fuller now. But that could only be his sight fading, as his sickness took hold.

'Father.'

'Sister Ganmor.'

Suddenly he knew with the clarity of the dying that he loved to say her name. Her name? Agony and delight split his cracked lips, and spread over his ravaged face. He had loved her, the

sister herself, loved her whole-heartedly for all these years. And
her virtue and grace had amply rewarded him. He loved her. The
knowledge spread through him with a joy beyond tears. How
blessed he was that God had permitted him to know the love of a
good woman, and enjoy it without sin.

He was weeping with gratitude. 'Ganmor?'

'Father?'

The door opened, and the stench came in with her. Lying in
his own filth, he had grown used to the stink, but this was something else. And her voice today was not as he remembered it. Fear
gripped his heart. Had she caught the sickness after all? Would
she die too?

He squinted up at the lean, black-clad form. She stood with
her back to the window, framed against the light. As always, her
head was bowed under the weight of her heavy wimple, and her
hands were folded submissively in her long black sleeves.

'Father?' she said again.

But her voice had changed. And suddenly she was growing,
filling the tiny cell. As she swelled, her black habit dwindled on
her frame till it became a slender tight-fitting gown, with a low
neck and narrow sleeves. The coarse wool softened into a
sensuous midnight velvet, and the hideous wimple dissolved and
re-formed as an elegant headdress with a gossamer veil.

He cried out in panic. 'Sister, is that you?'

'Father?' she replied.

And this time there was nothing pious in her tone. ' "Sister",
"Father", what nonsense that all is!' the strident voice ran on.
'You're on the edge of the grave, I'm going to a new life, we could
call each other by our names now, don't you think? But the
Christians took yours away when they took mine.' She laughed
mockingly. 'Father what? I don't suppose you can remember
what you're called.'

His brain laboured, and his heart pounded in his chest. 'I am
– I am –' But it would not come.

Again the cruel laugh. 'It doesn't matter. Your God knows
who you are.'

'My God?' he cried in anguish. 'Not yours?'

Her laughter chilled his soul. 'No, Father, never mine.'

'You are not Ganmor!' he screamed in dread. 'Who are you?'

'I am Morgan Le Fay!'

And suddenly she was beside him at the bed, leaning over him, trapping his helpless frame. Her eyes were like cartwheels of black fire, spinning in her head. Beneath the low opening of her gown, her red nipples burned and beckoned him.

'Why, Father,' she crowed, 'I am the mistress of this convent, did you not know? All these years, when you and your blind masters thought you ruled this place, you have done my bidding, and carried out my will. A lifetime ago, I was condemned here as a child. Ever since then I have worked to destroy the place.'

An Otherworldly glow spread over her face. 'Oh, it has not been easy, keeping the vow of darkness I made then. There are good souls among you Christians, and a powerful will. But you broke the hearts of the sisters for me, through the beatings, starvation and death-punishments your order imposed. After that, it only took a little, little plague to claim their bodies too.'

The Abbot groaned. 'You brought the sickness?'

White teeth gleamed in the mulberry mouth. 'It was not hard.'

The Father Confessor's soul was lost in a waste of pain. He could not weep. A lifetime's work lay in dust around his feet. All lost, to no avail.

'And now?' he said dully.

She gave a horrible laugh. 'Now I return to the world I left behind. I have a task that has been long a-brewing, and now is on the boil. In the meantime, I shall live as a great lady again.' She leaned into him and her breath scorched his face. 'I was born a queen. And now I go to make my son a king!'

She has a son. The young virgin, as I thought her, has a son. The Father Confessor listened in hopeless despair, beyond surprise.

The exultant voice went on. 'This house of wretched women will be no more. The Dark Mother has come to take the sisters home. This is Her day. Today they go to Her.'

The dying man moved his head in a slight nod. The Dark Mother, yes. Why was he not surprised? He used to know that the feast of Candlemas overlaid a darker rite. As a young priest, he had been taught that this day the Holy Spirit was sent to quicken the Virgin Mary with child, in order to win it back from the pagans who claimed it as theirs. What did they call it, Oimelc, Imbolc? For thousands of years they kept this as the day of the Dark Maiden, the Mother of love and death. All his life he had lit candles to the Virgin on this day, to keep the evil at bay. And now the forces of darkness had triumphed. They were here.

Here in this room.

He looked up at the devil woman with her eyes of fire, her pale skin like death and her gown as black as pitch.

And he had let her in.

The Father Confessor gasped, and fought for breath. The grave gaped for him, and he saw the flames of Hell. Now he faced God's judgement for opening the way to sin. Honest failure could be forgiven, or losing his flock to a God-sent plague. But harbouring a she-devil, aiding her and, God save us! loving her too – nothing but damnation awaited him now.

And the fire, the everlasting torment of the fire –

A thin scream bubbled in his throat and died. 'Ganmor – I beg of you –'

The figure in black was moving through the door. Her mocking laughter lingered in the cell. 'Farewell.'

With the last of his sight, he watched her glide away. It was all over: only the reckoning remained. And Hell itself could be no worse than his sufferings now. He turned his face to the wall, and closed his eyes. Soon, Lord. Let it be soon.

CHAPTER 50

The journey was long, but every mile revived Guenevere's heart. Afterwards she knew she had passed into a dream – time outside the common span of days and weeks. Lying in a curtained litter, she dreamed the days away, lulled by the plodding of the horses' hoofs. At night, Ina bathed her temples with rosewater, and brushed patchouli into her hair. She slept in the travelling bed with the curtains drawn back to the stars, and woke in the morning with a fresh spring of hope.

And all around her, the earth was reviving too. Along the wayside, tender pouting cowslips hung their heavy heads, and pale primroses sprawled in the undergrowth like fainting girls. The birds returning with spring filled every tree with song, and the hillsides carried the bulls' triumphant bellow from every wattle pen.

New life.

So she dreamed and drifted through each shining dawn. Soon they left the roads, and passed into the woods by hidden greenways hardly known to wayfarers of the human kind. The first time she followed these tracks she had been a young princess, travelling to the Lady in royal style, to learn the ways of the Great One herself. She had lived and studied with the Maidens of the Lake, in pure obedience to her mother's will, because all the queens of the Summer Country had done so too. But then she had come to love the Sacred Island, and above all the mystical ruler who lived, veiled and withdrawn, at its secret heart. For years she had dreamed of becoming like the Lady of the Lake, sovereign of her domain and of her own body, owing command and control to no man.

Later, she had made a second journey to the island with Arthur, to see what the Lady foretold. They had ridden out of Camelot in proud array, their banners dancing and lances glittering in the sun. These days she was no hopeful princess or ardent bride, but a heartsick woman in search of the healing that only love can bring.

'The children of Avalon may always return to me,' the Lady told all the Maidens when they left. 'Never be afraid to come back to your home.'

Mile after mile, swaying in her litter, Guenevere heard the distant call.

Avalon, Avalon, sacred island, home.

But as they drew near to Avalon, her doubts revived. *My husband betrayed me, and I betrayed my love. What hope of help or healing lies in that?* Twice she ordered the horsemaster to leave the woods, and make for Camelot, bypassing Avalon. But each time she changed her mind, and they turned back.

And by the time the sweet mist of the holy waters began to rise through the trees, she was calm again. Around her the men-at-arms grew subdued, and even the horses trod with greater care. With painful slowness they picked their way down through the dense forest to the plain of the Sacred Lake. And there it was, floating on its sheet of shining water, the island in the lake that the Old Ones called the Isle of Glass. Before them waited the boatmen of the Lady to ferry them across.

Around the lake, white drifts of blossom mantled every tree. At its edge, pale meadowsweet and golden kingcups admired their reflections in shallows as clear as glass. A light breeze danced over the still surface, and gold and silver fish slipped through the sunlit depths. Beyond the island lay the homes of the Lake-dwellers, strange contraptions rearing up on stilts. There, overhung by trees and shrouded in mist, they scavenged a living from the dark and brackish waters beyond the Lake, and hid from sight. But they were faithful followers of the Lady, manning the passage to the island night and day. Already they were loading up the boats to bring the newcomers and their possessions safely across.

Leaving the guard on the bank, Guenevere and Ina took to the first of the flat, slow-moving boats. Ahead of them the island slumbered in the midday sun. Along its shore, weeping willows trembled in the breeze, and above them lay Avalon's ancient orchards of apple trees. High above the clouds of pink and white blossom soared the great Tor of Avalon itself, the green hill shaped like the Mother lying at rest. Guenevere's eyes dwelt lovingly on the vast, spreading outline of the gently rounded body and grassy flanks. All the world, and all its secret knowledge, lay in there.

A small figure stood awaiting them on the low stone landing-stage.

'You were expected, Guenevere,' said Nemue, in the rusty tones of those who rarely speak. 'The Lady will see you at sundown. You may rest till then.'

But it was after dark before Nemue came for them in the small white guest-house where they had been installed. The night air was as clear as spring water, and a thousand stars glimmered in a cloudless sky. In silence they went up by the winding path, through the white apple orchards and dark groves of ancient trees. At the top of the hillside lay the Lady's house, a white stone structure built into the side of the Tor. As they approached, the doors opened without a sound.

Nemue nodded to Guenevere. 'Enter.' She held up her hand. 'Ina will stay with me.'

The great doors gaped on to a dark, echoing space. Guenevere's senses swam. When she lived on Avalon, the girls in the House of Maidens used to whisper that the Lady's house was not a house at all, but her enchanted way down to the Lake below. Gathering her strength, she stepped over the threshold into the warm, humid space. She thought her ears caught the sound of water far away, but she did not know.

The great doors clanged behind her, leaving her in the dark. Then a hundred tiny dragon-lamps began to glow, scattering pools of gold. They encrusted the ceiling like stars, and shone out from countless hidden niches in the walls. Slowly Guenevere's eyes adjusted to the light. She stood in a low, domed chamber, warm and welcoming, with a rich and heady fragrance filling the air. As Guenevere drank it in, she found herself trembling with joy. Many times in her dreams she had tried to get back to this place without success. Now the starlit roof and honey-coloured walls reached out to enfold her in their embrace.

Now she heard again the voice from her dream-time, from the time before thought. 'Come . . .'

Against the furthest wall stood a tall, strangely made throne bearing a silent, majestic shape. She was veiled in pale draperies from head to foot, and her headdress and fingers flashed with dragon-fire. One hand was raised in welcome, the other pointing to a low seat among the rich eastern carpets on the floor.

'Welcome, dear Guenevere,' came the low, vibrant sound. 'I am glad you have come home.'

Guenevere sank on to the stool, and fixed her eyes on the figure on the throne. Above the gauzy veil covering her face the Lady wore a moon-shaped diadem of palest gold, set with tiny pearls. On her second finger she wore the Goddess ring, and in her hand she held an orb of polished crystal bound in hoops of gold.

'So, Guenevere,' she said, 'you come to speak of Arthur, as I think?'

Guenevere felt the tears rising before she spoke. 'He has betrayed me, Lady. I shall never love him again.'

'Ah, Guenevere,' the Lady sighed. 'Never is too long a word to say. Love has a thousand lives. Fate spins as it will, and even the Mother cannot turn back the wheel.'

She could not bear it. 'Tell me what to do.'

A soft breath came from behind the Lady's muffling veils. 'You are Arthur's queen. He is the High King of all the Britons, and you are their queen too.'

Guenevere clutched her head. 'May I not escape?'

The Lady leaned forward. 'When you chose Arthur, he knew nothing but his power as a man. Through you he learned that women give life to the world, so the Mother ordained them to rule both love and life. You took him into the circle of the Goddess. You made him whole.'

There was a lengthy pause. 'Without you, he would never have been High King,' the low voice intoned at last. 'You made him what he is. Can you destroy him now?'

Guenevere could not speak. She hung down her head and wept.

The Lady's voice went on, 'When trust is lost, where does love hide its head? Look for the flower by the wayside, the pebble in the brook. Love may be driven weeping from the highest hill, yet live again in the smallest things.'

There was a sigh like the sadness of the world. 'All women have to watch men fail, and fall. This is why the Mother made us older and wiser, before we are born. For ours is the task of the world, to create and bear new life, and afterwards to endure its every pain.'

She raised her head, and the pearly diadem shimmered in the golden light. 'For this, the Goddess grants us three rewards, the bliss of ecstatic love, the joy of having a child, and the warmth of a life well lived. These are the three delights of woman, tokens of the Great One's own incarnation as Maiden, Mother, and Wise One. Each joy is appropriate to each stage. Some poor souls enjoy none of these, and many women are fated to know only one. The fortunate may know two.'

She raised a long pale hand. 'But hear me, Guenevere. Few indeed are born to enjoy all three. They are the blessed ones of the Goddess, and their lives echo Her own holy trinity. As maidens they find the key to their bodies, and pass through the gates of bliss. As mothers they learn the joy beyond joy that only a child can bring. And as Wise Ones in their old age, they can look back on a life fulfilled, and their human work well done. You, Guenevere –'

'Yes?' said Guenevere fearfully.

The pause stretched out to the very edge of hope. Then a soft laugh came from behind the veil.

'Think, Guenevere! Already you have known all three. You have not lived four decades, yet you have had the love of the two best men in the world. You have held your child in your arms for seven years, before the Mother took him for one of Her own. In the land that you love, your rule is secure, and your people bless your name. And you still have forty and more years of your life ahead.'

Guenevere lifted a tear-stained face, and felt again the disquiet of new things. 'Oh, Lady, can you see what lies ahead for me?'

The Lady nodded. 'Guenevere, it has long been written in the stars. You will return to Arthur, as his wife and his queen. But you will not live without love. A golden pathway lies ahead for you.' Her voice darkened. 'But it is not without danger.' She surged to her feet. 'Come!'

Behind the throne, a narrow opening gave on to a wide stone staircase descending into the dark. At once they left the friendly dragon-light for a midnight void whispering with unseen wings. Step by slippery step, Guenevere felt her way down through the blackness, till her feet met the softness of unresisting sand. Above them, she knew, slumbered the mighty Tor. But here below, the underground was alive with a thousand tiny scurrying noises as the dwellers in the dark slid away to their unseen lairs. Again the gentle sound of water reached her ears.

'Ho, there!'

The Lady clapped her hands, and Guenevere's eyes dazzled with flaring light. They stood in a soaring cavern of primeval rock, its every surface glistening with red and white. All round the crystal walls hung the treasures of the Goddess, gold chains and ropes of precious stones, and jewelled weapons richer than any dreams. Heaped up on the floor lay more priceless offerings, vast cauldrons of copper, gold plates and bowls of silver, and drinking cups of bronze.

In the centre of the chamber rose the waters of two springs, one white, one red. The Lady stood between them, her arms outstretched over two wide stone hollows carved in the living rock.

'The Body of the Mother,' she chanted, spreading her arms through the echoing space. She pointed to the red spring on her left.

'The blood of the Mother, which she gives to create us all.' Now her veiled arm floated to the right. 'The milk of the Mother, which she gives to feed us all.'

The long arms gave a serpentine flutter to embrace them both. 'The red spring and the white. The blood and milk of the Mother. The love of the Goddess as it pours forth to the world.'

Guenevere could feel the Lady's spirit expanding to fill the vibrating space.

'Draw near, Guenevere,' she called, 'and do not fear.' She raised her hand to her head, and unloosed her veil.

A glow filled the chamber, like the dawning of the world. For an instant Guenevere saw her mother's face. But then she saw a more-than-human radiance and the beauty of the Otherworld, a face alive with all the wisdom of the Old Ones and the sweetness of a child.

Guenevere's face was wet with tears. She could not speak.

The Lady turned. 'Come!'

At the back of the cave stood an altar of primeval rock. Arranged on its black surface were four shapes of antique gold.

Guenevere gasped. Her gaze roved over a massive gold plate, its edge embossed in gold, and a tall, two-handled drinking goblet patterned with strange symbols, big enough to send round a giant's hall. In front of them lay a long gold sword jewelled on both hilt and blade, and a slender lance of polished gold with a gleaming point.

'The Hallows of the Goddess!' she breathed.

The Lady nodded. With loving hands she touched them one by one.

'The great dish of plenty, from which the Mother feeds all who come to Her. The loving-cup of forgiveness, with which She reconciles us all.' Her hands moved to the weapons, and caressed them both. 'The sword of power. And the spear of defence.'

She turned on Guenevere, her eyes like pools of blood. 'These are the treasures of our Goddess since time began. And now the Christians claim them for their own!'

Guenevere gave a start of horror. 'The Christians?'

The Lady's lovely face darkened. 'King Arthur believes that they are men of faith, and that in their faith, we may all become one. And he is wrong. They preach of love, but they are full of hate. They seek the death of the Goddess, knowing that will bring loss and enslavement to women everywhere.' The Lady's low musical voice throbbed with scorn. 'Religion should be kindness. Faith should bring us love. Why would Arthur trust fine words on the lips of those who hate?'

'When I brought him here, he swore to defend our faith,' Guenevere moaned. 'He vowed to uphold the Goddess, on the honour of a king.'

The Lady's sigh came from far away. 'We cannot turn to him for assistance now.'

Guenevere's soul was dissolving. *Another betrayal, Arthur, another fall. Oh, Arthur, Arthur, why?*

'Do not judge him, Guenevere. He has pronounced his own doom if he breaks his word.'

Her hand flew to her mouth. 'Lady, what are you saying? Will Arthur die?'

There was a pause. 'All men must flourish and vanish in their time. The only truth is the everlasting dark. But Arthur is not ready for the last crossing of the water where he and I shall meet. No, another task faces us now.'

The Lady drew a deep breath and resumed. 'The Hallows must be taken from Avalon. Already the Christians are demanding their use. If we believe that all faith is love, they say, why will we not lend them our Hallows out of love? Soon, soon, I know, they will come and take them by force. Like all fanatics from the east, they believe in fire and the sword.'

She brooded for a while. 'You must take them, Guenevere. Once they are safely off the island, another must carry them to their final resting-place.'

She paused, and her deep, musical tones filled the air. 'And this is a task for a man who will travel alone, keeping faith to the death. One who loves you and the Goddess more than his own life. Who can you call upon?'

A cry of anguish ripped through Guenevere. 'I have no one! I have lost my knight, my true love and my life. I did not trust him, and I sent him away. And now I have lost my love and my life and all!'

'Ah, Guenevere.' The Lady's sigh was the breath that filled Avalon as the earth was born. 'One love dies, and another takes its place. When we fall, we must rise to dance again.' She leaned forward. 'It is the law of the Mother. One man alone cannot make all the music of the world. You must choose again. You have never needed a knight more than now.'

Her large luminous eyes raked Guenevere's face. 'Ah, my dear! You have lost a great and mighty love. But ahead there lies another love for you, one you dare not hope for – cannot dream –'

'Oh, Lady . . .'

Guenevere felt herself shrivelling with grief. 'I do not want to take another love. I loved Arthur, and that love fled. I loved Lancelot, and threw his love away. It is over now, and I must turn to other things.' She squared her shoulders. 'Give me the Hallows. I will not betray your trust.'

The Lady eyed her shrewdly. 'And for the rest? What of that?'

Guenevere calmed herself, and spoke steadily. 'I will keep the faith. I will return to Arthur, I will not destroy his life. I will live in my marriage, and find the way to love him as my husband once again.'

'You will indeed, dear Guenevere, for that is your fate.' The Lady drew herself up. 'But you must also obey your destiny. You will take the knight I spoke of, for you have no choice. He will take the Hallows, he will be yours to the death.'

'I cannot!' Guenevere cried in despair.

'Never is not a word for you to say.' Her voice grew deeper and more sonorous, ending the debate. 'Your quest has begun. Your knight awaits you now.'

The words of protest died on Guenevere's tongue. She bowed her head, and kissed the Lady's hand.

The Lady smiled her thousand-year-old smile. 'Go then, in grace and strength.' Her cool lips brushed Guenevere's overheated face. 'Remember that those who follow the Goddess can always enter the dream. May you awake from yours, and become that which you have dreamed.'

One love dies, and another takes its place –
But no man can take the place of Lancelot.

Weeping like a child, Guenevere climbed the steps to the upper world.

Another knight?

A new love?

What could she say to another man, after Lancelot?

Lady, Lady, she mourned, you always loved me like a mother. Now your desire to save the Hallows has made you cruel and cold. I cannot take a new love. I love Lancelot.

Lancelot, Lancelot, my only love, my loss –

Overflowing with grief, she stumbled down the hillside in the dark. The rough undergrowth by the path caught at her skirt, and she knocked her head on an overhanging branch. A wan-faced moon rode fretfully in the sky, obscured by drifting clouds. In the damp air, dew covered the leaves like tears and soon it would rain. The world was weeping for the loss of her love.

At last the white shape of the guest-house came in sight. As she made for the door, she saw the outline of a tall figure in the shadows, and behind him under the trees, the ghostly shape of a pale horse. Her heart leaped and pounded in her chest.

He was here then, her new knight, as the Lady had said. She shivered with dread. Faint shafts of moonlight glinted on a silver helmet, a coat of mail, and a tunic of woodland green. She wanted to scream, to run, to hide in the woods.

Then a voice she would have known anywhere reached her through the dark. 'Madame?'

CHAPTER 51

She could not say his name. Her hand flew to her mouth and she tried to hold back her little gasping cries. He came towards her and took her in his arms, and she quivered against his chest like a wounded bird. The wool of his tunic was rough against her face, and the muscles of his chest were hard and unfamiliar now. But he held her to him like a precious thing, he kissed her hair and soothed her as she wept, and after a long time, she grew still.

Now her body began to remember the feel of his, the tall, slender frame, the broad shoulders, the lean, supple hips. The soft stubble on his chin, his fine leather breeches, the dagger at his waist, his coat of mail were as familiar to her as her own skin.

They stood together in the glade, bathed in the glimmering light. Overhead the moon smiled to herself, and sailed on. The stars forgot to dance, and stood still in their tracks to gaze down. The forest air vibrated with the vital hum of life itself, and all the woodland creatures rejoiced with them.

A thousand voices cried through the moist night air.

'Live!' hissed the blind-worm, working through the earth.

'Love!' urged the owl, calling from the highest tree.

There was a pause longer than life itself.

'Lady?' he said.

The music of his accent stung her ears. She lifted her head and saw him truly for the first time. His bright brown eyes burned through the dusky night with their Otherworldly gleam. His thick chestnut hair glinted with fragments of fire in the moon's pale beam. A light shone in his face as he looked at her. He sighed, and she heard herself sighing too.

He brought her hand to his lips, and she felt the rising swell of life itself. She heard the crying of the white waves on the sea, and the laughter of the storm on the mountain-top. Her body remembered all his gifts of love, long days of beauty and endless nights of bliss.

'Tell me, lady, am I still your knight?'

His voice was calling from another world. And still she could not speak his long-loved name. Tears poured from her eyes and she cried aloud in pain.

'Ohh –'

'Hush –'

He kissed her lips as gently as a child. 'Hush, my love. Come indoors, let me bring you into the warm.'

May the darkness seize him now, wherever he is –

If he is – if he exists at all –

Had he seen him, curled up in that bed? Or was it a spirit shadow, sent for torment's sake?

Merlin clambered down from his mule, almost too tired to curse. The going had been hard on the rough mountain pass, and soon it would be night. Already the first stars of evening were coming out. Heartsick, he leaned on the mule's bony back, and sank into bitterness. How long ago had he embarked on this cursed quest? And when had he started to know that it had failed?

Perhaps the boy had died all those years ago, lost with the other newborns who were cast away. Perhaps he had perished of a childhood fever, as so many did. Perhaps the boys he had narrowly missed so far were nothing but fetches, designed to lure him on. Grimly Merlin recognised that he had been too ready to believe that Mordred lived. The hunger to find a Pendragon had seized his soul. Could Morgan have devised the whole thing all along?

He did not know. All he knew was that he must fall back to his cave in the Welshlands, and think again. He was almost on the Welsh borders where he stood. Once over this mountain pass, he could call himself home.

With a groan he secured the mule's bridle, turned it loose to graze, and lowered himself down. The stony ground struck cruelly hard and cold, punishing his lank haunches, but all he could feel was the turmoil in his soul. Had his power betrayed him, had his craft failed him now?

He clutched at his head, and tore his iron grey hair.

'I am Merlin the Bard!' he cried aloud to the uncaring sky. 'Bard and druid, seer and prophet, singer, dream-weaver and teller of all tales, I am old, I am young, I was dead, I am alive, *I am Merlin!*'

His scream rang round the high crags, echoing mockingly from peak to peak – *Merlin, Merlin, Merlin* . . .

'And grief upon me for this!' he keened, punching the air. 'Grief, grief, grief upon all my hopes!' He beat his head with his fist. Where had he gone wrong?

No, not wrong, that he would never believe. For many lives now he had borne the Druid mark, worn all the cloaks of power, prophesying in the shining feathers of peacock, crow and swan, and no man on earth had vanquished him in contest when his singing robes were on. In dreaming consciousness he had seen past and future, and often both at once. *And he had seen the boy.*

A faint comfort eased his wounded soul. Arthur had lain with Morgan, that he knew. Morgan had had a son, he knew that too. The boy lived, Pendragon lived, of that he had no doubt. And he would find him, however long it took.

The sweet mists of evening were rising to the mountain-top. The old enchanter gulped down great draughts of air, drawing in the life breath of the earth. But as his heart revived, his doubts did too. So many years in the search – the boy would be full grown.

'I wanted the child!' he cried to the barren crags. 'Another Arthur, to be mine from birth!'

Lovingly he recalled the infant that Arthur had been, his honest, slate-blue eyes and pale gold hair, his well-made frame. Fostered by Sir Ector, the boy had grown in grace and strength with every year.

'And I, Merlin, had the shaping of him, body and mind!' he proclaimed. 'Arthur was mine, he was only mine!'

With a start it came to him that those had been the best years of his life, in truth of all his many lives till now. Sir Ector had thought himself lucky enough to have the care of Arthur's body, rearing Uther Pendragon's child in his household as a brother for his own son. He had never done battle with Merlin for Arthur's soul. Merlin had always been welcomed by Sir Ector like royalty himself. As he was, he reminded himself touchily, being Pendragon born. Wherever he went, he should be fêted and adored.

Sir Ector . . .

Merlin's mind drifted off. How long was it since he had seen the old knight? Was he even still alive? A pity he had not kept in touch, for Sir Ector's estate lay hereabouts on the Welsh borders, not far away. For old times' sake, Merlin mused unhappily, he might have looked in on the kindly old man who had helped him to make Arthur what he was.

Darkness and devils, why dwell on triumphs of forty years ago? Merlin's yellow eyes glazed with bile. Go on, old fool, forget that your beloved Arthur is approaching middle age, and has no son. Forget that the house of Pendragon has no heir.

He leaped to his feet with a wail. 'I have abandoned Arthur for all these years to find his son. And I am no nearer to that than when I began!'

He surged to and fro on the mountain, railing at the stars. 'You have cursed me with the fate of a Lord of Light,' he wept. 'How many lives must I suffer to keep Pendragon alive?' Till the boy was found, the house of Pendragon hung on a thread. And who knew if his own thread would hold, or when the Old Ones planned to sever it?

'Why have I failed?' he begged the gusting winds. "I have denied the spirit woman access to my flesh. I have stayed away from her dark tower, and kept my body pure. I have communed with rocks and trees, I have cast the runes, lit sacred fires and called up visions in the smoke. I have criss-crossed these islands, and everywhere made magic older than the Druid kind. Yet still I cannot find if the boy lives!'

His lamentation echoed to the stars.

Find the boy –

Find the boy –

The echo mocked him from the highest crag. How much time had he wasted along the way? How long had he spent in the Orkneys, vainly courting the favour of Queen Morgause and her knight?

Morgause –

The shadow of blood passed over Merlin's twilight eyes. Ah, poor Morgause. Well, she had paid a high price for her love. But soon, very soon, the Queen would rejoin her love, where he waited for her in the world beyond the worlds. Together they would wander the astral plane hand in hand, never more to part. Through all eternity, Morgause would be with Lamorak. Their love was never perfect, but it was enduring, like the sea.

Fool that he was! He should have known the boy would not be there. Yet where?

'Where? Tell me where!' he screamed, in anguish, to the rising moon.

A huge indifference answered his heartfelt cry. Suddenly his old heart and brain could go no more. With the last of his strength he hobbled across to his mule, heaved himself into the saddle and pointed the patient creature down the mountainside.

The tears were pouring unchecked from his eyes. He had failed, Merlin had failed. There was nothing to do but fall back to the Welshlands, and take to his crystal cave. There he could hide, and rest, and pray to his Gods that his powers would return. He could roam with the wild pigs in the forest, ride a rutting stag under a horned moon, sing to the stars, and drink rock water for his wine.

The trusty mule picked its way down the rocky path.

'Yet I am Merlin still!' the old man sang. 'I am fire, I am frost, I am the tree, I am the leaf, *I am Merlin*!'

He did not know how many miles he passed this way. Day was breaking as he came off the mountainside and made his way down through the trees to the road ahead. As the woodland thinned out, he saw an old woman by the wayside, gathering twigs. Her long, lean body was bent almost to the ground, and her black garments were wrapped tightly around her against the cold. As he drew near, Merlin was swept with a hunger to hear her speak a word. The good wishes of old ones had a power he needed now.

'Greetings, mother,' he called.

The old woman straightened up, as far as she humanly could. Her smile was pleasant enough, Merlin noted, with a slight lifting of his burdened heart, and old age had not touched her deep black eyes. But her head sat sideways on her crooked spine, and one knobbled hand clutched at her ancient hip.

'Good day to you, father,' she returned in an old, cracked voice. 'D'you travel far?'

'Far enough,' he replied distantly.

She nodded, seeming unoffended by his tone. 'You'll be wanting to rest then, sir. A night on the mountain always takes its toll. There's not an inn hereby for miles around. But there's a good old knight who's known to take strangers in.'

Merlin's eyes turned colour. 'Hard by?' he said.

'Near enough,' she conceded. 'It's old Sir Ector, a good knight of these parts. I suppose you know him, sir?'

Merlin felt a wind from the Otherworld. 'I do.'

She cocked her head like a blackbird, and flashed him a piercing glance. 'Go on then, old sir. They are expecting you.'

Merlin rode past the old woman and did not turn his head. If he looked back, he knew, there would be no one there. He had not asked her how many miles it was. It did not matter, the mule would take him there.

Behind him, Morgan stretched her long body and resumed her natural shape. She smiled as she watched him riding on his way.

To Sir Ector, Merlin, go!

She uncoiled lasciviously, exulting in her power. Merlin would do her will as he did every time he came to her in her spirit body, begging her favour to answer his desires. And now she would see the fruition of all she had laboured for since Uther came.

Thunder and lightning convulsed her brain.

Go, Merlin! Seek and find!

And then beware, Arthur, beware!

To Sir Ector, yes, that was where he must go.

Merlin's mind was floating, beyond hope, beyond thought.

Sir Ector.

Could it be . . . ?

He had never considered Sir Ector, the old knight tucked away in his hidden valley hard by Wales. Sir Ector, the King's loyal vassal, Arthur's foster-father, the most devoted man alive –

would he harbour the child of Arthur's mortal foe? Yet if the boy came as a squire, how would he know whose son he was?

And where better to hide the boy than under everyone's nose? Sir Ector never left his lands to come to court. Arthur had not revisited his boyhood home in thirty years. Fond greetings passed between them, to be sure, but after a lifetime of fostering boys to train up as knights, would Sir Ector report to Arthur or anyone else if another young lad had joined him along the way?

The mule plodded on, mile after patient mile. At last they crested a hill, and the castle of Sir Ector lay below. Trembling in every limb, Merlin rode up to the gate-tower, and through to the inner court. A group of young lads on the verge of manhood were rough-and-tumbling round the courtyard in the sun, laughing and chasing like puppies at play.

Most of them took no notice as the old man rode in. With his grey-green grass-stained robes, ancient furs and well-worn boots, Merlin seldom attracted attention unless he chose. But one of the boys acknowledged his arrival with a wave. Breaking away from the group, he leaped towards Merlin in a graceful run.

'Good day to you, my lord!' he cried, as he came up.

He was taller than all the rest, with a slender, well-made body, and finely proportioned limbs. He carried himself like an athlete, and had a horseman's long, strong legs and clever hands. His dark wool tunic showed off an ivory skin and a head of thick black hair. His eyes were blue-black and smiling, large and lustrous, and fringed like a girl's. He had Arthur's open, trusting gaze, and he was the handsomest youth that Merlin had ever seen.

His voice was light and melodious, with the faintest hint of Wales. 'Can I help you sir?'

Pendragon . . .

The old man's heart soared and burst with love. He knew he was grinning like an ancient loon.

'Yes, indeed, my son.'

Cackling, he handed his reins to the boy, and leaned down to stare him in the face. 'Your name, young man?'

The boy fixed him with his hyacinthine eyes, and gave him a dazzling smile. 'It's Mordred, sir,' he said.

CHAPTER 52

They held each other for a moment as long as eternity, and whispered softly together, as lovers do. Guenevere was trembling so violently that she could hardly stand

'Can you forgive me?'

He paused, and held her tightly in his arms. 'There is nothing to forgive.'

'Oh, Lancelot,' she wept, 'say you can?'

He drew her more closely to his chest and tucked her head under his chin. 'I should ask you if you can forgive me.'

She pulled back astounded, and looked up at his face. 'Forgive you? What for?'

He shook his head. There was an expression she could not read round his long, full mouth. She closed her eyes and tried to compose herself. Only minutes before she had been stumbling weeping through the dark, and she still could hardly believe he was really here. He had led her gently inside the little white house, and drawn her down to lie on the narrow bed. A candle was shining to light their way in, and an applewood fire blazed cheerfully on the hearth. Now their bodies clung together in a hunger that could not be appeased.

She reached up to touch his face. The corners of his mouth lifted into a smile. Tenderly she stroked the long groove in his upper lip, and traced the clean, hard angle of his jaw. He turned to kiss the top of her head, and his glossy brown hair swung down to brush her face.

She sighed. 'What do I have to forgive you, Lancelot?'

'Oh . . .'

He turned away. She watched as his gaze shifted beyond the

rough whitewashed walls of the guest-house where they lay.

Lancelot closed his eyes. 'I am your knight,' he said, as if each word cost him pain. 'I chose you as my lady, above all the other ladies in the world. But when you doubted me, I was angry, and I rode away.' He caught his breath. 'I failed you, lady.'

She was pierced by a violent pain. 'No,' she cried furiously, 'no! You came to fight for me when I needed you. You saved my life.'

His distress redoubled. 'But at your trial, all men were against you, and you had no one but me. And I threw you my bloody sword, and rode off again.'

She saw again the green field of her trial, the dark armour of her accuser, the jury of black-clad monks, and her saviour the red knight, furiously spurring away. She could feel his body shaking with every word.

She held him tightly, and tried to soothe his pain. 'Lancelot, it wasn't wrong for you to be angry with me. I should never have doubted you about Elaine.' She stroked his neck, and hid her face against his chest. 'I was – I was half mad with jealousy when I thought you were in love. Gawain said you were going to marry –'

'My queen . . .'

He laid his finger on her lips. 'Elaine was like spring water, you are my soul's wine. I was not for her, nor she for me. May the Great One in Her mercy grant her peace.'

For a brief moment, the pale spirit of the lost Maid of Astolat hovered sadly between them, and was gone. Then Lancelot's head went up in the Otherworldly gesture that she knew so well. 'I could not love her, because I am yours.'

He turned his golden gaze full on her face, and her soul dissolved. She reached up and drew his head down for a kiss. His mouth was warm, and her longing for him was as sweet as summer rain. 'Oh, Lancelot.' she murmured in her throat.

His hand was already at her breast. 'Oh, lady – oh, my love . . .'

They came together like new lovers learning how to touch. He took her briefly and gently, and there were as many tears for both of them as cries of joy. After so long all they wanted was to become one again, to be whole. Then they lay together at peace, joined in a love closer than their skin.

A sudden sadness seized her, and she stroked his flank. 'All this while we've been apart – tell me, love, where did you go?'

'Back to my lady,' he said drowsily.

'Your –' She caught herself up in a fury of self-hate. *Guenevere, Guenevere, jealous again?*

She forced herself to smile. 'Who?'

'My lady,' he repeated, 'the lady who brought me up.'

Guenevere laughed with relief. 'Your foster-mother – the Lady of Broceliande?'

He nodded, his hair tickling her breast. 'The sister of your Lady here on Avalon. I was brought up in her crystal castle behind the waterfall. She and her maidens taught me all I know.' His bright brown eyes lit up. 'Men should be brought to manhood by women, because women remind men of the best they can become.' He laughed like a boy. 'Men only remind each other of themselves.'

She could not help but laugh along with him. Then somehow their laughter turned to kissing, and they made love again.

Daylight found them drowsing and talking, locked in each other's arms. They slept a little till the morning sun striking through the window bathed all the bed in gold. The water-fowl were calling from the marsh. Nearby, the otters whistled from their holts, and a thousand songs and cries reminded them of the life outside.

'Madame?'

Lancelot reared up on his elbow in the bed. Guenevere came to herself with a sudden pang. *Don't look at me*, she wanted to say. She was all too aware that the harsh daylight would show a face stained with tears, eyes swollen with weeping, and a skin that had long forgotten pink and white. *Do I look old? He must think I am.*

But Lancelot was gazing down at her with joy. He covered her face with kisses, then vaulted naked from the bed. He stood for a moment in all his unselfconscious glory, then held out his hand. 'Come, lady!' he beamed, 'come!'

With Ina absent, he had to help her to dress. Deftly he dealt with her skirts and underskirts, and the laces and ties of her gown. She chose a simple, free-flowing robe of silk in a forget-me-not blue that he had loved before, and she saw in his eyes that he remembered too. At last she was dressed, 'like a Queen,' he said, with pride. And hand in hand they went out of the house.

High above them loomed the vast green bulk of the Tor. They took the pilgrims' way round the hillside to the top, tracing the ancient winding grassy maze where the followers of the Goddess worshipped Her on high holy days with dancing feet. She noticed that Lancelot fell silent as they climbed, and grew sombre as they trod the intricate serpentines. Her heart darkened, and she feared to speak.

Slowly they traversed the loved shape of the Mother lying on her back asleep. Along the top, the Tor flattened out into a sunlit meadow bright with white and gold. All round their feet, daisies and celandines spangled the grass like stars, and further off grew tall gold kingcups and silver lady's smocks. A handful of white doves rolled and gambolled in the sky overhead. Guenevere felt the sun warming her soul. She turned with a surge of hope to the man at her side.

'Lancelot –'

And then she saw the hawk. A thin, dark outline sharp against the sun, he came down on the doves without warning, and struck at the leader in flight. She dropped from the sky, her white breast stained with blood, while her sisters gathered round her, flapping and screaming to drive the intruder away. The wounded bird fluttered off to the safety of a tree, attended by the rest. Lancelot followed Guenevere's agonised gaze, and took her hand.

'That was not Merlin,' he said gently. 'Merlin is part of the All-Life, a Lord of Light. He shares his being with every creature that runs, swims, or breathes. He would never attack a bird of the Goddess on Avalon.'

She shivered. 'No.'

He drew her into his arms. 'You feared the hawk because you fear Merlin's yellow eyes.' He sighed. 'Lovers who live in the shadows must always dread unwanted scrutiny.'

Now it was her turn to sigh. 'Must we always, Lancelot?'

He broke away. 'What else is there?' he cried. 'You cannot leave the King.' He gave a tortured laugh. 'And neither can I. I have sworn to serve him to my dying breath.'

He roamed up and down, clenching his fists. 'But neither can

I leave you. You have passed through me like wine through water, and changed my soul. You bound me to you for life when you made me yours. Neither of us may either go or stay. And so we suffer. What else can we do?'

Sorrowing, she reached out to stroke his hand. 'Our love is woven out of joy and pain.'

He ground her hand between his in mute response. She could feel desire for him pricking her skin, threading its way through every nerve and fibre, sinew, flesh and bone.

And that is how I love him, she thought. *Through every anguish, every ravishment that the human heart can know.*

And from this comes our mystical communion, our faith, our love. It is unfathomable, unknowable, inviolable, no matter how carnal is the feeling between us too. Our bodies come together so fiercely to burn away the dross. Then all that remains is the thing itself.

They were so close that he could hear her body calling, feel her thoughts. His eyes were on her, burning with desire. He drew her down to lie in the long grass, and they made one with the rhythm of the earth.

She slept then in the warmth of the midday sun. But as the day passed noon, the air grew cold, and she awoke to find herself alone.

Did I dream it? Goddess, Mother, surely you would not bring my love back to me, then send him away again?

She sat up wildly, casting around for him. But he was only a few feet away, staring down the hill and frowning, deep in thought.

'Lancelot,' she called.

'See, lady,' he cried harshly, beckoning her to his side.

From the top of the Tor they looked down on the landing-stage with its stone jetty thrusting into the Lake. The tiny people toiling far below looked scarcely human, like creatures of a lesser world. But they could see the wide barges of the Lake-dwellers disgorging a dozen new arrivals, each with his effects.

Guenevere gasped with shock. 'Monks!'

As they watched, another monk emerged from a building on the hillside, and hurried down to the jetty to greet the new arrivals. Soon all the monks were making their way back up to the stone-built house. Before the door, they stopped and genuflected to the white stone cross on the roof. Then one by one they trooped indoors.

Guenevere's heart set like stone. 'The Lady told me that they planned to take the Hallows by force,' she said, 'and here they are, bringing in more men.'

Lancelot nodded grimly. 'We are only just in time.'

In time to save the Hallows, perhaps.

But there will never be time enough for us, my love.

He read her face. 'My queen, don't be sad,' he sighed. 'Let us take the time we have.'

He raised his head, catching some unheard sound. 'Listen, do you hear that, on the mainland, far away?' His eyes were gleaming. 'Beltain is coming, lady. They're making up the fires. Soon they will celebrate the feast of love. As we will, lady – a love greater than others will ever know!'

CHAPTER 53

How long did they have on Avalon? Afterwards she could never say. Love's time is not like other days and weeks, and even then they knew they lived a lifetime in the time they had. By day they roamed the island, seeking out its hidden corners and thickly wooded ways. At noon they would lie in groves of whispering beeches, or rest on the soft white sand at the edge of the lake. Those who lived on the Sacred Island, Goddess worshippers and Christians alike, led lives of work and prayer with little time to spare. Day after sunlit day, they had the place to themselves.

Slowly the island ripened into spring. As the days lengthened, they spent all their time out of doors, not returning to the little white guest-house till the night mists rising off the lake drove them indoors. As the dusk drew in, they would sit hand in hand by the fire, savouring the sweet smoke of burning applewood and watching the shapes in the flames. They made love as freely as breathing, without thought. But above all, they talked.

They spoke of their boyhood and girlhood, both growing up with love, but in the deep loneliness that royal children know. She told him about her mother, Maire Macha, the great queen her people called the Battle Raven, and for a while the dead queen lived again in all her beauty, her loving, quicksilver ways, her undying smile.

Lancelot's face in the firelight lost the hard contours of manhood as he recalled a youth spent with no thought of tomorrow, only the eternal boyhood of the livelong day. He was an only son, and his mother, like Guenevere's, had gone to the Goddess before her time. He was lucky then to be fostered by the

Lady of Broceliande. Like her sister the Lady of the Lake, her spirit walked the world between the worlds, and taught his how to grow.

They talked of everything and anything, the topics of all lovers, great and small. But always they came back to the thing they could not change. With each 'I love you' came the following cry, 'What are we to do?' The sadness that had seized Lancelot on the Tor was with him still. She could not console him, for she felt it too.

He gripped her hand and stared into the fire. 'You are the Queen of the Summer Country,' he said at last. 'What you do is above reproach. Your people have had thigh-freedom since time began. And as queen, you may take a Chosen One at will.'

Her eyes flared. 'I do not follow my will. The Queen of the Summer Country takes a Chosen One for the good of all. She must maintain her vigour, when her vital life is the life of all the tribe. I don't choose for myself.'

'No?' He grinned with all the confidence of youth, and ran a knowing hand over her body, revelling in the effect of his touch.

Sharply she pushed him away. 'A queen marries her country, not one man. Champions fall in battle, men grow older, their flesh fails. So the Queen takes a new consort to restore herself. It is her duty to renew the marriage of the sovereignty with the land. And more – it is her right!'

His laughter fell away like summer snow. 'True,' he sighed. 'You may take a new knight when you please. But I have no right to enjoy your love. As Arthur's knight, I am betraying my lord. As his comrade in arms, I break the Fellowship of the Round Table by loving you.'

'Don't talk to me of fellowship!' she cried. 'The love of men and women is far above the love between men. Men together make only war and death.'

'Untrue!' he hissed in a passion. 'For men like my cousin Bors, the brotherhood of the knights of the Round Table is life itself.'

'But not for you!' she protested.

'True,' he agreed reluctantly. 'Oh, Madame, I cannot live without you, I know that now.' He drew a ragged breath. 'And I will never leave you from now on. All the suffering, all the separation we have endured has taught me this, that our love is as enduring as the earth.'

Suddenly he was on his feet, seizing her hands and pulling

her towards to the bed. 'Ask yourself, lady,' he demanded
heatedly, 'why would I leave the best love in the world?'

He threw her none too gently on the bed, and kissed her
passionately. His hands went swiftly to the front of her dress, as
his lips brushed the tears from her face. 'Where would I find
another Guenevere?'

'Oh, Lancelot,' she wept, 'I swear –'

He laughed like a boy, and kissed her on the mouth. 'No
more words, lady. You need loving now.'

So the days passed, and on the mainland Beltain came. For three
days and nights the sound of revelry reached them across the still
waters, and one by one the bloom of the bonfires turned night into
day. Sweet wisps of woodsmoke mingled with the first warm
breath of spring. A moon of hope lit the heavens, and bright stars
danced in the ripening sky.

The tribes had gathered from far and wide for the feast. By
day they drummed and sang, laughed, feasted and made games
to celebrate the life the Goddess gives. At night they crept into the
warm shadows of the roaring fires to join with the Mother in the
making of new life.

Safe in the shelter of their little house, Guenevere and
Lancelot listened as the rising wind brought its hope and comfort,
along with the sweet gurgling cries and moaning in the dark.
Their own yearning quickened as the faint echo of soft sounds
and sighs came trembling through the dark. Time and again they
found themselves in each other's arms. Afterwards a vast love
possessed them in its peace. At these times they passed together
into the Beyond, floating through the astral plane where two
souls become one. And as the barriers dissolved between their
worlds, they became more strange and lovely to each other with
each new dawn of knowledge, hope and trust.

'You are the traveller from the Otherworld, shining in the
night.' Guenevere said. 'You are the One I have looked for all my
life.'

'And you –' Lancelot could hardly speak. 'You are the
woman of the dream. Our love encompasses this world, the
Otherworld, and the world that is to come. If I lost you, I would
search all three worlds to find you again.'

The hours went by so swiftly that she hardly knew where his being ended and hers began. Their bodies, too, were like halves of the same whole. The days slipped by as sweetly as pearls on a chain But all the time they knew that it must end.

The knock came late at night, when the fire had burned down. Nemue stood at the door, her face pale and set, her eyes huge in the light of the little lamp she carried in her hand.

'The Christians are coming tomorrow to claim the Hallows,' she husked. 'The Lady says you must leave the island tonight.'

The next hours passed in a dream of misery. Numbly Guenevere prepared herself to leave, and watched as Lancelot did the same. Both moved through their tasks without protest, even with an occasional fleeting smile. In a calm beyond calm, they left the island with Ina, slipping silently from the stone jetty in a barge poled by Nemue alone.

They landed on the mainland in the silver haze of dawn. Through the half-light she could see a small group of Lake-dwellers standing with their horses and mules, and guarding a long wooden box, stoutly corded and lying on the ground. Inside, she knew, must be the Hallows, wrapped in silk and buried in a bed of straw. A new fear awoke in her. Plain as it was, a box of that size would make Lancelot the target of any outlaw or wayside thief.

Nemue read her thought. 'He must travel by night.' She turned to Lancelot. 'Sir Lancelot, this is your task.'

Lancelot heard the wind of loss and separation gathering force. For a moment he strove madly against his fate, his spirit beating against its unseen bonds. Then he struggled to settle his soul, and reached out to grasp Guenevere's hand.

'I am ready, lady,' he said to Nemue. 'What is your will?'

Nemue seemed to grow, gleaming with power, as she spoke. 'You must take the Hallows, and guard them with your life. You will travel far before you find them a home. They will not be safe wherever the Christians hold sway. But you will come to the place, and know where they must remain.'

She took a step back, and held up both her hands, palms outward, as if to ward him off. 'And when you do, tell no one where they are. The Lady is giving the Hallows back to the Great

One as freely as She gave them to us. Their fate must lie in other hands than ours. When the Christians come for them, we must say in perfect truth that we know nothing now.'

She gave a furious sigh. Tears as hard as diamonds stood in her eyes. 'The soul of Avalon goes out with them. For a thousand years, we have worshipped in this place. Now we must lose it all for a handful of brutal men.'

In the silence they caught the distant sound of a storm tearing through the mountain tops, destroying dwellings and uprooting trees. It raged by, gathering force, and swept on.

Guenevere pressed Lancelot's hand. 'But good men can keep the faith.'

Nemue bowed her head. 'Or else we are all lost.'

A silence fell. All around them the forest breathed lightly in its sleep. Only the soft jingling of the horses' harness came to them through the trees.

'So, then, this is my quest. I must take to the road while you return to Camelot.' Lancelot looked away. How would he ever find the strength to leave? 'Bid me farewell, my queen.'

A cold pain gripped her heart.

Farewell?

A wild protest mutinied in her soul, and died. *Fate spins as it will, and even the Mother cannot turn back the wheel. Farewell, my love, until we meet again.*

'Lancelot –' She turned towards him and kissed both his hands. 'Go with the Goddess, wherever She may lead. Wherever you go, my soul will be with you. You are my knight, my true love and my life. One day we may hope for a better world than this. One day I know we will be together again. Till then, every day of my life I shall give thanks for you, and the love the Goddess gave.'

He fixed his eyes on her. 'I will fulfil this task, however long and hard. But understand, my queen, that you are my true quest. I go to learn how to be worthy of you. Each day I will strive to live and love as you would wish. Every dawn and evening I will pray to you.' He gave a broken smile. 'Honour and dignity wait for us both apart. And service to the Great One who loves us all.'

He brought her hand to his lips, and turned away. She watched numbly as he crossed to the Lake-dwellers, and supervised the loading of the Hallows on to the strongest of the mules. Others were making his own horse ready for him, and behind them she could see mounts being led up for herself and Ina too. *He is going,* her mind tried to tell her, *and soon we will be gone. Treasure these last precious seconds, and prepare.*

Prepare to live a life of love apart.

She could not weep. *No tears, no fears, not now. You have a love stronger than life itself. You have the faith of the best man alive. You have a joy most women never know. You are blessed among women, Guenevere, take heart.*

With these and a hundred loving thoughts she tried to armour herself against what lay ahead. But nothing could stave off the moment when Lancelot had to say the words she was dreading to hear.

'So, lady, the time has come. One kiss, and then we part.'

CHAPTER 54

They could see the smoke above the trees from miles away. As they drew near, the smell of burning was overlaid by a sweeter, sicker stench. Sir Kay tried unsuccessfully to ease his bad leg in the saddle, and exchanged a look of foreboding with Sir Lucan and Sir Bedivere. They had all been on too many battlefields not to know the smell of bodies rotting to decay.

At the head of the troop, Arthur picked up the scent like a dog, and spurred his horse on to a breakneck speed. His face still wore its waxy sheen of dread, and he had kept up this punishing pace for hours. Still, it had to be over soon, Kay thought in dread. Any moment now they would learn the worst.

Yet nothing could have prepared them for what they saw as they rode through the convent gates. In the courtyard the bodies of half a dozen nuns lay sprawled where they had fallen, grinning cadavers black and crawling with flies. At the entry itself, what had been the Sister Gate-keeper still sat at her post, her ruined mouth open in a silent scream. All round the central square, charred walls and roofs lay open to the sky. Ahead of them, the chapel had burned out. Nothing remained but a heap of smouldering stones, with a thin column of smoke rising overhead. In the midst of the ruin, a broken cross lay at an unnatural angle, its tortured Christ seeming to live His final passion once again.

Arthur dragged his sweating horse to a violent halt. 'Morgan!' he howled.

Morganmorganmorgan cried the echo round the walls. Arthur sat sweating and trembling on his exhausted horse. Sir Lucan vaulted lightly to the ground.

'You!' he commanded the men with Sir Sagramore, 'take the northern block.' Sagramore raised his sword, and they were gone.

'Sir Dinant!' Lucan went on, 'the west range, and you, Sir Tor, the south.' His voice followed the knights and men as they galloped off. 'Whatever you find, bring it straight to the King.'

'Good, Lucan!' Arthur's eyes were glittering. He tried for a normal smile. 'And now –' He raised his sword and pointed to the building ahead, a low white cloistered structure slumbering in the westering sun. A harsh laugh racked him. 'Let us see what the eastern block holds.'

The answer was nothing, Kay agreed with Lucan and Bedivere afterwards, just as they had suspected from the start. Nothing but festering bodies in every cell, as the search of all the other dormitories found. Nothing but the cold remains of the Father Confessor, with the tears of his passing still wet on his face. And only an abandoned nun's outfit on the floor to give any hint of where Morgan might have gone.

Arthur stood over the crumpled black gown and white headdress with murder in his face. In a spasm of rage he drew back his booted foot, and kicked the empty wimple into the air. The great white shape soared up and fell back flapping like a wounded bird.

'Gone!' Arthur spat. 'She's gone.'

And we won't find her now, went through every mind.

Arthur laughed savagely. 'But she'll be back, I know.'

'Sire –' The gentle Bedivere stepped forward, and picked up the nun's gown. His light Welsh lilt gave a sad music to his words. 'Your sister suffered here cruelly as a child. Perhaps her sorrows are all paid for now.'

'He could be right, my lord.' Kay pointed to the dead monk on the bed. 'Their leader's gone. She's destroyed the chapel and all the buildings too. The Christians will never keep women here again.'

Sir Lucan nodded. His handsome face creased with unpleasant memories. 'Queen Morgan always knew what she wanted, sire. Surely she must have finished with this place now.'

'Ha!' Arthur's ravaged features showed the shadow of faint hope. 'Perhaps. At all events, there's nothing to keep us here.' He squared his shoulders, and gave a ragged grin. 'And if my sister's revenge is not complete, well, Madam Morgan knows where to come for me.'

A chill fell on the group. Lucan cleared his throat. 'Sire . . .'

'No matter.' Suddenly Arthur was calm and smiling again. 'But I have one last peace to make on this earth before Morgan and I meet again face to face.'

His grey eyes brightened, and his cry rang round the cell. 'To Camelot!'

Gawain stepped out of the tent to breathe the clean night air. All around him the forest slumbered, hushed and dim. Grimly he scanned the clearing where they were encamped. Weeks already on the road, at the pace of the slowest horse. Well, however long it took, they would all endure. And at least he did not have to suffer what Agravain did.

'Stay with him, both of you,' he threw over his shoulder as he left the tent. He did not wait for a reply. Neither Gaheris nor Gareth would leave Agravain's side, he knew. Both were well aware that they would pay with their lives if Agravain lost his.

For the pursuers were always with them, night and day. Not so much as a hoof-fall or the cracking of a broken twig, not a sound in the dark nor passing scent on the breeze had reached them to suggest that others were near. But with the certain instinct of an Orkneyan, Gawain knew that Leif and his two followers tracked their every move. He knew that they rode ahead, beside and behind, spinning an invisible web round them every day.

And he knew why. Sir Lamorak had been the Queen's Champion and her Chosen One. They were the Knight Companions of the Throne. Agravain had killed Lamorak. So Agravain had to die.

Gawain gritted his teeth, and shelved the terrible thought. It must not happen, he would see to that. Leif and his companions had their code, he knew. But a prince of the Orkneys had his, and no man on earth would take his brother's life. Every mile of the way, then, Gawain had stood guard over Agravain, or left Gaheris and Gareth as sentries in his place. But with every mile Agravain had defended what he had done, and loudly justified himself with every breath. Arrogant and vain as ever, he had showed neither sorrow nor remorse for their mother's grief, and at the end of the first day on the road, Gawain would gladly have killed his brother himself. But an Orkney man stood by his kin. And he had sworn an oath to bring Agravain to justice, to the judgement that only Arthur could provide.

Well, a few more days in the saddle, and they would be there. And Agravain's punishment was already under way. To be in the power of his brothers, night and day, was Agravain's deepest nightmare come to waking life. To be forced to obey Gawain's slightest whim, to have to sleep, eat, breathe and fulfil all nature's functions under the hostile gaze of Gaheris and Gareth too, had been the purest form of torment to his heart.

Yet he knew, too, that it was his only hope of life. For Agravain also had noticed the close pursuit, and lived every moment in fear. Already his hands were trembling, and his haunted face showed what he endured. In the weeks on the road, a strand of his hair had turned white, and now his dense black locks were scarred with a streak running back from his forehead, like the mark of Cain. There is some justice then, Gawain mused heavily. Blood will have blood, there is payment of the debt.

The night air was sweet and soothing on his face. Lost in thought, Gawain drifted away from the clearing and the little camp till he came to rest under a mighty oak. Through the thick thatch of leaves and cloud above he could still see the love star shining through the night. He breathed deeply, and sent his spirit into the void. Lamorak, Lamorak, he called silently, may the Great One speed your voyage through the Beyond. Hear my pledge as you wait for my mother to join you there, you will be avenged. On the oath of an Orkneyan, Agravain will pay for your death.

The love star dipped its light, and blazed up again. Far away he heard the hooting of an owl. Then, from a nearby copse, he caught the soft whoop-whoop of a night-jar calling its mate. His broad face creased in a smile.

'I hear you,' he chuckled. 'Come!'

From the depths of a thicket to his left, the shaggy form of Leif materialised and took shape. Behind him Gawain saw the shadow of Leif's two companions, the fellow-knights chosen to accompany him south. But behind them was another, a knight

Gawain knew at once as the best horseman of the Orkneys, fleet and fearless, and able to ride night and day. There could be only one reason why he was here.

'News, lord,' said Leif, in a voice like the raven in the night. He squinted his one eye at the horseman. 'Tell.'

The newcomer stepped into the moonlight. He was white with the dust of the roads, and wore the look of a stranger from the Otherworld. 'Our lord Sir Lamorak has been calling the Queen every night. Now she is with him, and they are both at peace.'

Gawain fixed his eyes on the love star and watched it glow. He could not speak.

Leif shouldered up to stand beside the messenger, with the knight companions closing in behind.

'She has gone to the Islands of the Blessed,' he grunted softly, 'to the kingdom beyond pain.'

He signalled to the horseman, and the two knights. All three drew their swords, and offered Gawain the hilts.

'You are our lord now,' Leif breathed through the night. 'We follow you.'

Gawain nodded. 'You are mine,' he said brusquely. 'Now hear my command. You will abandon the pursuit of Prince Agravain. He will live to face trial at King Arthur's court.'

Three pairs of eyes flared in the night like wolves. Gawain fixed a frowning gaze on Leif, and the knight companion stared back unblinkingly.

'We have a debt to our lord,' Leif said at last. 'And to our lady too.' His low grunting cry was full of pain. 'You saw her. You know.'

Gawain paused. It was true. He saw again Morgause raving in her granite hall, her face and hair all torn, her life destroyed. He saw her ending her days broken and alone, in the madness of despair, and made up his mind.

'A death is a debt,' he nodded to Leif and the knights, 'and it must be paid. Tonight you will find Prince Agravain alone. Tomorrow he will continue his journey with me, and you will return to the islands until I return. But what happens between those times, I do not wish to know.' He glared at Leif. 'Understand me, though, he is not to die. Nor to be injured. You may not shed his blood.'

A hungry grin was spreading over Leif's face. 'No death,' he promised. 'No blood.'

The horseman nodded, his thin smile chilling the night. 'No blood,' he echoed with a wide-eyed gleam. 'No knife, no blade, no blood.'

The knight companions behind him snickered softly as they thought of what was to come.

'So then,' Gawain said softly, 'he's yours till dawn. Then I want him back.'

'In one piece, lord,' Leif promised solemnly.

Together they followed Gawain back to the camp. They waited in perfect contentment as Gawain approached the tent, and lifted the flap at the door.

'Gaheris,' he called, 'and Gareth. Leave Agravain. Come here. I want you now.'

Now.

There was no need for speech. Leif and his three companions stood in the shadows of the trees till they could have been trees themselves.

Now, lord and leader, companion, knight and friend, your death will be avenged. Now your soul will be free to slip its shell, and wander in the world of fires and flowers.

One thought possessed them all.

Now the young wolf will pay for the death of his dam.

CHAPTER 55

Camelot, Camelot, fortress, palace, home –

High summer had never bloomed so gloriously. Leaving Avalon, they travelled through long purple evenings and warm rosy dawns. Rich swathes of golden corn covered the hills, and plump pigs and calves roistered in sunny pens. At every smallholding some sunburned harvester, toothless ancient or wide-eyed child would stop in their tracks to hail the Queen's procession with a cheer. Even the wayside flowers, wild rose and honeysuckle, poppy and marigold, thronged the verges to give her a welcome home.

At last they were cresting the final mountain ridge. Night was falling as the weary horses stumbled down the hillside through the trees. And there it was, the beloved stronghold of a thousand queens, its white towers and battlements glowing in the moonlight, its banners reflected in the ring of bright water below. Sighing with relief, she crossed the causeway, rode up the cobbled streets to the great gates, and allowed the old castle to enfold her in its arms again.

Camelot, Camelot, home –

At first, she could only lie on a daybed in the Queen's apartments, and watch the sun creeping along the wall. Hour by hour she relived the time she had spent with Lancelot, and her heart grew strong. In that short time on Avalon, they had had more joy, more truth, more sharing of souls and bodies than most people ever knew. She had had a love, a great and mighty love, and for that she would thank the Mother as long as she lived.

And she had him still. Every evening at sunset when the love

star bloomed, she lit a candle in her turret window to shine for
Lancelot, wherever he was. One night the flame flared up, and in
the heart of it she saw him far away. He was kneeling to pray in
the path of the setting sun, and the red-gold beams bathed all his
limbs with fire. She could even catch the words falling from his
lips, my lady, oh, my love –

From the angle of the sun, she knew he was travelling east.
Every dawn then brought the comfort that the rising sun would
tell her where he lay. So day by day she grew stronger, till she was
walking, and taking the air, and riding out again. Day after day
roses blazed from the castle walls, and the woodland beckoned
with its cool green shade. Night after night the roses poured out
their fragrance, and the song of the nightingale dropped through
the air like tears.

She lived now in full acceptance of the sadness at the heart of
love. There could be no joy like theirs without great pain. A
melancholy peace possessed her heart. Lancelot was with her, he
was part of her, and that was a truth as enduring as the earth.

But so was Arthur too. She had not seen him since the day
she rode away, and he had made no demands, seeming to
understand her need to be alone. Yet though absent, he was
present everywhere. Every day in Camelot she saw again the
Arthur of their youth. In those days he had loved Camelot, the
wind-tossed towers with their slender spires, the strong walls
and snug dwellings, and she had been overjoyed to have his
praise. The white castle had been their wonderland, their palace
of delight. When had they lost that love? How long had they kept
their kingdoms and their lives apart?

She did not know. But she knew that she had once loved
Arthur more than her life. He is your duty and your destiny, the
Lady had said. *What duty? What destiny?* were the questions that
tormented her now. And what would she say to him when he
came? For he came at last, as she knew he had to do.

He came on one of those days of cruel beauty at the peak of a long
hot summer, before the sun must die and leave the earth to the
cold. A dewy dawn had passed through a flaming noon, and the
evening shadows were lengthening when Ina came to her in an
arbour, and said, 'The King is here.'

He was standing in her apartments gazing out of the window, a bewildered, bear-like figure, quite alone. He wore a plain dark tunic with dark breeches, and seemed to have put off his royalty along with the cloak on the nearby chair. He looked tired and sad, and she had a sudden impulse to take him by the hand. But as she drew near, his air of hopeless resignation maddened her. Why had he bothered to come, if he already thought it was in vain?

'Guenevere –'

Arthur's heart constricted in his chest. Why did she look so remote? He had ridden every mile from Caerleon longing to see her, picturing the moment when he could take her in his arms. Now she turned a cold cheek to him, and his resolution died.

'Guenevere,' he began with an effort again.

'Arthur?'

He made no move towards her, she noted, with a spasm of pain. 'Welcome,' she said, in an empty voice.

Beside him on a table were a clutch of boxes, wood, ivory and silver, curiously inlaid. Guenevere stared at them with cold dislike. Did he think to buy her love back with his gifts?

Arthur noticed the direction of her gaze. 'Oh, just a few things I brought.' He waved at them with an indifferent hand. Dear God, he cried inside, why can't I speak? He had done all he could to make things perfect now. He had overcome his first mad impulse to ride straight to Guenevere, and had left her alone all this time, praying she might come to love him again. He had chosen the gifts so carefully, poring over them for weeks. Now the moment was here, he was throwing it away. He watched in hopeless fury as Guenevere drew near, then pressed the first of the boxes into her hands.

It was made of carved sandalwood, and no bigger than a glove. Inside, wrapped in red velvet, was a crystal mirror the size of a lady's hand. The glass was smoky and mysterious. As she looked into it, she saw another Guenevere, softer and happier, smiling in its depths.

The second box was of ivory, with woodland scenes and figures etched on the top and sides. As she lifted the lid, she saw what looked like a pool of starlight glimmering inside. It was a length of pale shining silk, as fine as the gossamer for a wedding gown. Her fingers snaked out to touch it in spite of herself.

'Ohh –' she cried.

Arthur's voice was low. 'I thought it might remind you of our wedding day.'

He reached out to pick up the third box himself. It was a square, flat silver casket, lovingly chased. His big hands stroked the surface, tracing the face of the full moon on the lid.

'The sign of the Queen of Heaven,' he murmured, 'for the Queen of my heart.' He opened the box. Inside lay a fine diadem of spun gold, spangled with bright stones shining like the stars.

Guenevere gasped, and tears leaped to her eyes. The loveliness of it was almost too much to bear. She thought of her mother, and wished she could see it too. A single sob shook her from head to foot. A moment later she had it in her hands.

Arthur's smile could not drive the sadness from his eyes. 'Take it, Guenevere, I had it made for you. You'll wear it as a queen, and a great one, too. You were born to rule, and you come of a great line.'

He stifled a sigh, and tried for another smile. 'All my life, I was only Merlin's boy. When I met you I was a king without a kingdom, riding on my hopes and little else.' He laughed sadly. 'You made me a man, Guenevere. You taught me my worth, and all I did was to outrun my strength.'

Guenevere nodded.

I made you king, yes, and High King too, when the Britons most needed a champion to unite the land and defeat the Saxon hordes. But the island's gain was fated to be my loss.

Arthur looked at Guenevere. 'Your mother loved you, and you were used to being loved. I did not love you enough.'

'Love is not all. Love and duty are the twin poles of life.'

'Ah, duty!' He let out a ragged breath. 'I failed you there as well. When we married, I swore to fight for you, and keep the worship of the Great Mother alive in these isles. I thought I could let Sir Mador make his challenge, and still check the Christians in their search for blood.' His voice was bleak. 'I was wrong.'

'Arthur, listen to me.' She paused. Why did it hurt her to see him suffering so? 'Kings and queens have power, but they do not have free choice.'

'No excuses, Guenevere.' The great head went back in

unconscious pride. 'It's all over now, in any case. I've come to make my final peace with you. Through my folly and vanity, I've lost two sons, and now I must lose you.'

'Lose me?' What gave him the right to decide what happened to them both? 'What are you talking about?' she said angrily.

'Morgan,' he said. He was very pale. 'She's here.'

An impulse of pure terror ran through Guenevere. 'Here in Camelot?'

Arthur gave a bitter smile. 'No. But not far away. She's destroyed the convent where she used to live. It's only a matter of time before she comes for me.'

'Arthur, Arthur,' she cried in anguish, 'you don't deserve to die!'

'Perhaps I do. But it's not for us to decide. The Great Ones spun our thread when the world was born.' He straightened his broad back, facing blindly into the dying light. 'And I am ready now, in any case. The sins of my father have to be answered some day.'

'No, Arthur, no, not yet! And you should not have to pay for what he did.' What was it about his mute dignity that moved her to tears, the tall heavy body stiffly braced for the worst? 'Listen to me, it can't be, and it won't!'

He came towards her and gently took her hands.

'Some day it must, we always knew that,' he murmured softly. 'Morgan will not rest till her wrongs are avenged. And when it comes, little one, you must not grieve.'

'I will, I will,' she cried, 'but it won't be yet!'

In a passion of fury, she tore her hands from his, and beat his chest. 'Arthur, listen to me! I saw the Lady in Avalon as I came here. She told me for sure that you're not going to die.'

'What?'

The words of the Lady filled Guenevere's mind.

Arthur's time has not yet come. He is not ready for the last crossing of the water, where he and I shall meet.

Slowly she repeated them to Arthur, word for word. 'The Lady never lies. Morgan means some mischief, yes, that must be true.' She took a breath. 'But whatever comes, we'll face it together, as we've always done.'

As she spoke, wild disbelief, then hope, flooded Arthur's face. Before she finished speaking, he was weeping with relief. He buried his face in his hands and his words came to her muffled by pain.

'Oh, Guenevere, could you find it in your heart? I don't deserve your forgiveness.'

The thought of Lancelot came as an answering pain. 'Don't say that, Arthur. There are some things you have to forgive me, too.'

He shook his head, smiling through his tears. 'No, Guenevere. You're a wonderful woman, and you've always been good to me. Whereas I –'

He turned away, and his eyes filled again.

'You're not a bad man, Arthur. Give yourself credit for the good you have done.' Her voice had a sharper edge than she would have wished.

He gave a tremulous smile. 'You don't change, Guenevere, do you know that?' Longingly his eyes caressed her face. 'You're still as beautiful to me as you ever were.'

'Oh . . .'

Guenevere waved her hand. She did not want his praise. 'You are my husband. And I care for you.'

'And I for you.'

He paused, then looked her steadily in the eye. 'Not even Amir was more to me than you.'

Amir –

'Ohhhh –' She could not help the sound that burst from her.

A moment later, Arthur had her in his arms. 'Cry, sweetheart,' he whispered into her hair.

He wrapped her in the shelter of his cloak. She clung to his broad chest, and the tears ran down her face.

Amir, my heart's darling, dearer to me than all.

She thought of her baby's little body, his round head, and his eyes, so like Arthur's with their wide, trusting gaze. She could feel his warm weight in her lap, and the satin smoothness of his rounded limbs. His fresh child's smell, as sweet as summer hay, came to her in a needlepoint of memory so sharp she could have cried aloud. *And all this sweetness gone with Amir, never to return.*

She felt Arthur's chest shaking as she clung to him, and knew that he was weeping too. Suddenly she was flooded with a new dimension of their mutual pain.

If I had been the cause of Amir's death –

If I had to bear that knowledge along with the grief of his loss, how would I live?

And this is Arthur's doom, his daily fate. Yet still he is loving to me, faithful to his knights, good to his people and kind to all the world.

'Arthur –'

Love for him surged through her like a tide. She raised her arms and threw them round his neck, drawing down his face for a kiss. Startled, he pulled back. The look of mingled hope and hurt on his face stabbed her afresh.

'Guenevere, you don't have to do this.'

'Don't speak.'

The last words of the Lady sighed in her ears like the sea.

Ah, Guenevere, you and Arthur will have many years together now. And love will come to you.

Gently she stroked his cheek. He looked at her with lovelight in his eyes. The dying sun lit up the golden stubble on his chin, and her fingers found the soft spot at his temples where the gold was turning grey. She could feel the old love rising from primeval depths. At the same time a new desire washed through her, and left her weak and panting in its wake. They stood for a moment clinging to each other like survivors of a wreck. Then she took his hand, and led him to her bed.

CHAPTER 56

In the Great Hall of Camelot, the two vast bronze thrones stood empty for Arthur and Guenevere, with Arthur's knights in attendance behind. Around them a packed court buzzed and hummed and held its breath. All knew that Sir Agravain had been brought to judgement by Sir Gawain. And as the word spread of how Queen Morgause and her knight had died, most of those present had no doubt what the judgement should be.

Gawain could feel all their eyes as he stood at the front of the court. Twitching with tension, he shifted from foot to foot. The endless journey dragging Agravain south had been almost too much to bear. Gaheris now had a new and bitter edge, and the gentle Gareth was cheerful and childlike no more. Gawain stirred again, and cursed violently to himself. Where was Arthur? When would their ordeal end?

But whatever the judgement, Queen Morgause and Lamorak had not gone unavenged. He did not know what had happened between Leif and the knight companions and Agravain, and he would not guess. All he knew was that the pursuers had been faithful to their oath. The experts in the art of inflicting pain, in the delicate play between sinew, bone and nerve, had kept their knives in their sheaths.

But in the morning they were gone, and their work had been well done. Agravain was lying curled up in a corner of the tent. At first he could only gibber and moan by turns, and when they forced him to eat, he retched and spewed like a dog. When speech returned, he would only scream or curse. They had feared then that he would never be right again.

The weeks on the road had brought a semblance of calm. But

the old sneering Agravain was no more. In his place was a creature who would carry his torment with him for ever more, as a snail bears its shell. Amid the ruins of his former peace, it gave Gawain some consolation that Agravain was paying for his crime.

And thank the Gods, it would soon be over now. Gawain sighed with relief as the voice of the Chamberlain boomed through the hall. He had done all he could in bringing Agravain here. It was in the hands of Arthur from now on.

Gawain looked sick and Agravain far worse, Guenevere noted, as she took her seat. What had happened to turn the darkest of the Orkney princes into a bleached shadow of himself? But by the time Gawain finished speaking, she understood. The horror of it was almost beyond belief. And these were Arthur's kin. What would he do?

Gawain was coming to the end of his address. 'I swore to my mother that Agravain would receive justice here. I beg you, sire, give judgement in this case.'

A deep hush fell on the court. Arthur leaned forward.

'Sir Agravain, you are charged with the death of Sir Lamorak. Killing a knight is a capital offence. What can you say to defend yourself from death?'

Agravain stepped forward, his thin body motionless, his hand clamped with a deadly rigor on the hilt of his sword. Only his eyes were alive in his staring white face.

'Lamorak was a traitor,' he pronounced, in a shrill monotone. 'He tried to kill me when I found him out. I had to strike him down in self-defence.'

Arthur frowned. 'Lamorak a traitor? He and his father were loyal all their lives.'

'To the house of Pendragon!' came the high-pitched reply. 'Not to the house of Lot. His father killed my father at the battle of the Kings. And Lamorak dishonoured my mother to complete his revenge.'

'Dishonoured her? How?' demanded Arthur.

'He lay with her as her lover, though he was young enough to be her son. He – he –'

'Sir Agravain –'

Gods above, what a loathsome thing he is!

Guenevere fixed her eyes on the contorted face, and forced down the revulsion that she felt. 'Every queen has the right to take a Chosen One. You dishonour your mother far more by saying this.'

'No woman would choose a man who had killed her husband!' Agravain shrilled. 'He must have forced himself into her bed.'

The image of Morgause rose before Guenevere, leaning back towards Lamorak with starlight in her eyes. With it came a sorrow too deep for tears. *Wrong, wrong, Agravain. How hateful and cruel you are.*

Arthur sat up with a sardonic laugh. 'So you're saying that Sir Lamorak was a rapist too? Tell me, sir –'

But Agravain was deaf. 'He used her, and refused to marry her,' he screeched. His voice rose to a new dramatic height. 'I was defending the honour of our house!'

Guenevere put her hand on Arthur's arm. 'All lies,' she said with quiet authority. 'Morgause told me herself that Lamorak begged her time and again to marry him. He was the son of a king, and he longed to make her his queen.'

'I know he lies with every word he says,' growled Arthur. 'Lamorak was the most loyal soul alive. Thank God his father hasn't lived to see this.'

Guenevere took a breath. 'So, what is it to be?'

Arthur paused. 'Agravain's a liar and a murderer. He killed Lamorak, and caused his mother's death. For both those reasons he deserves to die.'

'But?' she prompted gently.

He crushed her hand in his. 'But killing him will not bring Lamorak back,' he said heavily. 'There has been too much death. My father waded through blood to my mother's bed. What he did then is still with us today. Some day it has to stop.'

'If it can be stopped, Arthur,' Guenevere began. But she could see that Arthur was far away.

'And surely Agravain may be redeemed?' he went on, with hope and sorrow mingling in his voice. 'He is my kin. He and his brothers are all I have now.'

Guenevere shook her head. 'Think what he did to his mother. He would hurt you or those you love just as cruelly.'

A dull foreboding stirred in Guenevere's brain. *Yes, he would hurt you, Arthur, if he could. He would not scruple to destroy all that you held dear. We may think of this in times to come. Agravain's malice is not ended yet.*

'Yet blood is blood,' Arthur repeated, with sad emphasis.

'Banish him, then, Arthur,' she said quietly. 'Make him a homeless wanderer through the world. Then he will feel the pain of what he has done.'

Arthur's brow cleared.

'Stand forward, Sir Agravain,' he called. 'You must know that you have done a grievous wrong. We banish you from these islands, on pain of death.' He nodded to Gawain, agog at the foot of the throne. 'See that he takes ship immediately.'

'You are most gracious, sire,' Gawain said fervently. 'Give thanks to the King!' he barked at Agravain. Without waiting for an answer, he hustled his brother brusquely from the court. Grinning with relief, Gaheris and Gareth hurried along behind.

Arthur turned to Guenevere. 'And now –'

'Sire!'

Cutting through the gaily coloured court came two monks clad in sombre black. The taller of the two was the first to speak as they bowed before Arthur's throne.

'Great news, my king!' he cried.

He does not acknowledge a queen in her own kingdom?
Here are enemies bolder than any before.

'You are in Camelot, monk,' she said, raising her voice, 'where I rule with the King. Your names, good sirs?'

The monk turned towards her, raising his eyebrows with a subtly insulting air. 'Of course, Your Majesty,' he said smoothly. He gestured to the monk at his side. 'This is Brother Iachimo, and I am Brother Sylvester. We are Christians from the Isle of Avalon, and we bring tidings of great joy for the King.'

Tidings of joy?

'What?'

Guenevere started, her suspicions sharply aroused. But Arthur was leaning forward eagerly at her side. A memory of last night's loving passed through her mind, and she wanted to please him now.

'Speak, then,' she said.

'Sire –'

Again Brother Sylvester addressed himself earnestly to Arthur alone. 'We have received an embassy from Rome. Scholars there have been working on the origins of our faith. The night before Our Lord was crucified, He and His disciples broke bread, and shared a cup of wine. The next day, at His passion, He was pierced with a lance, and beaten with a sword. In all the centuries since Jesus died, these sacred relics have been lost to view.' His voice rose in triumph. 'But after all this time they have been traced again.'

No – they cannot do this – they would not dare –

A red mist was flooding Guenevere's brain. She leaned forward, gripping the arms of her throne. 'Monk, are you trying to say . . . ?'

But Arthur was already on the edge of his throne. 'The relics of Christ's passion?' he breathed, eyes bright and staring. 'Found again? Where?'

'Here, sire!' the monk cried. 'On the isle of Avalon.' He turned to Guenevere with a superior smile. 'Now we know why the ancients called it the Sacred Island. The holy women who have lived there were guarding a treasure greater than they knew.'

Goddess, Mother, the arrogance of these men –

'Hear me, monk,' she said levelly, fighting her fury down. 'The Hallows of our Goddess have been on Avalon since before your Christ was born. These sacred things belong to the Great Mother. They have nothing to do with Christianity at all.'

'They were thought so, madam, in that benighted time,' corrected Brother Sylvester smoothly. 'But God lifts the darkness of ignorance with the light of our faith. We know the truth at last.' He turned to Arthur again. 'A holy follower of our Lord, Joseph of Arimathea, brought them here. The vessels of the Last Supper, and the weapons of Christ crucified – it's a miracle, sire!' he cried enthusiastically.

'Praise the Lord!' put in Brother Iachimo at his side, rolling up his eyes. 'The Lord's name be praised!'

Arthur's face was pale with ecstasy. 'Christ's cup and plate?' he gasped. 'And the instruments of His passion – sirs, are you saying that you've found the Holy Grail?'

Sylvester's eyes bulged with triumph. 'We have indeed!'

They have the Holy Grail?

Guenevere gasped with fear. *If they have the Hallows, they must have followed Lancelot, and seized them from him.*

But Lancelot would never give them up. If he had lost the Hallows, he would have sent word to the Lady, to me, somehow.

And we've heard nothing. They must have killed him then.

Her heart failed, and she could hardly breathe.

Lancelot is dead, and they have the Hallows now.

The monk was grinning in triumph again. 'Yes, sire, we have found the Holy Grail!'

Once more he appealed to Arthur, ignoring Guenevere. 'I came to you, sire, as one who has found comfort in Jesus Christ, to share the good news. But there is sad news too.'

Now he will say that Lancelot is dead. That he died defending the Grail for the Christian cause –

With a face of sorrow, the monk spread his expressive hands. 'No sooner have we found the Holy Grail than it is lost again.'

'Lost?' breathed Arthur, transfixed.

'Vanished!' the monk cried. 'Spirited away! And the Lady of Avalon herself has no idea where.'

What is he saying?

Guenevere came to herself with a start. 'The Hallows have gone?' she demanded huskily.

'Without trace.' Brother Sylvester could not keep the anger from his voice. 'Removed in the night, we believe, and taken away, but where is not known.'

Goddess and Great Ones, praises on your name.

Oh, Lancelot, Lancelot –

The monk took an eager step towards the throne. 'But they may be found again. Will you help us, sire, to recover the Holy Grail? Think what a quest for you and your knights that would be!'

'It would indeed,' Arthur agreed. His face still wore the rapt, pale look of before, and his eyes were very bright. Guenevere stared at him in sudden alarm. She wanted to hit him, to scream, *No, Arthur, no!*

'The quest for the Holy Grail?' Arthur sighed, and fell into deep thought. At last he raised his head. 'But I have another quest before me now.'

He leaned down to address the monks and all the court. 'I have my duty here, to this land and this queen. She and I have ruled together for many years.' He turned to Guenevere and took her hand. 'It is time for me to renew my vow to her. She is my faith and my all.'

Oh, Arthur – oh, my love.

A low roar of appreciation swept through the crowded court. Guenevere could not move.

Arthur was clasping her hand. 'And I know she will wish to confirm our pledge herself.'

Guenevere found her voice. 'Thank you, my lord,' she managed.

She stood up to speak to the monks, her strength flowing through her with the power of her joy. 'Listen, sirs, and learn. What you call the Grail is our Lady's loving-cup, her vessel of power. It is the circle that contains us all, the cauldron of life itself. It signifies the Great One here on earth, like the Round Table, like the moon herself, all teaching us that in Her we are all one.'

'Madam –'

She waved him to be silent. 'In our faith, monk, each woman is a grail. Within her she bears life, and she gives life from herself. To the men who seek her, she is the one true object of life's quest. To her children, she is food, warmth, love and truth. To her man she is delight, transcendence, healing for the soul. In our faith, every woman is a priestess and every man a god. We do not need to crawl to your altars to be called sinners for enjoying and sharing the love our Goddess gives!'

All the court was on fire with approval now. 'The Queen! The Goddess!' they cried. 'Love and life to all!'

Arthur smiled. 'So, brothers, you are answered now, I think?' he said courteously.

'Thanks to Your Majesty, we are,' said Brother Sylvester, through gritted teeth. Like two black beetles, they vanished into the throng.

Guenevere took Arthur's hand and raised it to her lips. *You have kept your oath, my husband and my love. You have stood up for the Great One, for life and love. And both lie ahead for us now.*

'So, Guenevere?'

She looked towards the door. A faint disturbance was growing as Arthur spoke.

And there it was again, spreading through the palace, 'Merlin, Merlin, Merlin', came the cry of recognition on a hundred lips.

'Ohh,' Arthur wept. He turned to Guenevere with a face between grief and hope. 'Oh, Guenevere, can it be Merlin, after all this time?'

'Merlin!' came a roar at the door.

A tall figure burst in as the cry in the hall reached its height. He wore a long gown in Pendragon red, and a rich red velvet cloak that swept the ground. A thick band of gold held back his long grey hair, and gold earrings shaped like dragons writhed in his ears. Both hands were laden with rings like robin's eggs. He raised his arm in greeting, and the wand of golden yew he carried hummed and purred to itself with a wild, contented sound.

With him was a tall, well-made, dark-haired youth, dressed like a prince and looking about him in awe. He wore a black tunic edged with gold, and his cloak swung freely with the movement of his lithe, graceful form. He had a long, pale face of astonishing beauty, and a gift from the Otherworld, hyacinthine eyes.

Guenevere could not take her eyes from his face.

Who is he?

She could almost see Morgan's knowing smile.

You know who he is, Guenevere. Who else can he be?

Merlin strode through the throng with the youth on his heels. A strange and haunting air came in with them, and the people parted in awe to let them through. Together they came to a halt in front of the dais.

'Kneel, boy,' he cried.

With a flash of his indigo eyes, the youth fell to his knees. A mop of glossy black hair tumbled down over his shoulders as he bowed his head.

Merlin raised a joyful face to Arthur, and laughed with glee. His eyes blazed with a blue and yellow fire. Never had he looked more strange and wonderful. He stood by the boy, and pushed down his bent head.

'See, Arthur, see!' he cried.

Arthur surged to his feet, and strode to the edge of the dais.

Guenevere came hurriedly to stand at his side. Merlin's fingers were already parting the youth's hair. He jabbed a quivering hand at the back of his neck.

'Under the hairline, there, d'you see?'

Guenevere's eyes swam. In the roots of the blue-black hair, a blue-black outline shimmered and took shape. She saw two fighting dragons, closely entwined, each devouring the other's tail. It was the mark of Pendragon, identical to the tattoo Arthur and Merlin bore around their wrists.

'Pendragon born!'

Merlin's voice screamed and sighed, like the wind on the mountains of the moon. 'Embrace him, Arthur,' he cried. 'He is your son!'

CHAPTER 57

Arthur's eyes were closed. He stood swaying and moaning like a great bear in pain. Guenevere reached out and grasped him by the hand, caressing it frantically between both of hers.

'Arthur . . .' she began. Her voice tailed away. What was there to say?

The youth raised his head, his whole being taut with love and hope.

Who are you? Desperately Guenevere tried to read the upturned face. The thick black hair and ivory skin were Morgan's, without doubt, and the large, lustrous eyes midway between blue and black were all his own. But he had Arthur's broad shoulders and strong horseman's legs, and Arthur's capable hands. The handsome head, too, the well-shaped chin and jaw, the open gaze were Arthur to the life. Guenevere fought to control her rising fear. He was Morgan's child, and he was surely Arthur's son.

The boy's hand was on his sword-hilt as he knelt. The weapon rested in a scabbard that seemed to draw down the light, and whisper to its wearer as Merlin's yew wand did. Made of silver and plaited gold, it was set with jewels and ancient stones down all its length. Wandering in and out of the pattern of precious stones, faint runes down the shaft breathed out their spells of love. Guenevere bowed her head, and tears from long ago rose to her eyes. It was her mother's scabbard, the heirloom of the queens of the Summer Country, which Morgan had stolen from Arthur years ago. And now, years later, she had sent it back with her son.

'Arthur –'

She tried in vain to show him what she had seen. He stood frozen in an attitude of grief. In all the court, no one moved or spoke.

Merlin grew frantic. 'He's your son, Arthur! Speak to him! Mordred's here!'

Arthur made no move. Slowly the light died out in the boy's young face. He cast around for Merlin, but the old enchanter was staring at Arthur in an anguish that mirrored Arthur's own. Guenevere felt an impulse of pure rage. *You could not rest, could you, you meddlesome old man? Pendragon was all in all to you, and you have had your way. But when he was born, Arthur wanted him dead. What if he still feels the same way now?*

The youth looked from one to another for help. No one moved. White-faced, he rose to his feet and took Arthur's hand. With infinite dignity he touched it to his lips, bowed his head, and stepped back. As he turned away, Guenevere caught the word, 'Farewell.'

Farewell?

No, not farewell, there has been too much loss and grief.

Guenevere turned back to Arthur, and took his arm. 'Please, my love, will you recognise your son?'

Still Arthur did not move.

The boy continued his lonely progress down the hall.

Guenevere reached a hand up to Arthur's face. Never had she said anything as hard as this. 'Arthur,' she began, in a steady voice, 'listen to me. For the love between us, I beg you, welcome your son.'

Silence. Arthur was staring after Mordred as if a dead man walked.

She raised her voice. 'Arthur, it's Mordred. Won't you acknowledge him?'

'*Mordred!*'

With a cry, Arthur raised his head and came alive. In one wild move, he leaped after the departing figure, and caught him in his arms. Sobbing, he hugged the bewildered boy to his chest.

'Mordred!'

'Sire –'

The hurt and pain dissolved on Mordred's handsome young

face, and soon he was weeping too. Through their tears, one sound was heard again and again: 'My son – my son – my son –'

'Come – come, both of you, come.'

Guenevere reached up to put her arms round their shoulders, and led them from the hall.

'So you did it, you old fool – I suppose you always knew you would?'

Merlin stretched out in the velvet dark, and permitted himself a soft laugh. He extended an arm.

'Come here, my dear,' he said invitingly. 'No need to be cold and distant with me now. You've had your pleasure, playing with me all these years. And was I not a willing instrument when the moment came, and you were ready to hand over your son?'

Morgan stirred moodily, and renewed her fretful motion through the air. 'I always knew that Mordred would win Arthur's love. But what made you believe that Arthur would receive him well? After Amir died, he didn't care about having an heir.' She bit her lip. 'If he had, he would have left that barren bitch and given his love to me!' Her eyes flared red in the darkness of the cave. 'I would have given him twenty hundred sons.'

'Guenevere is not barren,' Merlin said equably. 'It is true that the Mother has not yet blest her again with child. But the springs of life flow in her, mark my words.'

Morgan clutched her forearms and hugged her naked breasts. 'Forget Guenevere,' she ordered. 'Tell me why Arthur loves Mordred, when the Pendragon line means less to him than the bitch.' She gave a coughing laugh. 'Growing up in Tintagel, Morgause and I knew we were born to be queens. Arthur never came to his royalty till he was full grown.' She laughed unpleasantly again. 'That's why he proved himself unworthy of me. He would not believe that royal brothers and sisters should rule together as the Pharaohs did.'

'Perhaps,' said Merlin peaceably. 'But remember, Arthur never knew his father, and he lost both his sons. He gave up his dreams of lineage long ago. Mordred is not a child of Pendragon to him.'

'Ha!' Morgan swung through the air with a snarl. 'Don't tell me he loves Mordred as my son!' Tears of fire and crystal scalded her shining eyes and scattered like brimstone, spitting where they fell. She rounded on Merlin, hissing fire, baring her fangs. 'The last time he saw me, he cursed me with his hate. Tell me, then, how can he love my son?'

Merlin's old heart ached. An infinite, weary pity flooded his soul. She loves Arthur still, he thought, she cannot choose. Whatever he does, she cannot change her fate. But then, neither can I. Nor Guenevere, nor Mordred, nor any of us.

He spread his withered hands, and concentrated on the raging spirit with all his force. A thousand stars bloomed in his golden eyes.

'Hear me, lady,' he said. 'King Arthur loves young Mordred for himself.'

Lightning passed through her long pale body, and she quivered with delight. 'Himself, yessss!' she hissed harshly, 'In himself he is precious like his father, he is fine.'

'He is indeed.' Merlin put a seductive note into his voice. 'He has his mother's beauty, and her magic too. All who see him love him. And Arthur most of all.'

'Yesss!' Morgan cried. 'This is his gift from childhood. I gave it him in his cradle, before they came to take him away from me.' Tears sharp as elf-arrows forced themselves from her eyes. 'King Ursien took my baby from my breast, just as Uther Pendragon took Arthur from my mother before!'

'But you got Mordred back,' Merlin reminded her. 'And you brought him up as you chose. '

Morgan's black temper ebbed like a midsummer flood.

'Yesss!' she agreed. Her nasal laugh snaked through the echoing void. 'Yesss, I had him with me a good deal. Who noticed the cook's child in the convent, the poor boy that Sister Ganmor in her kindness had to sleep in her cell, and taught how to read?'

Merlin chuckled. 'And sending him to Sir Ector to be reared with just the same knighthood training as Arthur had – truly, my dear, you have a spirit of incantation and the genius of sea-fire!'

Morgan stretched like a cat, purring at Merlin's praise. 'I knew it would be the one knight's estate where you would never look.' She threw back her arms, and her nipples glowed like stars. 'And it pleases Arthur, no, that his son had the same training as he had himself?'

'It means the world to him. Sir Ector was the only father he ever knew. He is truly content that his own son fared no worse.'

Morgan nodded. 'Sir Ector has made my son a fine young man.'

'He has,' Merlin said. He stepped up the soft insinuation in his voice. 'He is a prince indeed.'

'Yesss,' Morgan hissed contentedly. She drifted towards Merlin and allowed him to stroke her flank. The touch of her skin bit his fingers like scorpions. But the drive to caress, to probe, was stronger than the smart.

'You have seen Mordred, since Arthur took him in?' Merlin grinned to himself in the dark, not needing to ask. He had seen the old woman sweeping the courtyard steps as Arthur and Mordred rode out at the head of his knights. He had caught sight of the thin black cat slipping round the King's quarters as Arthur and Guenevere feasted Mordred in private, with their chosen few. And the Great Ones alone knew how many ravens and crows, black rats or beetles he had seen watching over Mordred in recent weeks. Yes, the spirit of Morgan had not been far from her beloved son.

Morgan did not deign to answer so foolish a thought. 'What you mean, old fool, is have I done with Arthur now? Will I leave him alone? Have I had my revenge?' Her black eyes gaped like pits of Hell. 'Wait and see.'

Holding her gaze in his steady golden flame, Merlin sent his soul spinning into the void, and prayed as he had never prayed in all his life. *All-Mother, All-Father, grant Arthur your peace. O You who are Earth and Water and dwell within the spirit of all things, spare him more suffering, let him live in harmony, at one with the evening sunset and the morning dew. Hold back the hatred of Morgan if it can be withheld, and help her to rejoice in Mordred's happiness. There is suffering, there is retribution, but there comes at last a time for hope and peace.*

Suddenly she was beside him, hissing in his ear. He knew that she had heard every unspoken word.

'Nothing for me, old man, no prayers for me?' she mouthed in his ear.

'Oh, yesss, madam,' he echoed her hissing voice. 'But you

already know what I want of you.' He drew her down beside him and kissed her damson lips, stroking her body with a practised hand. 'I want what you have given me since time began.'

CHAPTER 58

'Guenevere!'
'Here, Arthur.'
'Where?'
She laughed. 'Where I always am.'

The chamber was bright with the last of the winter sun, and snug and warm from the fire on the hearth. But outside the fields were spangled with frost, and as Arthur entered, an icy blast came in with him.

Guenevere looked up from the papers on her desk, and laughed again. 'Close the door, quickly, you're making it freezing in here.'

Arthur bounded up to her, and took both her hands. He smelt of the outdoors, of his leather jerkin, of his horse. His face was ruddy from the cold, and his eyes were as bright as a child's.

'Huddling indoors by the fire is making you delicate,' he said fondly. 'You should have come out hunting with us instead.'

She smiled, and squeezed his hand. 'Tomorrow I will. How was it today?'

Arthur pulled up a chair, and sat down by her side. In their new-found closeness, he could never bear to have her far out of reach.

'Truly, Guenevere, you should have been there. Mordred excelled himself. The going was rough, and he never faltered once. Hedges, ditches, he took everything in his stride.'

'He's a very good rider.'

'Horseman, swordsman, and fearless at the joust.' Arthur beamed. 'He's good at everything.'

Guenevere nodded. 'Sir Ector has made him into a fine young squire.'

'Yes, wasn't that wonderful?' Arthur marvelled. 'He'll be a good knight when the time comes.' His face grew serious. 'I think that was what made me see that Morgan meant well – that she sent Mordred for the same knighthood training as I had.'

'Mordred is a credit to you both,' Guenevere said.

'And to send back the scabbard –' Arthur's eyes moistened, and his honest face registered a heartfelt thankfulness and simple joy. 'Oh, Guenevere, wasn't that good of her? It shows she must have been sorry for what she has done. She's a different person now, I can tell.'

Guenevere paused, and chose her words with care. 'It is good to have the scabbard back again,' she agreed.

She did not want to remind Arthur how easily Morgan had stolen the scabbard before. But she had no doubt that whenever she wanted, Morgan could take it again. So she could not share Arthur's faith that Morgan had changed. Privately she doubted that Morgan ever meant well. And for that reason, she could never be entirely easy about Morgan's son. But Mordred was here now, and could not be sent away. And for the love of Arthur, she was determined not to disturb his ever-growing delight in his long-lost son.

For in the weeks since Mordred arrived, Arthur had passed from the first shock and shame to a constant delight. Almost every day he discovered something that thrilled his heart. Sir Ector had instructed Mordred in everything that long ago Arthur had learned as a boy. So for Arthur, getting to know Mordred had been like revisiting his past and meeting his younger self.

'When we come to make him a knight, as we must in a year or two –' Arthur broke off, and took her hand, plaiting her fingers in his. 'Oh Guenevere, do you think he will take the Siege Perilous when the time comes?'

Guenevere sat still. She had known this moment would come. The great chair with its carved canopy came into her mind, and she could read the prophecy in letters of golden fire: **He Will Be the Most Peerless Knight In All the World.**

Guenevere sighed. The small ghost of Amir flickered through her mind, and she gently put it away. 'It's a high destiny,

Arthur. And only the Great Ones know if it will be his.'

A moment of melancholy gripped them both.

Arthur pressed her hand, and stroked it lovingly. 'I know we always thought it was meant for Amir. If you don't want Mordred to be considered for it, tell me, and I'll never mention it again.'

She wanted to weep.

Oh my poor love, never free of the loss of Amir. But why should I use that against Mordred now?

My son lies in his grave by the sea. And another woman's son should not have to suffer for that.

'No, Arthur, I would never ask you to hold Mordred back.' She smiled painfully. 'And if that is truly his destiny, none of us could.' She was struck by a happier thought. 'Why not ask Merlin when he comes back? He will know. It is already written in the stars.'

'Yes, indeed.' A smile split Arthur's handsome face. 'He may not tell us, but he will surely know. And he'll tell us enough to decide what we should do.'

He heaved a wondering sigh, and shook his head. 'Can you believe it, Guenevere? You here, my son restored to me, and Merlin back with us too? Dear God, I think I'm the luckiest man alive.'

Guenevere took his face between her hands, and kissed him tenderly. 'You deserve it, Arthur,' she murmured. 'You're a good man.'

'I try,' he said gruffly. Tears stood in his eyes. 'And I know how much I still have to do.'

She patted his hand. 'We both do. We're lucky that the Mother has blessed us with the chance to begin again.'

He kissed her fervently. 'And we won't throw it away.'

There was a knock on the door, and Ina slipped in, smiling with delight. 'Prince Mordred is here.'

Arthur leaped to his feet and moved eagerly towards the door. 'Show him in.'

I must love Mordred, and I will, Guenevere thought. It should not be hard to love anyone who could put that smile on Arthur's face. The twinges of unease that she still felt would fade away, when there was so much to like about the boy.

She raised her eyes to the door. 'Mordred?'

'Madam.'

The youth who bounded in had all Arthur's passionate energy, and a more-than-boyish grace. He was tall for his age, and to judge by his slender frame, not yet full grown. But already his well-balanced body and handsome face were turning heads. It was to his credit, Guenevere and Arthur agreed, that he never noticed it.

'Mordred, welcome.' She extended her hand to be kissed. 'You had a good day, I hear. The King tells me that you outdid yourself.'

Mordred threw Arthur a glance of ardent love. 'My father is too kind to me, I think.'

'Nonsense!' cried Arthur happily. 'You're setting a great example to them all. Gawain was puffing so hard today that I think he must be getting old. Even Lucan had to exert himself to keep up. And Sagramore –' He burst out laughing at the memory. 'He's probably still trailing home with the stragglers, we shan't see them till owl-light!'

'Sir Sagramore was not well horsed for a country ride,' observed Mordred tactfully.

Arthur burst out laughing. 'At his weight, the Great Ones never yet made a horse for Sagramore!'

Mordred turned to Guenevere. 'Ride with us tomorrow, madam, if you can,' he urged. His eyes went to Arthur and back again. 'It's the finest thing I know, and to have you there . . .'

To have a mother and father, poor boy, for the first time in your life? Guenevere nodded. 'Tomorrow, yes, I will, I promised the King.'

Mordred turned to Arthur. 'There you are, sir,' he said, beaming, 'we can hold the Queen to that.'

'And you shall,' Guenevere laughed. 'Now be off, the pair of you, or I shall never finish these papers today.'

'Very well.' Arthur took her hand and brushed it with his lips. 'But I'll be back in time to take you down to the hall.'

Guenevere smiled in anticipation of the feast to come. She had always loved the evenings in the Great Hall, especially in winter, when the wine went round by candlelight and the fires on the great hearths played off the red and blue and silver of silk and mail.

She gave Arthur her hand. 'Till then, my lord.'

She stood for a moment and listened to them clattering out. Before they had reached the door, Mordred's light voice was already deep into some question that required Arthur's ear. The conversation between them had started as soon as Arthur took Mordred to his heart, and showed no sign of ending, in this life at least. She could hear Arthur's rumbling tones dying away, 'Well, my son, I believe . . .'

My son.

Yes, Arthur was a father now, at last. And who in the world could begrudge him that? Mordred could bring many blessings into Arthur's life. Morgan's malice must sleep now that her long-abandoned child had come into his own. And despite Guenevere's lingering concerns, there was no sign that any of her dark power had passed into her son

Sighing, she turned back to her papers, and worked on. It was some time later that she heard Ina's discreet cough. 'Two knights are here, my lady. Will you see them now?'

She knew at once it would be Bors and Lionel. They were plainly dressed for the road, but an air of suppressed excitement hung about them both. Above the dull grey-green of their riding cloaks, Lionel's skin glowed and Bors's eyes were bright.

'It's harsh weather, sirs, to take to the roads tonight,' Guenevere ventured, with a smile.

To her relief, Bors smiled back. 'It will be good for us, madam, to go adventuring again. We never concerned ourselves with the weather when we were boys.'

Lionel laughed, and tossed back his long hair. 'Better to catch cold on the roads than grow idle at court.'

There was a silence. 'You're going to Lancelot,' she said, with soft certainty.

The two knights exchanged a glance.

'To look for him, madam, at least,' Bors corrected. 'We don't know where he is. He said he did not want to burden us with his quest.' He gave a short laugh. 'Indeed, he did not even tell us what it was. All we know is that he has a great and worthy task to fulfil, and one he thinks that he must do alone. But we . . .' He nodded to his brother.

Lionel laughed tenderly. 'We beg to differ,' he said. 'We are sons of Benoic, and his nearest kin. So we mean to find him, and assist his quest.'

Guenevere stood still. *He did not tell us where he is,* Bors had said. That meant they had heard from him. She drew a shivering breath. 'You have news of Lancelot?'

Bors inclined his head. 'He was travelling northwards when he sent to us. He was well, he said, and fit from life on the road. His journey had been uneventful, and he told us that the pivot of his day comes every evening, when he sees the love star rise. Then he faces the west, looks into the setting sun, and prays for his star, his sun, his love.'

A sweet sadness filled Guenevere from head to foot. She trembled on the brink of joy and tears. 'When you find Sir Lancelot,' she said tremulously, 'tell him that I too watch for the evening star.'

'We have seen the candle in your window, lady,' Lionel said softly. 'We shall tell him that your flame calls to his, wherever you are.'

'Thank you.' Guenevere smiled. 'May the Gods go with you, sirs,' she said fervently. 'And the Mother herself guard every step of your way.'

She stood and watched them as they left the room. Outside, an early evening darkened the wintry sky. Warm memories and dear hopes, fond thoughts and tender dreams danced round her head and filled her heart and mind. She stood still, and let them come.

To love and be loved – to see love growing between those she loved – what greater joy than that? In the living moment she felt herself at one with the soul of things, with the spirit that lived in the mountain and the earthquake, in the heart of the violet, in the gaze of a newborn child. It came to her then that she knew the voice, the touch, the kiss of that secret now. She was part of that still centre, that ever-expanding circle of life itself.

Life, love, and the sorrow and joy of them both.

'Guenevere!' called Arthur from below.

She moved to the window, and lit the candle standing there. Its small flame flared up and burned steadily as the love star rose and bloomed brightly in the west.

'I'm coming, Arthur,' she replied.

THE CHARACTERS

Abbot, the Father   Head of the Abbey in London where Arthur was proclaimed King, leader of the Christian monks in Britain, implacably opposed to the worship of the Great Mother and the Lady of the Lake

Agravain   Second son of King Lot, brother of Gawain, Gaheris and Gareth, nephew and later knight to Arthur

Amir   'The Beloved One', only son of Arthur and Guenevere

Ann, Sister   *See* Morgan Le Fay

Arthur Pendragon, High King of Britain, son of Uther Pendragon and Queen Igraine of Cornwall, husband to Guenevere and father of Amir

Ban, King   King of Benoic in Little Britain, father of Lancelot, brother of King Bors, long-ago ally to Arthur in the Battle of the Kings

Baudwin   Knight of Caerleon, old servant of Uther, supporter of Arthur when he reclaimed his throne

Bedivere, Sir   Knight to Arthur, one of his first three companion knights

Bernard, Sir   Lord of Astolat, father of Sir Lavain, Sir Tirre and Elaine

Boniface, Brother   Monk of the Abbey in London, sent as emissary to the Lady of the Lake on Avalon

Bors, King   King of Benoic in Little Britain, brother of Ban, father of Bors and Lionel, ally to Arthur in the Battle of the Kings

Bors, Sir   Son of King Bors, brother of Lionel, cousin of Lancelot, knight to Guenevere

Clariva, Lady   Chatelaine of the Castle Fils de Dame in

Listinoise, mother of Sir Dorward and governor with him of the school for pages attended by Mordred as a child

Confessor, the Father Monk appointed by the Father Abbot of the Christians to take over the running of the Convent of Holy Mercy, formerly the Convent of the Holy Mother, where Morgan Le Fay was imprisoned as a child

Dinant, Sir Knight to King Arthur

Domenico of Tuscany Papal envoy from Rome to the Father Abbot in London, and supporter of his crusade against Avalon

Dorward, Sir Knight of the Castle Fils de Dame in Listinoise and son of Lady Clariva, with whom he keeps the school for pages attended by Mordred as a child

Ector, Sir Foster-father to Arthur, father of Sir Kay, knight to Arthur

Elaine 'The Fair Maid of Astolat', devoted to Sir Lancelot

Excalibur Sword of power given to Arthur by the Lady of the Lake

Gaheris Third son of King Lot, brother of Gawain, Agravain and Gareth, nephew and later knight to Arthur

Ganmor, Sister *See* Morgan Le Fay

Gareth Fourth son of King Lot, brother of Gawain, Agravain and Gaheris, nephew and later knight to Arthur

Gawain, Sir Eldest son of King Lot, Arthur's first companion knight, brother of Agravain, Gaheris and Gareth

Giorgio Monk sent from Rome to work with Boniface in the first Christian onslaught on Avalon

Gorlois, Duke Champion and Chosen One of Queen Igraine of Cornwall, father of Morgause and Morgan, murdered by Uther and Merlin

Guenevere Queen of the Summer Country, daughter of Queen Maire Macha and King Leogrance, wife of Arthur, lover of Sir Lancelot and mother of Amir

Hervis de Rivel, Sir Knight of the Castle Bel Espoir in southern England, governor of the school for squires attended by Mordred as a youth

Igraine, Queen Queen of Cornwall, wife of Duke Gorlois and beloved of King Uther Pendragon, mother of Arthur, Morgause and Morgan Le Fay

Iachimo, Brother Monk sent with Brother Sylvester to Avalon to support the Christians' attempts to claim the Hallows for their own use

Ina Maid to Guenevere

Kay, Sir Son of Sir Ector, foster-brother of Arthur and knight of the Round Table, one of the three companion knights of Arthur from the time he was proclaimed

Lamorak Son of Sir Pellinore, knighted by Arthur after the Battle of the Kings, later knight and Chosen One to Queen Morgause of the Orkneys

Lady of the Lake Ruler of Avalon, priestess of the Great Goddess

Lady of Broceliande Ruler of the Lake and waterfall of Broceliande in Little Britain, modern Brittany, Lancelot's foster-mother, sister of the Lady of the Lake and a priestess of the Great Goddess

Lancelot, Sir Son of King Ban of Benoic and Queen Elaine, knight of the Round Table and lover of Queen Guenevere

Lavain, Sir Elder son of Sir Bernard of Astolat, brother of Sir Tirre and Elaine, rescued by Sir Lancelot from an outlaw attack in the wood

Leif Leader of the Knight Companions of the Throne in the Orkneys, sworn to Sir Lamorak and Morgause, avenger of them both

Lionel, Sir Second son of King Bors, brother of Sir Bors, cousin of Sir Lancelot and knight to Guenevere

Lot, King King of Lothian and the Orkneys, one-time ally of King Uther Pendragon, husband of Morgause, father of Gawain, Agravain, Gaheris and Gareth, and later usurper of the Middle Kingdom and enemy of Arthur

Lovell the Bold, Sir Champion to Guenevere's mother before Sir Lucan

Lucan, Sir Champion to Guenevere's mother and her Chosen One, later Arthur's knight

Mador, Sir Young knight from the Meads, an estate on the Welsh borders, admirer of Guenevere

Maire Macha, Queen Guenevere's mother, Queen of the Summer Country, wife to King Leogrance, and lover of Sir Lucan

Merlin Welsh Druid and bard, illegitimate offspring of the house of Pendragon, adviser to Uther and Arthur

Mordred Son of Arthur and his half-sister Morgan Le Fay, cast adrift in a boat off the coast of Gore, and later found

Morgan Le Fay Younger daughter of Queen Igraine and Duke Gorlois of Cornwall, placed in a Christian convent by King Uther her step-father, also known as Sister Ganmor and Sister Ann, Arthur's half-sister and lover, wife of King Ursien and mother of Mordred

Morgause Elder daughter of Queen Igraine and Duke Gorlois, given as wife to King Lot by King Uther; Arthur's half sister, mother of Gawain, Agravain, Gaheris and Gareth, and later lover of Sir Lamorak

Nemue Chief Priestess to Lady of the Lake

Niamh, Sir Knight of the Round Table, early Champion of Guenevere's mother, and defender of the Mother-right

Patrise, Sir Knight of the Meads, brother of Sir Mador

Pelles, King Fanatical Christian King of Terre Foraine and the Castle of Corbenic, brother to Pellinore and father of Elaine

Pellinore, King King of Listinoise, ally of Arthur

Placida, Abbess Mother Superior of the House of the Holy Mother, the Christian convent where Morgan Le Fay was placed as a child

Sagramore, Sir Knight to Arthur

Sylvester, Brother Monk sent to replace Boniface and Giorgio on Avalon, to wrest the Hallows from the Lady of the Lake's control

Tirre, Sir Second son of Sir Bernard of Astolat and brother of Elaine, rescued by Lancelot from an outlaw attack in the wood

Tor, Sir Knight to Arthur

Ursien, King King of Gore, overlord of Sir Ector the foster-father of Arthur, and later husband of Morgan Le Fay

Uther Pendragon King of the Middle Kingdom, High King of Britain, lover of Queen Igraine of Cornwall and Arthur's father

Yvain, Sir Eldest son of King Ursien of Gore, sworn enemy of Morgan Le Fay

LIST OF PLACES

Avalon   Sacred island in a lake in the Summer Country, centre of Goddess worship; modern Glastonbury in Somerset

Bedegraine   Forest on the borders of Gore in the north of England

Bel Espoir, Castle   Seat of Sir Hervis de Rivel in the south of England below London, where he keeps a school for the training of squires, attended by Mordred

Caerleon   Capital of the Middle Kingdom, formerly the City of the Legions during the Roman occupation, seized by King Lot after the death of King Uther, held by a force of six vassal kings of King Lot, reclaimed by Arthur in a surprise attack, modern Caerleon in South Wales

Camelot   Capital of the Summer Country, home of the Round Table, modern Cadbury in Somerset

Canterbury   Base of the Roman Church in the British Isles, and site of first Archbishopric in England

Convent of Holy Mercy   Convent in the forest where Morgan Le Fay was imprisoned as a child, formerly the Convent of the Holy Mother, renamed when Morgan's activities come to light

Cornwall   Kingdom of Arthur's mother, Queen Igraine

Druid's Isle, the   Mona; modern Anglesey, off the north coast of Wales

Dolorous Garde   Castle of Prince Malgaunt, taken by Sir Lancelot and renamed Joyous Garde

Fils de Dame, Castle   Seat of Sir Dorward and his mother Lady Clariva in Listinoise, where they keep the school for pages attended by Mordred

Gore   Christian kingdom of King Ursien in the north-west of England where Arthur and Kay were brought up; modern West

Lancashire and Cumbria

Hill of Stones   Ancient burial site of the queens of the Summer Country, location of ritual queen-making and site of the feast of Beltain

Iona   Island on north-west coast of England, site of first settlement of Celtic Christianity in Britain

Island of the West   Modern Ireland

Joyous Garde   Sir Lancelot's Castle (*see* Dolorous Garde)

Listinoise   Kingdom of King Pellinore and his son Lamorak, modern East Riding of Yorkshire

Little Britain   Territory in France, location of the kingdom of Benoic, home of King Ban and King Bors; modern Brittany

London   Major city in ancient Britain, centre of Christian colonisation of the British Isles

Middle Kingdom   Arthur's ancestral kingdom lying between the Summer Country and Wales; modern Gwent, Glamorgan and Herefordshire

Mona   Known as the Druids' Isle, modern Anglesea

Orkney, Islands of   Cluster of most northerly islands of the British Isles, and site of King Lot's kingdom, later ruled by his widow Queen Morgause

Saxon shore, the   Site of invasions by tribes called 'the Norsemen', raiders from Norway, Denmark and East Germany

Severn Water, the   The Bristol Channel, estuary of the river Severn, dividing the Middle Kingdom from the Summer Country

Summer Country   Guenevere's kingdom, ancient centre of Goddess worship; modern Somerset

Terabil   Castle of Queen Igraine of Cornwall, defended by Duke Gorlois, taken by King Uther in siege where Gorlois lost his life.

Terre Foraine   Kingdom of King Pelles in northern England, modern Northumberland

Tintagel   Castle of Queen Igraine of Cornwall, capital of her kingdom

Val Sans Retour, Le   Estate of King Ursien in Gore, donated to Arthur, presented to Morgan Le Fay and the base of her power

Welshlands   Home to Merlin, modern Wales

York   Second most powerful centre for the Christian colonisation of the British Isles after Canterbury, and the second most senior archbishopric